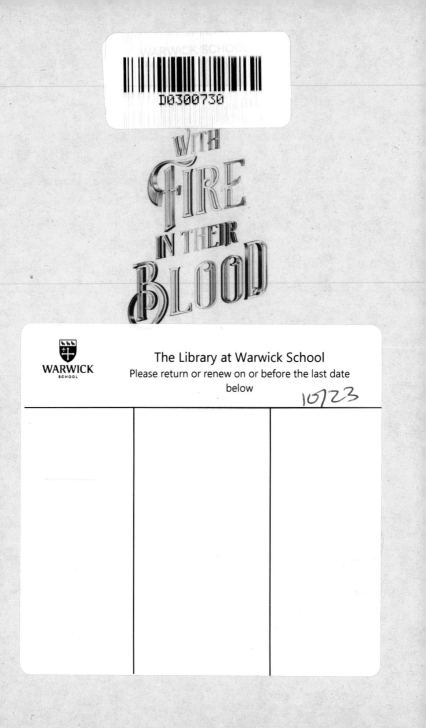

WARWICK
SCHOOL

The Library at Warwick School
Please return or renew on or before the last date
below

10723

# WITH FIRE IN THEIR BLOOD

# KAT DELACORTE

PENGUIN BOOKS

PENGUIN BOOKS

UK | USA | Canada | Ireland | Australia
India | New Zealand | South Africa

Penguin Books is part of the Penguin Random House group of companies
whose addresses can be found at global.penguinrandomhouse.com.

www.penguin.co.uk
www.puffin.co.uk
www.ladybird.co.uk

First published 2022

001

Set in 10.5/15.5pt Sabon LT Std
Typeset by Jouve (UK), Milton Keynes
Printed and bound in Great Britain by Clays Ltd, Elcograf S.p.A.

The authorized representative in the EEA is Penguin Random House Ireland,
Morrison Chambers, 32 Nassau Street, Dublin D02 YH68

A CIP catalogue record for this book is available from the British Library

ISBN: 978-0-241-48762-4

All correspondence to:
Penguin Books
Penguin Random House Children's
One Embassy Gardens, 8 Viaduct Gardens, London SW11 7BW

*For my parents, who told me I could*

*It is not upon you alone the dark patches fall,*
*The dark threw its patches down upon me also.*

Walt Whitman
'Crossing Brooklyn Ferry'

# CHAPTER ONE

On the drive up from Rome, the whole road was covered in mist. A good thing, probably: it prevented me from commenting on the scenery. Italy was supposed to be beautiful, but I had a lot of faith in my ability to be unimpressed. Rolling hills and ancient cities make good vacation spots, sure. But living there, being *forced* to stay – that's another story. Whatever charm the country had, I knew it wasn't going to work on me. At least in the mist I could pretend I was somewhere else. Preferably at home.

We had left Maine yesterday morning just before sunrise, and I'd frozen up on the way out the door, staring at the rambling yard and broken porch steps and thinking, *This is the last time.* I'd lived in the same place all my life, and it wasn't perfect, it wasn't even good, but at least it was familiar. My father put our house on the market as soon as he got the new job, and in a week the only home I'd ever known was sold. I considered leaving a note for the new owners, something to make them feel welcome.

*To whom it may concern,*
*My mother killed herself in the living*
*room. She tried to burn the place down*
*right before. Enjoy!*

In the end, though, I decided it wasn't worth it. I was afraid Jack would find out, and then I'd have to spend the whole plane ride shrinking from his disappointment. I was ten when my mother died, but I tried to keep my memories of her carefully blurred. Like faded Polaroids: too murky to hurt me.

It was different for my father. Losing Carly shook him to the core. Six years later, I still hadn't learned to fill the silence.

'So are we lost yet?' I ventured, staring towards the non-existent Italian landscape in the mist. 'Or is this supposed to be normal?'

We'd left the highway for a back road, and the GPS on the dashboard had cut to black. No signal. I could see grey shapes looming outside the car – a thick tangle of forest. In the fog, it was claustrophobic, almost eerie. The GPS wouldn't refresh no matter how many times I tapped it. My phone had lost reception ages ago.

'It's normal,' my father said. 'Castello's in a dead zone. The mountains interfere with the service.'

Castello. That was the place we were moving to. Not Rome, with its museums and boulevards. Not Florence. Castello.

It was somewhere in the middle of Italy, a tiny speck on Google Maps that didn't load properly when you searched it. The most I could tell was that there were woods around the city, and more woods around those woods. Also, apparently, mountains. On satellite view: a blurry shot of rooftops looming above the treeline. The image had dissolved into pixels when I'd tried to zoom in. Like the town was so unimportant that the rest of the world had forgotten it was even there. Which was why we were moving in the first place – so my father could help Castello modernize.

'If it's in a dead zone, how do we know where to go?'

'They sent a map,' Jack said, and reached for it under the dashboard.

All in all, this was riveting conversation, the longest exchange my father and I had managed since we'd left the States. We didn't talk much on a good day, and since the whole *we're moving to Italy* announcement, things were worse than usual. Every word out of my mouth sounded bitter now, had a dazed edge of disbelief – *how could you do this to me?*

My father was an engineer, one of those machine freaks who can take things apart and build them up again twice as quickly. When I was little, he'd made me toys: mechanical teddy bears and spinning ballerina dolls, a light-up mobile that I could squeeze on if I was afraid of the dark. I'd loved that thing to pieces until my mother decided it gave her migraines. The next day, it had vanished mysteriously.

After Carly died, my father retreated from everyone, me included. It was like a bad dream at first – the man who had read me bedtime stories and taught me to ride a bike, broken suddenly into dozens of shards, which threatened to cut me if I got too close. For months, I'd lived with a stranger, talked to the air when Jack was in the same room. Come home from school to find him staring at the patch of floor where she'd done it: on the flagstones by the fireplace.

When he'd finally dragged himself out of that haze, everything had been different. My father would never admit it, but he didn't want to look at me any longer. He spent hours in his workshop, fixing machines like he couldn't fix her. Pawning me off to after-school clubs or Gracie next door for babysitting – forcing pleasantries and avoiding me in the hall and never, ever saying it out loud: *I loved her more.*

Then the job offer came from Italy. Cloistered city seeks assistance entering current decade. Housing and transportation provided.

I should've known Jack wouldn't be able to resist. Italy was my mother's country, and my father had been morbidly fascinated by it since she died. I'm sure he'd have preferred moving to Venice, Carly's hometown, where he could have retraced her childhood footsteps through the winding streets and dazzling canals. But Castello was hiring, so Castello would have to do.

Not that this was the explanation I was given. Jack had pitched the move as a fresh start, a thrilling adventure – a real change for both of us. I couldn't roll my eyes hard enough. Or at least I would've been rolling my eyes if I hadn't been so busy being furious.

Outside the car, the mist was starting to dissolve, and I could see snatches of muddy road, carrying us further into the mountains. Jack glanced at the map and said, 'It'll be around the next bend.'

I crossed my arms, holding back an unnecessary comment, like, *It's never too late to crash!* Then we turned a corner, and I felt my breath catch.

We had come out of the woods at the edge of a narrow gorge: Castello was built into the mountaintop on the other side.

The city rose from the mist like a kingdom in a fairy tale, the kind of place I'd never expected to see in real life. Glittery marble buildings piled up against the sky, a sea of red rooftops framed by the dagger silhouettes of two watchtowers. Between the towers, in what I imagined was the centre of town, there was a colossal church dome, casting long shadows over the houses below. And the wall. It was carved directly out of the mountain like the battlements of a massive fortress, protecting Castello from the world outside.

'See?' my father said. 'I knew you'd be impressed.'

He sounded vindicated, like the fact that the city was gorgeous made up for him forcing me to move here. It didn't. And besides I wasn't *impressed*. That implied approval or respect, sentiments I certainly did not feel about Castello.

*Mesmerized*, though. That was better. Because something about Castello seemed very powerful to me. The closer we got, the more imperfections I saw. The city was old and worn; the wall was crumbling; the rooftops sagged. But the sense of power remained, a kind of timeless authority, like we were approaching the castle of an ancient god. It made me suddenly wary about entering Castello – as if the god that lived there might be angered by our intrusion.

'Navigate for me?' my father asked, as we wound our way across the gorge towards the city gate. He handed me the map like a peace offering.

Castello's insignia was stamped at the top, a gold cross below a trinity symbol. I recognized it from the welcome package we'd received in the mail, containing the keys to our new house and a list of local shops – all bearing that same golden mark.

Reluctantly, I ran my finger across the map, tracing a snake-like route towards our address: Building 62, Via Secondo.

'It's straight,' I muttered. 'Then right at the corner.'

We passed under the city gate, a row of huge iron teeth open halfway to let a car through. Torches were lodged on either side of it, bright bowls of fire like beacons in the fading daylight. Above them, there were two marble angels, sculpted with their wings spread, heads bent, fingers gripped around carved bouquets of roses.

It should've been a pleasant image, except that the angels were missing their faces. Centuries of wind and rain had washed their features away, leaving nothing but the hollows of their eyes. I stared up at the statues as we drove through the gate, wondering why I was suddenly convinced they were watching me back.

Inside, Castello was silent and decaying, more than it had seemed from a distance. The streets were narrow, paved with uneven cobblestones, the houses crooked and weather-stained. Chips of plaster littered the side of the road. Ours was the only car in sight.

*So we've moved to a ghost town*, I thought, watching the sun slide out of sight behind the city rooftops. *At least Venice would've had people in it.*

Lines of graffiti twisted across the building, along with yellowing posters of some kind. I could make out Castello's trinity symbol at the top, but had to squint to read the letters printed underneath. SALVEZZA

I was pretty sure that meant *Salvation*.

It was dusk when we pulled up in Via Secondo. Building 62 looked the same as every other one we'd passed, tall and bent, with warped rows of sooty windows.

'We're on the third floor,' my father said, and went to unlock the front door. I watched him from the car, a chiselled figure diminished by the massive scale of the architecture. It was tempting to do something dramatic while he was occupied: climb into the front seat and drive away. But one look at the blank GPS cancelled that plan. And it was getting dark.

By the time I made it upstairs, I was covered in cobwebs, out of breath from dragging my suitcase. Apart from the third floor, the rest of the building was clearly abandoned. My father was fiddling with the bolt on our apartment door, running an appreciative hand over the mechanism.

'It's a warded lock,' Jack said, explaining to me like he'd done when I was little. 'In the Middle Ages, this was the height of security.'

'How reassuring,' I said. 'Can we go home now?'

'Very funny, Lilly,' my father called after me, as I shoved past him into the apartment.

I was met with a sprawl of hollow rooms, all of them old and dismal, a recurring theme I was beginning to sense with Castello. I held my phone up as I walked, looking for service. There was one bar near the living-room window, two in the hallway. Definitely no Wi-Fi. I felt a sharp stab of disappointment, watching the text I wanted to send to Maine bounce back undelivered. So much for telling Gracie I'd arrived safely. For all she knew, I could've been dead on the side of the road. And this was supposed to be my life now.

At the end of the hall, past the master suite, I found my new bedroom, big but mostly empty, with rickety furniture looming in the dark. Then I flipped on the overhead light and noticed the paintings.

The room was covered in a giant mural: chipped and fading, but still visible in all its gruesome glory. The scene was a battle, something from history, I presumed, but nothing I recognized.

Two dirt-streaked armies rode against each other on horseback, trampling the bodies of fallen soldiers underfoot. Flags waved in an invisible wind on both sides of the battlefield. One was painted with a rose, the other with the curved and spreading wings of an angel. Between the armies, etched into the sky like a heavenly apparition, was a dagger crossed over a golden key.

For a long time, I stared at the mural, torn between awe and horror. Transfixed by the hatred on the faces of the soldiers, the blood from their armour dripping down towards my bedposts.

*Sweet dreams, Lilly*, I thought. The overhead light flickered and burned out with a pop.

It took a while for the power to come back on. Jack was unfazed by the outage – after all, replacing the electrical grid and wiring up the internet were what Castello had brought him here to do. But I resented the fact that we could be cast into darkness at any moment. It made me feel like we'd left the real world behind the second we'd passed through the city gate.

When the power finally returned, we ate dinner: bread, cheese and olives, provided for us by the man who had hired my father, the same one who had mailed us the map and keys. He signed his letters *The General*, but Jack had told me he was some sort of preacher and the political leader of Castello. When I'd asked about the military title, my father said he didn't know.

It was the first real meal the two of us had shared in ages, and the scrape of cutlery in the silence put me on edge. I was used to eating alone, microwave dinners in my bedroom or sprawled out on the couch in front of the TV. Sometimes I'd slip out and eat with Gracie, the woman with the farmhouse next to ours. My father had hired her to take care of me for a while after Carly died, and she'd been my childhood hero, with her shiny white hair and wool sweaters for every season, putting things right in my life where my mother had shattered them. Before we'd left Maine, Gracie had hugged me once, firm and silent. Like she'd thought she'd never see me again.

'Are you excited for school?' Jack asked, when the silence at the table had stretched beyond reasonable proportions.

I stared at him. Popped an olive in my mouth.

'I heard they have a music elective.'

In seventh grade, I'd been dying to learn piano, but I'd stopped trying by eighth.

'I quit.'

My father frowned, fiddling with the rim of his glasses, a boyish habit that reminded me how young he was. Barely thirty-six, his soft brown curls untouched by grey. But it was easy to forget because the grief had changed him so much: carved permanent circles under his eyes and stunted his dimpled smile. Or maybe that was wrong. Maybe it was *me* who had changed him. It was a feeling I couldn't shake sometimes – that all those months he'd spent staring into space weren't just because Carly was gone, but because he'd been left with me instead. A wide-eyed ten-year-old, bad at math and terrified of thunderstorms. Nobody wanted that. At least that's what my mother would have said.

She still spoke to me now and then, a cool whisper in the back of my mind, ready to pounce whenever I let my guard down. The voice that told me I was dangerous, that I ruined the things I touched. The voice that told me to run and hide.

'Lilly, I know you're upset,' Jack said. 'And I'm sorry for that, truly. But this is a second chance for us. It's an opportunity.'

'An opportunity to do what?' I asked. 'Start a flashlight business? Train carrier pigeons? Or maybe we could go into grave robbing, since this whole city looks practically dead –'

'Lilly –'

'Castello's creepy,' I said. 'We're in the middle of nowhere, my phone doesn't work, and there's a war mural in my bedroom.'

'Castello is *different*,' Jack corrected. 'You saw the shape the roads are in – the city's been secluded up here for decades. That's why I've been hired. I'll have the Wi-Fi working in no time, but for now you should think of this as a cultural experience. Italy is in your blood. Lots of people would consider it a privilege to live here.'

'Then you should've given my plane ticket to one of them instead.'

For a moment, my father looked wounded. I hated making him feel that way; couldn't help it at the same time. It seemed to come to me naturally.

'Lilly, please,' Jack said. 'This could be good for us. Chin up, remember?'

I flinched. It was an old saying, one he'd invented on the day of my mother's funeral: the two of us in that stifling black hearse with her coffin in the back. When I was refusing to get out of the car because we were going to bury her, and I was afraid she'd reach out of the grave and drag me down, too. My father had turned around in the front seat, tapped my chin and raised my face to look at him. This was before he'd decided to lose himself, shut me out completely. Changed from being my father to a strange, empty man called Jack Deluca who I hardly recognized at all.

*Chin up, Lilly*, he'd said. *Be strong. We can do this.*

I shook my head, pushing my chair back hard, not caring if I scraped the tile floor.

'That doesn't work on me any longer.'

It took me ages to fall asleep. The house was stone, so I expected it to be dead silent, but instead it seemed to be breathing around me, moving the way old, cunning things do: behind your back, in the shadows. Pipes creaked, mice scurried across the floor of the attic. Once, I was even sure I heard footsteps up there. Shivering a little, I slipped out of bed and went to the window.

From my room, I had a panoramic view of Castello, and the city looked sharper in the moonlight, less decayed. Eternal. As if centuries could pass and it would still be here, a sleeping beast coiled under the night sky. Biding its time, watching, listening. Waiting for new blood. Because cities never really die, just the people in them.

When I slid back into bed, I knew I'd have nightmares. As a child, I'd tried to stay awake to avoid them, pinching my wrists for hours in the dark. But eventually I'd learned it was pointless. Sleep is cruel like that. The harder you try to fight it, the more power it has. And then the dreams come.

I was walking through the city in the snow. White flakes swirled around my body, enclosing me in a cage of absolute silence. Castello was in ruins all around me, the aftermath of a war. Burnt-out buildings, piles of broken furniture on the sides of the road. Then suddenly: the high curl of a voice.

There was a figure up ahead, a black silhouette against the murky background. I couldn't see her face, but I knew it was my mother because she was singing, laughing, coaxing me forward. Nursery rhymes she'd taught me when I was little. About roses, and rings around them, and people falling down and something else, too, something important.

*Ashes*, my mother said. *It's about ashes, Lilly.*

Her dark hair was matted with blood, the way it had looked on the day I found her body. She threw her head back and spun in circles in the snow.

Only it wasn't snow. It had been ashes all along.

My mother smiled at me, and I saw that her sharp white teeth had blood on them, too. Then she began to walk away.

*Wait*, I called, stumbling after her. *Wait for me. Don't leave.*

My mother glanced back over her shoulder, curious in a detached way, like an angel watching mortals fall apart. There was knowledge in her eyes, bottomless, unearthly understanding. The answers to questions I desperately needed to know. And I was going to ask her, I was going to *demand*, but then the pavement was slipping underneath me, and I ended up on my knees in the middle of the road, sealed alone inside a cloud of swirling ash.

My mother smiled gently, compassionately, and kept on walking.

No, I begged her. *You have to help me. Please, Mom. HELP ME.*

But she was gone.

# CHAPTER TWO

I woke the next morning to my phone alarm buzzing erratically, showing a low-battery warning along with the unpleasant notification that it was now 7 a.m. I slammed the alarm off, feeling disoriented and spectacularly unrested, as if I hadn't slept at all. For a while, I lay in bed, wondering if I should even bother getting up. The night hadn't exactly been pleasant, but I could hardly imagine it being worse than the day ahead.

There was a metallic taste in my mouth, my lower lip bleeding sluggishly like I'd bitten through it. I frowned, running my tongue over the damage. It had been ages since I'd hurt myself in my sleep. Ages since I'd dreamed so clearly. Ages since I'd seen my mother.

Annoyed, I dragged myself out of bed and went to clean my lip, watching my reflection ripple and distort in the fractured bathroom mirror.

The girl staring back at me was pale and shadowed, her dark hair a tangling mess. Something feral about her, difficult to tame. I was glad of that, because it hid how brittle I felt on the inside. Like there was another girl, a scared, lost one, locked below my ribcage, threatening to claw her way to the surface if I didn't watch out. First the dream and now this – it bothered me how quickly Castello was unravelling my defences.

On my way to the kitchen, I passed my father's bedroom, saw him poring over work papers with a mug of coffee in one hand. He glanced up at me in greeting, but I ignored him. I didn't trust my temper this early in the morning.

I found a packet of airline crackers on the table, which I ate while examining the map of Castello from last night. The city was perfectly symmetrical, divided down the middle by a massive town square and the cathedral I'd seen yesterday from the road. My new school, like our house, was on the south side of town, marked by the Castello insignia and the words *Scuola Lafolia*. I made a face.

In Maine, I'd taken the bus every day to the public high school in the next town over, where they grouped the kids from rural areas together. I'd loved that anonymity: the ability to float unnoticed through the corridors, no one knowing or caring where I'd come from or what I'd done. All year, I'd sat with the same girls at lunch, and none of them had ever thought to ask about my dead mom.

But middle school had been a different story. The kids there were from my hometown, and the rumours they spread had been vicious – that Carly was crazy so I was probably crazy, too. Avoiding me in hallways, switching desks if I tried to sit next to them. Staring at me so hard sometimes I felt like I'd snap.

That was what I was afraid Castello would be like. I was the new girl here, the one it was acceptable to look at and laugh.

I considered my original plan again: dropping back into bed and forgetting about everything. But I figured my father would find out if I went truant on day one.

It was nearly eight o'clock when I got outside, but the streets were still grey and muted, as if the sunlight was being blocked by the slanted buildings. I walked slowly – deciding I could at least be late for school if I couldn't skip – taking in the sights of the city. Dingy shops with metal grilles over the windows, a butcher unloading pig carcasses from a truck, a pair of workers in dirty overalls. Thrilling stuff.

The only things that stood out to me were the posters. Most of the buildings were covered with them: big yellowed notices like I'd seen last night from the car. Each had the word SALVEZZA stamped in bold letters, with Castello's cross and trinity symbol above. At the bottom: a spidery signature, which I recognized from my father's letters.

*The General*

Around the next corner, the streets began tilting uphill, leading me towards the centre of town. The posters were sparser here, overtaken by graffiti. One line caught my attention in particular, because someone had tried to erase it with red paint.

*THE SAINTS LIVE*, said the graffiti.

19

I had no idea what that meant, but the person with the red paint clearly didn't agree. They'd drawn an angry slash across the words and written something else off to the side, a savage muddle of letters that looked like they'd been scrawled in blood.

## ALL WITCHES BURN

I sighed. So even the graffiti in Castello was about five hundred years out of date.

At the end of the street, I discovered the town square, which was as long as a football pitch and paved in glistening white marble, shockingly bright after the bits of the city I'd seen so far. And then there was the church.

It towered over the back of the square, almost inhuman in its dimensions, by far the largest building I'd ever set eyes on. I found myself enthralled by it: the bronze dome sparkling in the sun, the glittery windows of stained glass. Curving marble staircases led up to a terrace before the main doors, like a podium where a speaker could address the square below. And the church had two identical wings, flanked by those two identical watchtowers. Perfect symmetry, just like my map had shown. The north and south halves of Castello were exact reflections of each other.

My school was on a street off the square up ahead, so I walked along the edge of it, glad that I didn't have to cross over to the other side. I couldn't explain why, but I felt it would've been dangerous to do so. For one thing, there were no people around, and all the storefronts were abandoned, their windows boarded over. A neat, organized kind of empty, like a neighbourhood that had been evacuated after a chemical spill. As if the whole town had been told that the square was simply the wrong place to be.

I got to Scuola Lafolia around eight thirty, a respectable half-hour late, drawn in by yet another cross and trinity symbol, this time in chipped gold over the door. The lobby was vacant and crumbling, and as soon as I was inside, I realized I had no idea where to go. I could hear a distant buzz of voices, lessons happening nearby, but there was no helpful front office to give me directions. Maybe being late hadn't been such a brilliant idea, after all. All I knew was that I was meant to be in eleventh grade – Year Three in this town.

I was wandering around aimlessly, wondering if I could leave again if I claimed I couldn't find my classroom, when I backed into a boy. I felt a pulse of heat where my fingers brushed his wrist, like static electricity, making me jerk my hand away in a rush.

'Sorry,' I said in English. 'Did I hurt you?'

The boy blinked. He seemed about my age, slender and pale, with sandy curls tumbling down into murky blue eyes. But for a second, when he looked at me, I had the strangest feeling – my heart picking up, my head going fuzzy – as if I was slipping away from reality, sinking into a pool of dark water. Dragging him along. Or maybe he was dragging me.

A flicker of panic crossed the boy's face, his lips parting.

'Do I know you?' he asked. In Italian, of course. My mother's tongue. Slick, gorgeous and deadly. Which meant I had to answer the same way.

'Not yet,' I said, hoping my grammar wasn't wrong. I'd been almost fluent in this language as a child, but after Carly died it was just another thing I wanted to forget. 'I moved here last night.'

'*Certo*,' the boy said. *Of course*. Shaking himself a little, like he was coming out of a daze. A flush rising on his cheeks when he realized he was staring at me. 'Sorry. It's just, no one else is ever this late to school. I can't believe I have competition.'

'Well, I try,' I muttered. Willing myself not to stare at *him*, either. He reminded me of something from a painting – delicate and ethereal like a Renaissance angel. But there was a dark undertone to his beauty, too: shadowed circles below his eyes, his curls a knotted mess, his clothing loose-cut, swallowing his body. As though he wanted to hide what he looked like. It wasn't exactly working.

'Do you know how to get to Year Three?' I asked, when we'd stood there long enough not-staring at each other. The Italian words were coming easier to me now, rising up from wherever they'd hidden themselves inside my brain. 'Keep in mind that if you say no I get to go home. And your lateness record will remain undefeated.'

'Unfortunately, I do know,' the boy said with a rueful smile. 'It's my class, too. I can show you.' He nodded for me to follow him towards a grimy staircase at the back of the lobby. 'I'm Christian.'

'Lilly.'

'Lilly,' he repeated, like he was testing the word out. Eyes darting to my face and away again in teasing flashes of blue.

Together, we climbed the stairs to the second floor, a web of narrow hallways lined with classroom doors labelled by grade. There were more posters on the walls here, but now SALVEZZA was not the only thing being advertised. There was also UNITÀ, ONORE, VITTORIA and SACRIFICIO.

*Unity. Honour. Victory. Sacrifice.*

Underneath the posters, the plaster was so worn it was almost peeling off.

Wind swept the landing, October air spiralling in through a series of broken windows, making Christian pull his bomber jacket close. I was dying to ask about the state of the school – if the budget in Castello was so tight that they couldn't even afford wall paint and windowpanes, or if this was just the kind of city that didn't believe in funding education. But I didn't want to be rude.

Christian seemed to guess my thoughts anyway, because when I glanced over he just shook his head. 'Take it up with the General.'

Year Three was the last classroom we came to, identified by a tarnished gold plaque on the door. I'd never have found my way here if Christian hadn't shown me; like Castello's streets, the school was a maze.

Someone had taped a sign on the wall nearby, hand-written in black marker. It said:

*LASCIATE OGNI SPERANZA, VOI CH'ENTRATE.*

My Italian may have been rusty, but I believed that translated to: *Abandon all hope, you who enter here.*

'Dante's *Inferno*,' Christian said, following my gaze. 'It's the line on the gates of Hell.'

'Charming,' I said.

He grinned. 'Do you have a uniform? No one wears them most of the time, but today they're required.'

I shook my head, wondering why my father hadn't warned me. Thinking it was bold of Lafolia to require uniforms when they couldn't be bothered with basic repairs.

'It's not a full uniform,' Christian said, reading my mind again. 'More like a token. Something to show your respect.' He hesitated, then reached up to his collar, pulling a loose tie from around his neck. I caught a glimpse of a necklace below it, fragile gold against his skin.

'Here,' he said. 'This should do.'

He took a step forward and paused, teeth sunk into his bottom lip, like he was asking permission to put the tie around my neck. I felt a dizzy pang of anticipation, realizing all of a sudden how badly I wanted this boy to touch me. Inclining my head to tell him what to do.

But the moment his fingers brushed my skin it happened again: that electric shock, the pulse of heat lighting me up. Christian's eyes gone wide, his body swaying towards me

24

like he couldn't stop himself. And the falling sensation – like we were slipping into each other. This time, it felt good enough to take my breath away.

Christian clearly disagreed. The next thing I knew, he was stumbling back from me, cradling his hand against his chest like I'd burned him. Face ghost-white, flooded again with panic.

'I'm sorry,' I stammered, thinking of my mother clutching my arm in the grocery store, hissing, *Don't touch a thing.* 'I swear this doesn't usually happen –'

'It's fine,' Christian said. But there was an edge to his voice now, his shoulders tensed like he was expecting an attack. My heart sank when I realized what I was seeing: he was afraid of me.

Before I could question it, Christian was moving, pulling open the door to the classroom and stepping past me inside. I watched him go, feeling disoriented, reaching up automatically for the tie he'd left around my neck. The fabric was soft from too much washing, still warm from his skin. Dangerously intimate. Shaking myself a little, I tucked the tie under my sweater and followed him into Year Three.

The first thing I saw was a boy with a knife. He was lounging on the sill of one of Lafolia's broken windows, keeping watch for something in the street below. The drop to the ground must've been staggering, but the boy didn't seem bothered. A silver switchblade spun through his fingers like he'd been born with it, moving so fast the metal blurred.

'Any sign, Nico?' said a kid with wild corkscrew curls, who was inexplicably wearing a gas mask.

The boy in the window – Nico – shook his head.

'Still clear,' he said. 'Do you really think I'd let them sneak up on you?'

'That's super,' said the gas-mask kid, rubbing his hands together like a very cheerful mad scientist. 'I need to defuse my cherry bombs.'

Nico rolled his eyes. 'Don't die.'

He was the opposite of Christian in every way, except that they were both beautiful. His skin was tan, his hair dark, his ears studded with metal. Broad shoulders in a white T-shirt, black tattoos snaking across his collarbones. Something raw about him, rough at the edges. Magnetic. My eyes lingered helplessly on the contraction of his muscles as he spun the knife.

The classroom around him was a wasteland of scattered desks and balled-up paper, highlighters and textbooks strewn across the floor. I thought of my old school, with its sterile rows of metal desks and the drilling bell that shuffled you from room to room. This was like entering a hurricane in comparison. A dozen or so kids sat around, talking or throwing things at each other. As far as I could tell, none of them was wearing a uniform, either. And there was no teacher.

Someone had spray-painted a caricature of Castello's panorama across the back wall: the church dome, the watchtowers, big rats standing in the gutter. The trinity symbol was there, too, but drawn upside down, like a satanic perversion, dripping fresh paint over the horizon. A boy with gelled black hair and an armful of aerosol paint cans, who I assumed was the artist, was having an argument about it with Christian.

'It's not my fault you got here too late to stop me,' the boy was saying. He had model-sharp cheeks, wore a leather jacket with chains that clattered together when he moved. 'I was hit by a bolt of divine inspiration and had to follow through.'

'Divine inspiration to get arrested,' Christian snapped, glaring at the trinity. 'Alex, you can't seriously be planning to leave that up for testing –'

'It's *fine*,' said the boy named Alex. 'Just help me hide the paint.'

He dumped half the cans into Christian's book bag and nudged him back towards the hallway, bickering as they went. I told myself I didn't care that Christian avoided looking at me when he passed.

At the front of the room, a girl with dirty blonde hair sat with her legs propped up on the teacher's desk, holding a paper airplane and a cigarette lighter. As I watched, she set the tail of the plane on fire and threw it into the air. It spiralled a few times, bright like a comet, then burned out over the desk. Ash dusted her hair, reminding me of my dream: wandering lost through Castello's burnt streets. Shaken, I turned away. And found myself locking eyes with Nico in the window.

At first, he just seemed surprised, but then his face changed, became a cool mask of hostility. The knife in his hands went still. This caught the attention of the gas-mask boy, who turned around to see what the matter was. When he noticed me, his eyes bugged out.

'Wow,' he said. 'Where did you come from?'

I froze. The classroom was very quiet all of a sudden, the kids turning one by one in their chairs to stare me down. I got a tight feeling in my throat, the weight of their gazes stealing my breath away. This was what I'd been dreading.

*Say something*, I thought sharply. *Anything. Do it.*

'Um, hi?' I tried.

Silence. More stares. Suddenly I was glad that Christian had left class, so he didn't have to watch me make a fool of myself.

Then someone said, 'Enough ogling. This isn't the zoo.'

It was the girl from the teacher's desk. She had gotten to her feet, slight and agile, and came towards me, still holding the cigarette lighter.

'I mean it,' she snapped at the kids. Then to me, 'Just ignore them. They're in shock. We never get new people in this dump.' She swept her long hair off her shoulders, offering me her hand. 'I'm Liza.'

The way she spoke was quick and musical, her Italian words blurring together like an incantation. Rosy cheeks, freckles on her nose, green eyes that burned like flames, fierce and dazzling. The eyes of a fighter. I was hypnotized.

'Lilly,' I managed to say.

'*Perfetto*,' Liza murmured. 'Come with me.'

She led me through the obstacle course of crumpled notebooks and overturned pencil cases to a two-person desk in the centre of the classroom, unwinding a black bandana from her slender wrist.

'Here,' she said. 'For the smoke, in case Iacopo accidentally sets off one of his cherry bombs. He plants them all over the place, and every time a teacher steps on one we all get the week off.'

She nodded at the gas-mask boy, who was now lying flat on the floor, fiddling with something below the blackboard. When I glanced back at Liza, she was smiling a little, her green eyes sharp on mine. I felt warm under her gaze, drawn towards her inexplicably. Wanting to please.

'Welcome to Year Three,' she said. 'I hope you don't like following the rules.'

We sat down together at the desk, knees bumping under the surface. Liza was wearing light skinny jeans and a T-shirt with the sleeves rolled up, showing the pale stretch of her arms.

I cast another glance around the classroom. Some of the kids were *still* shooting me looks, but most of them had the decency to pretend they were busy when they saw me looking back. Except Nico. He was spinning his knife again, keeping watch for something out the window – displaying absolutely no interest in me at all. I allowed my eyes to rest on him while he was turned away, tracing the shape of his golden body, the tantalizing curve of his lips.

'You think he's pretty, don't you?' Liza said, toying with the flame on her lighter.

'Sure,' I said, unable to deny it. Nico's looks weren't the debatable kind.

Liza laughed, a slight edge to her voice, like she begged to differ. I wondered if she'd seen the way he'd looked at me before – the disdain in his eyes.

'Anyway,' I said, eager to change the subject, 'when does class start?'

'Oh,' Liza said. 'Well, we used to have trigonometry at eight. But the professor was tragically incapacitated. Giorgia put glue in her coffee.' She nodded to a redhead in the corner, who was flipping through a very outdated fashion magazine. 'Besides, you've come on testing day. So things are a little different.'

'Testing?' I asked. 'Like an exam?'

Liza glanced at me sideways. 'Not quite.'

She paused, like she was waiting to see if I'd catch on to some hidden meaning in her words. I had no idea what she was talking about.

'It's written into the truce,' Liza said helpfully. 'There's mandatory testing on the first of the month for both sides of town. The General says it's how we maintain order and purity in Castello.'

She sounded like she was reciting from an instruction manual, her voice flat but tinged with faint sarcasm. I stared at her, wondering if my Italian was failing me. None of this made sense.

'You shouldn't worry, though,' Liza said, oblivious to my confusion. 'They haven't found a Saint in ages. I think the General's just entertaining himself at this point. God forbid he lets us forget who's really in charge –'

'Haven't found a *what*?'

'Don't listen to her,' someone snapped. 'She'll get you both locked up for talking like that.' It was the girl at the desk in front of us, whirling around to glare at me. Her pinched face was just visible through a curtain of mousy hair. 'Testing is the most important day of the month,' she said. 'And the General's our saviour. Not that you'd know it from Liza. She'll drag you to the dark side if you don't watch out.'

'Susi,' said Liza very calmly, 'I will punch you.'

The girl named Susi squeaked. 'You see what I mean?'

She whirled back around in a huff. Liza narrowed her eyes, waving her lighter through the air like she was performing an exorcism on the back of Susi's head.

'Our Father, who art in heaven,' she chanted, 'please deliver this sad lost soul to Jesus, amen.'

'Liza,' I said, when she'd finished, 'who exactly is the General?'

'The General's the leader of Castello,' Liza said matter-of-factly, then cast a sly glance at Alex's mural. 'At least for now.'

'Like the mayor or something?'

'Sort of. I'd call him more of a peacekeeper, though. He negotiated the ceasefire between the Paradisos and Marconis twenty years ago and then just decided to stick around.'

'Paradisos and *who*?'

Liza arched an eyebrow at me. 'Castello's split down the middle, haven't you noticed?'

Slowly, I nodded.

'Right,' Liza said. 'Because there have always been two families in town. Clans, I guess you'd call them. Marconi down here and Paradiso up north, across the boundary line. They used to fight each other. A *lot*. It was like ... total war for centuries. Then one day the General came along and made it stop. The end. We all live happily ever after. Our saviour, like Susi said.' The sarcasm was back, biting at the corners of her words. 'So now we just have to do everything he tells us.'

'Like the testing,' I said. 'The testing that's not an exam.'

'Exactly.'

'So ... what is it, then?'

Liza made a dismissive gesture. 'Just a pinprick. To make sure you're not, you know. Different.'

'Different how?'

For a moment, Liza seemed to struggle with herself, weighing her options. I had the impression that she'd been trying to shield me from something dark and unpleasant, but had realized there was no way around it now.

'Lilly,' she said, 'how do you think the General did it? Made peace between the clans? Got people who'd been hating each other for centuries to suddenly just stop?'

I shook my head, at a loss.

'He gave them a new enemy,' Liza said. 'Someone they could all hate together.'

'Who?' I asked.

'I already told you,' Liza said. 'The Saints.'

# CHAPTER THREE

From the window, Nico said, 'They're here.'

The whole class seemed to freeze. Then everyone was moving, rushing to put their desks back in order, shoving textbooks and pencil cases away in their bags. Iacopo stuffed his cherry bombs into his pockets and wrenched the gas mask off his head. And now I saw the uniforms appearing – or at least pieces of them, what Christian had referred to as tokens of respect. Suddenly everyone was wearing something formal: ties or faded suit jackets that looked like they'd once belonged to a prep-school set. The air in the room had changed, too, become thick with tension.

'Liza, what's a Saint?' I asked, thinking of old paintings, people with stigmata on their hands. 'What exactly are we getting tested for?'

'It really doesn't matter,' Liza said. She was being evasive again, dusting ash off her clothing and extracting a tie of her own from her bag.

Out of the corner of my eye, I saw Nico slide down from the window sill and head for his seat, a single desk near the blackboard. Even in the tension, I couldn't help but notice how gracefully he moved, his beat-up jeans hiding a kind of deadly elegance, like an assassin trained to walk without any noise.

'I told you they haven't found a Saint in ages.' Liza was fiddling with my clothing now, smoothing out the tie Christian had given me – readying me for some kind of ritual. 'And you're not even from here. So you'll be totally fine –'

'How do you know?' I demanded, shaking out of her grip, starting to feel uneasy. 'Why won't you just tell me what they're testing for?'

'The thing is, Lilly,' Liza said with a bitter smile, 'you wouldn't believe me if I tried.'

The door to the classroom burst open. A man in a grey uniform entered, followed by half a dozen others all dressed the same: gun belts and military boots, the trinity symbol pinned to their breast pockets in bright gold. I didn't think they were going to like Alex's wall art very much. A hush descended over the class. This was the moment everyone had been waiting for.

'Who are they?' I asked Liza, watching the men line up like soldiers before the blackboard.

'Enforcers,' she whispered. 'They work for the General.'

The man at the front of the pack turned to face us. He was taller and younger than my father, striking in a way that felt dangerous – a predatory glint in his eyes. It was like that with some men: you knew you had to fear them. He wore his uniform loose, almost casually, the collar unbuttoned and the sleeves undone. Long black hair licking at his shoulders. A faded scar ran like a claw scratch down the left side of his face, breaking on his eyelid.

'And that's Tiago,' Liza said.

'Year Three,' said Tiago, smiling blandly. 'A pleasure to see you again. Today is the first of October. A new month and a new opportunity to cleanse the unworthy. You will each have the honour to stand before me and prove your loyalty to our city. On behalf of the General, I wish you all luck and purity.'

I glanced at Liza, wondering if I'd misunderstood. *Luck and purity?* I mouthed. But she just shrugged.

Tiago waved a leather-gloved hand towards the hallway where a pair of enforcers were standing guard, telling them to shut the door. Someone slipped into class just before they did so: Alex with his glass-cut cheeks, black eyes bright with strong emotion. Maybe anger. I expected Christian to be on his heels, but there was no sign of him at all.

'Kind of you to show up,' Tiago said, as Alex swept by him without a second glance.

'I know, right?' Alex said.

Behind him, the door clanged decisively shut, the enforcers sliding the bolt into place from the hall. I shot another glance at Liza, wanting to ask her what kind of test required being sealed in a room with a bunch of soldiers. But she was studiously looking the other way.

Tiago reached down to the leather holster on his belt, and for a heart-stopping moment, I thought he was going to draw his gun. Instead, he took out a machine, like a tiny ticket scanner, sleek and metallic and small enough to fit inside his palm.

'Now I lay me down to sleep, I pray the Lord my soul to keep.' Tiago pressed a button, making a red light blink steadily on top of the machine. 'And if I should become a Saint I pray the Lord my soul to break.'

'Amen,' someone said. It sounded like Susi.

'Get Carenza,' Tiago told the enforcers.

A pair of them marched to Nico's desk, seized his shoulders and dragged him roughly to his feet. Forcing his hand forward to Tiago's scanner like they thought he'd lash out if they let him go. Nico seemed bored by it all, uninterested in causing trouble.

'You don't have to make them do this every time,' he told Tiago. 'I don't bite.'

'So you claim,' Tiago said coldly.

A needle descended from the bottom of the scanner and punctured the pad of Nico's finger. Blood pooled on his skin, the whole class deathly silent while the machine ran an analysis of some kind. I held my breath, expecting an alarm to go off, something wild and ear-splitting, but nothing happened. The red light on the scanner continued to blink methodically. A negative result. So Nico was not a Saint. Whatever that meant. And the whole thing was a blood test.

Tiago drew the scanner back, lip curling disdainfully. 'Saved again, Carenza. One day, you'll have to tell us how you manage it.'

When he moved on to the next desk, the enforcers shoved Nico back into his chair and returned to their posts at the blackboard. Apparently, no one else needed to be treated like that.

I watched Tiago change the needle and prick Iacopo's finger, feeling a panicky anticipation build inside my chest. Running over scenarios in my head – trying to remember what blood tests were used for. Detecting sickness, I thought. So maybe being a Saint was an illness of some kind. Except that the enforcers didn't look worried about contagion. They seemed almost hungry instead. Eager to pounce.

*At least it's simple*, I told myself. *All you have to do is hold out your hand.* But you couldn't cheat a blood test, either. If you were a Saint, you were a Saint *inside*. You couldn't hide it from them.

Iacopo tested negative, and then Tiago was pricking Susi's finger, looming over the desk in front of us. She went all breathless waiting for her result, like she really thought there might be something wrong with her blood. There wasn't. Afterwards, she flushed pink and gave Tiago a simpering little curtsey. Liza made a very quiet gagging noise at my side. Then it was her turn.

'Mezzi,' Tiago said. 'Shall we?'

Liza rose to her feet and held her hand out. She didn't flinch when the needle went in, regarding Tiago with those steel-green eyes. The red light blinked rhythmically over her finger, declaring her normal. Tiago seemed almost disappointed.

'You know I always wonder about you,' he said. 'Because of your tainted bloodline.'

Liza's eyes flashed, but she didn't deign to respond. Tiago turned to me.

I felt it clearly, the moment his gaze hit my body, because it was like being stripped – like he was seeing through my clothes, his hunter's eyes finding secret, hidden parts of myself and ruining what they touched.

'And who might you be?' Tiago said.

I swallowed, forcing myself to my feet the way the rest of the kids had done.

'Lilliana Deluca.'

'*Ciao*, Lilly,' Tiago said, shortening it without asking. He walked a slow, deliberate circle around my desk. 'Have you visited us before?'

I shook my head. 'We just moved here.'

'Well, don't be frightened,' Tiago said, taking my hand in one shiny leather glove. 'Everyone has a first time.'

He jammed the needle into my finger. I jerked back, feeling pain spiral up my arm. Heart pounding hard, watching the red light flash and willing it not to falter.

Around the room, the kids were staring at me, twisted around in their chairs for a better view. Their faces were a little too curious, a little too sharp. Like maybe they were expecting me to fail the test. Only Nico seemed uninterested, picking at a piece of splintered wood on his desk, eyes downturned, lips set into a tiny frown. *Look at me*, I thought, feeling a sudden rush of defiance. *Look at me, I dare you.* But he didn't move.

The test couldn't have lasted more than a minute, but to me it felt like an eternity. Blood dripped down the side of my finger, the scanner running its analysis, the red light blinking steadily to show I was clear. Just below the desk, Liza squeezed my free hand so hard I was afraid she'd crack something.

'And there you have it,' Tiago said, smiling benevolently as he drew the scanner back. 'You're pure.'

I sank into my chair as soon as he moved on, waiting for my heart to settle, wishing I could erase the oily feeling his eyes had left on my skin. There was something very wrong about what was happening here – the idea of testing for purity. I didn't understand how we were meant to prove something like that, or why we should have to. But I was desperately relieved that I'd passed.

Tiago had moved to the back of the class now: the two-person desk where Alex sat next to an empty chair that I presumed belonged to Christian. The inverted trinity symbol looked bold and dark on the wall above his head. Tiago flicked his eyes over it, a muscle jumping in his jaw.

'Getting creative, are we, Latore?' he said, pulling Alex to his feet by one narrow wrist and pricking his finger.

'Me?' said Alex. 'I definitely didn't draw that. But you have to admit, whoever did is pretty talented –'

Tiago reached abruptly for Alex's bag and turned it upside down. A waterfall of notebooks, markers, glue sticks and comic books exploded on the floor. But there was no spray paint. Alex flashed a smile and popped his bloody finger in his mouth, watching Tiago through a dark sprawl of lashes. His test had come back negative. Tiago was not amused.

'Where's your other half?' he snapped, turning to Christian's chair.

'He went home,' Alex said. 'He's sick.' He coughed once, deliberately, in Tiago's face. 'He caught it from me.'

For a moment, it looked like Tiago was considering whether he could hit Alex and get away with it. Then he seemed to decide it wasn't worth his time. 'Tell Asaro I'll be making a house call,' he said. 'I always enjoy the chance to see his father.'

Alex deflated at that, taking his seat without reply. A curl of wariness shot through me, wishing I knew what was going on – if Christian was really sick, or if this had something to do with the way Alex had seemed angry coming into class, like they'd been fighting.

The test ended soon afterwards, with the redhead presenting a manicured finger to the scanner and passing easily. Then Tiago returned the machine to his belt and resumed his position at the front of the classroom. There was no doubt in my mind that he was disappointed now. He'd clearly been hoping to find a Saint or two among us. Something to feed the starved eyes of the enforcers flanking him on either side.

'Year Three, I congratulate you,' Tiago said. 'This month, all of you are pure. All of you are loyal. May you keep your minds and souls turned towards the light.' He touched two fingers to his lips like a kiss and pressed them to the gold pin on his jacket. 'Hail the General.'

Around the room, my classmates responded in one voice, trained to perfection. 'For he alone protects.'

# CHAPTER FOUR

'See, I told you,' said Liza, supremely relaxed all of a sudden. 'No Saints. We *never* have any Saints. I knew it would be fine.'

'That was messed up,' I said, staring down the hallway where Tiago and the enforcers had vanished into the next classroom. 'What were they looking for in our blood?'

'Who cares?' Liza said. 'The test is over. Why dwell on it?'

'Because I want to know,' I said sharply. 'What did he mean about purity?'

But Liza was having none of it. 'Come on,' she said. 'I'll give you a school tour on the way out.'

'Out?' I reached for my phone to check the time, only to realize the battery had died. 'But it can't be past ten.'

'Testing day has early dismissal.'

Sure enough, kids were packing up their things, chattering as if nothing out of the ordinary had happened. I felt like I had whiplash: the tension hadn't melted out of me yet.

'But don't worry,' Liza said. 'Since you're clearly desperate to have proper lessons, you'll be delighted to know we've got history tomorrow. Veronica Marconi's all business. I'm sure you'll learn loads.'

'Marconi,' I repeated. 'Like the clan?'

Liza nodded. 'Before the truce, she was the leader of this side of town. Now she works with the General for peacekeeping.' The sarcasm was creeping into her voice again. 'To remind us of all the incredible things he's done.'

We left class together, overtaking Nico in the hallway. He moved his body smoothly to the side when we passed, like the idea of my shoulder brushing against his was too horrible to bear.

'Thanks,' I snapped, turning back for a second to stare him down.

Liza led me through the school corridors, pointing out important landmarks as we went: a chemistry lab full of broken beakers, a library with bare bookshelves, a sunken courtyard with bullet holes in the walls. Everything had a beaten-down look to it, coated in a thick layer of grime. My father had definitely been misinformed about the music elective.

We were approaching the main staircase when the redhead from Year Three appeared out of nowhere and pounced on me. Tiago must've finished testing another classroom because there were younger kids in uniform milling around the hallway now, trying to descend the stairs. The redhead paid no mind to the traffic she was stopping.

'Oh my *gosh*,' she said breathlessly, grabbing my wrists like she thought I might make a break for it. 'I've been trying to find you for ages! Liza's just stolen you away, hasn't she?'

Liza shot me a long-suffering look. 'Lilly, this is Giorgia. Giorgia, Lilly.'

'Look at you,' Giorgia purred, stroking my hand like I was a rare and precious animal. A boy with an oversized backpack tried to push through our blockade; Giorgia swatted him expertly away. 'A real foreigner in Castello. That's never happened before. You're absolutely a *phenomenon*.'

'It's nice to meet you, too,' I tried to say, but found myself drowned out by her continuous stream of conversation.

'You're lucky they've put you on the good side of town, of course. I really shouldn't mention it, but the Paradisos are *evil*. You're much too sweet; I'm sure they would've slaughtered you.'

'Giorgia,' said Liza sarcastically, 'stop violating the truce.'

Giorgia paid her no mind. She hooked our elbows together and headed down the stairs at an extremely leisurely pace, plying me with gossip. 'So I was *positive* Alex was going to get himself arrested today. I swear he's got a death wish. And Christian, going home sick like that? A scandal. Maybe I should check on him –'

'Good idea,' said Liza. 'You can ask him out again while you're at it. Since he's turned you down the last four times.'

Giorgia flushed bright pink and skittered off, suddenly remembering she had somewhere to be. Liza smirked, taking up the vacant spot at my side. 'And good riddance,' she said.

We passed through the school doors together, accompanied by the flood of children Giorgia had been blocking – glancing up automatically at the gold trinity symbol overhead. Sculpted into the wall behind it, I could just make out the faded lines of a crossed key and dagger.

'The gold one is the General's mark,' Liza said. 'In case you hadn't guessed by now.'

'It kind of looks like a holy trinity.'

'Sure, if by trinity you mean Marconi, Paradiso and the General in between. But I wouldn't call it holy.'

'What about the key and dagger? I've seen it before. It's painted in my bedroom.'

'That's Castello's original coat of arms,' said Liza. 'It represents the founding key to the city. The legend was, whoever had the key was the true leader of town. Which pretty much explains why the clan wars started. The General tried to get rid of all the old symbols when he took over, but medieval stone is surprisingly durable.'

Liza grinned, linking her pinkie in mine and tugging me up the street; I'd told her my address, and she'd offered to walk me home so I wouldn't have to use the map. Someone had brought out a football, and I saw a few of my classmates joining in the game. Ahead of us, a silhouette in black leather was just turning into the town square.

'Is that Alex?' I asked, squinting.

44

'Yes, unfortunately,' Liza said. 'Discount Michelangelo is your neighbour. Building sixty-one or something. His mum works for the General.'

'Where does Christian live?' I asked before I could help myself. Liza's eyebrows shot up, as if to say, *Not you too*.

'Never mind,' I said quickly.

We passed along the edge of the square, which was still devoid of human life, eerily quiet in that evacuation-zone kind of way. It was less intimidating with Liza than it had been on my own, but I didn't like the barren glint of the marble, the way the sunlight seemed to reflect back at us like thousands of little daggers in the ground.

'See the boundary line?' Liza asked.

If I shaded my eyes, I could make out a slab of metal running through the pavement in the middle of the square, marking the barrier between the north and south sides of town.

'It was a wall before the truce, but the General made it retractable and decided to roll it down. Very daring of him. We're still not allowed to *cross* it, obviously. The last person who tried got executed for treason.'

'Executed?' I said, snapping my head around.

'Don't fret – it was eons ago. And besides it's what they deserved for being stupid enough to go north in the first place.' Contempt turned Liza's voice cold.

'You really don't like them, do you?' I said, trying to remember the name she'd used for the other half of Castello. 'The . . . Paradiso clan.'

Liza shrugged. 'Old habits die hard. And hating Paradisos is ancient.'

'Why exactly? I mean, what's so wrong with them?'

Liza's eyes narrowed. 'Apart from the fact that they tried to destroy us for centuries? Let's see.' She ticked a list off on her fingers. 'They're heartless; they think their ancestors owned Castello; and they've got all the good stuff over there – all the marble and mills. We just have dirt and dead things.'

I frowned. 'What about the Saints, though? I thought you were supposed to hate them instead of each other.'

'Of course we're *supposed* to.' Liza dropped her voice, leaning close like she was worried about eavesdroppers. 'It's just, the Saints have never actually done anything to me.'

'If they've never done anything, why are they the enemy?'

'Not so loud,' she hissed. 'I said the Saints have never done anything to *me*.' She stopped, tugging me towards her, preparing for a secret.

'Look at the church,' Liza said. We were standing near the southern wing of the cathedral, the only building that straddled the boundary line. 'Twenty years ago, a couple of Saints decided to burn it to the ground. They did it at midnight mass when hundreds of people from both clans were inside. It was a massacre. Everybody died.'

'That's horrible,' I whispered.

'Well, you'll be glad to hear we got rid of them after that,' Liza said flatly. 'And not just the kids who set the fire. Suddenly all the Saints had to go.'

I frowned again, wondering at her word choice. 'Got rid of them? How?'

'Permanently,' was all Liza said. 'Anyway, the General was practically a child when the fire happened, but then he came up with the blood tests, which made him a hero. He convinced the Marconis and Paradisos to sign the truce, stop fighting with each other and take on the Saints instead. And he rebuilt Icarium, to prove that evil never triumphs.'

'Icarium?'

Liza motioned to the church. 'It was called Saint Peter's Cathedral before the fire, but the General had to give it a new name. You know how we feel about Saints in Castello.'

Our eyes met, and I found myself nodding automatically, captivated by the lure of her.

'Icarium sounds better, anyway,' Liza said. 'The General's a sucker for metaphors.'

'Meaning?'

'Don't you know the myth? That Greek kid Icarus gets a pair of wings because he decides he wants to fly. Which is totally great for a while until he gets too close to the sun and just sort of . . . falls out of the sky.'

I almost laughed at her rendition of the story, but decided it would be inappropriate, given the context.

'The point is,' said Liza, 'people who reach for heaven always burn in the end. There can only be one supreme authority.'

'Are you talking about God or the General?'

'I think he wants us to forget the difference.'

*

47

Liza left me at the end of Via Secondo, reassured that I wouldn't get lost once my house was in sight. She'd rattled off a list of Castello's rules for me on the way, some of which I'd already guessed, like steer clear of the boundary line, and don't talk about the Saints in public. Others were new to me, like the curfew, which was set for a strict 8 p.m.

'It's a peacekeeping thing,' Liza said. 'Apparently, people get bolder in the dark.'

The apartment was silent when I got upstairs, long shadows crawling through the hallway, making it seem like evening already. That fit my mood – I couldn't wait for the day to end. Liza had explained Castello's structure like it was the most natural thing in the world, but now that I was alone the strangeness of it sank into me like cold fingers down my spine. The more I thought about this city, the more unsettling it became.

I found a discarded page from my father's welcome packet on the kitchen table and grabbed a pen. Hesitated a moment, then wrote: *There are mafia clans in Castello. They hunt people called Saints.*

I was hoping the words would look stupid written down, a big joke. If I sent this on a postcard to Gracie, she'd think I was going mad. And yet . . . there was a needle prick in my finger. Liza's cool voice, saying, *We got rid of them . . . permanently.*

I should've pressed her more, asked her what she meant. Permanently sounded bad. It sounded like death. But I refused to believe that.

I paced around the house for a while, infuriated by the lack of internet, which made it impossible for me to get answers on my own. I wanted to look up Saints, or the General, or even the uses of blood tests. But no – like this, I was completely helpless.

I had no idea what Jack's new job hours were because it hadn't occurred to me to ask. As a child, I'd been fascinated by what he did, had loved going into work with him so I could watch him create things. He'd been barely more than a kid himself back then, bright-eyed and full of possibility, guiding my hands over bolts and wires – teaching me to make metal come alive. But after Carly died, he'd started banning me from his workshop. Sealing himself in for days at a time, eating and sleeping there. Eventually, I'd stopped counting on him to come home.

I spent the afternoon listlessly sorting through my suitcase, unwilling to commit to unpacking, but afraid that things would get crushed if I left them inside too long. I hadn't brought much – mostly books and clothes, and trinkets I was too old for but couldn't bring myself to let go. The rag doll Gracie had knitted to ward off nightmares. The music box Jack had built me for my ninth birthday, one of his cleverest machines. It was rigged with a silver ballerina on top, who spun in circles to *Für Elise*. When her spinning stopped, there was a trick: her metal eyes blinking at you curiously, fitted with tiny motion sensors. Most people tried to touch her, feel around for a lock. But only if you stood perfectly still in front of the ballerina did the box open up.

Inside, wrapped in a piece of faded velvet, were things I'd inherited from my mother. Two blown-glass figurines from Venice, shaped like winged lions. A pair of pearl-drop earrings and an expensive bottle of perfume. Carly's dazzling life boiled down into objects. That was my mother's specialty: dazzling people. Everything about her made you stop and stare. Her bright laugh, her melodic accent. Her ridiculous beauty.

When I was little, I'd wanted nothing more than to be like her, had followed her around the house, trying on her lipstick and repeating her Italian words. She told me stories of her childhood that sounded like fairy tales – midnight outings on the Venice canals, the soft lights of the city glowing on the water. Those were the times when I'd believed I could make her happy, that we could lift the veil that hung between us and become a normal mother and daughter somehow.

But those times never lasted. After a while, Carly always changed. Her charm would spark out like a broken fuse, and I'd be left with dull eyes and cold indifference. Or worse: anger. Breaking mirrors and tearing my art projects up, driving miles into the woods and threatening to leave me there. Hiding me away so deep and quiet it was like she wanted to forget I was alive at all.

Once she was gone, I'd had the urge to throw away everything of hers I could get my hands on, burn it up along with my memories. But I'd ended up sorting guiltily through her belongings instead, wearing her clothes and reading her old schoolbooks – trying to understand what I'd done to make her turn on me.

It was a losing battle. Nothing of my mother's was familiar any more. Her clothes had lost their lilac scent, and her margin notes had faded. Even her name was foreign, written in cursive script on the first page of every book. *Leonora Carlina Tale*. She'd never used Leonora when I was alive. She had always been Carly instead. Carly was elegant. Carly could slice you apart.

It was almost evening by the time I finished with my suitcase, arranging my trinkets and stacking my mother's books on top of the wardrobe: wilting volumes of Shakespeare and Milton. Afterwards, I collapsed on to my bed, staring at the war mural on my wall and fiddling with Christian's tie, still looped around my neck. Resisting the urge to press it against my nose and discover what his skin smelled like.

I must've dozed off eventually because the next thing I knew I was jolting awake in the middle of the night, gasping for breath, snapshots of a bad dream fading from my mind. The moon was up, coating my bedroom with pale light, making it perfectly visible from all angles.

And yet I couldn't shake the feeling that someone was standing in the corner, watching me.

# CHAPTER FIVE

I woke without an alarm the next morning, disoriented and tangled in sheets, skin hot like I'd burned through a fever. The window in the far wall had blown open, and the books I'd stacked on my wardrobe were scattered all over the floor. *Good start*, I thought, and lugged myself into the shower.

My father was already in the kitchen when I got there. He must've come back last night while I was sleeping, but I could tell from the circles under his eyes that he'd worked late and rested little. There was a pager hooked in his belt, sleek and black like the machine Tiago used, and dozens of work papers on the table. But Jack wasn't looking at them. Instead, he was holding a leather-bound book, which I recognized immediately. It was one of my mother's diaries.

She'd kept journals for as long as I could remember: secret, coveted things that Jack had claimed the right to read after she died. It was like he was searching for a reason in those pages – the answer to why she'd left him behind. No matter what my father said about fresh starts in Castello, he seemed to be behaving exactly the same as usual.

'So how's the power grid going?' I asked, louder than necessary, flicking the kitchen light on and off for emphasis.

My father started like he was coming out of a trance, slamming the diary shut. 'Lilly,' he said. 'You're awake.'

'Clearly,' I muttered, stealing a piece of his toast, Christian's tie dangling from my wrist. I noticed that my father tensed up when I approached, like he thought I was going to snatch the diary out of his hands. I couldn't have cared less. I'd stopped trying to understand my mother years ago.

'Did you sleep well?' Jack asked with a hint of forced pleasantry. 'How was your first day at school?'

'Educational,' I said, taking a second piece of toast. 'There were blood tests.'

'What?' he said. Distracted now – sweeping his papers off the table and out of sight. So maybe the diary wasn't what he was keeping from me, after all.

'Blood tests,' I repeated. 'They were looking for people called Saints. Do you know anything about that?'

For a moment, my father seemed to freeze, papers clutched in one hand, eyes darting up to meet mine. Then the pager in his belt started to buzz erratically, and his attention was gone again.

'Well, have a great day!' I heard him call, long after I'd left the kitchen. I resisted the urge to bang my head against the wall.

I got to school slightly earlier than the day before, but wasted a lot of time wandering around, trying to remember where the Year Three classroom was. Clearly, I should've paid more attention when Christian had shown me the way. After a while, I found myself in a dusty corridor in what I took to be an unused wing of the building, because the dirt on the ground was so thick I practically left footprints in it. I would've turned back immediately if not for the voices ahead.

There was a huge washroom at the end of the corridor, acting as a storage space now, with cracked mirrors and marble sinks on one side and piles of broken desks on the other. A coil of exposed piping dripped water down the wall. And there, like I'd conjured him: Christian, leaning against one of the sinks, fiddling with a thin leather bracelet on his wrist. Alex was with him, rummaging through the pile of desks, retrieving the spray-paint cans he must've hidden there the day before.

'I covered for you,' Alex was saying, tossing the cans into his open book bag. 'As usual. But you have to tell me what's going on.'

'I *did* tell you,' Christian said. I tried not to fixate on the arch of his neck, the golden tangle of his curls. The way I suddenly wanted to run my hands through them. 'I felt weird so I went home. It's not some big conspiracy.'

Alex snorted in disbelief, throwing a paint can harder than necessary. He seemed different than yesterday, more serious. It was as if their roles had been reversed. 'You've been doing that a lot lately. Feeling weird. Vanishing –'

'Alex, stop,' Christian said. Flicking a handful of water at Alex's forehead – making Alex face him with a scowl. 'You're being paranoid. Everything's totally fine.'

'Really?' Alex said. 'So your dad didn't care that you decided to ditch testing? That you had to let Tiago in the house?'

Christian was suddenly very quiet. Alex narrowed his eyes and crossed the room, took Christian's jaw in his hand and turned it to the side, examining something I couldn't see. For a moment, they were both still, bent towards each other like a sculpture: all fluid edges and curving lines.

'You're such a shit liar,' Alex said. 'Especially with me.'

I was halfway down the hall again, realizing I'd already seen more than I should have, when I heard Alex say, 'What about the girl?'

There was a pause, a hesitation, and I found myself freezing in place, heart in my throat for no reason I could explain. 'What girl?' Christian said at last.

Disappointment spun through me like liquid heat.

'That one,' Alex said.

I whirled around to find him standing in the washroom doorway, arms crossed, staring daggers at me – and cursed myself for not getting out of the hall fast enough.

'It's Deluca, right?' Alex said. 'Didn't they teach you it's rude to spy on people where you came from?'

Christian appeared behind him a second later, something bright and vulnerable flashing in his eyes. 'Lilly,' he said, and suddenly all I could think of were his fingers yesterday, brushing my neckline. From the slow bloom of colour on Christian's face, I wondered if he was thinking about it, too.

Alex made a disgusted noise, like he knew exactly what was on our minds. 'Where *did* you come from, anyway?' he demanded. 'Any chance they'll take you back?'

'Alex,' Christian said. 'Seriously?'

But Alex just shrugged. 'Welcome to Castello,' he snapped, shooting me an icy smile. 'Don't stay too long.'

He slammed into my shoulder as he passed, disappearing down the hall. *Great*, I thought. *Another one*. Maybe he and Nico could form a club.

I expected Christian to follow, but when I glanced back he was still in the doorway, frowning a little. A hesitant curl to his posture, like he wanted to ask a question he couldn't put into words. The air between us felt thicker than usual, warm and heavy at the edges.

'Don't pay attention to Alex,' Christian said. 'It's me he's really mad at.'

'It's fine,' I said. Eyes skating instinctively over his face, resting on the spot of darkness at his jawline. A bruise, spreading like an ink stain. What Alex had been examining before. And there it was again: that urge to reach out and touch him. Cradle his face between my palms.

Then I asked myself where on earth these thoughts were coming from, and vowed never to think them again.

*What girl*, Christian had said.

Except, he still had made no effort to leave the hall.

'I brought your tie,' I said, in an attempt at normal conversation, unravelling it from my wrist and holding it out to him. 'Thanks for lending it.'

But it was a mistake. Because the instant I moved, Christian seemed to come to his senses – lurching away from me, that familiar panic cutting through his eyes. Just like yesterday. I should've known.

*He doesn't want me near him again*, I realized. *He's afraid I'll shock him. He thinks I'm a freak.*

A flash of humiliation ran through me, making my muscles burn.

'Keep the tie,' Christian mumbled. 'It suits you.'

He stayed two steps ahead of me the whole way to class, and I wasn't stupid enough to try and get closer.

It was long past eight o'clock again when we got to Year Three, but it didn't seem to matter – there was no teacher there yet. The desks were all scattered about, and no one was doing anything remotely resembling schoolwork. Iacopo was lurking at the window with a fistful of electrical wires, determined to catch a bird from the roof outside. Nico was sprawled next to him on the sill, teaching him how to make a snare.

'Not too tight,' he explained, testing the ring of wires with his pocketknife. 'Or you'll actually hurt it.'

He glanced up automatically when I came into class, and I saw the perfect lines of his face harden at the sight of me, eyes narrowing in distaste. This time, the heat that rushed through me had edges, sharp and dangerous. *What exactly did I do to you?* I wanted to snap.

Across the room, the wall clock above Nico's head smashed to the floor, missing him by inches. The hook behind it must've given out.

'There's something wrong with me,' I said furiously, slumping into my seat next to Liza, who was balanced backwards on two legs of her chair, shooting rubber bands at Susi's head. 'Nico hates me, Christian acts like I've got

57

the plague, and Alex told me to go back where I came from.'

'Well,' said Liza, letting her chair slam down with a bang. She was wearing a pleated skirt, a faded button-down hanging loose off her shoulders. 'Nico's moody, Christian's tragic, and Alex has a grudge against anyone Christian talks to. But, if it's any consolation, I think you're perfect.'

'Thanks a lot.'

'No, I mean it,' Liza said. She wrapped one hand around my wrist and dragged my chair closer, hitting me with one of her low, tantalizing smiles. 'Boys are so tedious, aren't they?'

For a moment, my brain seemed to short-circuit, the sweet vanilla scent of her washing over me. Suddenly, I couldn't remember why I cared what anyone else thought. Then Susi cleared her throat with excessive volume, and Liza released me to snap her with another rubber band.

'Do you have a charger by any chance?' I asked, gathering my wits enough to pull my phone from my backpack. 'Mine only fits into American outlets.'

'*Che bello*,' Liza said, snatching the phone and turning it over a few times. 'I've never seen one of these in real life.'

I gaped at her. 'You've never seen a cellphone?'

'Not a nice one,' Liza said. She pulled an old flip phone from her backpack and compared it to the touch screen on mine. 'Everything we have here is at least twenty years old. The General doesn't allow new technology. He says it interferes with our spiritual connections.'

'The blood tests are pretty advanced,' I pointed out.

'That's different. The General invented those scanners himself. It's the stuff from outside that he doesn't permit. Like smartphones. Or internet that actually loads.'

I made a mental note to relay this to my father – I wanted him to know I wasn't the only one desperate for Wi-Fi.

'That's why my dad came here,' I told Liza. 'He's helping the city modernize.'

'Really?' Liza strung another rubber band between two fingers and released it against the back of Susi's head. 'I wouldn't have thought so. The General seems to like things just the way they are.'

Before I had time to reflect on that, Professor Marconi walked into class. I knew it had to be her because Liza sighed and reached automatically for an oversized history textbook, *City of Castello: Then and Now*. But I couldn't stop staring at the woman.

My first thought was *Carly*; not because they looked alike, but because they were both beautiful, excruciatingly so. Cold beauty, the most powerful kind.

'Veronica Marconi,' Liza said with a certain amount of grudging respect. 'In another life, I'm pretty sure she was royalty.'

She was much younger than I'd been expecting, my father's age, if that. Her hair was dark, tied in an elegant knot at the back of her head, her body long and slender. She wore a white silk blouse, a black pencil skirt and stiletto heels – simple but commanding. Her eyes swept the room in one glance, missing nothing.

'Iacopo Rossi,' Veronica said, 'release that pigeon immediately.'

'But, *professoressa*,' Iacopo spluttered, trying to hide the pigeon behind his back while it flapped its wings and pecked at his fingers. Nico's snare had clearly been a success. 'It's my comfort animal.'

'Within the hour, please,' Veronica said. Authority made her voice severe, but I could detect a hint of affection underneath. Iacopo groaned, but let the pigeon flap to freedom out the window.

'Thank you ever so kindly,' said Veronica. 'Now we can begin.'

She took her seat at the teacher's desk, sorting through a pile of papers. 'I hear we have a new arrival in town. Lilliana Deluca. That's a pretty little name.'

Her eyes found me in the centre of the classroom, and she smiled. It was genuine, but also calculating, just on the edge of sharp. 'The General told me you'd be joining us. I hope the students haven't been too uncivilized?'

Automatically, I glanced at Nico. For once, he was looking back at me, dark eyes bright with a challenge. Daring me to disagree. 'Not at all,' I said coolly.

'Very good,' Veronica said. 'Everyone will be pleased to know you're fitting in.'

The way she said *everyone* made me uneasy, like there was a secret commission just out of sight judging my behaviour. Determining whether I was worthy of living in Castello. Maybe it was the same commission that judged the Saints. Or maybe it was just the General, solitary and supreme. For some reason, that seemed like the worst scenario of all.

'We left off with the fall of the Roman Empire last week,' Veronica was saying. 'But, since the anniversary of Icarium is coming up, the General has asked us to spend today in remembrance.'

Liza knocked over the stack of erasers she'd been building, clearly displeased by this development.

'We'll start with the video, as usual,' Veronica said, looking towards the hallway, where a small boy was struggling to roll a bulky old television in from the class next door. 'Yes, *grazie*, Paolo,' she said, when the boy showed signs of lingering after the TV was in place. He scowled and ran out.

'Lights, please,' she said, and Susi sprang up to switch them off.

'What're we watching?' I asked Liza, as the television came alive with static.

'It's a history of Castello according to the General,' Liza muttered. 'Professor Marconi shows it to us once a year, around the anniversary of the church fire.'

'Icarium,' I said.

Liza nodded. 'There'll be a big memorial ceremony next month, but in the meantime –' she pointed at the screen – 'the General wants us to remember how he saved the city. Can't have people thinking they were better off before.' Liza slid down in her chair, arms crossed. 'At least *you'll* enjoy it,' she said broodingly. 'It explains all about the Saints.'

# CHAPTER SIX

The film began with staticky music, heroic and full of trumpets. The General's symbol flickered patriotically across the screen. *CITY OF CASTELLO*, said the opening titles. *WE ROSE FROM THE FIRE*. A man's crackly voice began to narrate.

'*In the beginning, there was a war.*'

Castello's panorama appeared in black and white. Then shots of the streets: gaunt houses with bullet-ridden plaster; the town square full of rubble like the aftermath of a bomb strike.

'*Centuries of senseless violence: it tore our city apart.*'

The boundary wall that Liza had shown me yesterday was rolled all the way up, twenty feet of sheet metal and barbed wire running like a barricade down the centre of the square. Dark splashes on the marble pavement – maybe blood. Two processions of coffins moving towards the church, draped in flags with familiar coats of arms. Roses for the Marconi victims, angel wings for the Paradisos.

'*Marconi and Paradiso clans: an ancient rivalry perfectly matched in military strength. The Paradisos lived by industry,*' *the Marconis from working the land. Each claimed a blood right to rule Castello, but neither could gain the upper hand in battle. And so the war dragged on. And on.'*

'And on,' Liza muttered. 'Like this video.'

'Mezzi,' said Veronica coolly. 'Restrain yourself.'

*'But, while we fought against each other, the real enemy was growing in the shadows.'*

The film showed slanted figures disappearing into a dark alley. It was like a B-grade horror movie – I didn't know whether to shiver or roll my eyes.

Then a woman appeared on screen, suspicious and guarded. A rose in the corner of the frame indicated that she was from the Marconi side of town.

'We always knew there was something wrong with the family next door,' she said. 'There would be noises in the middle of the night, crashing furniture. Once, we saw the little boy lift the backyard table with his eyes. It was monstrous.'

The woman was replaced by a wizened old man. Angel wings labelled him a Paradiso. 'Some people in town can do things,' he said gruffly. 'Unnatural things. We used to call them Saints, like the miracle workers. Never gave us real trouble before, but now they're suddenly wanting to burn us up in church.' His eyes narrowed. 'Demons, they are, instead of angels like we thought.'

*'In the turmoil of our war against one another, we had become blind to the darkness within. Castello was about to come under siege. We had been polluted by an unholy evil.'*

THE SAINTS! screamed letters on screen.

'One of them lived down the street,' a little girl said. She looked about nine, clutching a straw doll in her hands. 'Whenever we played with our skipping rope, she'd snap her fingers and it would swing by itself.'

'My cousin was one,' said a young man. 'If he got angry, the whole house would shake. Dishes flying off the shelves, pipes bursting, doors slamming all over the place. Almost killed me when I couldn't get out of the way.'

A mother and her sons appeared last, picturesque in their normalcy. 'My husband was murdered in front of me,' said the mother. 'By a *child*. She pointed at his throat, and he suffocated.' She clutched her sons bravely by their shoulders. 'The Bible says *thou shalt not suffer a witch to live*, so what I want to know is why do we let them?'

The film went silent long enough to let her message sink in. I shifted uncomfortably, wondering where this was going. Still half gripped by the urge to laugh it off, but unnerved by how serious these people were. The things they were saying were crazy. But they really seemed to believe them.

'*Who were the Saints?*' asked the narrator. '*Why were they in Castello? No one could say for sure. All we knew was that they were children of evil, born with tainted blood in their veins. Their abilities went against the laws of God. And yet we had let them live among us for decades, disguising themselves as our neighbours, our children, our friends. Spreading their poison through both sides of town, plotting against Marconi and Paradiso alike. Preparing to exterminate us all.*'

The screen was suddenly full of flames. Billowing smoke clouds, blocking out the sky. It was the church burning down.

'*Our eyes were opened by the fire. Two Saints joined together from opposing clans. With their powers combined, they were stronger than we had ever imagined. They united to start a massacre. Hundreds died in the church that night. The good people of our city – slaughtered by forces of total darkness.*'

A picture of a blonde boy flashed up, like a mugshot without the booking number. I felt an instinctive pang of sympathy for him, despite what the narrator was saying. The boy looked the same age as me.

'*The two Saints who set the fire were hunted for their crimes. The Paradiso boy was captured; the Marconi girl escaped. But we citizens of Castello had learned our lesson. The Saints were abominations. They had overcome clan rivalries to destroy us – in order to destroy them, we would have to do the same.*'

The church was a pile of embers now, with a rickety podium standing in front of the ruins, and a boy in a cloak speaking to people in the square. His figure was blurry because the video was old, but the power he had over the crowd was unmistakable. When the camera zoomed in, every face was full of rapture.

'*Joining Marconi and Paradiso in a truce had once been unthinkable. But now we were blessed with a peacemaker, a prophet who came in our darkest hour to show us the way. The General devoted himself to uniting Castello. He knew that the curse of perpetual war on our city could be broken for good. We only had to rid ourselves of the witches among us. Both clans together – we had to purge the Saints.'*

The town square again. The boundary wall had been rolled down; in its place was a pyre of wood with a stake rising from the middle. I dropped the pen I'd been holding when I realized what I was looking at. The boy from the mugshot was tied to the stake. A tall, handsome young man with a torch circled him from the square below. Dread ripped through me like ice water, all the pieces clicking into place. I thought of what Liza had said, the casual way she'd tossed it off yesterday: *We got rid of them.*

They were going to kill the boy. They were going to burn him.

A wave of sickness rose inside me, and I tried to stand up, needing to get out of this room, to escape what I was seeing. Liza's hand closed over my wrist and tugged me back into my seat.

'You can't,' she whispered.

'*The General himself made the ultimate sacrifice,*' the narrator was informing us, as the boy's pyre began to flame. '*Turning his own brother over for purification. Then he assembled a neutral squad of enforcers, who used blood tests to hunt Saints on both sides of town.*'

Groups of men in grey uniforms, crowded into military jeeps with guns slung over their shoulders. Pounding on doors, raiding houses, handcuffing people and hauling them away. Families waved enthusiastically from their windows and doorways.

'*Finally, the good citizens of Castello had learned to recognize their true enemy. Marconi and Paradiso no longer fought each other in the streets. Thousands of innocent lives had been spared.*'

Children holding hands before the newly built church. The General in his cloak on the marble terrace outside. To his right was Veronica Marconi. She looked about seventeen, young but hardened, her beauty unmistakable even in the shaky film reel. To the General's left, a man in a heavy trench coat was leaning on a cane. The Paradiso representative, I assumed.

'*Under the General's guidance, the leaders of the clans met for the first time in peace.*'

The Paradiso man reached across the General and shook Veronica's hand. It looked patronizing to me, like he thought she was a little girl.

'*A permanent truce was forged. The clans vowed to remain united against the Saints for all time. And they made the General custodian of Castello, to help them keep their sacred oaths. He would be a humble, impartial ruler, caring equally for north and south.*'

Workers plastering posters on to buildings, easy to recognize because they were still there today. SALVEZZA, UNITÀ, VITTORIA, SACRIFICIO. Filling the city until they were impossible to avoid. The General's trinity symbol was hoisted up above Lafolia's doorway, replacing Castello's old key and dagger.

'*With the General in control, the remaining Saints were purged from our city in a few short years. Castello was declared clean.*'

A final shot of the town square, new church and all, with a single wooden pyre before it. A girl tied to the stake. Maybe the last Saint to be burned. At the General's direction, that same handsome young man descended from the church steps with his torch. I squeezed my eyes shut, fighting back a wave of horror – refusing to witness this. But I didn't dare cover my ears. So even with the scratchy audio quality, I could still hear the girl screaming.

By the time I opened my eyes again, the screen was back to Castello's panorama, gloomy and dull against the sky. Closing titles hovered over the image: *At the time of this taping, there have been no Saints in Castello for more than eighteen months! But the General reminds you to remain vigilant. Compliance with blood testing is mandatory. Report all abnormal behaviour. Collaboration between north and south is crucial to our security. Persons found in violation of the truce will stand trial before the General to be punished at his discretion.*

Blaring trumpet music like the opening.

*City of Castello. We rose from the fire.*

And then three little words. *HAIL THE GENERAL.*

My classmates answered automatically from around the room, and I found myself speaking along with them this time, too numb to fight it – compelled by the power of the crowd.

'For he alone protects.'

# CHAPTER SEVEN

The video screen fizzled to black. Darkness reigned over the classroom, broken by a smattering of sarcastic applause.

'What a masterpiece,' I heard Alex say. 'Where's the Palme d'Or?'

'No commentary needed, Latore,' said Veronica. She flipped on the lights.

The room came into sudden focus. Liza was watching me, her eyes sharp and biting, waiting for my reaction. Veronica had gone back to sorting papers, proceeding smoothly with her lesson plan.

'Always an informative film,' she said, 'if slightly out of date. I've been asked to give you some more recent statistics.' She located a page and read out loud. 'The General reminds you that on November the first we will commemorate the twenty-year anniversary of the fire at Icarium. No Saints have been discovered in Castello for over a decade. The truce between north and south continues to be enforced without complication. The curfew remains set at a strict eight p.m. Attempts at cross-clan violence are considered crimes against the city, and may result in imprisonment or death.' She set the page down. 'Meanwhile, we'll be heading into the Middle Ages next week. Would anyone like to present on Castello's founding?'

Susi's hand shot up sky-high. Veronica sighed. 'Would anyone *besides* Susi like to present?'

Susi glowered. 'I'm sorry, dear,' said Veronica. 'It's been you every time.'

I pressed my fingers against my cheeks, trying to make myself feel something. The video seemed to have frozen me from the inside. In a way, I guess I should've seen it coming – Liza had tried to warn me, after all. About the rivalry, and the truce, and the General's rise to power by persecuting Saints. She'd as good as told me they'd been killed. I had just refused to believe it. It seemed too far-fetched, too impossible. You couldn't set people on fire and get away with it. And yet that was exactly what Castello had done.

*They burn witches*, I thought dizzily. *They still burn witches in this town.*

Except witches didn't exist. So that made it even worse.

*The General invented it*, I realized. *He needed to scare people, give them something to rally against. So he told stories about demons, and the town believed him. The Saints are a creation. And people burned them, anyway.*

'Lilly.' Liza was shaking my shoulder insistently. 'You're going all pale. We don't have a school nurse or anything, so if you faint it'll just be Giorgia pouring water over your head.'

I blinked hard, forcing myself to focus – grasping for something normal to say after what I'd just seen. 'I'm fine,' I mumbled, which was a wicked lie. 'Just shocked.'

'The Saints,' Liza said wisely.

I nodded. 'I didn't expect –' *What?* I asked myself. *To see them die like that? To hear them screaming?* 'I didn't expect them to be made up,' I said finally. 'When you wouldn't talk about them yesterday, I thought it was because they were really horrible somehow. Not because they were fake.'

'Oh,' said Liza, sounding apologetic. 'But they're not.'

'What?'

'The Saints aren't fake, Lilly.'

'Is that supposed to be a joke?'

'No,' Liza said flatly. 'But if you're going to laugh, do it now. While Professor Marconi's distracted.'

I glanced around. Veronica was engaged in a heated debate with Iacopo, to whom she had assigned the duty of presenting in Susi's place. Iacopo seemed on the verge of exploding a cherry bomb in his own face to get out of it.

'I hoped you'd understand once you saw the video,' Liza said, fiddling with a strand of hair. 'It would've sounded delusional if I'd tried to tell you before, but the stuff on tape is pretty clear.'

'Clear?' I repeated. 'They were talking about witches and demons and superpowers. That's not clear, Liza, it's psycho.'

'It's just history,' she said, shrugging. 'It's how things work in Castello.'

72

I stared at her, cheeks heating with frustration. Liza was the first person I'd chosen to trust in this town – I didn't want to discover that she was secretly losing her mind.

'Are you telling me you believe the General?' I demanded. 'That you really think there are people walking around with some kind of . . . magical ability to suffocate you and blow out your kitchen appliances?'

'Not magic,' said Liza, almost offended. 'The Saints have *power*. And they're certainly not walking around any more.' Her brilliant green eyes locked on to mine. 'Haven't you been paying attention? We burned them all.'

'But how?' I heard myself stammer. 'How could that be allowed to happen? Why didn't someone make it stop?'

'Like who?' Liza asked, genuinely curious.

'Like *anyone*. It's not the fourteen hundreds – there are laws about things now. You can't just *kill* people you suspect of witchcraft –'

'Can't you?' Liza said. 'No one really comes to Castello. And no one leaves much, either. So we do what we want here most of the time. Secretly, I think a lot of towns are like that.'

I recalled the muddy road we'd taken to get here – the gorge we'd crossed, with the mountains and woods on either side. The image on Google Maps, too blurry to make out. All of a sudden, I wondered if a whole town could be forgotten. If it was lost up in the hills for long enough – if people stopped coming and going. If the man in charge wanted it to stay that way . . .

But then why had he hired my dad?

73

'Besides,' Liza said, cutting through my thoughts, 'the Saints weren't *suspected* of witchcraft. They were the real deal.'

'Sure they were,' I muttered. 'They were real witches – that makes *so* much sense –'

'You don't have to take my word for it,' she said. 'There's plenty of evidence. Before he executed them, the General would make the Saints use their power. As a reminder to anyone who might have doubts about how dangerous they were. It's all stored on video down at the archives. Open to the public if you want to go –'

'No,' I said sharply. 'I'll pass.' Dropping my voice, aware that some of my classmates were shooting me looks now, listening in on the argument. Maybe they were afraid I was going to report them to NATO for burning people at the stake. Or maybe they thought I was a witch. That they were going to have to burn *me*. I felt incredibly out of my league all of a sudden, treading water in the deep end of a very dangerous pool.

Options flashed like fireworks in my mind, my childhood survival instincts resurfacing from the place I'd buried them. *Run. Hide. Keep your head down and they won't have a reason to hurt you.*

I could do that, I told myself. I'd had plenty of practice with my mother.

'Okay,' I said finally, taking a breath and meeting Liza's gaze straight on. She looked worried about me, but annoyed at the same time, like I'd failed her by refusing to believe that Castello had once been a hotbed of supernatural activity. 'About the Saints. We're just going to have to agree to disagree, I guess.'

Liza smiled thinly. 'You're stubborn, aren't you?'

'I like to think of it as being logical.'

'It's not logic if there's *proof.*'

'Nobody can prove witches,' I snapped. 'That's ridiculous.'

'Lilly,' she said pityingly, 'what do you know?'

All afternoon, I was tense, pacing around the house, my body still reeling from the shock of the video. I'd flung open the windows, letting the cold air sweep through the rooms, hoping it might soothe me. The city smelled like smoke, and, underneath that, rotting. Wilted flowers discarded in the streets. Not that I'd ever seen actual flowers in Castello. Just the elusive image of the Marconi rose.

By the time my father got home, it was almost dark. I'd already repacked my suitcase and left it by the door, but he didn't notice, head buried in a work folder even as he was stepping inside. I caught a glimpse of faded blueprints, electrical diagrams, sketched symbols like an ancient language – before Jack noticed me peeking and snapped the folder shut. Just like this morning: hiding things from me.

'What's so top secret about setting up the internet?' I asked.

My father gave me a distracted smile. 'The General likes to keep things close to his chest.'

I wondered what that was supposed to mean, then decided it didn't matter.

'I'm going home,' I said.

Jack paused in the process of rolling up his sleeves. The fabric was plaid and grease-stained, and I knew exactly what it smelled like, even though I'd barely been in touching distance of him for years. Peppermint and lemon, cut through with the tang of motor oil. The scent of my childhood. The good parts, anyway.

'You don't have to come with me,' I said, ploughing ahead with the speech I'd prepared. 'I can live with Gracie if you'd rather stay here. I just need car keys and directions to the airport.'

'Lilly, honestly,' Jack said in his 'patient parent' voice. 'School can't be *that* bad.'

'School's not the problem.'

'Then what . . .?'

'It's the Saints.'

Something dark crossed my father's face before he could hide it.

'So you've heard of them, then? I thought so.'

'Only in passing,' Jack said. 'Connected to a whole slew of superstitions. But I was assured they weren't a concern any longer –'

'Witches,' I cut in. 'People think they're witches. And they *kill* them –'

76

'Past tense, Lilly,' my father said quickly. 'People *used* to think that. But it was decades ago. They've come to their senses now, thank God –'

'If they've come to their senses, then why is our blood still being tested?'

'Is it?' This time the flash of darkness on my father's face looked almost like fear.

'I told you yesterday, not that you were listening – some men came to school. Enforcers for the General. They tested all of us. Liza says they do it every month.'

'An old habit, I'm sure,' my father said, frowning. 'But you'll stay home next time. I don't want you to feel unsafe.'

'I *am* unsafe, though,' I snapped, the hallway light flickering to prove my point, on the verge of another outage. 'This whole town is unsafe. I want to go back to Maine.'

'You know that's not possible,' Jack said firmly. 'We live here now. We have to give it a try. I'm not shipping you off like some kind of orphan –'

'Why not? Afraid it might spoil our loving family dynamic?'

My father flinched, and I felt a pang of regret, a burnt feeling in my throat. 'It's just, we barely talk. We never see each other, anyway. So I don't understand why I can't go home –'

Jack's eyes flashed. 'Because I said so.'

It was the sharpest thing I'd heard from him in ages, made me bite my lip and hold my tongue. My father looked so tired all of a sudden, disappointment etched clearly on his face. The only emotion I knew how to make him feel.

Something wounded ran through me like a heatwave, building and building, until the sudden shatter of the overhead light bulb pulled me back to earth.

Both of us jumped, hands thrown up to shield our faces from the shower of glass.

*You see?* I wanted to yell into the darkness. *This place is cursed.*

But I knew a lost argument when I saw one. Jack was the only person more stubborn than I was. Sometimes I thought I'd inherited the worst of both my parents: my father's destructive willpower, and my mother's fury.

'I'm sorry you're unhappy here,' Jack said finally. 'I'm sorry this is hard. But it's just an old town, Lilly. You can't let the superstitions get to you. And besides . . . we won't be here forever. I just need some time with this job. I have to –'
He broke off, struggling with something.

'Have to what?' I whispered.

But Jack shook his head, closing in on himself. 'Never mind.'

'What's the General like?' I asked, after we'd stood there long enough, facing each other in the dark. 'I mean, he's your boss, right? So what do you think of him?'

Jack didn't answer right away. When he did, there was something in his voice that I didn't like at all. It sounded like admiration.

'He speaks well.'

# CHAPTER EIGHT

The rest of the week was surprisingly average. No more enforcers, and no mention of the Saints. I couldn't decide if that was a relief or not. Snapshots of the video kept surfacing in my mind: the screaming girl on the pyre, the magnetic figure of the General preaching to the crowd. Sometimes I caught myself staring at my classmates – Iacopo experimenting with liquids from the chemistry lab, Giorgia painting her nails behind a textbook – and thought, *They believe in witches. They believe in killing them.*

In those moments, it took every ounce of self-control I had not to run for the city gate. But the knowledge of the no man's land that lay beyond always managed to hold me in place. I hated to admit it, but without my father I would have no idea where to go.

It didn't help that Castello seemed to be making me physically ill. I wasn't sleeping much, plagued by dreams almost every night, like those torturous months after my mother died when I could barely get into bed without waking up screaming later on. I didn't scream any more, and the dreams were different, but the fear still tasted the same – a thick, dark desperation, the sensation of being trapped with no way out. Lately, I'd started to see a boy too: a hazy silhouette in a cloud of smoke. Fire-stained curls and the bright flash of blue eyes. He made me ache with longing, turned me hollow and sick with the desire to reach him. But it was no good. I never got close enough.

After the dreams, I'd feel jittery and unsettled all day, my skin hot, a headache building behind my temples. It was as if there was a storm brewing inside me – like my body was rebelling against the town.

At least I didn't have to concentrate very hard in school. Besides history with Veronica Marconi, none of our teachers was overly concerned with lessons. Most of them just seemed glad to get in and out of our classroom unscathed by the general mayhem. I'd learned a little more about how the two sides of Castello worked – economics lectures on the Marconi farmlands and Paradiso factories; art history class where we analysed photos of the marble quarry in the north . . . all followed by lengthy homilies about how visionary the General was for making the clans share their resources. I felt that if Liza rolled her eyes any higher she was at risk of losing them in the back of her head.

By the end of the week, I'd done what I'd promised myself: blended in and become unimportant. A threat to no one. Except Alex, apparently, who never lost an opportunity to throw me a nasty look. And Nico, of course. He really did hate me, and I'd given up trying to figure out why. Instead, I shot him back the same waves of disdain I was receiving, deciding that if we were destined to be enemies I would give as good as I got.

Most of my first weekend in Castello passed with me shut up in my bedroom, trying to do homework for history class. Jack was at the office, as usual – I'd taken to slamming cupboards and doors so loudly whenever he was home that I almost didn't blame him for fleeing.

Our homework was a worksheet about Castello's founding as a medieval kingdom on the ruins of a Roman town. The legend was that the first kings had dug the city key up from the ground and made it the symbol of the royal bloodline. Passed it down from ruler to ruler – through plague and prosperity, flood and famine – until a king had the misfortune of having twin sons, and both had decided it was their right to succeed him. Each son had taken his own dynastic name as a way to distinguish himself from his brother: Vittorio of the House Marconi and Angelico of the House Paradiso. And each dynasty had claimed ownership of the key. Enter the clan wars.

At least the murals in my room made sense now: those ancient knights marching against one another with their rose and angel-wing flags. The key had been lost early on in the battles, but the clans had kept right on fighting, anyway. And they hadn't stopped. Even building the boundary wall had made no difference. So the General's video wasn't exaggerating. Before he came along, the war had been practically eternal. It was a miracle he'd managed to bring peace at all.

*No, not a miracle*, I told myself. *He murdered people. The Saints died for that peace.*

'What do you think?' I asked the knight above my bed, who had a sword stuck through his chest. 'Were they really witches? Am I supposed to accept that?'

My knight didn't answer. He was too busy bleeding.

On Sunday afternoon, Liza rang my doorbell. I was barely out of my pyjamas, had felt dizzy all day after another poor night's sleep. Christian's tie was wrapped around my wrist again, a bad habit developing. I knew I should probably get rid of it, this reminder of the boy who'd flinched when I'd tried to touch him. But I couldn't make myself take the plunge. Couldn't escape the memory of him in that hallway: his blue eyes on mine, the helpless way his cheeks had flushed. The air between us, warm and heavy and electric. Some nights I even allowed myself to believe that the boy I was seeing in my dreams was *him*. But then I told myself I was being foolish. Because during the daytime, Christian seemed dead set on pretending we'd never met.

'How did you get in?' I asked, when I opened my apartment door and found Liza waiting on the landing.

'The downstairs was unlocked,' she said, although I swore it wasn't. 'I had a feeling you were moping around alone up here. We can't have that.'

It took a while, but eventually she convinced me to come outside. I figured it was better than talking to my walls and brooding over a boy's tie.

The sky was still bright overhead, but the torches on the buildings had been lit in anticipation of evening and I discovered that there was something charming about that fire in the daytime. It gave the shadowy, decaying parts of the city a mystical feeling, like a scene from a folk tale. I was forced to admit that Castello had probably been very beautiful once upon a time.

Liza led me through the streets, past the city gate, those iron teeth hanging stark against the horizon. Far above them, enforcers with guns kept watch, dark silhouettes on top of the wall.

'Are the guards there all the time?' I asked, trying to recall if I'd seen them when we'd first driven into Castello. Back then, I'd been too distracted by the city's sights to notice much else.

'If the gate's open, then they're up there,' Liza said. 'They check who's coming and going. The General likes to know what's happening inside his town.'

I grimaced, trying not to let that unsettle me – another nail in the coffin of any potential escape from Castello. We turned down a side street, entered a dingy shop like the ones I passed on the way to school. It was a convenience store, with shelves of candy in crinkled cellophane and cigarette cartons behind the counter.

'What do you want?' Liza asked, heading for the chocolate display at the back of the shop.

'I didn't bring any money.'

She laughed. 'So?' Running a hand expertly over the shelves, curling candies between her fingers and secreting them in the pockets of her cardigan.

'*Liza*,' I hissed, glancing around to see if anyone had noticed.

'Oh, come on,' she said, catching my eye. 'You're not *that* good.'

And how could I disappoint her?

We ended up on a stone bench in a little courtyard, Liza's haul of chocolates spread out between us. She dug in immediately, but I ate slower, more interested in people-watching. I saw dirt-streaked men in farming overalls, women with wicker baskets of shopping. They all looked dated to me, hunched and worn down, like they'd stepped out of a black-and-white photograph.

'Liza,' I found myself asking, 'did the General ever say where the Saints got their powers from?'

She whipped around to stare at me, a chocolate halfway to her mouth – shocked that I'd decided to bring this up, given our well-established difference of opinion. But, no matter how hard I tried, I couldn't seem to get the Saints out of my head. Couldn't escape the knowledge that every person walking by us believed in them unequivocally.

'I mean, did they have to sell their souls to the devil or something like that?'

'They didn't sell their souls,' Liza said slowly. 'They didn't do anything at all.' She cast a look around the courtyard, making sure we wouldn't be overheard. 'The

General gives a lot of speeches about how the Saints are demons, but, when it comes down to it, some people just grow up that way. There's a misfit in every family if you look hard enough.'

'But being a misfit isn't the same as having superpowers,' I argued. 'I don't understand how people can grow up to be *witches* –'

'Because of the town,' Liza said without hesitation. 'It's just something to do with the town. There have been people with power in Castello for as long as anyone can remember. Rumour has it even the old kings ruled that way. And the clans – they've known about the Saints for ages. They used them in the war, trained them as soldiers and put them right on the front lines. Not that the video mentions that.'

She flicked a strand of silky hair over her shoulder, fixing me with her vivid green stare.

'The point is, the Saints have always existed here. The General wasn't the first one to figure out they had power. He was just the first one to kill them for it.'

We were standing up to leave when a sharp noise hit the courtyard: the rev of engines and the screech of tyres on cobblestone. A motorcade, hurtling suddenly around the corner.

Two enforcers were in the lead, riding sleek black bikes with Castello's trinity symbol on their wheels, followed by a black sedan and a rusty military truck carrying a dozen more enforcers in the back. Townspeople scattered before the procession, shutters slamming closed, door locks turning hard. Fear shot through me: the sudden conviction that the enforcers were here for us. They knew we'd been talking about Saints, and now they wanted to punish us.

But the motorcade whipped straight past us, skidding to a halt at the end of the courtyard instead.

'What's going on?' I asked Liza, watching enforcers swarm out of the truck bed to pound on locked doors. Tiago dismounted from one of the bikes and drew his gun. Only the black sedan remained completely still, its passengers hidden by tinted windows.

'It's a raid,' Liza said. 'They do this sometimes. Random checks for loyalty, to make sure no one's hiding evidence of Saints.'

I winced, watching the enforcers shove their way into a house with a few well-aimed kicks. Inside, there were clattering noises: tables and chairs being overturned. A woman screamed. The brutal efficiency of it all made my stomach churn.

'It's weird, though,' Liza murmured. 'They just hit this area last month. Sometimes I don't think the raids are random at all. Sometimes I think they're looking for something specific.'

'Like what?'

But Liza just shrugged. 'We should probably go now. Before Tiago has a go at us for loitering.'

I cast one last look at the enforcers funnelling in and out of buildings, tossing confiscated books and household trinkets into the truck bed. Metal candelabras; old picture frames; a tray of rusting silverware. It was hard to imagine how any of that stuff could be interpreted as disloyal.

I was turning to go when the black sedan caught my eye again. Through the tinted window, I saw a flicker of movement. Just the slightest thing, like a head turning. As if someone inside was now looking at me.

'Who's in the black car?' I asked Liza, as we headed away up the street.

She hesitated, lips turning down, something in her eyes making me suddenly dread the answer. 'It's not confirmed,' she said. 'I mean, there are some people who think he never leaves the church. But ... technically, it belongs to the General.'

That night, I dreamed of burning. I was standing in the square, watching a girl on a wooden stake catch flame. A dozen other girls stood around me, each of us chained and waiting to climb the steps to the pyre. I could feel panic in my throat, my body straining uselessly against the shackles. I wasn't supposed to be here; there had been a mistake. I wasn't meant to die this way.

I was next for the fire when I spotted the boy. He was moving across the square through the smoke, woven in a web of golden light. Features blurred by haze and distance – and yet I recognized him anyway, deep down in my body where all the secret things lie. I recognized that I needed him. That if could just get to him, somehow, then the flames wouldn't be able to take me. Because the boy would have me instead.

*Christian*, I thought. *Christian, please* –

That was the exact moment when the girl on the stake turned her head, looked straight at me and began to scream.

# CHAPTER NINE

The following week, on the way to school, something was different. The abandoned town square was buzzing with life: workers unloading wooden poles and piles of fabric from trucks, supervised by a swarm of enforcers. I steered clear, keeping my head down, acutely aware after the raid of how dangerous they were. But . . . I could've sworn they were putting up circus tents.

'Something's going on out there,' I informed Liza, joining her in class on Thursday. I'd already dealt with Iacopo's mischief of the morning: a strip of nearly invisible dental floss strung across the door like a tripwire. I'd spotted it in time to step over, but Susi had not been so lucky and had ended up flat on her face.

'Carnival is next weekend,' Liza said darkly. She was sitting on top of our desk, swinging her legs and scribbling nonsense answers on yesterday's art-history worksheet. 'They're already setting up.'

'Carnival?'

'It's one of the General's peacekeeping strategies,' she explained, pausing where she was writing *this painting is about death* next to a black-and-white image of some water lilies. 'He organizes events where both sides of town can mingle. For Carnival, it's like a glorified debutante ball. We're supposed to wear masks and gowns to hide our identities, so we can remember how we're all just the same deep down –'

Her disdain was so strong I could practically taste it.

'Liza,' Giorgia said, swooping in out of nowhere, 'just because *you* hate fun doesn't mean you get to ruin it for the rest of us. I'm sure Lilly will *adore* Carnival. Dressing up and fighting with the Paradisos – doesn't it sound *quaint*?'

'Does it?' I asked, alarmed. Liza snickered.

'Of course you'll need a gown,' Giorgia said, forging on valiantly. 'But I think you'll fit into one of mine.' She was examining my body proportions, pinching my waistline and moving my shoulders aggressively up and down.

'Ow,' I said.

'I've got a little thing that will look *spectacular* with some added lace. A Giorgia Alba original. You're welcome in advance.' She scurried off to jot a note in her planner. Liza kept snickering until I kicked her in the shin.

True to her word, Giorgia showed up to school the next week with a carnival gown for me, an extravagant white dress crumpled into a paper bag. I shook it out warily and then stuffed it away again just as fast, hoping that Christian hadn't noticed.

Since that dream of the pyre, I found it hard to keep my eyes off him in class. It was like something in my body had shifted, linked itself to him without my permission – carried that achy longing from my dreams straight over into reality. There were days when I felt furious with it, had to fight the urge to march up to him and demand to know what was going on: why he had infiltrated my mind, when all he did was avoid me in real life. Why sometimes, out of the corner of my eye, I swore I saw him looking at me back.

But whenever I turned to meet his gaze, he was maddeningly focused on something else. I was hoping at least that meant he hadn't noticed the dress Giorgia had made for me: a see-through mess with a tiny skirt and plunging neckline.

'I can't wear this,' I hissed at Liza, who today was occupied with dipping the ends of Susi's hair in white-out. 'I might as well be naked.'

'Giorgia's mum makes the uniforms for the enforcers,' Liza explained. 'Think of this as her teenage rebellion.' Then, taking pity on me, 'Tell you what – why don't you come over to my house on Saturday? We can do each other's make-up and be miserable together.'

It was almost humiliating how quickly I said, 'I'd love that.'

Liza lived on a street that was exceptionally steep and narrow, even by Castello's standards. She'd offered to meet me at the end of Via Secondo on Saturday afternoon so I wouldn't have to find my way to her house alone, and I was grateful for it. I'd never been to this part of the city. The pavement was torn up in places, littered with broken bottles and cigarette butts. Once, I almost stepped on a metal grate in the ground, but Liza yanked me sideways at the last second.

'Watch out. I don't want to lose you to the catacombs.'

'The what?'

'Catacombs,' she repeated. 'They're like tunnels under the streets, but full of dead people. It's what we used to use for a burial ground.'

I grimaced. As if Castello wasn't already bleak enough.

We came to Liza's house a few minutes later, a grimy door in a grimy building. 'Sorry,' she said, fiddling with the lock. 'It's not exactly the lap of luxury, but.'

'No, it's nice,' I said, following her inside.

'Don't lie to me,' Liza said coolly. 'I hate liars.'

The house was a labyrinth of dark air. What I'd come to think of as the 'Castello smell' hung over the place: rotting flowers buried under the floorboards. There was something almost tantalizing about the sweet decay. We climbed a staircase and came out into Liza's apartment.

'Ta-da,' she said unenthusiastically, flipping on a light. I knew better than to comment this time.

A cramped combination kitchen and living room lit up around us: faded yellow walls and bare Formica countertops. There was a wooden cross hanging above a ragged sofa, and not much else for decor, save a few cherub figurines on the counter, painted haphazardly so their faces looked like they were dripping off.

'That's why you should never give children art supplies,' Liza said, following my gaze. 'I made those in nursery school.'

'I bet Alex was painting the Sistine Chapel by then,' I muttered, unsure why I was bitter about it.

Liza dropped her bag on the couch, and I jumped back when a huge white cat sprang from the cushions. 'Oh, I forgot to tell you,' she said. 'This is Cat. He's the worst pet. All he does is eat and sleep.'

Cat hissed loudly, like he was protesting this defamation of his character. His fur was matted and dyed blue in patches – another one of Liza's failed art projects, I supposed.

'Doesn't he have a real name?' I asked.

'Cat is perfectly sufficient,' said Liza. 'Careless abominable termite. Creeping antiquated tea bag. I can change the words whenever I think of something less complimentary.'

'Why did you dye him blue?'

Liza seemed to stiffen. 'I didn't.'

She swatted Cat off to sulk in the corner, and nodded for me to follow her down the hallway to her room. It felt different from the rest of the house, hazy and almost fantastical: dark velvet draperies on the walls, half-burnt candles on the window sill. Liza sat on a threadbare swivel desk chair, spinning in circles while I took it all in. There was a family photo on the bookshelf – a pretty woman with dark hair holding a tiny blonde girl by the hand. Even as a child, Liza had been striking, staring defiantly at the camera with vivid green eyes.

'You're adorable,' I said. 'Is that your mom?'

'Yeah,' Liza said. 'Before she started working at the slaughterhouse. Now she looks about a hundred years old.'

'My dad's like that, too. Tired a lot of the time. My mom died a while ago.'

Liza's eyes sparked. 'Lucky.'

I froze.

'Sorry,' she said. 'I didn't mean it like that. Just.' She shrugged. 'If you're going to be abandoned, death is so much easier. Because then they didn't *choose* to leave. So you never have to wonder if it was because of you.'

'My mom killed herself. Definitely a choice.' I wasn't mad at Liza, which was the strange part. I was sort of transfixed. Then again, I often seemed to feel that way around her.

'Oh, sorry, that's –' Liza was going to apologize again, but I shook my head. She leaned forward, shamelessly curious. 'How did she do it?'

'Wrists,' I heard myself say. 'In the living room, by the fireplace. They had to bleach the blood out of the floor.'

'Why?' Liza asked. 'I mean, why did she want to –'

'I don't know.'

I'd never talked about Carly's death before, never wanted to. The memories felt too dangerous to me, like a bottomless well that would swallow me if I dipped in so much as a finger. Sometimes I thought that was why I'd had trouble making friends back home – because they could tell how much I was holding back.

It was different with Liza, though. There was something about the way she'd asked me . . . like I wouldn't shock her, no matter what I said. As if she was promising not to look at me differently afterwards. All of a sudden, I found myself willing to talk.

'My mom was depressed,' I said slowly. 'At least that was the official explanation. But it always felt like more than that to me. She was really young when she had me, and I know she never wanted kids, but my dad thought it would be good for them. Except it wasn't. Not for her.'

The words were coming faster now, tumbling over themselves to get out.

'She tried in the beginning, but . . . it was like I had a glitch or something. Like she was ashamed of me. The older I got, the more I think she wished she'd gotten rid of me when she had the chance –'

I broke off, feeling the well open inside my mind, threatening to drag me under. Liza watched me steadily, unfazed by what I'd said. Just like I knew she would be.

'It's funny, isn't it?' she murmured. 'Everyone who's meant to take care of you – keep you safe – they mess it up one way or another. People like us can't rely on anyone but ourselves.'

*People like us.* There was an implication in it, which sent a flicker of quiet joy through my body: that we were bound together somehow. That we were the same.

'So who messed you up?' I asked.

'Guess,' said Liza.

I shot another glance at the photo of her mother, sensing that it was the wrong tack. There was no sign of any other family members in the house. 'Where's your dad?'

Liza's green eyes flashed. 'Got it in one.'

'What happened to him?'

'Nothing,' Liza said. 'He gave me bad blood. And then he walked out.'

I shook my head, not understanding, until she said, 'He went back to his own side of town.'

I stared at her. 'Your dad's a *Paradiso*?'

Liza smiled sharp enough to cut glass. 'Surprise.'

'But – how?'

'How do you think?' she said impatiently. 'During the purges, when everything was chaos, he met my mum and ... whatever. I was a mistake, though. Evidence. I mean, he already had a wife. And he's got other kids, too. Legitimate kids who he doesn't have to be ashamed of.'

'So that's what Tiago meant,' I said. 'On testing day, when he was talking about –'

'My tainted bloodline?' Liza muttered. 'Yeah. Tiago has this idea that people who are ... different, somehow, are more likely to end up, you know. Witchy.' She shrugged. 'Maybe it's true.'

'Do you ever talk to him?' I asked. 'Your father, I mean.'

'*Talk* to him?' Liza snapped. 'Have you been missing the memos? Paradisos are filth. It's better that he never claimed me. I'd rather be dead than one of them.'

'Isn't that a little harsh?'

96

Liza laughed. It was cold, but also fond somehow. Like she found my naïvety charming. 'Wait until you meet them. You'll see.'

She stood abruptly and turned away from me, pacing the room in short, restless strides. 'We should probably make sure your dress fits properly,' she said.

But she made no move to take it out of the bag. Neither did I. I'd almost forgotten the real reason I was here – to put on make-up and wear something pretty. I couldn't think of anything less appealing right now. We were swapping secrets, and there was a thrill to that, which got better the more dangerous the secrets were.

'I just keep thinking,' Liza said. 'There has to be another way. The General wants to own us, and the Paradisos want to wipe us out. Everyone who lives in this town is stuck somehow. No fighting back. No escaping. Everyone except –' She caught herself just short of saying it, but I could tell where she was going, anyway. Straight to the most dangerous secret of all.

'Except . . .?'

'Except them,' Liza said and tugged a cord on her wall. The drapes pulled back in an instant, and I gasped.

The walls of her bedroom were plastered with grainy photographs, black-and-white mugshots like the one from the video we'd watched in class. The faces of Castello's townspeople stared back at me, some old and grizzled, some painfully young, all tense and frozen before the camera. A bolt of ice ran through me when I understood: I was looking at the Saints.

Around the photos, Liza had pasted a messy collage of news clippings, scrap paper and scribbled notes – all labelled and colour-coded with different pins and ink. The whole thing had an obsessive quality to it, like someone tracking a serial killer. Or trying to imitate one.

'Liza,' I whispered, 'what the hell is this?'

'History of the Saints,' she said. 'As best as I can figure it out.' She glanced at me, a glitter of triumph in her eyes. 'I told you there was proof.'

# CHAPTER TEN

I turned a dizzy circle in the centre of the room, body strung tight with fear and something else – exhilaration. The Saints in the mugshots stared down at me accusingly. *Look at us, Lilly*, they seemed to say. *We're just as real as you are.*

'This is insane,' I breathed. 'If the enforcers found out –'

Liza waved that away. 'They never raid this area, don't ask me why. Unless you're planning to tell on me?'

She flashed a sly, dangerous smile.

'Shut up,' I said, pacing the room again. Eye catching on the far wall: a cascade of photographs that Liza had placed separately, like a kind of shrine. I saw a smoking pile of ruins; charred bodies tangled together on the ground. The aftermath of a fire. Two more Saints were pasted above it all like gods. A boy with blonde hair and wide eyes, whose mugshot I recognized from the video. The General's brother – the first Saint to be burned. And next to him: a girl.

She was sketched instead of photographed, depicted amid pillars of smoke, pleats of dark hair whipping across her face to hide her features. White dress stained with soot;

hands outstretched and greedy as if she wanted to break through the paper and step into the room with me. The drawing looked old, like Liza had ripped it out of a long-forgotten book, but there was something awful about it all the same – an incomprehensible power stored up inside the girl's body. The photo of the boy looked practically cherubic in comparison.

'Who are they?' I whispered, even though I was pretty sure I already knew. Liza smiled again, satisfied, like she knew she had hooked me, easy as breathing.

'Those are the princelings,' she said.

'Princelings?'

'It's what people called them. The two kids who –'

'Set the fire in the church,' I finished. Feeling dread prick at the back of my throat, cut with a dark pulse of anticipation.

'Boy and girl from opposite clans,' Liza said. 'He was a Paradiso, she a Marconi –'

'Why *princelings*, though? It makes them sound like royalty.'

'That's the point. They decided they were.'

Liza came to stand beside me, her hand just barely brushing against mine.

'In real life, those kids were worthless. Just two more Saints raised up to fight in the clan wars. But, with their power, they realized they could be so much more. They didn't have to die for someone else's glory – they could take control of their lives. So the Paradiso boy, he named himself prince. And the Marconi girl, she was his queen.

They had a plan when they set that fire: to overthrow the clans and rule Castello *together*. Kind of like the General's strategy, only better. Because the people with real power should be the ones in charge.'

'That sounds delusional,' I said.

'I don't know,' Liza murmured. 'I think it's pretty brave. Because they saw something they wanted and they took it. Or at least they tried to.'

'Liza, they were killers,' I said sharply. 'They were bad –'

'Please,' she said disdainfully. 'Everyone's a killer. Just give them something to use.'

I turned to stare at her, caught off guard by the conviction in her voice. The remorseless green steel of her eyes.

'You think they did the right thing?' I demanded. 'Burning down a church, murdering everyone, just so they could take over?'

'I think if you push people hard enough, they push back,' Liza said. 'I mean, wouldn't you? If you'd been hurt enough? If you got really angry?'

'No,' I said, less steadily than I meant to. Wondering what it was she saw inside me that I didn't know about. *People like us*. 'No, of course not.'

Liza just laughed. 'Come on, Lilly. I told you I hate liars.'

'Well, the princelings failed in their plan for world domination,' I snapped. 'All the fire did was start a witch-hunt. They got themselves killed, along with a lot of other people.'

'Other *Saints*, you mean,' Liza said. 'Besides, one of the princelings survived. The Marconi girl, the one called queen.

She disappeared after the fire. Nobody knew her identity, so it was impossible to track her down. Even the General couldn't lure her out of hiding. And, trust me, he tried. The princelings were in love or something, so he was sure that if the enforcers tortured the boy badly enough she'd come running out to save him. But she never did. She let him burn alone.'

I felt sick all of a sudden, the erratic beat of my heart echoing painfully inside my head. The sketch of the girl was taunting me from the corner: her hidden face, her midnight hair, her savage hands, pressing against the edges of the parchment.

'So she was a coward,' I said. 'On top of everything else.'

'Are you kidding?' Liza said. 'The General would've killed her the second she showed her face. Why should she die for some boy? No, that girl was clever. She knew better than to let anyone drag her down.'

Liza faced the shrine with her shoulders set, sunlight weaving an aura around her body. It almost looked like fire.

'That's the kind of person I want to be,' she said. 'Someone who makes their own rules. Who doesn't need anybody else.'

So we'd come to it at last: the truth this conversation had been leading towards the whole time.

'You admire her,' I whispered. 'The princeling girl. You admire *all* the Saints. That's what the research is for, and the photos – you're trying to discover how to be like them. You want power, too.'

Liza turned to face me, her eyes unnaturally bright, ruby-red lips curled into a smile. 'I thought you'd never figure it out.'

I sank abruptly on to the bed, drawing my knees to my chest, too shaken to stand all of a sudden. Realizing that I barely doubted what Liza was saying any more. Maybe it was the mugshots on the walls, watching me with their unblinking eyes. Or the resolve in her voice, the unflinching determination. But it dawned on me in a rush that I was starting to believe in the Saints. I was starting to believe in power. People might think I was crazy from the outside, too. But those people had never been to Castello.

'The princeling girl, whoever she was,' Liza said, 'she brought this city to its knees. She found a way to control her own destiny. That's what power is: freedom from fear, from pain. From being trapped. From being nothing.' She took a quick step towards me, lips shiny, eyes aglow.

'And I know if I can just figure out how she planned it – who she was, and how she got out of here – then I can follow her. I can do it, too.'

'And leave a trail of bodies behind you?' I whispered. 'Burn the rest of us down?'

'Maybe,' Liza said with a shrug. 'Or maybe, if you ask nicely, I'll take you with me.'

In that moment, it didn't matter that alarm bells had started ringing in the back of my mind, telling me she was dangerous; that this was a dark road, which you couldn't come back from.

In that moment, all I knew was that she'd said she'd take me with her. And I wanted her to.

# CHAPTER ELEVEN

'You really better put the dress on,' Liza said. 'Carnival starts at sunset.'

I blinked, trying to focus. The real world seemed very far away right now. I felt like I was surfacing from a lake, half drowned, only the lake was Liza's mind, and I hadn't yet managed to pull myself all the way out.

'Do we have to go?' I asked.

'Yes, unfortunately,' said Liza, crossing the room to rummage in her closet. 'Attendance is mandatory. And the Paradisos will be dying to meet you.'

I made a face. I'd almost managed to forget about them.

'Stop pouting,' she said, turning back with a gown in her hand. It was green silk, lush but fraying from use. 'You're not allowed to hate this night more than I do.'

She pulled her shirt over her head without preamble, revealing her bare chest. I dropped my eyes a second too late, feeling my cheeks go hot.

Liza laughed at me. 'You can look,' she said. 'I don't care.'

Slowly, I chanced a glance at her, warmth curling in my stomach. Drinking in the sight of her body: the sharply angled shoulders and the trail of freckles on her ribcage. Liza watched me watch her, smirking a little. Slipped the gown over her head in a tangle of silky straps.

'Your turn,' she murmured.

I swallowed, peeling my shirt off – very aware that Liza's eyes were still on me. It made my thoughts swim, my skin tingling under the slow drag of her gaze. Breath hitching a little as I tried to squirm into Giorgia's dress. It was tight and short and lacy, with cut-outs along my sides. I hadn't been kidding about being practically naked. I fidgeted in place, feeling itchy and unglamorous. The last time I'd worn a dress was for my mother's funeral.

When I glanced up, Liza had that smirk on her lips again, curled like a promise.

'What?' I snapped. 'I know I look stupid.'

'Really?' she said. 'You could've fooled me.'

Something buzzed loudly from outside, and I jumped.

'Giorgia,' Liza muttered, and tugged the cord on her wall, making the drapes cover up the Saints again. I was glad of that; coming back to reality felt easier without the dizzy promises of those photos haunting me.

'Oh my God!' Giorgia shrieked, bursting through the doorway. She looked fairy-like in a pale pink gown, her hair done up in an artful bun. 'Lilly!! I knew you could be pretty!'

'Thanks a lot,' I said, but still let her fuss over me, smoothing out bits of the dress and chattering unstoppably while Liza did my make-up.

When we were finally ready to leave, Giorgia handed out the masks she'd brought – slender things that covered our eyes and tied at the back of our heads with silky string. A pink one for herself, green for Liza and white for me. Cat slid out from under the couch as soon as the masks made an appearance, pawing at them hopefully like they might be toys.

'Bad kitty,' Liza said, shooing him away down the hall. She returned a moment later with a long satchel over one shoulder, half hidden under a travelling cloak.

It was fully dark when we left the house. I realized that I'd never been outside in Castello past sundown, but I assumed curfew was suspended for this occasion. The city was a foreign land at night, the streets dense with shadows, broken here and there by the glow of torchlight. My body felt slightly feverish, a low throb of pain beating in my forehead, my vision narrowed by the eye slits in the mask. Balance thrown off by the high heels Liza had made me put on.

As we approached Castello's centre, the streets began to brighten. Turning a corner, I saw a pathway of torches, different from the ones on the buildings: huge bowls of fire that led like burning signals towards the town square. Music swirled eerily in the wind. The carnival had begun without us.

A pair of enforcers was stationed at the bottom of the street, inspecting the crowd heading into the square and sorting people into two lines: boys on the right side, girls on the left. Giorgia, Liza and I were herded unceremoniously to the left.

'Why are they splitting us up?' I asked.

'For the dance,' Liza said. 'It's how you get into the carnival.'

'Dance?' I said uneasily. 'Like, with a Paradiso?'

Giorgia shuddered. 'God *forbid*. We'd all murder each other if that was the rule. *Disastro totale.*'

'It's with someone from your own clan,' Liza explained. 'But the point is to share the space. We enter the square from different sides of town, but by the time the dance is over we're all mixed together in unity. Get it?' I imagined she was wiggling her eyebrows behind her mask. 'Symbolism.'

I nodded. I could see snatches of the town square through the line of girls in front of me: a large red carpet rolled out before the church, a swirl of dancers moving across it while a live orchestra played. And beyond that: tents and vendor stalls lit up in hazy neon. The carnival. There seemed to be no way to reach it besides passing through the dance.

'Look at Christian,' Giorgia said, gripping my elbow suddenly. 'Isn't he *pretty*?'

I followed her gaze almost reluctantly, knowing by now what it cost to look at him: the useless wanting that would bloom in my chest. He was standing with Alex in the line of boys, hair golden in the firelight, cheeks hollowed out below his mask. And for the barest second, I thought I saw his head turn – like he could feel my gaze on him; like he couldn't resist. My pulse quickening in my neck, my body tight with anticipation.

*Please see me*, I thought. *Just this once, tell me why you're in my dreams.*

But then Christian seemed to catch himself, turned his head away.

'I desperately need to get paired with him this year,' Giorgia was saying. 'I've been waiting forever. Last time I got stuck with Iacopo, and he practically broke my feet.'

I let her voice wash over me, focusing back on the square. The closer we got, the more surreal it became. It was like a veil had been lifted from Castello, and I was seeing the city as it had been hundreds of years ago. Dripping in riches, decked out in firelight. An era of lords and ladies, jokers and knights, all masked and corseted and styled to perfection. Women with silk gloves and trailing gowns, men in tailcoats and doublets or tunics with cloaks. And the dancers – swirling in a synchronized ritual that I alone was unfamiliar with.

'Don't worry,' Liza said, whispering to me under Giorgia's continuous stream of chatter. 'It's not as bad as it looks. And your partner will know what to do.'

'We can't choose who we dance with?'

Liza shook her head. 'Why? Who were you hoping for?'

I shrugged, knowing it was pointless to say Christian's name. 'I guess I was hoping for you.'

For some reason, Liza found this hilarious. 'Yeah right,' she scoffed. 'Like they'd let that happen.'

'Why not?'

'We're both girls, Lilly,' she said, as if I was being very dense.

'So?'

'*So*,' Liza said. 'It's Castello.'

I frowned, glancing around at the neat lines we'd been sorted into – feeling like I'd confessed to something dangerous without realizing what it meant. Wondering why Liza had watched me undress if she was just going to laugh at me now. 'Well, that's stupid,' I said. 'It shouldn't matter.'

Liza seemed to consider this, head tilted to one side, watching me curiously. And I had the sudden urge to lean towards her. See how close she'd let me get before she pulled away.

'Anyway, you'll be fine,' she said, breaking the moment as we reached the front of the line. 'Just steer clear of the Paradisos. You never know when someone might pull something clever.'

'How will I be able to tell who they are? We're all wearing masks.'

'You'll know,' Liza said simply, and flashed me one of her tantalizing smiles. 'See you on the other side.' She shoved me into the square.

In an instant, I was trapped in the glittering fray of bodies, forced to move or be trampled. I spun around, looking to the side for the boy who was supposed to catch me. At first, there was no one there, and I was sure I'd be left alone to drown in the crowd. Then someone grabbed my hand. At first, I was relieved, until the boy spun me to face him, and we both froze.

Nico.

# CHAPTER TWELVE

He was underdressed compared to the rest of us, in a black mask and loose black tunic, his collar open to show tan skin and the dark curl of tattoos. I could see the change in his eyes when he recognized me standing before him: shock, confusion, then icy dislike.

'Don't worry,' I said coldly. 'I didn't want it to be you, either.'

Nico's eyes narrowed behind his mask, and I was almost convinced he would toss me back into the crowd. But there were probably rules against that. Instead, he brought his hand up to my waist and sealed it deliberately over the bare skin below my ribcage. My body seemed to light up at the sensation, his fingers warm and sure in a way I hadn't expected. I bit my tongue, hating him for this – making my body betray me at the first hint of a touch. For a long moment, we just watched each other, Nico's hand flexing against my waist like he was daring me to react.

'You should breathe,' he said finally. 'I'm not catching you if you pass out.'

Then he pulled me forward, and we were dancing.

It was like being on fire, spinning through the dark with just the heat of him to guide me. The pain in my forehead sharpened in response, setting all my senses on edge. The music picked up, a forceful rhythm that I recognized. It was from a ballet: *Romeo and Juliet*, which my mother had loved. Surging downbeats, a clatter of horns; Nico moving effortless and lazy, leading me almost faster than I could keep up. It felt as if he was waiting for me to make a mistake, miss a step – fall and make a fool of myself.

'You think too much,' Nico said, right on cue.

'You give me too much to think about,' I shot back.

'That's funny, because I don't remember ever speaking to you in my li—'

Someone slammed against us from the side, making us stumble. I whipped my head around and saw a retreating figure, a tall blonde girl in a blood-red dress. She wasn't looking at us, but now that I'd bothered to glance around I realized other people were. Dozens of dancers had turned our way, watching us through their masks. And Liza was right: I knew exactly who they were.

The Paradisos were stunning. They seemed to part the crowd before them, cutting across the carpet like they owned it. Wealth clung to them like a second skin, their costumes studded with diamonds, bodies draped in fur and gold. Suddenly I was aware of how cheap I looked in my second-hand dress – how cheap we all looked on the Marconi side. The women I'd thought so stylish a few minutes ago seemed like knock-offs now. And the way the

Paradisos carried themselves: like they knew exactly how glamorous they were, how cultured and beautiful. Like they knew we could never measure up.

'Why are they so rich?' I heard myself say furiously. 'I thought the General made everyone equal in the truce.'

Nico's eyes glinted with disdainful amusement. 'You really believe that stuff?'

'I don't know what I'm supposed to believe.'

It was true. Nothing about Castello made sense to me. I never knew when I was being lied to or manipulated. When I was being told the truth, but the truth wasn't something I wanted to hear at all.

Someone smashed into us again, a sharp shoulder-check. The retreating silhouette of another Paradiso flitted by. And I knew it was deliberate this time – that they were *trying* to hurt us. I just didn't know why.

'Don't look at them,' Nico said. 'It'll make it worse.'

But I couldn't help it.

The Paradisos had formed a cage around us, isolating us from the rest of the dance. Their laughter was loud in the air, their gowns and coat-tails slapping against my ankles. The girl in the red dress seemed to be everywhere – crawling into my mind like a parasite, her mask white and cruel, bloody tears gathered below both eyes.

'Is this normal?' I demanded. 'Did I do something? What do they want?'

'They're not here for you,' Nico said. 'They're here for me.'

This time, when the blow came, it made him fall forward, gripping my waist for balance. *Now who's catching who?*

I wanted to snap, but held him up anyway, my hands curling into his collar, the warmth of his chest pushing against my knuckles. The Paradisos were coming at us faster now, trying to knock us down before the dance was over. And it *was* almost over, I could sense it: the red carpet nearly run out below our feet, the glow of the carnival lights growing closer and closer over Nico's shoulder. If we could just hold on a few more seconds, we could make it to the end –

The final attack came from the girl in red. She swerved in with her partner, a boy in a sailor suit, and abandoned all subtlety, flinging a hand out towards our heads, a set of brass knuckles glittering in the firelight. Nico ducked and pulled me sharply sideways, missing her hand by a millisecond. The girl's hair streaked past my face, leaving a trail of flowery perfume. I couldn't be sure, but I thought she hissed *traitor* at Nico as she spun away.

Abruptly, the music cut out. We tumbled ungracefully off the carpet, clinging to each other, my ankles protesting in Liza's stupid heels. The string on Nico's mask snapped, bringing his face into sudden view before me. It was the first time I'd seen him close up, and I'd never bargained on it happening like this: with his body tight against mine, the denim and metal scent of him pressing into me. All his anger, all his impossible beauty – suddenly within my reach.

For a moment, we were frozen like that, my heart beating hard, head throbbing, muscles tense with the expectation of another attack. Nico's eyes were burnt-looking, filled with shame, or maybe fury. But for once there was no hostility there. No dislike for me. I felt dizzy with the sensation: finally being seen by him and not cast out.

It didn't last. A second later, Nico seemed to come to his senses, cold rising in his eyes. Pulling away from me so fast it made me stumble, swaying before him like a rejected bride. Humiliation stinging my skin from the way he was looking at me now: like he couldn't believe how close he'd been holding me an instant ago.

'What just happened?' I asked. 'What did they want from you? Who was the girl in red?'

'It's none of your business,' Nico said.

He turned his back on me, quick as blinking, and melted into the crowd. I stared after him, disoriented and furious at myself for letting my guard down. For believing, even for one second, that there could be something between us besides disdain.

The pain in my forehead seemed to crest and shatter, sending a wave of angry heat through my body. Something sparked on the ground at my feet, a curl of smoke rising towards the hem of my dress. When I looked down, I froze. The carpet was on fire.

It was a tiny blossom of orange flame, like someone had dropped a match next to me. My mouth dry, my hands trembling. The pressure in my head beating in time with my heart. And, for a second, watching the flames dance up towards my carnival gown, I had the strangest thought.

*I did that.*

Then I shook myself. There were torches everywhere, the air thick with ash and embers. Anything could light up at any time. Dazed, I stamped the fire out. Just in time.

'Lilly!'

It was Liza, sweeping in from the left, her silky gown trailing behind her on the marble. 'Thank goodness, there you are. Giorgia got Iacopo *again* – can you believe her luck? He stepped all over her dress. But you made it here in one piece.'

There was a forced lightness in her voice, something very un-Liza-like about the cheerful air she was putting on. I knew she must've seen what had happened during the dance, the way the Paradisos had come for us. From her tone, I could tell she was hoping to put me off asking questions. But I had to know.

'They tried to hurt Nico,' I said. 'The Paradisos. The girl in red.'

Liza made a non-committal noise, fiddling with her satchel and not meeting my eye.

'Liza, why did they do that?' I demanded. 'Tell me what's going on.'

'Well,' she said, 'I may have forgotten to mention. Technically Nico's a Paradiso.'

# CHAPTER THIRTEEN

'Why didn't you tell me?'

Liza shrugged, breezing through the carnival. We had entered the main cluster of tents, that fire-lit paradise everyone had worked so hard to get to. There were food carts piled with sweets; popcorn and cotton-candy machines; a tarot reader in a circle of candles and a spinning wheel of fortune.

'Liza, I'm serious,' I said, pushing through a group of Marconi boys throwing darts.

'I didn't think it mattered,' she said. Then, pointing to a vendor, 'Candyfloss?'

I ignored her. 'If Nico's a Paradiso, what's he doing on our side of town?'

'He was exiled a while back. The Paradisos are mad because they don't think it was a good enough punishment. They wanted his head. So every year at Carnival they make a point of trying to get it.' She turned to face me in the jostling crowd, crossing her arms over her chest. 'Now are you *sure* you don't want candyfloss?'

'What did Nico do?' I asked.

Liza narrowed her eyes. She seemed exquisitely bored by this topic, and a little angry, too, like she couldn't understand why I was so interested.

'To be exiled, Liza, what did he do?'

'He killed someone, if you must know,' she said thinly. 'At least that's what the Paradisos said. They couldn't prove it, though. Not really. Which is why Nico's still hanging around with us instead of dead on an execution block.'

I had stopped walking without meaning to, her words rocketing around my mind like the darts the boys were throwing. *He killed someone.* I waited for the fear to hit, remembering his hand on my waist, his tight, uncompromising grip. But no fear came. Because, of course, I'd liked it. A sinking feeling took hold in my chest, turning my limbs to lead.

'Who did he kill?' I asked.

Liza glanced back, frowning when she noticed I'd fallen behind. 'His father.'

The sinking feeling got worse. The crowd was brushing past me on all sides, laughing and chattering behind their masks, but I felt detached from it, rooted to the spot by a mix of fear, shame and pure morbid curiosity.

'Why?' I said.

'Who knows?' Liza said exasperatedly. 'It's all just rumours, Lilly.'

'Tell me the rumours, then.'

Liza's lip curled back, and I was afraid for a moment that she would refuse point-blank. But that wasn't fair.

*I wanted to dance with you*, I thought. *But you threw me to the wolves, and this is the wolf who came for me.*

Finally, Liza seemed to relent. 'You have to understand. Nico's dad was important. He trained the Paradiso military before the truce. So, naturally, they all worshipped him. Then one day, a few years back, he turned up dead. Not a scratch on him, mind you. Could've been suicide, since they found him in the garage with the car engine on. But the Paradisos didn't buy that for a second. They were convinced it was staged, and someone had done him in. So – with a locked house, between Nico and his little brother, who would you suspect?'

'Nico,' I said.

'Exactly. The Paradisos thought so, too. They had the General put Nico on trial before both sides of town – that's what happens when you mess up really badly. He was only thirteen, but, growing up with his dad, everyone figured he'd have been trained to kill. And he wouldn't talk. Not even to say he didn't do it. The case basically made itself. Except . . . Veronica Marconi kept intervening. She said he was just a child, and no matter how much training he'd had, he couldn't overpower a man as strong as his father. Eventually, everyone got so fed up with the back and forth that the General declared the trial inconclusive and exiled Nico to the south. He had him branded first, though, for disturbing the peace.'

'Branded?' I stammered. 'Seriously?'

'Believe me, that's getting off easy. The Paradisos were ready to hang him by the end of the trial. They've been trying to finish the job ever since. As you noticed tonight.' She sighed dramatically. 'There. End of story. Are you happy now?'

'Not really.'

'Oh, just eat some candyfloss,' Liza snapped. 'It'll cheer you up.'

But, for some reason, I still couldn't make myself move.

'Lilly, I mean it,' she said. Her voice had changed now, hardened at the edges. Become a warning to me. 'Nico Carenza is a train wreck. He's never going to be worth your time.'

She was right, of course. That was the problem. I had to stop letting him get to me.

'Okay, fine,' I said. 'Cotton candy it is.'

Except that Liza was already gone. I glanced around, trying to spot her in the crowd, expecting her to be a few paces ahead, waiting for me to catch up. But she wasn't.

'Liza?' I called, scanning the vendor stalls. 'Liza?'

Nothing. The carnival seemed to have grown louder in her absence, a writhing mass of bodies. It was like someone had told the crowd I was alone, spread the word to the Paradisos. Told them to come back for me.

I took a quick step sideways, out of the main crush, retreating into a shadowy tent filled with costume racks. It looked deserted, cloth walls swaying lightly in the wind. But then I heard movement behind me, the rustle of footsteps – glanced around and squinted into the dark.

'Hello?' The word seemed to echo back to me in the hollow space. 'Liza?'

'Not quite,' someone said.

I froze. It was the girl in the red dress. She was standing at the back of the tent, her face shadowed, her blonde hair standing out in the dark. Almost like she'd been waiting for me. I couldn't explain why the sight of her felt so dangerous, only knew that it was. My heart started to pound.

'Who are you?' I whispered.

'Guess,' the girl said, and lifted her mask. I caught my breath. Even in the shadows, I recognized her: sharp cheekbones, creamy skin, burning green eyes, hypnotic and deadly at the same time. It was like a variation on a theme, a different version of a face I knew well. I thought of Liza in her bedroom, saying, *Legitimate kids who he doesn't have to be ashamed of.*

'You're her sister, aren't you?'

'Close,' said the girl. 'I'm more like her daydream. When she closes her eyes, she pretends she's me.'

She came forward into the murky light, letting me see her properly, and I felt my stomach drop. Liza was beautiful, obviously, but this girl was more than that. She was a kind of perfect I'd never seen in someone my age. Like a superpower: the ability to stop people from looking away. Envy twisted through me, leaving a bitter aftertaste.

'I guess I'm your daydream, too,' the girl said, and curtseyed lightly, gathering up her dress. 'Chrissy Paradiso. Your turn, Lilly.'

'How do you know my name?'

'Intuition,' Chrissy said. 'It fits you. Flowers are such breakable things.'

'I'm not breakable,' I said coldly.

'Well, *cara*, I suppose we'll see.'

She came towards me across the tent, the brass knuckles lacing over her fingers like a metal crown. I felt my hands curl into fists at my sides, wondering if I was going to have to relive the dance – if she was going to lash out at me. The nearby costume rack shuddered in the wind, like it sympathized with my plight.

'What do you want?' I asked, resisting the urge to back away from Chrissy. Not that there was anywhere to go. I could sense the wall of the tent behind me, trapping me in place.

'Want?' she said innocently. 'Just to make your acquaintance. You're famous, you know. Talk of the carnival. The new girl dancing with Nico Carenza. I heard you looked positively star-struck.'

'I doubt it.'

'It must've been quite a shock for you,' Chrissy murmured. 'Someone who looks like him, paying you attention. I'm surprised you didn't faint on the spot.' She leaned in, bringing the flowery smell of her hair close to my face. 'Although ... I did hear that he didn't want to touch you. I heard he had a long, hard think about it – whether to put his hands on you or not. Had to prise you off him at the end, too. A bit of a sad scene you made. I mean, he's a liar and a traitor and the worst person in this town, but he *still* didn't want to get his hands dirty on your little dress –'

It would have been better if she'd just hit me. *So everyone knows*, I realized, feeling shame twist through me. *Everyone can see how much he hates me –*

'You need to check your sources,' I said. 'All I remember is some girl in a red dress who brought brass knuckles to a dance but missed every swing she took.'

I stepped sideways the next second, head pounding, needing to get away from her, but Chrissy snaked a hand out and seized my arm, pinning me roughly against the costume rack. I was stunned by how strong she was for someone so slight, like she'd been trained from birth in combat, waiting for a war that hadn't yet come.

'Not so fast,' Chrissy said sweetly. 'We're still getting to know each other.'

'Let me go,' I hissed. 'I have nothing to say to you.'

'Then you can listen. I just thought you'd like to know the reason Carenza can't stand you. In case he's dead when we're finished with him this time.'

'Let me *go* –'

'It's this, right here,' Chrissy said, digging her nails into my arm. 'Weakness is a disease. He doesn't want you to infect him.'

The costume rack behind me smashed to the ground in a shower of cloaks and ballgowns. The impact sent us both sprawling, Chrissy against the tent wall and me on to the floor before her, my mask skittering away into the dark. For a moment, I just lay there, not even caring about my dignity. Hands shaky, muscles tinged with heat, an electric rush of anger burning through me. *I hate her*, I thought. *I hate this girl.*

'Well,' said a familiar voice from the doorway, 'you've both looked better. You might want to find a mirror, Chrissy. I think one single hair is out of place.'

There was a hand in my field of vision a moment later, and I took it automatically, letting Liza drag me to my feet. Chrissy was already standing up across the tent, flicking a speck of dust off her dress, unfazed.

'Hello, Liza. Come to collect your new toy? I was just breaking her in for you. But I have to say I'm a little disappointed. She's not much, even by your standards. Then again, pickings must be slim in the slums.'

Liza's eyes flashed. 'No one asked for your opinion, Chrissy. Go and harass someone else.'

'Oh, if you insist,' Chrissy said and then threw me a bright smile. 'I hope you got a good look at Carenza's face. I doubt you'll recognize him later on.'

She swept out of the tent, red dress cutting through the air behind her. I watched her go, still burning with rage.

'Hey,' Liza said, waving her hand in front of my face. 'Lilly. Are you okay?'

'Fine,' I said. 'You just have the worst sister on earth.'

'Paradisos,' Liza said grimly. 'I warned you.'

I rubbed my arm where Chrissy had dug in with her nails, furious with myself for letting her put her hands on me. *Weakness is a disease.*

'What about Nico?' I said. 'She's going to hurt him again.'

'Obviously,' said Liza. 'I told you the Paradisos want his head.'

'So we have to tell someone. The enforcers could –'

'Hold him down while Chrissy punches?' Liza suggested.

'What? I thought they were supposed to keep the peace.'

Liza shrugged. 'No one likes a traitor, Lilly.' The cold edge in her voice told me she couldn't quite believe we were having this conversation again. 'I'm sure he'll be fine. Just think – if they kill him this time, they'll have no fun left over for next year.'

I gaped at her, momentarily shocked by how much she reminded me of the girl who'd just pinned me against a costume rack. Then Liza rolled her eyes, and the similarity passed.

'Give Nico some credit,' she said. 'He's made it this far without you looking after him. Now come on. We're already late.'

I let her grab my hand and lead me out of the tent, too exhausted to argue any longer. But, as we ploughed through the carnival a second time, I couldn't help wondering –

'Did you leave me on purpose?' I asked. 'Before, it was like you'd vanished. I couldn't find you anywhere.'

Liza threw me a look over her shoulder, as if she was offended that I'd even asked. 'Why would I do that?' she demanded.

But she hadn't said *no*.

# CHAPTER FOURTEEN

Liza led me back to the front of the square, where the orchestra was still playing, but the dance had ended, the red carpet replaced now by a huge bonfire. Pillars of sparks filled the air, casting an orange haze over the stained-glass church windows above it. Liza shot a glance at one of the watchtowers along the edge of the square, reading the clock face, the steel hands pointing to 9.50 p.m. She swore and doubled her pace.

'What's the rush?' I asked.

'I've got an appointment,' she said. 'Delivering my colossal almond trapeze.'

'Your *what*?'

'Cat, Lilly. My cat.'

A crowd was forming around the bonfire, people of all ages and both clans attracted to the smoke and the smell of burning. As we got closer, I realized there was something stuck in the flames: a life-size straw man tied to a crude wooden stake. Laughter from the crowd, pointing fingers; children tossing sticks at the man's head. A wooden sign hanging around his neck, visible even through the ripples of heat. It said:

### SAINT

I froze in place, heart in my throat all of a sudden – thinking of my dream. The flames and the pyre, the terror, knowing it was going to be my turn next. The boy in the smoke, always just beyond my reach.

A flash of blue made me snap my head around, half-convinced I was dreaming right now: searching for him before I could think better of it. Christian was standing across the bonfire with a tall, handsome man who I assumed was his father. His mask was pushed up into his curls, delicate features criss-crossed by shadows. Looking just like he did inside my mind, where I never had to pretend I didn't want him.

'You're staring, Deluca,' said a voice. 'It's not a good trait.'

I jolted, glanced sideways to find that I had stepped forward without meaning to, moved deeper into the crowd. Liza was gone, and Alex Latore was standing next to me instead. He wore no mask because he'd painted one on himself: an intricate web of black skulls and roses around his eyes. It was gorgeous, but I wasn't about to let him know.

'You stare at me all the time,' I pointed out, thinking of all the nasty looks I'd had to endure in school.

'That's different,' Alex said. 'I'm being rude. You're just being . . .' He trailed off, letting me fill in the blank. *Pathetic*.

I bit my tongue, knowing that I couldn't deny it. Wishing I had the willpower to stomp it out – the bright thing in my body that pulled towards Christian like a compass.

'Wow,' Alex said. 'No comeback? You've got it bad.' He scowled. 'Not that I blame you. But here's the thing, Deluca. If you actually care about him, you'll leave him alone. He doesn't need you messing him up any worse than he is already.'

'What is that supposed to mean?'

Alex just shrugged. 'You tell me.'

I frowned, watching firelight reflect on Christian's lips, the man at his side bending down to speak in his ear. A strange pulse of urgency ran through me at the sight: the sensation that I knew this man, and should get away.

'Is that his dad?' I asked Alex. 'He seems familiar.'

Alex shot me a look. 'Think hard,' he said. 'It'll come to you.'

I was still trying to place him when the doors of the church opened up. It was a harsh sound, like dragging chains, emphasized by the sudden silence as the orchestra cut out. A hush fell over the crowd, hundreds of heads turning to stare at Icarium's marble terrace. At the figure who was stepping outside.

He wore a hooded cloak, like a monk's robe of rough brown burlap, the hood hanging so low that all I could see of his face was pale skin and a slashed red mouth. The man walked smoothly to the edge of the terrace and spread his arms out. His shadow reflected across the church facade, magnified a hundred times over, big enough to envelop the whole town. With the hood and oversized sleeves, he reminded me of a Halloween image of the Grim Reaper. Like Death himself.

'Hail the General,' someone said.

Around the square, people fell to their knees in unison, as if they'd been blown over by the wind.

'Now who's leaving who?' Liza hissed, appearing next to me in time to drag me to the ground.

Slowly, the General turned his head from side to side, taking in the crowd, the carnival, the sprawling city at his command. He never spoke, never needed to. We were already under his spell. I could feel it in the awed pulsing of my heartbeat, see it in the reverent faces of the people in the crowd. Suddenly Castello's organization made perfect sense to me. If there was anyone who could unite a war-torn city, it was the man in front of the church. He had simply taught people to worship him until they forgot everything else.

The General stayed on the terrace a moment longer, a human figure casting a god's shadow on Icarium's wall. Then he lowered his arms. In an instant, his robe seemed to fold around him, blending him into the darkness. Like the end of a magic trick: fade to black. The only sign that he had returned inside the church was the ghostly scraping of the doors as they swung shut.

The crowd rose to their feet a little at a time, me and Liza with them. When I looked around for Alex, he had vanished. I shot another glance at Icarium, feeling strangely hypnotized, as if the General had left me in a trance.

'You think that's impressive?' Liza said. 'Wait until you hear him preach.'

'Ladies and gentlemen!' someone called. It was Tiago, standing by the bonfire in his grey uniform. 'Please welcome, as anointed by the General, our citizen leaders: Enrico Paradiso and Veronica Marconi.'

There was a subdued round of applause, and I saw the crowd part to let them through. I recognized Veronica immediately, approaching from the south side of the square in a sleeveless black ballgown, evening gloves and a black satin mask. A single red rose was pinned to her breast.

The Marconis in the crowd bowed their heads as she passed, women curtseying, children who'd seen her at school waving from behind their mothers' skirts. Veronica smiled graciously, curtseyed back at them. *Royalty*, Liza had called her once, and I could see it now. People were enamoured with her, captivated by her youth and beauty. Just . . . not quite as captivated as they were by the General.

Veronica reached the bonfire, the exact centre between the two sides of town, and paused. Waiting for something. At my side, Liza was suddenly antsy, trying to make me move again. 'Come on,' she said. 'This part is stupid.'

Her hand in mine, tugging. But I resisted. I wanted to see what happened next.

Then, from somewhere deep in the northern crowd, I heard tapping. *Click-clack*, *click-clack* on the marble. Like a cane.

'Lilly,' Liza said urgently. 'Come *on*.'

An ageing man was emerging from the ranks of Paradisos, wearing a long trench coat, leaning on an ebony walking stick. He had no mask, so I could see his face clearly even from a distance: deep-set eyes and pockmarked cheeks, greasy silver hair tangling around his shoulders. It was the man from the video we'd watched in class – the one who'd shaken Veronica's hand and signed the truce on behalf of the north. Behind him, Chrissy Paradiso cut a powerful figure in her red dress.

And it dawned on me, then, with Liza's hand locked like a vice around my wrist. 'Oh my God,' I whispered. '*That's* your dad. He's head of the clan.'

Enrico Paradiso met Veronica Marconi in front of the bonfire and bent to kiss her fingers. He looked old and frail, and yet I feared him, anyway. There was something coiled about his movements, like a snake in a box. Full of deadly possibilities. Tiago watched the two of them interact with hawk eyes, reminding me of a football referee.

'We are thankful every day to our citizen leaders for helping the General preserve our peace. Next month, we will celebrate twenty years of unity – tonight, we pave the way for twenty more. Let the carnival continue!'

The orchestra kicked off again with a jovial little waltz, and the crowd returned to its chatter. Veronica and Enrico remained standing stiffly by the bonfire, doing their civic duty. I chanced a look at Liza, found her eyes narrow and hard on mine, daring me to comment about her father.

Slowly, I shrugged. 'It could be worse. At least he has good bone structure.'

Something dark crossed Liza's face. 'Sure,' she muttered. 'That's one way to look at it.' Then, shaking herself, 'Come on. You might as well finish meeting the family.'

She moved decisively away from the bonfire, digging around in her satchel and hauling out a very squirmy handful of white cat. I did a double take.

'Have you been carrying him around all night?'

'Sadly, yes,' Liza said, heading towards the entrance to another shadowy tent, Cat swinging wildly from one hand. 'See, he's not really my cat. I mean, he's not *only* my cat. I sort of share him.' She swept back the flap of the tent and ducked inside. 'With Sebastian Paradiso.'

# CHAPTER FIFTEEN

The tent was long and dark, littered with carnival rejects: overturned chairs, painted scenery boards, a funhouse sign. A roll of black carpet had been unravelled down the middle of the floor, carving a velvet path across the marble. At the end of the carpet, there was a throne. It was made of sleek dark wood, like a theatre prop, larger than life. Skulls sprang from the armrests, biting roses in their bony teeth, and angel wings spread across the high back.

A young boy was slouched on the throne with his legs kicked out, palms wrapped around the skulls like they were weapons he could pick up and use. He looked no more than thirteen, skinny limbs dwarfed by the size of the chair he was sitting in, but there was something instantly commanding about him all the same.

He didn't have a mask, but his costume screamed *Paradiso* all the way – a vivid gold tunic hand-woven with intricate patterns and crusted with jewels on the collar and cuffs. Like a baby king: all he was missing was a crown. His hair hung in loose waves around his ears, not as pure as

Chrissy's blonde, but less dusty than Liza's. And those green eyes, bright and dangerous, a family trait. I decided he had to be their brother.

'You brought the new girl,' Sebastian Paradiso said.

'Well spotted,' said Liza. She had stopped just inside the door, like this was a stand-off and she wasn't going to be the one to approach first. Cat, oblivious, wriggled out of her hands and flopped to the ground, instantly throwing himself into a pile of discarded fabric. 'Oh, for God's sake,' Liza snapped, and bent down to get him back.

Sebastian flicked his eyes to me. 'Lilly Deluca,' he said. 'I've heard about you.'

'Great,' I said. 'Who hasn't?'

Sebastian's eyes sharpened, as if he knew my mind had gone directly to Chrissy. 'I'm not her,' he said coolly. 'I can't choose who I'm related to.'

There was a hint of accusation in it – like he was daring me to be better than the kind of person who judged someone by their blood. No matter that it was what everyone else did in this town. And yet, against all odds, I found I was ashamed of myself.

'You're right,' I said. 'I'm sorry.'

Sebastian pushed himself off the throne and came towards me down the black carpet. On his feet, he was slight but compact, hardened in a way only Castello could teach. Here wore an assortment of jewellery, not polished like that of the other Paradisos, but old and dirt-stained. Gold rings thick on every finger, heavy chains around his neck, crosses and pendants that left smudges of grime on his fancy tunic. I felt there was something defiant about it all, as if he'd donned the jewellery in protest. The one part of his costume that was truly his own.

'I like your necklaces,' I said, offering an olive branch.

Sebastian glanced up at me, eyebrow raised. 'My father says they're junk.'

'Junk is okay. Besides, I think he's wrong.'

Sebastian's eyebrow arched higher, reminding me of Liza. I shrugged, thinking of my own father, a long time ago, teaching me how every old machine and broken circuit board had its own story to tell. 'They're artefacts, right? Pieces of history.'

My eyes lingered on one of the necklaces, which had a rough gold medallion on the end, carved with the symbol of an ancient thorn-encrusted door. A Latin inscription was etched across the top, too worn for me to make out. There was something vaguely familiar about the whole thing, but I couldn't explain what.

'Why do I recognize that?' I asked Sebastian. He followed my eyes down, tensing slightly when he realized which necklace I was looking at.

'It's a Janus coin,' he said. 'The Roman god of gateways. They believed he controlled all endings and beginnings. Even life and death.'

'Can I see it?' I asked, gripped by the sudden need to have that coin up close.

Slowly, Sebastian offered it up for me to hold. I felt a pull as soon as I touched it, a rush of exhilaration – like the coin was gripping me by the throat, dragging me hard and fast through the dark. The gold seemed to burn against my skin, eating me from the inside.

'What is this?' I breathed, wondering if Sebastian had heated the metal somehow before handing it over.

'It's a coin,' he said again, and tugged it away from me a little roughly.

I felt sick without it, head throbbing, a burnt taste in my mouth. Sebastian was watching me strangely now, like he was afraid I might bite.

'Well, I give up,' Liza said, reclaiming our attention as she rose to her feet. She'd extricated Cat from the fabric pile, but now he was lying flat on his back, paws pointed at the ceiling like an overturned bug. 'Take him or leave him – I don't care. He's a brat.'

Sebastian wrinkled his nose and bent to scoop Cat into his arms. 'Don't worry,' he told the animal. 'She doesn't really mean that.'

He retreated to the back of the tent, glancing at us once over his shoulder before vanishing into the dark. Liza kept her lips pursed, arms crossed, the picture of indifference. Only after Sebastian had disappeared did she relax her guard.

'Congratulations,' I said. 'Your family is officially not all terrible after all.'

'Not all terrible *yet*,' Liza said. 'Wait a few years: we'll see how he turns out.'

I frowned. 'If you think Sebastian's going to be evil, why do you share your cat with him?'

'Technically, it was his cat first. I don't really have a choice.' Liza seized my wrist and led me out of the tent, scuffing her toes maliciously on the marble. She had tugged off her green mask and was swinging it around with her free hand, keeping time with our footsteps. 'One year, at Carnival, Sebastian asked me to take his kitten because Chrissy was trying to drown it in the apple-dunking bin. That was ages ago, mind you, before she'd moved on to torturing humans. Anyway, I tried to give the stupid animal back to him the next year, but Sebastian said Cat had probably got used to me and would be *sad* and *maladjusted* if he never saw me again.'

Liza tossed her head, like she couldn't believe how absurd that was. 'So then Sebastian asked me if I wanted to share his pet. I mean, what kind of a question is that?'

'Well, you obviously said yes.'

Liza glared at me. 'Temporary insanity. I should've just drowned the monster myself. We've been passing that cat back and forth every month for three years now. Sometimes I really do think I'm mad – playing house with a *Paradiso*.'

The word was acid on her tongue, something to be spat out before it could devour her.

I thought of the accusation in Sebastian's eyes, telling me to be better than all of this. 'Liza, he's your brother,' I said. 'He isn't bad just because of his name. They can't all be bad because of where they come from.'

Liza looked at me disdainfully. 'Thanks, Lilly, that's really deep. I'll remember that next time Chrissy and her friends come for you or, God forbid, your boyfriend Nico.'

'He's not my boyfriend,' I said sharply. 'You know he hates my guts. And, besides, I bet the General would be happy if he knew about the Cat-sharing. You and Sebastian are everything the truce is supposed to be working for.'

'Screw the General,' Liza said. 'Screw the Paradisos, too.' Her voice was ruthless but soft, mindful of eavesdroppers. 'Long live the Saints.'

We were directly in front of the church now, where the bonfire burned steadily on. Probably the most dangerous place Liza could've chosen to make that statement, but nobody seemed to have heard. Absurdly, I found myself smiling, swept up in the danger of saying forbidden things under the General's nose.

*You're not* that *good*, Liza had told me once. And maybe she was right. Maybe I wasn't. Maybe that was why my mother had hated me so much.

'Long live the Saints,' Liza said again, louder this time, feeding off my smile. Grabbing my hands and spinning us in a circle, our hair swinging, dresses swirling out. 'Long live the Saints, long live the Saints, long live the *Saints*.'

We came to a staggering halt by the bonfire, gasping for breath and clutching each other. The straw man was still stuck on the stake, doing a jittery dance as the flames devoured him, and I felt the smile die on my lips in an instant. Because the Saints didn't live. Of course not. Quite the opposite.

'Don't think like that,' Liza said, following my gaze.

Bending suddenly and snatching a charred piece of wood from the bonfire – reaching up and drawing two quick stripes of soot below my eyes. Like war paint. I held my breath, watching her mark her own skin to match me, soot blurring over her freckles. And then we were both leaning in at the same time, not so much a kiss as a sticky brush of lips, Liza turning her head at the last second and pressing her mouth to my cheek instead. My heart pounding hard and heavy, head a mess of want and confusion: wondering how I could spend so much time thinking about Christian and still crave Liza's touch this badly. How two such different people had both taken over parts of my mind.

Liza was laughing when we separated, her eyes bright and full of triumph, so I laughed, too. Trying to live in the moment – convincing myself I didn't want to lean back in and ask for more. Distantly, I thought that she could break me if she wanted to, that it would be very easy for her now. But I couldn't bring myself to care.

'You and me,' Liza said. 'We're going to be different.'

# CHAPTER SIXTEEN

In my dream, I was hidden.

It was very dark, but I could sense walls around me, the familiar press of floorboards under my feet. I was a child again, curled in the closet under the rack of winter coats. Waiting for my mother to let me out. Only there was a new element to it now – something bitter snaking its way through my lungs. The air thick and filled with ripples of heat. It took me a second to realize: I was breathing smoke. Which meant that somewhere else, there was a fire.

Fear shot through me, driving me to my feet and scrambling for the door. It felt impossible to reach, buried behind mounds of old clothing that tangled around my legs as I moved. And all the while the smoke grew thicker, as if someone had lit the closet on fire from inside. Like there was someone else in here with me.

The second I thought it, I knew it was true. I heard footsteps at my back, a girlish patter. Saw a flash of black hair and a white, sooty dress. *It's her*, I realized, my grown-up consciousness filtering down into the nightmare. *The girl from Liza's drawing. She's coming for me.*

Desperately, I threw myself forward, colliding with the wooden closet door, tugging at the handle. But it wouldn't budge. I could hear the rattle of the bolt, slid into place from the other side. The door was locked. That was the problem with being hidden. The door was always locked.

'Mom,' I screamed, banging my fists against the wood. 'Something's wrong. Let me out of here.' The air glowing red around me, the fire closing in. 'Mom, please. I'm sorry, let me *out* –'

No answer. Just my feet slipping in a sudden mess of liquid on the floor. Metal-scented and sticky, like the day I'd come home from school and found her lying there; when her blood had soaked into my skin before I'd realized what was happening.

That was how I knew she was gone already. I supposed in a way she'd been gone from the start.

A rush of pain swept through me, melding with my panic – filling me up with electric heat. I felt so alone all of a sudden, so forgotten. Trapped with the princeling queen in a tide of rising flame. Aching for Christian in his golden haze. *Where is he?* I thought. *Why is he letting this happen to me?*

Convinced that I would burn here, in this room, with the girl's breath teasing the back of my neck.

*Unless you fight.*

The words rang out like a dare inside my mind, making the electricity in my blood intensify. It was coursing through my veins, all my fear and anger crystallizing into a vivid swirl of heat. Forbidding me to go down so easily. Pooling in my palms like a weapon.

*Unless you fight.*

Slowly, I turned to face the princeling queen. She was framed by rolling banks of fire, wild hair whipping in front of her, hiding her face. Swiping out a hand possessively, ready to claim me.

But I refused to be claimed.

The last thing I was aware of was the heat in my palms, exploding out of me, shattering the dream apart.

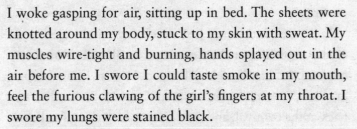

I woke gasping for air, sitting up in bed. The sheets were knotted around my body, stuck to my skin with sweat. My muscles wire-tight and burning, hands splayed out in the air before me. I swore I could taste smoke in my mouth, feel the furious clawing of the girl's fingers at my throat. I swore my lungs were stained black.

*It was a nightmare*, I told myself. *Not the first you've had and not the last.*

But it had felt like more than that.

My body was still ringing with that white-hot electricity. It pulsed below my skin like a second heartbeat, lighting up every nerve and inch of me, brightest in my fingertips. I felt dizzy, buzzing on a kind of high. Wild and dangerous. Invincible. I felt –

*Power.*

The word sent a thrill through me, a sickening twist of need and horror. The heat in my fingers seemed to jump in response, making something rattle nearby. That was when I bothered to look around for the first time.

All the furniture in my bedroom had lifted off the floor. The dresser, the wardrobe, the night table – hanging above me in a semicircle, like puppets on invisible strings. They looked warped in the moonlight, almost concave, as if some force was pressing them backwards towards the walls, making them bend unnaturally. Keeping them away from me. Keeping me safe. Only my bed remained untouched, an oasis at the centre of a storm. And the rattling noise I'd heard: it was the lamp from my night table, overturned and dangling by its cord in mid-air, knocking against the side of the dresser.

For a long moment, I just stared, my mind wiped clean of any rational thought. Looking from the furniture to my outstretched hands and back again. Heat swirling through my bloodstream, daring me to understand. Suddenly I was back at the carnival, and the carpet was catching fire below my feet. The rack of costumes exploding when Chrissy had cornered me. Because I'd been angry and afraid, and then I'd made something happen –

*Power.*

Very slowly, muscles trembling, I lifted my hands higher in the air. My eyes were narrowed at the furniture, but I was focusing all my attention on the heat in my blood. Imagining that I could shape it: commanding it to obey my will. *Up*, I thought. *Make it go up –*

My bedroom seemed to distort around me, a current of electricity spreading out from my body like a wave. Then, with a shudder, the furniture began to inch upward. It was a tenuous thing, fragile and on the verge of collapse. My breath coming in sharp bursts, hands burning with the effort of keeping the heat steady. But it was real, and it was happening. I was controlling it.

*Power.*

Triumph laced through me, a bolt of euphoria, lifting my heart in my chest.

*Power, power –*

Then the fear came.

My body seemed to liquefy, my muscles going slack all at once. Hands dropping uselessly to my lap, the heat flooding out of me like leaking gasoline. A second too late, I realized what that meant.

With an earth-shattering crash, all the furniture in my bedroom slammed to the ground.

I squeezed my eyes shut, pressed my hands to my ears and curled into myself defensively. Even after the noise stopped, I could still hear it inside my head: an echoing disaster. Smashing apart everything I knew about myself. Leaving me in pieces.

*What are you?* I thought deliriously. *What are you, what have you done –*

Vaguely, I was aware of footsteps closing in from the hallway. A tentative knock on my bedroom door. 'Lilly?' My father's voice, softened by sleep. 'Is something wrong? I heard noises.'

I blinked my eyes open, trying to focus. Everything I'd felt a second ago – the heat, the strength, the power – it was evaporating now, leaving me hollow and shaky, about to crash. It was like coming down from an adrenaline rush, realizing you've pushed your body further than it was meant to go. Like the heat had stolen something from me when I'd used it, energy or life force, and now I was fractured, muscles throbbing like I'd been smashing up the furniture with my bare hands. My mind hazy, caught in a loop of *what are you, what have you done* –

'Lilly?' Jack was knocking again, harder now. 'Are you awake? What's going on?'

A slight pause, then the squeak of the door handle turning.

*No*, I thought, and raised my hand, seizing the last scrap of heat as it fled my body – channelling it out through my fingers. The air hot around me, the lock on my door clicking into place from the inside.

'Lilly, open the door,' Jack said, rattling the handle. 'Let me in.'

'It's fine,' I said. My voice sounded hoarse and smoke-stained, my throat raw. 'I just dropped something. I'm going back to sleep now.'

Hesitation in the hallway, the handle turning uselessly again. I counted to ten, praying that my father would listen to me. Knowing that if he bothered to get a skeleton key I couldn't stop him from coming in. Not any more. That last pulse of heat had pushed me over the edge, and I could feel myself sliding towards unconsciousness: black spots behind my eyes, the welcome tug of oblivion. The only way to shut off my feverish mind.

*What are you, what have you DONE –*

I was slipping under when I finally saw Christian. He came to me like a hologram, shiny and gorgeous but impossible to pin down. Smoky curls and a flash of blue eyes. Trapped across an abyss of fire, always too distant for me to reach.

And in that moment I understood something. I couldn't explain where the heat had come from – maybe it was a twisted kind of destiny, something that had been inside me all along. Or maybe it was bad luck, cold and cruel. But Christian Asaro?

In some way, he was a part of it. In some way, he had done this to me.

# CHAPTER SEVENTEEN

When I woke again, I had no idea what time it was, only that it was morning. I was curled on top of my comforter, at eye level with Gracie's rag doll, which was twisted unnaturally like someone had snapped its neck. My body felt as if it had been raked over hot coals. Even turning my head to the side was a monumental task. For the longest time, I lay still, refusing to move. But eventually, I knew I had to.

Slowly, steeling myself, I shoved my elbows under me and levered myself up in bed. A wave of dizziness hit me instantly, my head rebelling against the sudden change in position. When it was over, I blinked out at my bedroom.

My furniture looked like it had been hit by a hurricane. My dresser drawers hung open, my wardrobe tilted sideways on a split leg. The lamp from my night table had been reduced to a ceramic pile. In the daylight, the whole scene was surreal, an impossible dream that had followed me over into reality. I closed my eyes, taking stock of my body, probing tentatively for the heat that had burned through me last night. Torn between dread and anticipation at what I'd find. But there was nothing. I felt drained, crippled by exhaustion, emptied out of everything useful. Completely average.

Relief shot through me, my eyes fluttering open in a rush.

*You must've imagined it. You imagined the heat. The whole thing was just a really long nightmare.*

I wanted to believe it so badly I could taste it on my tongue. Never mind the damage to my furniture – that could be explained away. Maybe there really *had* been a hurricane last night. Or I'd had some kind of massive sleepwalking accident.

*Very well, but what about the carnival?* said a sharp voice in my mind. *Did you imagine that, too?*

I shook my head, trying to shove the voice away.

*You made those things happen*, it hissed. *You lifted your furniture. You locked the door. There was power inside you, and you could control it –*

No, worse than that.

*There was power inside you, and you* liked *it.*

I shuddered, an image flashing unbidden behind my eyes. That woman from the video we'd watched in class. *Thou shalt not suffer a witch to live*, she was saying. *So what I want to know is why do we let them?*

'Stop it,' I breathed, cutting off the surge of panic that was suddenly threatening to overwhelm me. 'Just stop.'

I wasn't a witch. I couldn't be. It was ridiculous.

Whatever had happened, last night and at the carnival – was just a fluke. Now it was over, and the heat had gone away. So I didn't have to worry about it ever again.

To prove my point, I lifted a shaky hand and pointed at my night table. Concentrated hard and imagined it lifting off the ground. I felt ridiculous doing it, like a kid impersonating their favourite superhero. Nothing happened besides another dizzy spell overtaking me.

'See?' I said, addressing the audience of bleeding knights on my walls. 'I'm normal.'

The words seemed to hang in the air longer than necessary, like they were taunting me.

'Oh, shut up,' I muttered and swung my legs out of bed.

Then I stopped. It was just – for the barest second – I thought I'd felt something. The tiniest spark in my fingertips. And, out of the corner of my eye, I swore I'd seen the night table twitch.

It took me ages to clean up my bedroom. I swept the broken pieces of lamp off the floor, sorted through my tangled clothes and books and jewellery, shoved my dislodged wardrobe back into place. My muscles screamed in protest the whole time, my brain glazed over with fatigue. Sometimes I felt a little bolt of fear, threatening to break through the haze I was in.

*Thou shalt not suffer –*

But I pushed it back.

I was just about to crawl into bed again and sleep for the rest of the day when I noticed a note stuck under my door. It was from my father.

*Lilly, I'd like to talk to you*, it said. *Let's meet at church.*

Church. I'd forgotten.

I leaned my head against the door frame, resisting the urge to scream. There was meant to be a mass today, something to prepare us for the anniversary of the church fire in November. The General himself would be speaking. Attendance was mandatory.

According to my phone, it was 10.30 a.m. The service started at 11.

I was dragging myself resentfully towards the shower when I noticed something in my wardrobe. There was a yellowing piece of parchment sticking out from the side panel, which I knew I hadn't put there myself. I had no time to spare, and yet I found myself backtracking anyway, kneeling down to prise it out. Wrinkling my nose when I discovered how mouldy it was, like it had been stuck in the dark for ages.

The parchment showed a blueprint of a massive building with a familiar shape: broad nave and two symmetrical wings. There was an inscription at the bottom, stamped next to Castello's original key-and-dagger coat of arms.

CATTEDRALE DI SAN PIETRO

*Saint Peter's Cathedral.* I stood uneasily in the centre of my bedroom, trying to make sense of what I was looking at. Someone had drawn all over the blueprint in faded red ink:

circles by the church doors, a huge arrow on the altar, a scrawled word in the upper corner, nearly illegible from dirt.

*gasoline*

And all at once, it dawned on me exactly what I was holding. It was a battle plan. From the princelings' fire.

Dread laced through me, a prickly feeling on my skin, and I snapped my head up, heart in my throat, staring around my bedroom. Suddenly convinced I would see her there, just like I had in my dream. The princeling girl coated in soot. Reaching for me.

But my room was empty.

When I glanced back at the blueprint, it felt dangerous, almost alive with spite. I had the urge to rip it up, destroy it somehow, but I couldn't. Because some nagging instinct was telling me that if I got rid of it the princeling girl would never forgive me. She'd track me down. She'd make me pay.

In the end, I tossed the parchment into the back of my wardrobe, shutting the splintered door with a thud. Wishing I had a padlock to seal it with.

But I had to hurry if I wanted to make it to church.

The town square was packed when I got there.

People from both clans stood around, talking in low voices, waiting for their turn to climb the massive marble staircases into Icarium. It was easy to tell the Marconis from the Paradisos based on which stairs they used, and the difference in the quality of their clothing. But still – the common theme was formality, which made me feel out of place in my old jeans and a cardigan. I hadn't had time to consider the dress code.

Enforcers were stationed around the square like riot police, keeping a close eye on the milling crowd. There was something else off about the whole scene, but I couldn't quite put my finger on it. All I knew was that it was unnaturally quiet, considering how many people were out.

*You just have to survive today*, I told myself. *Then you can go back to bed and never get out again.*

Steeling myself, I joined the stream of townspeople heading for church. More enforcers were waiting on the terrace at the top of the staircases, handing out flowers: red roses for the Marconis, white orchids for the Paradisos. I accepted my rose with my head down, allowing the crowd to sweep me forward into Icarium.

Then I stopped short.

I'd heard people say that churches were the houses of God, and if that was true then Icarium was his palace. Nothing had prepared me for the sheer size of what I was looking at: marble walls rising up for miles, a domed ceiling light years above my head. Distant balconies crisscrossing through the air, stained-glass windows depicting the Icarus myth in shimmering colours. Everywhere there were sculptures, columns, paintings, lavish flower displays. Golden relics and jewelled censers hanging over the aisles on shiny chains. It was the most beautiful building I'd ever set foot in, and the most intimidating.

The north and south wings of the church were identical, both packed with ornate wooden pews. Between them stood the altar, a raised platform of blinding white stone, with two velvet thrones and a marble pulpit. Black cloth banners streamed down from the ceiling, the General's trinity symbol sewn on them in gold. Combined with the enforcers standing guard, I had the sensation of being at a political rally instead of a spiritual event. Or maybe it was both.

I caught sight of Liza halfway down an aisle, wearing a sunshine-yellow dress, her head tilted back to examine the tall marble columns with a critical eye. As I made my way towards her, it finally occurred to me what was so off about this whole scene: there were no church bells ringing.

'There you are,' Liza said, shooting me an absent glance. 'I was worried you'd forgotten.'

I shook my head, suddenly caught in the memory of her lips on my cheek at the bonfire. It made my stomach flip. But Liza clearly had other things on her mind. She was gazing up at the church architecture like it was the first time she'd been here, which I knew couldn't be true. I pretended not to be disappointed that she wasn't looking at me instead.

'Why aren't the bells ringing?' I asked. 'Church is never this quiet.'

'It's bad memories,' Liza said. 'Bells symbolize disaster. Before the truce, they would ring all day long. It meant people were shooting each other in the streets. But they haven't made a sound since the General came along.'

She had tucked her rose into the loose curl of her bun, a shock of red against her neck as she craned her head back.

'What's so fascinating up there?' I demanded.

'I'm just thinking,' Liza said. 'It must be hard to set this much stone on fire.'

I froze, the blueprint from my bedroom burning in my mind's eye.

'I mean, the princelings must've found some kind of flaw in the system –'

'Can we not talk about them?' I said sharply.

'Why not?' Liza asked, turning to face me for the first time. There was a smear of glitter on her cheeks, left over from last night's make-up. 'Aren't you curious?'

I swallowed hard, trapped by the green glint of her eyes, feeling as if I was being tested – like every time I thought I was getting close to her, she demanded I follow her one step further over the cliff edge.

'Oh, come on,' Liza said. 'You can't be going soft on me already. We've barely even started. Besides ... I know you'd burn this place down in a second if you could catch *them* in the middle of it.'

She was looking at the front doors; the Paradiso family had entered church.

The crowd scattered before them like mice with cats on the prowl. Enrico Paradiso led the way, bent over in his trench coat, his ebony cane click-clacking on the marble. Sebastian came next, wearing an impossibly fancy suit. He kept his head high, chin stuck out, cool eyes fixed forward. And yet, for an instant, I swore I saw him glance my way.

Then it was Chrissy's turn. She looked despicably perfect in a sky-blue dress, cinched at the waist and trailing out behind her over the marble. Her white orchid was woven into tumbling waves of blonde hair. My stomach sank at the sight of her: that familiar churn of envy and hate.

She had one hand curled possessively on the shoulder of a younger boy, tan and dark-eyed, around Sebastian's age. I saw a ripple in the crowd as they passed: Nico pushing his way forward to watch. The Paradisos must've caught up with him last night because his face was a minefield of bruising, his right eye swollen, his bottom lip busted apart. But still: his resemblance to the boy was obvious. It had to be his brother, left on the Paradiso side of town when he'd been exiled. So he belonged to Chrissy now.

'There he is,' Chrissy said brightly, squeezing the boy's shoulder as they spotted Nico in the crowd. 'Tell him what you think of him.'

Numbly, the boy walked up to Nico and spat at his feet. 'Traitor,' he said, and then turned away.

Nico's eyes flashed, dark with anger and something else – like bone-deep pain. Chrissy looked so delighted she might've been clapping her hands.

'You see?' Liza murmured, reading the outrage on my face. 'Some people deserve to burn.'

And she was right. In that instant, it scared me how much I believed it – how glad I would've been to see Chrissy's dress go up in flames.

Something sharp and dangerous twisted in my chest. It almost felt like heat.

I took a stumbling step backwards, heart in my throat all of a sudden, thinking, *Thou shalt not suffer –*

Turning abruptly from Liza and pushing my way into the crowd. Trying to flee from my panic – head bowed, fists clenched – as if I could outrun my own mind if I just moved fast enough. Which was how I ended up slamming into him, for the second time since I'd moved to this town.

For an instant, we were both frozen, our gazes locked, bodies tense with surprise. My breath suddenly quick, my head swimming: like on that first day of school, when his fingers had touched my neck and the whole world had stopped.

'Lilly,' Christian said, 'I was hoping we'd moved past this part.'

# CHAPTER EIGHTEEN

He looked different from the way I remembered him. Skin ashy, cheeks gaunt, eyes red-rimmed like he'd just risen from a sickbed.

*What happened to you?* I wanted to ask. *Why haven't you let me close enough to help?*

But I couldn't speak. Because this time the heat in my chest spiked *hard*.

It seemed to rise from some hidden place inside me, a wounded animal clawing out of a trap. Battered and weak, but not dead. Not gone. If anything, it was getting stronger. Like Christian was drawing it out.

I felt another flash of panic, a rush of *not here, not now, this can't be happening* – but then it was replaced by a lethal kind of need. All of a sudden, I knew I would die if I couldn't touch him. That I'd been waiting my whole life to get to this place.

'Can you feel that?' I whispered, desperate to know I wasn't alone in this – that the pull went both ways. 'God, please tell me you can feel that.'

'I don't know what you're talking about,' Christian said. But it was a lie, I was sure of it. Because he looked terrified. 'Goodbye, Lilly,' he said, and stepped away from me, trying to vanish into the crowd. Like every other time we'd come together: pretending that he felt nothing. That he didn't need me like I needed him. Pretending he could survive this on his own.

'Wait,' I said, and grabbed his wrist.

It was like my body had caught fire. The instant we were touching, the heat was everywhere – ripping through my blood, like the night before but a hundred times stronger. My skin was pulsing with it, my heart soaring, every one of my senses sharpening to a point. The air distorting around us, crosses swinging overhead, ornate vases of flowers tottering on their stands.

*This is power*, I thought, unable to deny it any longer, and strangely relieved at the fact. *You know it's power, you KNOW* –

And then I wasn't thinking at all, because the world was dropping away, and I was falling into him.

My vision flooded black, and then there were images: white walls, cigarette butts in water, an iron box draped in chains. A locked room and a shadow man with snakes in his hands. The bitter tang of fear. Not mine: Christian's.

With a jolt, I realized, *I'm inside his mind*.

The whole thing couldn't have lasted more than a second. Then Christian was wrenching his hand away, slumping back against one of the church pillars, breathing ragged. Jacket slipping from his shoulder, sweat on his throat. Eyes wide and accusing, watching me like I was a monster who had escaped her leash.

I watched him back, feeling sick, as if he'd ripped one of my organs out when we'd separated. The heat in my blood had gone weak again, a sputtering flame. Begging me to touch him a second time.

'What was that?' I said. 'What's happening to us? Are you –'

'No,' Christian said roughly. Like he knew what I was going to ask, even though I'd barely formed the question.

*Are you like me?*

Which really meant, *Do you have power?*

Slowly, Christian seemed to gain control of himself, running a hand through his hair and pulling his jacket up. Shoving the fear from his eyes, replacing it with something deadened that I didn't like to look at. 'You should find a seat,' he said. 'The service starts soon.'

This time, when he walked away, I didn't dare to stop him.

I stood in place, trying to make sense of what had just happened – what was going on inside my body. The heat was still there, a quiet throb in my blood, something that felt almost natural now that I wasn't resisting it so hard. It reminded me of a sixth sense, a new kind of instinct, one I trusted despite myself. After last night, I'd been so desperate to believe it was a mistake, a one-shot deal, something that had slipped from me in the daylight. But the heat had never left. I could admit that now. I'd just used too much of it, drained my strength when I'd lifted the furniture. It had needed time to recover, to build itself back up again. Needed something – someone – to cling to.

Needed *him*.

And it had found him, now.

*Maybe I* am *a witch*, I thought. *But I swear I'm not the only one.*

I sensed eyes on me, turned abruptly to find Alex watching me from a nearby pew. He was slouched between his parents, a stern-looking man and an impeccably dressed woman in pastel, who was telling him off for his outfit: skinny jeans and smudged eyeliner. But Alex wasn't paying her attention. He was putting all his effort into glaring at me. I realized he must've seen what had passed between me and Christian – the way I'd reached for him, after Alex had warned me not to. *If you actually care about him, you'll leave him alone.* But it was a little late for that.

'Why did you run off?' Liza demanded, appearing out of the crowd and jolting me from my reverie. 'You dropped your rose. We're supposed to give them to the General as an offering after the service.'

I took the flower she was thrusting at me and allowed her to lead me towards an empty pew. It occurred to me on the way that I hadn't spotted Jack yet. 'I'm supposed to meet my dad here,' I said. 'But I haven't seen him.'

'Maybe he got an exemption for work,' Liza said. 'My mum has one, cos she's on the early shift this morning.'

'No, but he told me –'

'Shh,' Liza said, picking up on some cue I'd missed. Tugging me down into my seat.

Silence was falling over the church, slowly at first and then with sudden viciousness. The crowd went still, all eyes raised towards the altar, so I looked, too, expecting to see the General. Instead, I found Veronica Marconi, poised on one of the velvet thrones, looking elegant as always in a beige wool coat. Enrico Paradiso occupied the chair next to her, hunched over his cane. Like the crowd, they both seemed to be waiting for something.

Then, from the back of the church, I heard chanting. Low male voices, in a rhythm like the beating of a massive heart. '*Dies iræ, dies illa, solvet sæclum in favilla.*' A procession of enforcers wound up the aisles in hooded black cloaks, swinging censers, perfuming the air with sweet smoke. Tiago led the way, the silver scar on his cheek glinting in the haze. When he reached the altar, he made for the pulpit, while the rest of the enforcers fanned out in a line behind him.

Tiago cracked open an old leather book and began to read, his lilting voice amplified to a ringing sound by the hollowness of the church. 'Father, have mercy on us, for we are seekers of the light.'

'Father, have mercy on our souls,' the crowd replied.

My eyes glanced across the altar platform, scanning the enforcers lined up there – catching on one of them instinctively. A dark-haired man with his arms clasped behind his back. He was very familiar to me, but I couldn't quite place him . . . until I realized that I'd hardly ever seen that face without glasses.

'Dad,' I said, feeling the breath go out of me all at once.

Jack was wearing a long black cloak and a crisp grey suit with the General's trinity pin, his face cool and attentive as he listened to Tiago speak. *So this is why he didn't want to leave town*, I thought with a horrible sinking feeling. *He's decided he belongs here. He's decided he's one of them.*

I was on the verge of tears all of a sudden – squeezed my eyes shut and gripped the pew hard, a pulse of heat pooling in my fingers. Trying to tell myself that my father didn't have a gun. He didn't have a blood scanner. So he wasn't really an enforcer. For all I knew, this was just how the General expected all of his employees to appear in public. Like a show of loyalty.

Except . . . Alex's mother worked for the General, too. And she was sitting with her family.

Something cracked below me, and I realized with a jolt that the heat in my hands had made the pew splinter a little. It seemed to respond to my emotions, spiking up strongest when I was scared or angry – telling me to defend myself. I bit my tongue, glancing from side to side, terrified that someone might have noticed. But all the faces around me were looking straight ahead. Even Liza hadn't seen.

*You have to control it*, I told myself. *Like you did last night. You have to make the heat obey you, or they'll figure it out. They'll see what you can do. And then –*

I stopped the thought before it could go further, shoving my hands under my knees. Resolving to keep my emotions in check; scanning the church for something to take my mind off it all. Gaze resting on Christian in the front row.

He was seated with his father, that tall, handsome man who made me uneasy for no reason I could explain. Christian's head was turned slightly to the side, lashes feathered down, like he couldn't bring himself to face the altar all the way.

The heat in my blood gave a kick of joy at the sight of him – not the kind of kick that told me I was about to explode something. More like a bright, aching pull. My body squirming in place, telling me it would be so good for me, for him, for *both* of us if I could just be near him again –

'There is great fortune to be lavished upon us, if we should be called children of the light,' Tiago was saying. 'But we must prove ourselves worthy! We must wear the armour of heaven and fight the devil on earth. For there are demons in the shadows spreading death and eternal war. They are witches.'

'And they burn,' said the crowd.

'In the black days, when the Saints were among us, our city was cursed. Misery, misery. Blood and ashes. But then, in our darkest hour, a prophet rose. He saved us from destruction. He carried us with him into the light.'

Tiago raised his leather-clad hands, and the congregation swelled forward in response. 'Worship the General as he deserves. Praise him.' He bowed his head. 'Let us pray.'

'Our Father, who built this city,' the crowd breathed, 'hallowed be thy name. Thy kingdom come, thy will be done.'

I heard a door creak open, caught a glimpse of fluttering robes, bare feet and a dark hood at the back of the church.

'Lead us not into temptation, but deliver us from evil. Deliver us from Saints.'

The crowd was on the edge of their seats now, wound tight with anticipation. *He's here*, I thought, possessed by a wild reverence I could hardly comprehend. *He's coming.*

Tiago closed the leather book and stepped away from the pulpit. 'Hail the General,' he said.

'For he alone protects,' said the crowd.

Finally, the man showed himself.

He came up the centre aisle, moving towards the altar, a hooded figure in a burlap robe. Red footprints spread in his wake as if his feet were bleeding. The people sitting along the aisle fell to their knees as he passed, reaching for the tail of his robe like beggars in a marketplace.

When the General neared Christian's pew, Christian tensed, and I felt a familiar tugging sensation, my head filling with images. Icy room, locked door, dirt floor, with a chained box in the corner. The same scene I'd glimpsed when we'd touched before. So I could still get into his mind.

A guilty pulse of relief ran through me, the bone-deep reassurance that we were connected, no matter what Christian said. I thought of his silhouette in my dreams – of the longing that I felt for him, carried inside of me like a wound, refusing to vanish in the daytime. Of the way I'd been so sure that whatever was happening to me came back to him in the end.

As far as I could tell, there was only one explanation for it: that we had the same heat in our blood. The same power.

And, in Castello, having power meant only one thing.

*That we were Saints.*

The General swept up the altar steps and moved to the pulpit, facing the crowd. Slowly, he lowered his hood.

'Welcome, my children,' he said. 'Come and join me in the light.'

# CHAPTER NINETEEN

He was young.

It was my first thought, frivolous but unavoidable, because it was the exact opposite of what I'd expected. The General wasn't withered or priest-like. He looked almost boyish: brutally handsome, with perfect, chiselled features, like he'd been carved from stone. His skin was unmarked by time, his eyes rimmed in circles of ash, his head shaved in a military undercut. Black tattoos snaked up his neck and coiled at his temples. Etched into his forehead was a gruesome crown of thorns.

'Surprise,' I heard Liza say. 'The General's inked. When he was a kid, he probably wanted to be a rock star.'

*And now he wants to be a god*, I thought. *Even better.*

'Citizens of Castello,' the General said. His voice was dark and silky, built for persuasion. 'We are gathered here to remember. To celebrate. Twenty years of peace. Twenty years of purity. Twenty years of standing united.'

He glanced to one side of the church, then the other, bringing the Marconi and Paradiso wings together under his gaze. On the altar platform, Veronica tapped her fingers distractedly on the arm of her throne.

'Today, we are allies, one people made equal by our devotion. Our city is a holy place, blessed by the light. But, citizens, recall our history,' the General said. 'Recall and repent – for there is terrible wickedness in our past. Though it was commanded *love thy neighbour*, we forsook that oath and fell into hatred. We were a divided people, torn apart by greed and strife. The north fought the south; death and chaos ravaged our city. In those years, we were sinners, fallen from the light. Our sins were a blanket of darkness covering Castello. And, in that darkness, the devil came to town.' The General's lips curled up in a cold little smile.

'And the devil had a name,' he said. 'The devil was a Saint.'

*The devil was a Saint.*

It made me shiver instinctively, a tangled mass of *shamehateterror* rising inside my chest. But the emotions weren't mine. They were coming from Christian again.

'The Saints were the children of hell,' the General said. 'Born blighted and unnatural, with fire in their blood. Stained dark by sorcery and loathsome in the eyes of the light. For the Saints did not bow down for judgment, but rejoiced in their witchcraft and desired to rule over our world. And the Saints saw that the people of Castello were weak and sinful. They knew they could thrive in our city, for we would let their evil grow. Swiftly, cunningly, these creatures crawled into our homes. They entered our families, wearing the disguise of human flesh, though underneath they had no souls. The Saints spread among us like a disease, and while we fought against one another they plotted to destroy us all.'

The next time I looked at the altar, I was surprised to find Veronica Marconi staring right back at me. Her eyes were sharp and calculating, reminding me of how she'd looked the first day I'd met her: like she was waiting for me to prove myself. Even after I lowered my gaze, I swore I could still feel her watching.

'Citizens, remember the fire!' the General called. 'Remember how it raged! The Saints attacked us here, in this place of holy worship. North and south together, we were slaughtered in this church. And, while the embers fell on the ruins of our city, the Saints laughed, for they believed they had conquered us all.' He leaned forward on the pulpit, gripping the marble with his skeletal hands. 'But, my children, remember how we defied them. Remember how we rose from the ashes. For, in that time of darkness, I came to you and showed you the path of the light.'

'Bless us, Father,' chanted the crowd. 'Lift us up.'

'I alone survived the massacre at Icarium,' the General said. 'I alone was chosen. I brought peace to Castello. I brought salvation. I gave you revenge on those who wronged you. I purified your town.'

Christian's body was very stiff in front of me, something fragmented and deadly growing in his mind. The iron box with the chains. The icy room with the locked door and the shadow man with the snakes. I tried to block it out, not wanting to spy on him, but I couldn't bring myself to truly fight the link.

*He's like me*, I thought, more sure of it than ever. *He's like me, he has to be.*

And yet ... I couldn't actually see any power in Christian's mind. I found myself searching for it instinctively, skimming past his memories, looking for signs: the thrill and the heat and the dangerous mistakes. But there was nothing there. His thoughts were stuck in a loop, full of dead ends and repeat images. Always the man and the snakes and the box with the chains.

The box fascinated me for some reason, and I imagined reaching out and lifting the chains off – leaning down to see inside. Heat surging up in my fingers, telling me to do it, *do it now* –

'My children, stand strong with me!' the General called. 'Do not falter in our great purpose. Every Saint we burn is a beacon of light, casting the devil from our town. While the righteous and obedient are spared, the witches will be punished!'

The crowd burst into feverish applause, pounding their feet on the floor, filling the church with the sound of rolling thunder. The box in Christian's mind gave a sudden shudder, like the thing inside could sense my presence, wanted to fight its way out to meet me.

*Yes*, I thought. *Good, please* –

But Christian shook his head and focused every ounce of effort on keeping the box shut.

Up on the pulpit, the General ended his speech with his

arms spread wide, robe swirling. The crowd was in a frenzy, spilling out of the pews with their flowers, rushing to meet him. The General stepped around the pulpit and knelt down, lowering his bony hands into the mob.

'Behold the prophet!' Tiago called out. 'Behold him who wipes away the sins of the world!'

The crowd was pawing at the General, pressing their flowers greedily into his hands. The box in Christian's mind shook harder, the thing inside desperate to escape now. I felt light-headed with anticipation, heat burning through me, urging the chains to crack. Sensing that this was it, the root of everything. The answers I'd been looking for.

*Lilly, stop*, Christian said sharply.

I reeled back, his voice ringing through my mind as clearly as if he'd spoken out loud.

*Just stop it.*

*How can I hear you?* I thought, floored. *What's going on?*

*Please*, Christian said, and turned to face me, rising to his feet across the empty rows of pews. His blue eyes were glassy with fear, skin drained of colour, sweaty curls stuck to his forehead. *Don't open it*, he said. *Don't you dare –*

But it was too late.

The box was breaking already, the chains falling away. The rusty lid slamming back with a crash. The thing inside was climbing out.

I prepared for the worst – expecting to see darkness and monstrosity, something bad enough to explain Christian's desperation to keep it locked away. Instead, I saw a hazy light, white-gold and humming.

The thing in the box was his power.

*I knew it*, I thought with a furious rush of triumph. *I knew we were the same.*

Power poured over the edges of the box, flooding Christian's body and settling into his blood. I couldn't imagine how he'd been able to hide it in the first place, locked so tight without any traces in his mind. It was like he'd found a way to stop it from existing at all.

*Because he hated it.*

The realization hit me hard, a blackout wave of loathing crashing down from Christian's brain to mine. He hated his power more than I could believe.

Our eyes locked across the church, and I saw him sway on his feet, gripping the pew for balance, weak from the way it felt: the heat like poison under his skin, dissolving him from the inside out. I could sense his terror, vivid as daylight between us, and his denial. His need to refuse and refuse and refuse.

*The devil was a Saint.*

Viciously, Christian thought, *No, I won't be*, and then he was out of the pew and pushing into the crowd, forcing his way through the chaos towards the church doors. I rose to my feet, following him instinctively, shrugging off Liza when she tried to stop me – knowing that if I lost him right now I would never get him back again.

But in the end, I wasn't fast enough.

By the time I made it to the doors, Christian had already vanished.

# CHAPTER TWENTY

Icarium's terrace was white marble, swept clean by the wind. The church doors slammed shut behind me with an echo that seemed to rattle the whole town. Then there was silence.

I was sure Christian had gone already, but to my surprise I found him leaning against the terrace railing with his back to me, looking over the square. Relief thudded through me, making my body thrum.

'I thought you'd left,' I said.

Christian didn't answer, didn't move, stayed tensed up and staring across the city. My window into his mind had snapped shut the moment he'd passed through the church doors, and now there was only emptiness behind my eyes, black pools where his thoughts had been before. The heat in my blood, which had been reaching for him so fiercely – spurned and rejected now, reduced to a simmer. It was like he'd found a way to lock his power up again, force it back inside that metal box. Shredding the link between us in the process.

'Christian,' I tried again. 'What's going on? What are we?'

Finally, he turned. His eyes were dull but no longer panicked, the wind twisting his curls across his forehead. I thought, not for the first time, of some kind of angel, who had been kicked down into the darkness of the human world.

'Haven't you figured it out yet?' Christian said.

And I had. I just didn't want to say it.

*The devil was a Saint.*

I let the words hover in my mind like a neon sign, dissolving a little at a time, until there was only one part left.

*Saint.*

'But how?' I breathed, feeling a delayed pulse of fear. 'I'm not even from this town. This shouldn't be happening –'

'Trust me,' Christian said. 'That's what I thought, too. The day I met you, you made my power go haywire. But I thought, no way. It can't be her. She's too new. She can't be cursed already.' His lips curled down. 'Except it *was* you. It's always been you.'

I winced at his tone, the bitter edge to it. The way he'd said *cursed*.

'I could hear you before,' I said slowly. 'I was in your head. I felt your power. But now there's nothing left.'

Christian's shoulders tensed a little, and I was afraid he might turn away again. But I had to know.

'Christian, where did it go?' I said. 'What did you do with your power?'

Slowly, he shrugged. 'I made it stop.'

That was when I noticed what he was holding: a small metal cylinder with a needle on the end. Like an old-fashioned syringe. And his jacket sleeve – rolled up to the elbow, showing bare skin where the needle had stuck in.

'What is that?' I asked.

'It's an injection,' Christian said. 'To kill power. It's basically a miracle drug. At least it used to be, until I met you.'

'Injection,' I repeated.

'They were the General's brilliant idea during the purges. When the enforcers needed a way to stop Saints from resisting arrest.' Christian rolled the syringe between his fingers, as reverent as a caress. 'One shot of this and your power just sort of . . . dies off. It comes back after a while, but I guess by then everyone had been burned.'

'If the injections are from the purges, how did you get them?'

'My dad has a stockpile,' Christian said. 'He used to be an enforcer, before . . .' He let it hang. 'So I started stealing from his supply as soon as I realized I was, you know. Abnormal.'

There it was again: the bitter edge to his voice. The raw hatred of his power cutting through his blank facade.

'How long has it been?' I asked. 'I mean, how long have you been hiding what you are?'

'Three months, give or take,' Christian said. 'But I felt it coming for a while before that. Like . . . a tide building inside me, waiting to break. And then one day I just –'

'Made something happen?'

'Kind of.' There was a dark glint in his eyes, the echo of a bad memory. 'At least it was easy to deal with at first because the injections were strong. I could do one shot, and the power would disappear for ages. Then you moved here. Now the injections hardly last at all. My power doesn't like to stay dead when you're near me. It's like it's fighting back because it knows there's someone else, someone it can reach for. I need a shot every day just to kill it off. And when you touched me before –'

He shuddered. I thought about how it had felt when I'd held his wrist in church – the heat surging up inside me, fierce and blinding – and realized it must've felt like that for him, too. His power, rattling the box in which he'd chained it. Desperate to reach me.

'You brought it to life,' Christian said. 'You always do that. You let my power out, so I have to stop it.'

'So that's why you've been avoiding me,' I said, feeling the understanding dawn with a guilty rush. 'Why you've been afraid of me this whole time. You could tell I'd end up with power somehow, that I'd make things worse –'

'I wasn't sure,' Christian said. 'I didn't want to believe it. But that first day, do you remember? Touching you messed me up. We were supposed to get tested, but I couldn't do it. I was sure Tiago would find out what I was. I've been trying to stay away from you ever since. But – I don't know. It's like I can't help it sometimes. My power wants you.' His eyes were on mine again, lidded and dazed. 'It wants you now. It's so hard to keep hidden when you're around.'

'I'm sorry,' I whispered. 'I had no idea. I've been using power without meaning to. I didn't even know what it was until last night –'

'It's not your fault,' Christian said. 'It's just how power is. Everything good gets turned into a nightmare.' He turned the syringe through his fingers again, almost compulsive. 'It wouldn't even matter if I had more shots. But at this rate they'll be gone by the end of the month.'

'What do you mean?'

Christian shrugged. 'Since you moved here, I've been going through them way too fast. My dad had dozens of injections stored away, but not hundreds. The thing is . . . I'm running out.'

I was still processing that when the church doors scraped open.

'Well, well,' Tiago said.

I recognized his voice even before I turned around: that faint curl of humour with something dark below it. He was coming towards us across the terrace, black cloak billowing in the wind, hands smooth in his leather gloves.

'Skipping out on church, Asaro?' he asked, giving Christian a leering smile. 'Your father will be so disappointed.' His eyes slid to me. '*Tesoro*, yours too.'

I had a sudden flash of Jack standing on that altar, and realized that Tiago must know him now. That they worked together. That my father had just become my enemy.

'We weren't skipping,' Christian said coolly. 'I got sick, so Lilly was helping me –'

'Sick again?' said Tiago. 'I'm sensing a pattern. Of course, with your family history, it's hardly a surprise. Still, leaving during the service is an unfortunate choice. Sickness or otherwise, you were raised better than to disrespect the General.'

'It was an honest mistake,' Christian said. 'We were just going back inside.'

He moved sideways to prove it, aiming for the church doors, but Tiago blocked the way.

'You know,' he said, 'I often wonder what exactly went wrong with your father. Such a fine man, and yet he lost his mind so fast –'

'Don't talk about my dad,' Christian said sharply.

'We've got a few theories going around. Some people are convinced it was your mother's fault. She had quite a reputation. But the rest of us think it was down to *you* –'

'Stop,' I snapped, grabbing Christian's arm as he lunged forward – squeezing myself in front of Tiago instead. 'Can we stay focused, please?' I asked him. 'You were supposed to be telling us what horrible people we are for leaving church.'

'*Ma certo, angelo,*' Tiago said with false sincerity. 'I wouldn't want to disappoint you.' Slowly, he reached out a gloved hand and rubbed a strand of my hair between his fingers, making me hold my breath to keep from flinching. 'Lilliana Deluca,' he said, 'it's the strangest thing. You remind me of someone.'

'Who?' I whispered.

But then Tiago froze. His attention had been caught by something over my shoulder, and it made his whole face sharpen. Gone was the humour and the taunting. I was standing in front of a hunter now.

'Boy,' Tiago said. 'What's in your hand?'

I glanced back, saw Christian's fingers curled tight below his jacket sleeve, the flash of silver between them. It was the syringe.

'Nothing,' Christian said, voice thick with indifference. 'Is it illegal to make a fist in this town?'

'Show it to me,' Tiago said, shoving me unceremoniously sideways and reaching for Christian instead.

Christian lurched away from him, slamming against the terrace railing, hands gripped tightly behind his back. 'I *said* there's nothing.'

Tiago's lip curled, like he couldn't believe what he was hearing. I wondered if anyone had ever disobeyed him before. From the manic glint in his eyes, I was guessing not.

'Asaro,' Tiago said, 'I think you've gone as mad as your father.'

He reached out and seized a fistful of Christian's hair, dragging him roughly forward, making Christian twist and gasp in pain.

'Get off him,' I said furiously, trying to step between them again, only to find myself swatted backwards, hitting the ground hard. My head collided with the marble, mind a haze of panic, knowing that the moment Tiago saw the syringe we were dead.

Then – 'That is quite enough,' someone said. It was a woman's voice, full of authority. 'There's no need for indelicacy on holy ground.'

Tiago turned, one hand still gripping Christian's hair, bowing Christian's head towards him like a supplicant. His eyes were narrowed, as if the voice had triggered a primal instinct inside him, made his hackles rise.

'Hello, Veronica,' Tiago said. 'I must've misheard you. Surely you weren't interfering with an enforcer's work?'

'Surely you weren't going to relieve the boy of his scalp?' Veronica Marconi said. She crossed the terrace, heels clicking on the marble, and I scrambled to my feet in a rush, embarrassed that she'd seen me fall.

'What's he done this time?' Veronica asked Tiago. 'Stolen the altar wine?'

'There's something in his hand,' Tiago said coldly. 'He doesn't want to show it to me.'

'What a terrible offence,' Veronica said. 'How can we ever punish him properly? Oh, wait. I have an idea. Asaro – open your hand.'

Christian obeyed, twisting out of Tiago's grasp and offering his palm up. It was empty now. I assumed he'd stuffed the syringe up his sleeve.

'Look at that,' said Veronica, smiling tightly. 'It seems we've averted yet another peacekeeping crisis. All thanks to your diligence, no doubt. Now, if that's all . . .?'

She beckoned us forward, but Tiago held his arm out.

'I don't think so,' he said. 'They both walked out of church. The General might enjoy having a chat with them. Remind them of the importance of respecting our traditions.' Tiago flashed a nasty smile. 'Goodness, I could even take them in for treason –'

'Don't be ridiculous,' Veronica said. 'There's nothing in

the truce that forbids stepping outside for a breath of fresh air. I should know – I signed it.'

'You did,' Tiago said. 'But sometimes I think you had your fingers crossed behind your back.'

Veronica's eyes flashed. Tiago seemed to revel in it, nodding at her like a challenge. 'It's been twenty years, Vee. When are you going to realize that you don't matter any more?'

For a moment, I was sure Veronica was going to do something to him – what exactly, I couldn't say. But, in the end, she just gave Tiago her most charming smile. 'Fortunately for this city,' she said, 'I will always matter more than you. Now come along.' She motioned sharply to me and Christian. 'I'm taking you home.'

We were already at the top of the Marconi staircase, Veronica's arms placed protectively around our shoulders, when she glanced back at Tiago one last time. 'You know, we all used to think you'd grow into it. But no such luck.'

It took me a moment to realize she was talking about his scar. I just had time to see his reaction – the bolt of pure rage in his eyes – before Veronica was shoving us unceremoniously down the steps and out of sight.

I went without protest, letting her lead us into Castello's labyrinthine streets, too relieved to think twice about it. But, after a while, I realized Veronica was cutting a path through the city I'd never walked before. The buildings around us were shabby and broken down, even by Castello's standards. It made Liza's neighbourhood look practically pristine.

'I think my house might be the other way,' I ventured.

'I'm aware,' said Veronica.

A ripple of uneasiness passed through me. I thought of the service: glancing up at the altar and seeing her looking back at me. The hard edge to her gaze, like she was waiting for me to prove myself. It occurred to me that letting her take us to such an isolated part of town might not have been a good idea.

'Where are we going?' I demanded, pulling against her grip. 'People will start looking for me if I'm not back soon.'

'Really?' Veronica said. 'Like who?'

I opened my mouth to say *my father*, and then shut it tight. Veronica smiled faintly and herded us onwards. I chanced a look at Christian, wishing I could still read his mind – trying to ask questions with my eyes.

*What now? Do we run?*

Christian's response was an almost-smile, devoid of humour. *Where to?*

Veronica came to a stop before an abandoned building with a battered wooden door, a metal gargoyle protruding from the centre of it. The gargoyle's mouth was open, showing gaping rows of dagger teeth. Veronica plunged her hand inside.

'You two got very lucky today,' she said pleasantly, finding a switch somewhere in the gargoyle's mouth that triggered a lock on the door. It swung open silently, revealing a long dark tunnel. 'Tiago arrived too late to realize what you were hiding. But really,' she said, ushering us inside, 'if you're going to discuss your power, you should not do it in public. You never know when the wrong person might come along.'

# CHAPTER TWENTY-ONE

There was darkness everywhere. Heavy, damp air enveloped me like a blanket. I couldn't see Christian or Veronica, couldn't even sense them standing next to me. All I heard was my own breathing, a harsh, unsteady sound. It felt like being buried alive.

Then, out of the black: the scrape of a match being lit. Veronica's face came into view, illuminated by a torch. The firelight showed a new sharpness in her features, something dangerous lurking in the corners of her smile.

I cast a quick glance around the tunnel, saw a low ceiling dripping water, a dirt floor littered with bullet casings and tiny animal bones. Across the way, Christian was feeling the walls for an exit, searching for the outline of the door we'd just come through. But that had vanished, too, devoured by the dark.

Veronica patiently watched us discover we were trapped. 'The only way out is in,' she said. 'Shall we?'

I looked at Christian again. Fire reflected like diamonds in his eyes. Slowly, he shrugged.

Veronica began to walk deeper into the tunnel. I followed

her reluctantly, running through options in my head. She'd heard us talking on the terrace, so she knew what we were. But she'd stepped in before Tiago could find out and hurt us. Why?

*Maybe she wants to hurt you herself.*

Heat spiked in my blood, a pulse of power ready to defend me. *I can hurt her back*, I thought. But it didn't reassure me as much as I would've liked.

We'd been walking for what felt like ages when I finally saw another door up ahead. It seemed to glow in the dark, fiery with rust, fitted with a wheel mechanism like a bank vault. Veronica lodged her torch in the wall and spun the wheel around until a bolt clicked. Slowly, she gripped the metal door with both hands and rolled it back on its hinges.

Beyond it, there was pure black again, but Veronica moved ahead of us, lighting candles as she went – bringing things into view a little at a time. I gasped.

We were standing on the edge of what looked like the ballroom of a long-deserted palace. It was a massive open space paved in marble, the walls covered in moth-eaten velvet and hung with chipped gold picture frames. It must've been gorgeous once, but had now fallen into deep decay – the fireplace collapsing in a pile of rubble, the plush furniture deflated and covered in spiderwebs. A wooden banqueting table ran the full length of the room, piled high with a strange assortment of objects: gold coins and silver daggers like an ancient treasure trove, mixed in with the cool dark metal of dozens of handguns. Gnarled candelabras bloomed from every surface, fitted with red candles that dripped bloody wax down to the floor.

'What is this place?' I breathed, taking an involuntary step forward, captivated despite myself.

'The centre of the world,' Veronica said. 'My family has spent centuries fighting for Castello from in here.'

'It's a safe house,' Christian murmured, joining me. 'Where you retreat to when you can't win the war.' He glanced at Veronica. 'I thought the General made you give up all your hideouts when you signed the truce.'

'He tried,' Veronica said. 'But there are parts of this city that will always be beyond his reach.'

She moved to an oversized desk in the corner, set on a raised platform to offer a clear view of the room. Above it, a giant portrait was mounted on the wall, showing a dark-haired young man in royal regalia holding a shield with Castello's key-and-dagger coat of arms. Out of everything in the safe house, the portrait alone seemed well preserved, cared for meticulously when the rest of the place was left to rot.

'People have wasted lifetimes trying to snatch Castello out of my family's control,' Veronica said. 'The Paradisos used war as their weapon; the General chose peace instead. So far, none of them has succeeded. This place is proof of that.' She pressed her palms flat on the surface of the desk, like she was gathering strength from the wood. 'The General believes he owns this town, but he doesn't know half its secrets.'

I stared at her, wondering what I was missing. Surely

that couldn't be mockery in her voice? I'd heard her talk about the General in class a dozen times, always perfectly respectful and obedient. And yet –

'You look stunned,' Veronica said. 'Is it really so surprising? Did you honestly think I would roll over and let that man steal my legacy? No. This was my city first. I haven't given up on it yet.'

Christian narrowed his eyes, like he didn't trust a word she was saying. I had no idea what to think.

'What exactly do you want from us?' I asked, playing for time.

'*Want* is the wrong word,' Veronica said. 'I'm trying to give you something.' Then, when we didn't react, 'I'm trying to help you.'

'Why?'

'I told you,' said Veronica. 'This was my city first. And in my city we never burned anyone. Not even Saints.'

Out of nowhere, Christian laughed. 'Sorry,' he said. 'But I mean – you don't actually expect us to believe that.'

'I certainly do.'

'Yeah, right. You're sworn to the General. You've been teaching his laws for decades. He hates the Saints, and so do you –'

'Don't be naïve, child,' Veronica said. 'When the General took power, anyone who opposed him ended up on a pyre. I wasn't going to die like that. I swore loyalty to survive. For twenty years, I've done what I have to do to protect myself. I may teach his laws, but that doesn't mean I *believe* them. Not everyone is so easily led astray.'

Her eyes were harsh on Christian's face, and I wondered all of a sudden if she was talking about his father. The man Tiago said had lost his mind. Christian seemed to curl in on himself, wounded, and I had the urge to stand in front of him, shield him from her scorn.

'So you're not actually planning to kill us?' I asked instead. I was fairly reassured by now, but it was always good to clarify.

Veronica sighed. 'No, Lilly. Like I said, I'm trying to help you.'

She reached under the desk and drew out a small iron chest with a broken padlock. A wave of dust rolled off when Veronica flipped the lid up, and only after it settled could I see what was inside. Dozens of metal syringes packed into neat, gleaming rows.

Christian took a shuddering step towards them, unable to help himself. The shot he'd had outside the church had killed his power for now, but it would come back eventually. The chest of injections was like salvation to him.

'Where did you get those?' he said.

'During the purges,' Veronica said, 'I thought it would be useful to have a sample of the General's weaponry. And some of the enforcers in this town were quite fond of me, once upon a time.'

'Not Tiago,' I muttered.

Veronica shot me a look. 'No. Tiago has only ever been fond of things he can own. But that is of no consequence.' She motioned us forward, pointing to two decrepit armchairs in front of her desk. 'Come. Sit. These injections are for you now.'

Slowly, we went.

'There are twenty-four shots in this chest,' Veronica said. 'That's a year's supply for two Saints. You'll need one on the first of every month for testing day.' She removed two syringes from the box and rolled them towards us across the desk. 'Those are for November. When the month is up, you'll return to me, and I'll give you each another.'

I reached for my syringe automatically, but Christian just stared at her. 'You're kidding, right?' he said. 'One shot a month?'

'Do you find that unsatisfactory?'

'It took a shot a *week* to kill my power when I was on my own. Now that there's two of us, we'll need twenty times that. Or it all comes back after a few hours. Less if we're close together.'

'Fascinating,' Veronica said, glancing between us like we were of purely clinical interest to her. 'I've only ever heard stories of Saints strengthening each other's abilities. But perhaps if you choose to spend significant time –'

'It's *not* just spending time,' Christian said. 'It's anything. Being in the same room as her. Looking at her. Even when she's not here, and I –' He bit back the words, cheeks flushing. 'It's constant,' he said with a kind of numb finality. 'She does something to my power. I need more shots.'

Veronica seemed to contemplate it. 'Are you saying you think your power is linked together somehow?'

Christian said nothing, like he thought the answer was too obvious to voice.

I said, 'We can read each other's minds.'

A pulse of genuine shock crossed Veronica's face. 'Can you? That's remarkable. Though I suppose, in certain circumstances . . .' She looked between us again, much more carefully now, letting her eyes linger on Christian. I almost thought she seemed hungry. Then it was gone.

'If I had to guess, I'd say your connection comes from your rarity,' Veronica said. 'The first two Saints in over a decade – your power can sense how fragile your existence is. It binds you together to help you both survive. Nonetheless, I am confident the injections will work when you need them to. One shot each on testing day, and Tiago's scanner will find your blood perfectly clear.'

'And what about the other days?' Christian said, a hitch in his voice. 'How am I supposed to get rid of my power the rest of the time?'

'You don't,' said Veronica shortly. She shut the chest with a harsh metallic sound. Christian flinched. 'Power runs in your veins. You shouldn't try to fight it. It's foolish to deny what you are.'

'No, I have to fight it,' Christian said. He looked almost feverish in the candlelight, the flush on his cheeks like a permanent stain. 'I didn't ask for this, okay? I don't want power. I don't want to be a demon. I don't want to be wrong.'

The words spilled out before he could think about what he was saying, and I could sense the sting of humiliation that hit him afterwards. He wished he hadn't spoken; he knew he couldn't take it back.

'You're not a demon,' Veronica said. I was afraid she'd mock him again, but her voice held only pity now. 'It doesn't matter what the General says. You have a gift. There's a reason they called you Saints in the first place. Once upon a time, the people of this city believed you had come to save them.'

'Yeah,' said Christian. 'And then we killed them all.'

There was silence after that. The candelabras dripped tears of deep red wax on to the desk.

'What's done is done,' Veronica said finally. 'You can't blame yourself for the tragedies of the past. The Saints have paid for them already, far more than they deserved. Two misguided children started a fire, and in exchange the General annihilated an entire generation. That wasn't justice, only slaughter. What I'm trying to spare you from.' She was looking at us steadily, daring us to argue. 'Now take the injections, and be grateful I had any to give you at all.'

I took mine without speaking, stuffed the cold metal cylinder into the pocket of my cardigan. Christian swiped his hatefully off the desk. His gaze was fixed on the chest that held the other twenty-two, so tantalizingly close, yet still out of reach.

*I will not beg*, he was thinking. *I will not beg her.*

I could hear the words distantly, like an echo at the end of a telephone line. His last injection was fading faster than I'd expected it to. His power had already begun to rattle the lid of its box. It made him restless, itchy in his own skin, reaching up to brush sweaty hair off his forehead with a twitch.

'Of course,' said Veronica, 'there is an alternative.'

I was on the verge of standing up, assuming we'd been dismissed, but something in her voice made me stop. A hint of slyness, as if she'd only just come to the real point of this conversation.

'Alternative to what?' I asked.

'*This*,' Veronica said, bringing her palm down suddenly on the desk. 'Persecution, living in fear all the time, relying on a drug to survive. The enforcers testing you like lab rats. Bowing to a man who burns people alive.'

I shot a look at Christian, wanting his reaction, but he was tuned out, eyes glazed over, lost in his own mind.

'What are you talking about?' I said.

'Isn't it obvious?' Veronica demanded. 'I'm talking about fighting back. The General may have stormed my city, but don't believe for a minute that I've stopped thinking of ways to throw him out. I've been watching that man for twenty years. I see the things he thinks he's hiding. I know where his weakness lies.'

'Weakness,' I said sceptically.

'Yes,' said Veronica. 'Would you like to guess what it might be?'

I shook my head. All I could think of was the way the crowd had rushed the General at the altar, desperate for a touch of his skeletal hands. He didn't seem like a weak man to me.

'It's fear,' Veronica said. 'The General is afraid of the one thing he's devoted his life to destroying. All his hatred for the Saints – it's because he fears you, deep down. He's terrified of what you have: true power, which he knows he can never compete with. Which tells me that power is the only way to bring him down.'

'How are we supposed to bring him down if he's trying to burn us all the time?'

'I never said it had to be *your* power, did I?' Veronica had begun to pace behind her desk, eyes darting up to the portrait of the young man with the key-and-dagger shield.

'There are other ways,' she said. 'There are weapons stronger than you can imagine. The Saints don't exist in a vacuum: you're part of this town. You were *created* by it. Which means that real power – raw power – it has to come from Castello itself. Why else would this place be so coveted, for so many millennia? The clans weren't the first to go to war here, you know; there have been empires rising and falling on this land since the beginning of time. The Etruscans, the Romans, the kings of the Dark Ages – sacking and killing and mutilating each other, all for the chance to rule this miserable scrap of a town. It makes no sense unless they knew Castello was different. Unless they knew there was power to be had.'

Veronica's eyes had taken on a hypnotic glow, making me lean forward in my chair despite myself. 'And, if power comes from Castello, then what the Saints can do with it is just the tip of the iceberg. You're genetic accidents, born with the capacity to absorb a tiny fraction of what this city offers up. Bound by the limitations of your human bodies – susceptible to exhaustion and weakness and pain. If we want to defeat the General, we need to do better than that. We need a way to control *all* the power in the town. The heart of Castello at our command. *That's* a weapon. That's how a rebellion starts.'

'Rebellion,' Christian said. I swung around to look at him, glad that he was speaking, but wary of his tone, which told me he thought Veronica was the stupidest person on earth. 'You want to start a *rebellion*.'

'Why not?' she said. 'Haven't you ever gone to sleep at night and dreamed of waking up in a better world?'

'No time,' Christian said coldly. 'I'm too busy trying to stay alive in this one.'

'Exactly. Which is why someone has to change it.'

Christian's lip curled, like he wanted to laugh at her again, but couldn't be bothered. His eyes were as hard as I'd ever seen them, fingers gripped furiously around the one syringe Veronica had been willing to give him. And I understood, all of a sudden, how impossible it was for him to sit here and listen to her talk, when all he wanted was her chest full of shots. That was the real solution to his problems, and Veronica had denied it to him point-blank.

'Rebellions don't work in Castello,' Christian said. 'The last time your family tried to start one, we ended up with a clan war instead. Besides, whatever you think you know about the General, you're wrong. Trust me. He changes people. He's unbeatable. He owns this place now.'

'He may seem unbeatable,' Veronica said, 'but he's not eternal. Someone ruled before him, and someone will rule after him, too.'

'No, you don't get it,' Christian said. 'There's no one before or after God. And that's who the General thinks he is.'

Veronica just smiled. 'Luckily, we aren't all believers.'

# CHAPTER TWENTY-TWO

We came out of the safe house into a grey afternoon. Christian was walking a little ahead of me, his hair a tangled glow of dirty gold at his neckline. Head down, fingers still gripped tight around his syringe. For a while, his mind had been full of staticky anger at Veronica, but now it had faded to desperation. All he cared about was injections. Stealing them, breaking into buildings, bribing enforcers –

'You have to stop thinking like that,' I said. I was scared of how strong it was, his all-consuming need to kill his power. I was scared of how far he'd go to make it happen.

Christian glanced over sharply, eyes dark. 'You can hear me?'

I nodded. His panic flickered bright at the edge of my consciousness. 'It's coming back,' he said, and pushed up his sleeve. He was lining up the injection before I could process it, pressing the needle tip into his inner arm.

'What are you doing?' I snapped, grabbing his hand at the last second. 'Veronica said to save the shots.'

'I don't care,' Christian said. 'I've got six more at home. After that, I don't know. I'll figure something out –'

'Christian, stop,' I hissed, fighting him for the syringe. 'Just think about this for a second.'

'You don't understand,' he whispered. Our eyes met, and I was stunned by the raw need I saw in his, the tension thrumming through every inch of his body. 'I *have* to do it.'

'So this is what you meant,' said a voice behind us, 'when you said everything was totally fine.'

We both spun around.

'Alex,' Christian said.

He was perched on the stoop of a building at the end of the street, his leather jacket blending in with the shadows. Christian seemed to freeze at the sight of him, heartbeat kicking up in his chest.

'Well, don't stop on my account,' Alex said coldly. 'I mean, fighting over needles in alleyways is completely normal behaviour.'

'What are you doing here?' Christian stammered.

'Waiting for you,' Alex said. 'You weren't exactly subtle about leaving church. I got out just in time to see Professor Marconi taking you both away. I figured I should stick around and make sure she was planning on letting you go again.' His black eyes flashed over Christian's face. 'Given how poor your self-preservation skills have been lately, I thought someone should be watching your back. But clearly, getting kidnapped is the least of your worries.'

Alex kicked off the stoop and rose to his feet, anger pouring off him in waves. 'Clearly, I'm the stupid one for believing I had any *idea* what was going on.'

'Alex,' Christian started, 'I can explain. This isn't what you think –'

'Which part?' Alex demanded. 'You're not a freak of nature? Or you haven't been hiding it from me all term?'

Christian winced, and for a second I thought Alex might take it back. But he seemed too furious to care.

'I know what that is,' he said, pointing at the syringe still gripped in Christian's hand. 'I know they used to use it on the Saints. Because you're one of them, aren't you? You probably have been for a while. It makes perfect sense now that I think about it. It explains why you've been going around half dead for months, making me lie for you.' His eyes flashed again, something dangerous inside him needing to lash out.

'Honestly, I should've figured it out on my own. But I was stupid. I kept thinking that if something was really wrong, if it was really important, then you'd actually have bothered to tell me –'

'I couldn't,' Christian said. 'You don't understand. This is bad, okay, and it's not your problem –'

'Oh, so *this* is where you draw the line?' Alex snapped. '*This* is where things stop being my problem? Good to know. I'll remember that the next time you show up bleeding on my doorstep –'

Christian winced again, but Alex didn't seem sorry about it any longer.

'It's funny,' he said, 'how close you let people get when you need something from them. But then you find someone better.' His eyes darted to me and away again, like a little arrow of fury shot at my heart. 'I'm guessing she's a freak, too? That's why you've been obsessed with her this whole time? Acting like you don't care and then talking about her non-stop . . . Except she's hurting you, too. I can tell. You've been falling apart since she moved here. Like, worse than usual. But somehow you still trust her more than me.'

'That's not true,' Christian said. He seemed shell-shocked by what was happening, thoughts tumbling over themselves in his head. 'This isn't about her, I swear, just let me explain –'

'Don't bother,' Alex said with a quick shrug, dripping disinterest. 'I know when I've been replaced. Next time, just have the decency to tell me to my face.' He shot me another look, plastering on an awful smile. 'Congratulations, Deluca. Enjoy the mess. He's all yours now.'

Then he was gone, melting into the shadows as fast as he'd appeared. Christian stared after him, eyes wide, paralysed.

'Are you okay?' I said.

Slowly, he shook his head. 'He's right. I should've told him. And I wanted to, honestly. But . . . I couldn't. Saying it out loud would have made it real. And, besides, bad things happen to him when he's with me. Bad things happen to everyone. I guess I thought, if he didn't know, then –'

*I wouldn't lose him.*

There was an image pressing at the front of his mind, muddled and full of fear. I pulled away, trying to create space between our thoughts, not wanting to see things that weren't meant for me. Christian shot me a glassy-eyed look, like he could sense me falling into his head again, and was daring me to tell him he shouldn't make it stop. The syringe glinted dully between his fingers. So we were right back where we'd begun: fighting over needles in alleyways.

'It's not a big deal,' Christian said, reading the frustration in my face or mind. 'I have to do a shot sooner or later. That's what I was trying to tell you before. I can't go home with power. Or my dad will know. He can track it from a mile away. It's like he smells it.'

'So don't go home,' I said.

'Yeah, well, there's a curfew –'

'No, I mean – I have a couch.'

The words sounded much less smooth out loud than when I'd planned them in my head, but they made Christian's lips twitch, the first sign of humour I'd seen from him in a while. And as soon as I said it, I realized how badly I wanted him to come with me. It wasn't just about power – the biological demand of the heat inside me, telling me I needed him close. It was a kind of protectiveness I hadn't known I was capable of. The conviction that if I lost sight of him, even for a second, something terrible would happen.

For a long time, Christian said nothing, watching me with those hooded eyes. Flashes of his thoughts brushed up against mine: what it felt like with his power crawling back, weaving through his bloodstream, so much stronger than he'd ever let it get before. How sick it made him feel; how desperately he wanted it to stop.

'It's bad, right?' I murmured. 'Being near me.'

'Of course it is,' Christian said. Then, incomprehensibly, 'Take me home.'

On the way to Via Secondo, I checked my phone. I had three missed calls from Liza, followed by the message: what the hell Lilly are you dead??

Not yet, I shot back. Gripped by a low pulse of dread at the prospect of having to explain all this to her. It's a long story. I'll tell you tomorrow.

There were also a half-dozen calls and messages from my dad, the most recent one from half an hour earlier. I waited for you at church, it said. But now you're worrying me, Lilly.

I wanted to feel vindicated by this – Jack *had* noticed I was missing, despite what Veronica had said. But then I thought of him standing by that altar with Tiago and the General, and just felt cold instead.

Leave me alone, I wrote, and switched my phone off.

By the time Christian and I got to my apartment, it was nearly dusk.

'So that's the couch,' I said, pointing helpfully.

'Thanks,' he said and shrugged off his bomber jacket. He was wearing a faded military T-shirt underneath it, black leather bracelets on both wrists, a slender gold crucifix around his neck. I watched him toss his jacket over an armchair, realizing all of a sudden how dusty everything was. I'd never actually used the living room since moving to this house. Now I felt guilty for telling him it would be a good place to sleep.

'You want to see some creepy murals?' I asked. 'I mean, if you're into that kind of thing.'

Christian looked surprised, like he'd actually expected me to walk out and leave him for the rest of the evening. 'Why not.'

My bedroom was still a little wrecked from what I'd done to the furniture, but Christian didn't seem to notice. He took one look at the bleeding knights on my walls and grinned. 'You have to show these to Alex. He's got a fixation with artistic deaths.'

I arched an eyebrow, feeling like Liza – doubting very much that Alex would ever speak to me again.

'He's your neighbour, you know,' Christian said, going for a closer look at the paintings. 'He basically lives behind this wall. I've been there a million times, but I never stopped to wonder what was on the other side.'

'He could turn us in,' I said, deciding that someone had to put it out there. 'If he wanted to, he could go straight to Tiago –'

'No,' Christian said. 'He couldn't. He's not like that. Trust me.'

He said it with so much conviction that I couldn't bring myself to argue.

I watched him wander restlessly through my room, examining things as he went: pausing by the wardrobe to take down one of my mother's books. It was from her Shakespeare collection, an old edition of *Richard III* bound in leather. I tried not to stare at his arms as he moved, the constellation of needle marks from the injections clustered on the inside of his elbows like tiny stars.

'*I am a villain: yet I lie. I am not,*' Christian read out loud. 'Why did you highlight that part?'

'I didn't. It was my mom's, before she died.'

'I'm sorry,' he said quickly. 'I didn't know –'

'It's fine,' I said. 'She wasn't – I mean, we weren't close.' It felt like an understatement, but it was easier than saying, *She liked to pretend she didn't know me in company.* 'Parents are overrated.'

Christian flinched. Something flashed in his mind – that other memory from church: the locked room and the shadow man with the snakes. He took a quick step backwards and sank down on the edge of my bed, Carly's book hanging loose between his hands.

'Parents,' he said numbly.

And out of nowhere, it dawned on me why his father had looked familiar this whole time. It was so obvious that I felt stupid for not realizing it sooner. He was the man from the video we'd watched in class: tall and handsome and holding a torch.

Christian's father was the one who set the Saints on fire.

# CHAPTER TWENTY-THREE

Silence fell between us, sudden and suffocating. I tried to think of something normal to say that would break the tension, stop the slow crawl of dread spreading through the room. But every time I thought I'd found a way to change the subject, my mind seemed to stall – linked too closely to Christian's, consumed by the silhouette of that shadow man closing in on me.

'What did he do to you?' I heard myself say.

'It doesn't matter,' Christian said.

But it did matter. I had a feeling it mattered a lot.

Slowly, I went to him, sat down on the bed with my knees curled up to my chest. I could feel warmth radiating off his skin – too much warmth, like he was running a fever. His power seemed to do that to him. It was like he'd become so used to killing it off that having it back sent his whole body into shock.

*Maybe I should leave*, I thought. *Maybe this wouldn't be so bad if I just left him alone.*

But when I tried to move again, Christian reached for my wrist, held me there next to him. He did it without looking at me, without moving in any other way at all. My head went instantly light, a delirious feeling rushing through my body – basking in the closeness of him, hardly daring to believe that after all the times I'd fantasized about touching him, he had reached for *me*.

*My power wants you*, I thought. But it felt like more than that.

For a long time, we stayed still, barely breathing, or maybe breathing too much.

'What Tiago said before,' Christian said finally. 'That my dad went mad? I guess it's true. But it wasn't his fault. He was just trying to do the right thing.'

His voice was quite even, unemotional, but I could sense something desperate buried below the surface: a plea for me to understand.

'He was our age when the church burned down. The Saints killed his whole family. Everyone he cared about walked out of the house one night and never came back. Wouldn't that drive you a little crazy, too?'

'Sure,' I whispered. Eyes wandering across his face, discovering little things I'd never known about him before. The tiny freckle below his bottom lip, the sealed-up piercing in his left ear, his perfectly angular nose.

'My dad was the enforcers' first recruit when the General put out the call. By the time the purges were over, he was in charge of everything. He caught more Saints than all the rest of them combined. Tiago still hates him for it. But the reason he was so good was because it was personal for him. It was an obsession. He really believed that light and dark stuff the General talks about. He thought he was sending demons back to Hell.

'The problem was, eventually all the Saints were gone. There was no one left to burn. But my dad couldn't stop. He just got more paranoid, seeing them everywhere, dragging people in for testing when they'd already passed. He was convinced the Saints were regrouping, preparing to attack again. When I was little, he decided my mum was one of them.'

Christian stopped suddenly, his breath catching in his throat. The circles below his eyes were as dark as bruises.

'You don't have to tell me,' I whispered. 'We don't have to talk about it –'

'I barely remember her,' Christian said. 'I feel so bad. I know I should, but I don't. I just remember *him*. Telling me she was a witch. That her blood was cursed, and she was going to take me away from him and curse me, too. That it was better this way.'

The image flashed in his mind, lightning-quick: a man's hand holding a woman's blonde head underwater. I bit my tongue, trying not to flinch, not sure if Christian had meant for me to see.

'Even the General wouldn't let my dad go back to work after that. I guess everyone knew he'd finally snapped. Tiago got his job instead. But at least he still had me. He could still protect *me*. So he did. In his own way, he was just trying to keep me safe.'

It was happening again – Christian's thoughts flooding my head, so hard for me to shut out when he had his guard down. Right now, I felt like I *was* him: young and full of dread, on my knees in that locked room. His body seemed so small to me, so impossibly fragile.

'My dad was afraid I'd turn out to be a demon like my mum,' Christian said. 'That all the bad stuff from her blood was going to end up in mine, too. So . . . he tried to fix me.'

Out of the dark came the shadow man with the snakes. But this time I could see them for what they really were. Not snakes: it was coiled leather in the man's hands.

A second too late, I understood what was coming – tried to tear my mind away. But I still felt the pain, lacing down my back like burning oil. The sound of skin breaking under leather, wet and slick.

'Shit,' Christian stammered, as I reeled away from him, grasping for my back – needing to convince myself I wasn't bleeding. 'I didn't realize you could feel –'

I shook my head, eyes squeezed shut, running my fingers desperately across my own skin. Unable to believe that he had survived this, over and over again.

Carefully, Christian touched me, fingers pressing against my neck, trying to root me in the present.

'Lilly, look at me. It's okay.'

*You're a liar*, I thought. *How could this ever be okay?*

But at least, when I met his eyes, the pain began to fade.

We were both silent for a long time, linked together on the bed, coming down from the memory. Christian's curls were falling across his forehead, and I reached up without thinking, brushed them behind his ear, felt him turn his head to follow my touch. His lips trailed against the edge of my palm, slow and tantalizing. His fingers moving against my neck in dizzy circles, until I was leaning in to him, unable to help myself, and he was leaning in too, both of us raw and vulnerable and needing each other so much.

'The thing is,' Christian said, 'my dad was right. All that time, he was only trying to fix me because he knew I was cursed. And I am. I grew up to be everything he was afraid of. No matter how hard I tried, I ended up being a demon anyway.'

'Christian, don't,' I whispered. 'Your dad's sick – you know that. You're not cursed for having power, and neither am I. I don't know why we ended up like this, but I think it's just part of who we are.' I hesitated a moment, gathering my courage. 'The truth is, power feels kind of good to me. It feels kind of normal –'

'Of course you'd think that,' Christian said, and dropped his hand from my neck. 'You haven't hurt anyone yet.'

'Maybe,' I said. 'But at least I'm not hurting myself.'

His eyes flashed to mine, and I knew he wanted to deny it – say there was nothing wrong with killing his power off. But in his mind, I saw that he knew exactly how dangerous it was. Running through shots like water, skin burning from needle points, his power fighting tooth and nail to escape its box. Fighting like something with survival on the line. Yes, he knew it was dangerous: the problem was, he didn't care.

'I just want it gone,' Christian mumbled. 'I hate the way it feels in my blood. I can't deal with it.' He turned away from me, staring at the far wall, daring me to challenge him. 'I know my dad kind of ruined me,' he said. 'But the point is he was ruined first. That's why none of it's his fault. Before the fire, he would never have hurt anyone. I've seen photos, from when his family was alive. He was happy, and the Saints took that away. They're the reason he is who he is. Maybe not all of us are demons, but the princeling kids, the ones who burned the church – they really did come from Hell.'

I had no argument with that. Thinking of the fire-drenched girl from my dream, and shivering a little. 'I feel like I can see them sometimes,' I said. 'Well, like I can see *her*. There are nights when I'm sure she's in the room with me.'

Abruptly, I rose to my feet and went to my wardrobe, dragging the old parchment from the back. Unsure of what had compelled me to do it, only feeling that Christian deserved to see it somehow.

'I think this was their battle plan. It's a blueprint of the church. They circled all the places they wanted to burn.'

Christian took it warily, like it might bite. 'Christ, Lilly. Where did you find this?'

'It was in the wardrobe. Maybe the girl lived here before the fire. She was the Marconi, right?'

Christian nodded, rubbing at the parchment with his thumb, scraping away layers of mould. Uncovering more of that scribbled writing: a wiry and girlish signature in the corner.

*Lecta*

Christian frowned. 'Do you think that was her name? No one could ever figure it out. They just called her –'

He stopped short, another layer of writing coming into view under his thumb.

*queen queen they will
bow before me I am the queen*

I sat back on the bed, feeling cold. 'She was crazy,' I whispered. 'She had to be.'

'Maybe,' said Christian. 'Or maybe she just really wanted to rule.'

He was still staring at the blueprint, transfixed despite himself. Like looking at crime-scene photos: gruesome and hypnotic at the same time. There were dozens of notes hidden in the parchment now that I was paying attention – slanting words on the terrace, screaming *LOCK THE DOORS!!!* A line on the altar that played like a chant in my head: *Valio is the prince I am the queen and I will make them see.*

'Who's Valio?' I asked.

'The General's brother, I think,' Christian said. 'The other princeling. According to my dad, everyone used to call him Val.'

I stared down at the map, thinking, *Val and Lecta. Lecta and Val* – transfixed by the sound. Then it occurred to me that all the notes were in the girl's handwriting. There was nothing from the boy. Maybe because it was her map, signed and left behind in her bedroom. Or maybe because she'd been the one planning the fire from the start. She'd come up with the idea, the target, and the boy had gone along with it because –

'He was in love with her,' I murmured.

'Yeah.' Christian glanced up. 'That's what people say.'

'You don't think it's true?'

He shrugged. 'Sure. But she didn't care much about him. You know the story, right? The General turned his brother in, and they tortured him publicly, so the girl would be able to see. Everybody was positive she'd come and save him, but –'

'She let him burn alone.'

Christian nodded. The blueprint was still in his hands, and he seemed to become aware of it all at once – shoved it off the bed like he'd just realized the horror of what he was holding. Slumped back against the wall, fiddling restlessly with one of his leather bracelets. I watched him for a moment, wanting to ask what he was planning to do when his injections ran out, if he really thought he could steal more from the enforcers. If he had a backup plan. But when I spoke, there were different words on my tongue.

'If you hate power so much, why don't you hate me?'

Christian flicked his eyes up. They were unnaturally bright, a crystal blue. And I could tell, right then, that he didn't know what he was doing – why he was here, so close to me, after avoiding me for ages. Why he kept making parts of our bodies touch.

*Because it feels good*, I thought, not sure if the realization was in his mind or mine. *It hurts, but it feels good at the same time*.

'I tried to hate you,' Christian said. 'I tried really hard. I just – couldn't. Read to me,' he said, and slid Carly's Shakespeare volume across the bed.

I hesitated, watching him collapse face down on to my pillow, then leaned up against the headboard with *Richard III*. The bit I opened to involved a couple of children being sent to their deaths. I flicked around, searching for a more soothing passage, but no luck. The play was a real slaughter. Eventually, I gave up and began reading from the start.

The next time I glanced over, Christian's eyes had slipped shut. I tucked the book under my pillow and slid slowly down the bed until our bodies matched, pressed my hand between his shoulder blades. I could feel the warmth of his skin through his T-shirt, the web of scars from his father's whip in ridges across his spine. And I imagined what it would be like to take some of his pain away, soak it up through my fingertips. Wash him clean. My hand was still on his shoulders when he opened his eyes.

'Lilly,' Christian said, half asleep and dazed from it.

'Sorry,' I said and pulled away. Christian reached up, threaded his fingers in my hair and kissed me.

All I could think was, *Finally*.

It was like a dam breaking inside of me, all the fear and longing I'd stored up since moving to this town suddenly crashing free. He tasted like smoke and fever, a hungry, desperate pressure on my lips. The air turned charged around us, buzzing like a storm: my power and his, tangled together the way it was meant to be.

I trailed my hand down his waistline, felt him tremble above me, leaning in to my touch. Relief a sweet haze in my mind, hardly daring to believe that he was letting me have this. The heat of his mouth and the drag of his body – the walls he'd built around himself to hold me back crumbling away in a rush. Every perfect inch of him, fitting against every inch of me.

'I dreamed about you,' I said, when we parted for breath. 'Almost every single night since I moved to this town –'

'I dreamed about *you*,' Christian said. A ragged catch in his voice, blinking down at me with dizzy eyes. 'Even before you came here, I used to see you all the time. I thought I was losing it.'

'I wish you'd told me. Just once, I wish you'd told me you felt something too –'

'I couldn't,' Christian said. 'I couldn't let myself do it. I think I knew if I had you – if I got close enough – then I wouldn't be able to stop.' He pulled back a little, shaking his head, curls brushing at my temple. 'It doesn't make sense. I shouldn't want you this much, not when I know the consequences. But I do. God, I do anyway.'

Abruptly, Christian squeezed his eyes shut and pressed his forehead into my collarbone, the weight of what was happening catching up to him all at once. The thick rush of power in his blood, so strong where it linked with mine – and the way, for the first time in his life, he wasn't fighting it. Despite all his fear and all his instincts: the way he was trying so hard to let it in.

*We could be good together*, I thought. Holding him tight against me, feeling the shaky pull of his breath. *I can help him get used to his power. I can make it worthwhile –*

'Stop thinking, Lilly,' Christian mumbled, ghosting a smile against my neck. 'It's loud. Just . . . don't let me go.'

So I didn't.

The princeling girl was in my dream again that night. The moment my eyes slid shut, she was waiting for me: bathed in flames, hair swirling around her face. I tensed for the inevitable fight, sure that she would make a grab for me. But the girl didn't move. Instead, she raised one talon-like finger and beckoned. Telling me to come to *her*.

'Don't go,' someone said – Christian at my side, woven in hazy light. 'Stay with me. You promised.'

But I couldn't. The girl had been taunting me for too long. Watching me from the corner, trying to claim me as her own. I had to know why.

Slowly, dreading it, I followed the beckoning finger. Let the flames curl around me – parting my lips and charring my lungs. Facing the princeling girl straight on, ready to know what she wanted.

But she never said. The girl never spoke at all. All she did was reach her clawed hands towards her own face and sweep her hair away, showing me her features for the first time.

Her eyes were black, her bones hollowed out and alive with darkness. My first thought was that I was looking at myself.

Then the girl smiled, and I realized I was looking at my mother.

# CHAPTER TWENTY-FOUR

I sat bolt upright in bed, horror rising like bile in my throat – leaning towards the floor, afraid I would be sick. My mouth was dry, my stomach tightened into knots. The room was completely dark around me, cut through by a single beam of moonlight. I could feel Christian at my side, body warm and vulnerable in sleep. He'd shifted a little when I sat up, and I realized that I was clinging to his wrist, fingers locked in a death grip, the way he'd held on to me before. I forced myself to let go.

Carly's Shakespeare volume tumbled off the bed, spine cracking against the floor. The title page fell open, and in the moonlight, I could see my mother's name written at the bottom in looping cursive. Her full name, the one I always managed to forget.

*Leonora Carlina Tale*

My eyes darted to the blueprint where Christian had tossed it. *Lecta*, said the scrawl in the corner. *Lecta*. The letters seemed to swirl, coming to life, parading across the parchment in front of me.

*Le c·ta*

Not a real name, more like a nickname, cobbled together from the ruins of something else, from –

It was there on the title page of the book: *Leonora Carlina Tale*.

Her handwriting was slender, curled in all the right places. Neater in the book, not as childish as on the blueprint, and maybe that was the difference that had blocked my mind, prevented me from realizing –

*Leonora Carlina Tale*

*queen queen they will bow*
*before me I am the queen*

Something snapped inside me. I lashed out at the pages on the floor, kicking them against the dresser as hard as I could. The book went, but the blueprint stayed put, winking up at me.

*Impossible*, I thought. *This is impossible*. My mother was from Venice. I'd spent my childhood listening to her stories, cradling her glass lions in my hands. She'd never been to Castello in her life.

And yet.

It was her name on the blueprint. I knew it in a

fundamental way, the deepest intuition I'd ever had. It was her writing, a scratched and angry version of the notes she'd left in her schoolbooks. It was her smile in my dream, the same one I'd seen as a little girl, the smile that had hurt me. I'd never doubted my mother's ability to be cruel. I'd just never assumed she was a killer.

'Please, no,' I whispered. '*Please*, God, no –'

God didn't answer, but Christian did. I felt him move behind me, dragging himself out of sleep, mumbling, 'What's going on?'

I shook my head, heart slamming in my chest, thinking, *My mother my mother the queen –*

'Lilly.' Christian sat up by my side, becoming aware of things at intervals: the way I was shaking, the harsh sound of my breath. 'What's wrong?'

'It was her,' I said. 'It was my mother. She was the one. She burned them.'

'What are you talking about?'

I pointed at the floor. The blueprint lay in the pool of moonlight before us, *Richard III* crumpled by the dresser. Christian ran a hand across his eyes and reached down to gather them both up.

'I don't understan–'

Then he stopped. He'd opened to Carly's signature in the book, where the *L* swooped like *Lecta*, stupidly obvious now that he was paying attention. I sat very still while he put the pieces together, moving only to shy away when the edge of the blueprint threatened to brush my leg.

'No way,' Christian said, fingers white around the

215

papers, comparing the writing side by side. 'It's a coincidence – it must be.'

I shook my head again, not believing it. Knowing he didn't, either.

'It was my mother,' I said.

I felt sick, still, but also distant now, speaking from somewhere far away. 'She did it. She set the fire. She burned them, half the town and your family. She burned your *family*, she drove your dad insane –'

Christian's eyes flashed. I flinched, suddenly aware of his fear, his anger, rolling off him in waves. Like thinking you've outrun all the bad things behind you, only to discover they've just been waiting up ahead.

He blinked it away after a second, but I knew what I'd seen. He was afraid of me. For real this time, and with good reason.

I stumbled to my feet, pushing across the room, trying to put distance between us. Unable to believe how stupid I'd been: lying there, wanting to take his pain away. Thinking I could be *good* for him, when it was me who had made him hurt so badly in the first place. Me and her, the blood-soaked princeling queen. The woman who'd raised me.

My shoulders slammed against the door frame, and I realized that I had to leave now, leave quick, before I could wreck him any more than she already had.

'Where are you going?' Christian said.

He looked dazed in the moonlight, an animal with a trap closing around him on all sides. Part of me wanted to go to him again, sink to my knees and beg his forgiveness.

But the other part wanted to disappear. I knew there was no way I could have him after this, and the realization hurt so much I feared it would rip me open. I couldn't bear to look at him a single moment longer, knowing what I'd just lost.

*Mom, why did you have to do it?* I thought. *Why do you have to destroy everything that counts?*

'I'm so sorry,' I whispered, reaching for the door handle, body primed to flee. 'I like you so much. I swear I didn't know –'

'Lilly, wait,' Christian said. 'We have to talk about this. Just wait a second –'

But I was already running.

I tore through the streets, turning corners at random, wanting the city to claim me like a sacrifice to make up for what my mother had done. Breathless and uncaring, unwilling to stop – until I was forced to by a sudden dead end. I had reached the city wall.

It seemed to rise for miles above me, a gargantuan fortification of crumbling stone, making me crane my neck back to see the top. The city gate was cut out in the middle, but the usual spots where the enforcers patrolled were empty. Because the gate was locked. The iron teeth were dug deep into the ground, cold metal doors blocking any view of the road beyond. It shouldn't have been surprising –

I'd always known that Castello was a prison – but facing the locked gate straight on made my skin crawl.

There was a rudimentary staircase built into the wall, narrow but very steep, heading up towards the slowly lightening sky. It felt like a dare to me, the town testing my resolve.

*You can't leave, Lilly*, it seemed to say. *So you might as well face it. Come up and see the mess your mother made.*

Numbly, before I could think better of it, I began to climb.

The ascent felt endless, reality dropping away around me as I pushed higher and higher into the dawn. My head went tight, my eyelids strange and heavy from the vertigo, my hands frigid where they gripped the stone bannister.

Then, just when I was sure I could climb no further, the stairway ended, and I was stepping on to a flat stone walkway flanked by waist-high parapets on either side. Like the battlements of an ancient fortress. The top of the wall.

Wind hit me instantly, a vicious chill snapping at my clothes. I took one uneasy step forward and stopped, holding the parapet for balance, taking stock of the sight below me. There was a sheer drop down the cliffside to the gorge that ran along Castello's wall, and from this height, I could make out a river thundering at the bottom of it, the mountains locking us in on all sides. It seemed impossible to imagine a world beyond this hilltop, a place where normal people went about normal lives. The city stood alone here, like a sealed universe. A self-devouring ecosystem. Fed by blood and fire.

'Planning on jumping, Lilly?'

I whirled around. It was Veronica. She cut an unfamiliar figure in the dawn: no make-up, no elegant clothing, her hair loose in the wind. It could've made her look weak, but she seemed fiercer than ever instead.

'What are you doing here?' I stammered.

'What are *you* doing here is the more pertinent question,' said Veronica. 'Surely you realize you're breaking curfew?'

I winced. I'd forgotten all about that.

'Residential buildings are armed, from eight at night to five in the morning. You set off quite a few alarms.'

'I didn't realize,' I mumbled.

'Clearly,' Veronica said. 'But I told the General I'd take care of you before he could set Tiago on your tail. Once again, you're lucky.'

I almost laughed at that. Lucky was not how I was feeling at the moment.

'So,' Veronica went on, when it was clear I wasn't going to thank her for saving me yet again, 'dare I ask what prompted this new display of carelessness? After what happened at church, I hoped you might think twice –'

'My mother was the princeling queen,' I blurted out.

Veronica froze. Surprise flashed briefly in her eyes, then faded to something I couldn't comprehend. It looked like resignation.

'Did you hear me?' I demanded. 'My mother –'

'I heard,' Veronica said and then sighed, as if she'd just realized she was going to have to stay up on this freezing wall for quite some time. 'I know, Lilly.'

# CHAPTER TWENTY-FIVE

'I don't understand.'

I was pacing back and forth on the walkway, hands balled at my sides, feeling like if I stopped, even for a moment, I would crumble to bits. 'The girl was never caught. No one knew her identity. So how can you possibly *know*?'

'Because she told me herself,' Veronica said patiently. 'Your mother and I were very good friends once upon a time. We shared everything with each other. Everything but power.'

I recoiled from her, then, feeling like I'd been slapped. 'Friends,' I breathed. 'You were *friends* with her?'

Suddenly it was all real, beyond questioning. If there had been any hope that I'd made a mistake – that the writing on the blueprint was a fluke – it was gone now. Veronica had known my mother. Veronica had been *friends* with her. Which meant Carly had never been from Venice. She'd lived in Castello the whole time.

*She lied to me*, I realized with a sick jolt of understanding. *Every single story, every memory she shared, all a lie.*

I thought of her glass lions, which I'd guarded so carefully through the years: nothing but props. And I'd been stupid enough to cherish them. I'd really believed they were clues to her past, something that could bring her closer to me.

My head swam, and I gripped the parapet again.

'Perhaps you should sit down,' Veronica suggested. 'Before you fall.'

'Why didn't you tell me?' I asked. 'All this time you knew, and you never said –'

Veronica shrugged. 'I felt it would be cruel. It's not the kind of burden a child should have to bear.'

I shook my head, thinking of the girl in the corner of my bedroom, how she had taunted me for so long. Of the moment in my dream when she'd brushed her hair back, and I'd been convinced it was me I was looking at.

No matter what Veronica said, I felt like I'd been bearing this burden from the start.

*At least now you know*, I thought. *This is who you are. This is where you come from. This is your heritage.*

When I turned to face Veronica again, I felt the weight of it settle into me, heavy as stone. 'I want you to tell me everything about my mother.'

For a moment, I thought she was going to refuse. But then her shoulders seemed to soften, and she nodded. 'Come here,' she said. 'Look down. What do you see?'

I crossed the walkway and joined her, followed her gaze out over the city. The crowd of rooftops, the watchtower spires, the church dome tinted grey in the early light. 'It's just Castello,' I said.

'Not very notable at a glance, is it? Some marble, some brick, some scraps of gold. And yet this place has always been a battleground. People in this town crave things – blood, recognition, power. They'll do anything for that fix, and they don't care what the cost is. Your mother was one of those people. I believed I was, too, in the beginning. And we were drawn to each other through that: wanting more than what life had dealt us.'

I shot her a look, her perfect profile sharpened by the morning light. 'What did you want, exactly?'

'We wanted to rule,' Veronica said. 'Not just half the city. The whole of it.'

A shiver ran through me, which had nothing to do with the wind.

'You must understand, it felt quite noble at the time. The war had been dragging on so long – people were sick of it. We wanted to find a way to end it for good. Two little girls with delusions of grandeur ... but some days I really believed we could do it. That together we might accomplish what no one else had.' Veronica smiled ruefully. 'But then, of course, your mother became a Saint. And I began to see how different we really were.'

'What do you mean?'

'Your mother wanted to rule this town, but she never loved it. She saw it as a means to an end. Something to control for the sake of controlling. She would kill for this city, but she would never die for it.'

'And you would?'

'Castello is my birthright,' Veronica said. 'If I can't die for it, then I don't deserve it at all.' A pang of bitterness came into her voice. 'Unfortunately, I wasn't the one who ended up with power.

'After your mother became a Saint, she had no time for me any more. Suddenly she could demand things from people – bend them to her will. Real friendship lost its meaning. I'd like to say power made her ruthless, but I believe it simply revealed what had been inside her all along. She still talked of ruling, but now she believed it was the Saints who deserved to take control. And then she met the boy.'

'Val,' I murmured, thinking of the blueprint. 'What was he like?'

'Angry,' Veronica said. 'And trapped. The Paradisos used Saints on the front lines of their army – Val had no desire to die like that. Your mother opened up a whole world of possibilities to him. They whispered rebellion plans to each other through holes in the boundary wall, like a regular Romeo and Juliet. What if power ruled instead of blood? What if they could change their own destinies?'

'And then they started a fire.'

'And then they started a fire. Midnight mass on a very special occasion. One of the only times they knew the church would be packed.'

'What occasion?'

'All Saints' Day, of course.'

I felt abruptly dizzy, bit my tongue until the feeling passed. A question pricking at the back of my mind: Christian's father's family dying in one stroke.

'Why weren't you there?' I asked Veronica. 'Why didn't you go to church that night?'

'When I was sixteen years old, the Paradisos killed my father in a bombing. I had very little taste for God after that.'

'That was fortunate,' I murmured.

Veronica's eyes flashed. 'Was it?'

I shrugged. I had lost the ability to know what was and wasn't cruel any more.

'It took the better part of the night, but by morning the whole church had burned down. Any hope that it might've been an accident was dashed when we realized the doors had been locked from the inside. And only one person had survived.'

'The General.'

Veronica inclined her head. 'The General.'

'He was fortunate, too, wasn't he?'

'Very,' said Veronica. 'Although fortune didn't figure much in the way he told his story. He was barely more than a child, but when he crawled from the ashes that day he realized he could make himself a king. People had been gathering in the square all night, and the General told his story to them like some kind of messiah. He explained what had happened during the mass – how two Saints had started the fire. How they were plotting to take Castello for themselves and leave the rest of us for dead. The General said he knew their plans because his own brother was one of them. And then he began to preach: to save our city, we had to burn the demons out.

'You should've seen him, Lilly: a fourteen-year-old

224

boy bringing grown men and women to their knees. It was as if once he started talking, you simply *had* to listen. Besides, people were so vulnerable, then. Crippled by grief, desperate for someone to blame. The General knew exactly what to feed them.

'And so the witch-hunting began. Valio was one of the first to be burned. It set a brilliant precedent. The General proved that family, friends, loyalty – none of it meant a thing. All that mattered was killing Saints.'

'How could he bear it?' I asked Veronica. 'Sending his own brother to die like that?'

'I imagine it was very easy,' she said. 'He simply refused to see him as human any more.'

'And my mother let it happen. She left him to burn –'

'That,' said Veronica, 'was Val's own fault, really. Anyone who thought your mother loved them was a fool. That girl only ever loved herself.'

I wanted to shy away from the words, to deny them, but I didn't know how. After all, wasn't this what I'd been afraid of my whole life?

'I can't believe they never caught her,' I mumbled. 'All that effort hunting Saints, and they couldn't find the one person who was really guilty.'

'No, your mother was too clever for them,' Veronica said. 'She was gone from this town as soon as the flames died down. But she came to see me first. Strange and wild, covered in ash. Scared, too, for the first time since I'd known her. She told me something had gone wrong in the church. That she'd never meant anyone to die that way.'

'You didn't believe her, did you?'

Veronica seemed to consider it. 'I don't know. Killing in numbers like that – she must've known it would turn the city against her. She was reckless, yes, but never stupid . . .' Veronica shrugged. 'In the end, though, it made no difference. By the next day, she had vanished. For a time, I had a notion that I'd be able to track her down, but it proved impossible. Imagine my surprise, then, twenty years later, when you show up in my classroom. You look exactly like her, *amore* – I thought I was hallucinating. I asked the General for your file: "Jack and Lilliana Deluca", it said. An innocent little family of two. "Carly Deluca – deceased."'

Veronica shook her head. 'She always despised her name, so I could understand the change. But *deceased* –'

'She killed herself,' I said.

Veronica seemed surprised. 'Really? That's not the girl I knew.'

'She killed herself because of me.'

'Don't be silly.'

'No, it's true.'

I couldn't ignore it any more, couldn't pretend not to see. Couldn't block out the memories, no matter how much I wanted to. This was it: the black hole that lived at the bottom of my mind.

'My whole life, there was something wrong between us. She tried not to show it in the beginning, but the older I got, the more she fell apart. Because she knew what was coming – that I'd grow up to look like her, talk like her. To *be* like her. That's why she hated taking me places, why she wanted me gone so badly. That's why she hid me away. Because I reminded her of herself, and in the end she decided it was easier to die than have to face all the ways we were the same –'

'That's a lie,' Veronica said sharply. 'This is why I didn't want to tell you. However your mother behaved in her lifetime, it has no bearing on you. She was selfish and obsessed with power. You're not responsible for the crimes she committed. You're not bound by her mistakes –'

'I am, though,' I said. 'We all are. She broke this city, and nobody can fix it. Nobody can fix *him*.'

In an instant, Veronica's voice turned cold. 'So this is about the boy, then.'

I turned on her furiously, daring her to challenge me. Of course it was about the boy.

'Don't you know what my mother did to him?' I demanded. 'She burned his whole family. Except his dad – him she drove mad. He's been telling Christian he's cursed practically since he was born, and Christian believes it. You saw how he was yesterday, with the injections. He's addicted to destroying his power. He's going to get himself killed trying to steal more shots, or doing too many, and I don't even know how to talk him out of it because I'm the reason he needs them in the first place –'

'I'm sorry about Christian,' Veronica said. 'Truly I am. But blaming yourself won't change anything. If you want to look in the mirror for the rest of your life and see your mother staring back at you, that's your choice. But, if I were you, I'd choose a different path. I'd take control of my legacy.'

'What does that even mean?' I snapped.

'It means be different, Lilly. It means fight back.'

I stared at her. Exhaustion was creeping up on me more strongly now, dulling my mind. But Veronica seemed suddenly unwilling to let me tune out.

'You think your mother broke this city?' she demanded. 'Well, darling, you're right. But not just because she started a fire in a church. Those deaths were a tragedy, of course, but the real tragedy came afterwards. The fire gave us the General. That's your mother's true crime: she let a murderer take over Castello. When she killed, people called her a witch. But when the General does it he's a saviour. Which means he'll never have a reason to stop. The blood tests, the fear, the hatred – people like Christian growing up convinced they're cursed, hunted like dogs for an ability they can't control –

'As long as the General rules this town, the Saints will suffer. And the cycle of death that your mother started will go on and on. Unless someone decides to end it for good.'

Veronica took a step towards me, her eyes fiercely bright, impossible to look away from. 'This city's been broken, but you're wrong to say it can't be fixed. If you want to distinguish yourself from your mother, then, for God's sake, help me undo what she did.'

'What are you talking about?' I whispered.

'I'm going to overthrow the General,' Veronica said. 'I know how to do it, but it will be very difficult on my own. I want you with me.'

# CHAPTER TWENTY-SIX

'You're talking about the city's power, aren't you?'

'We need to harness it,' Veronica said. She was pacing before me along the walkway, a dark silhouette in the morning glow. 'The General has too many advantages: a private army of enforcers, the loyalty of a people who believe he saved their souls. Only Castello's power can give us the upper hand.'

'But how are we meant to harness something that lives in the town?'

'The same way you open any door,' said Veronica. 'Turn any lock, enter any gateway: you only need a key that fits.'

It took me a moment to piece together, Liza's voice ringing suddenly in my head, saying, *The legend was, whoever had the key was the true leader of town.* Telling me stories about the old kings – saying they used to rule with power.

'Castello's founding key,' I said slowly. 'You think it can access the city's power?'

'I don't think it,' Veronica said with a hint of triumph. 'I *know*.'

I must've looked sceptical, because she made an impatient gesture, and said, 'Didn't you pay attention in history class? The founding key has always represented the right to rule this town. The old kings dug it up when they settled here, but it existed long before them. Dynasty after dynasty, going to war for Castello, only stopping when they had the key in hand. But why fight for something so trivial if not because it could access the city's power? If not because it gave them the raw strength they needed to lead? I've thought about every possibility, every option, and this is the only one that makes sense. The key can't just be a symbol of power – it has to be a weapon, too.'

'But I thought it was just a legend,' I said. 'I mean, a long-lost key that everyone fights over, isn't it a bit . . .'

'Far-fetched?' Veronica prompted. 'Says the girl who turned out to be a witch.' She smiled thinly. 'You of all people should know, darling: in this town legends have a way of coming true.' Her eyes narrowed. 'Besides, the General seems to think it's real enough. He's looking for it, after all.'

'He's *what*?'

'Haven't you ever wondered what the raids are about? Posting enforcers on corners, spying on people, confiscating anything that looks old and valuable –'

'I thought they were checking for loyalty.'

'They serve that purpose, too. But all those objects the enforcers take away, do you know what the General does with them?'

I shook my head.

'He has them scanned,' Veronica said. 'For power.' She was pacing more quickly now, her face hard with anger. 'For years, that man has been ripping my city apart, inch by inch and building by building, trying to find the founding key. Searching for traces of power that go beyond the Saints – that come from Castello itself. That's the ultimate threat to him, after all: if people were to realize the Saints are not abominations, but natural products of this town. That power is everywhere in this place, and we are all heirs to it, one way or another. That it could be turned against him.'

Her eyes flashed. 'That would be the end of his reign, wouldn't it? So he wants the key gone. He'll destroy it if he can find it. And then no one will ever be able to rise up again. We cannot allow that to happen.'

'But on the raids,' I said slowly, 'he doesn't just take keys. He confiscates everything.'

'Because he has no idea what the key looks like,' Veronica said. 'No one does.'

I stared at her, waiting for the punchline. But she seemed perfectly serious.

'This land has changed hands too many times,' Veronica said. 'Each civilization had its own symbols, its own ways of depicting power. After a thousand years, it's impossible to tell which representation is the original one. I suppose, in a way, the founding key is our own Holy Grail. Lost for so long no one remembers exactly what they're looking for.'

'This is mad,' I breathed. 'How are we meant to find something before the General does if we don't even know what it looks like?'

Veronica raised an eyebrow. 'You're a Saint, and I'm the heir to this city's throne. Surely we can outsmart a glorified priest in a baggy cloak?'

'You just said the key was like the Holy Grail,' I snapped. 'In case you didn't know, no one's ever found that, either –'

'No one who looked for the Holy Grail was me,' Veronica said coolly. 'Besides, we'll start simple: see what ground the General's already covered and work from there. He's got a lab at the enforcer headquarters set aside for this project. They're building clever new power scanners, but the security is clever, too. That's where you come in.'

'Me?'

'You can access the lab,' Veronica said, like it was obvious. 'You can get us one of his maps and one of his scanners. And you won't leave a single trace behind.'

'Don't be so sure,' I muttered. 'I barely know what I'm doing with my power. I lose my temper all the time, and it just explodes –'

'Then you'll have to regulate yourself. All your anger, your emotions – try to channel them into something useful. A little self-control, darling. That's all it takes.'

I crossed my arms, feeling like I was being accused of something: thinking of the raging girl in my dreams. Thinking of my mother.

Right on cue, Veronica said, 'I asked her once, you know. Just after she became a Saint. I asked her if she could sense where the key might be hidden. And she claimed she could feel it. A place where Castello seemed to brighten and intensify, narrowing in on itself, forming a pipeline to the city's power.' Veronica looked at me thoughtfully. 'I wonder, Lilly – can you feel it, too?'

I hesitated, put on the spot. Remembering the first impressions I'd had of this town: like a coiled beast, more powerful and dangerous than I could understand. Slowly, I shut my eyes and tried to tap into it. Imagining Castello's power brimming under my feet, waiting to be accessed. Trying to sense the pipeline Veronica was talking about. Trying to find the key that would open it up.

And maybe I *could* feel something, a slight buzz in the back of my mind. But it wasn't concrete. It wasn't helpful. Annoyed with myself, I shook my head and opened my eyes.

'No matter,' said Veronica. 'It was just a thought. We'll need one of the General's power scanners, then. It's the quickest way.'

She sounded brisk now, quite businesslike, and I wanted badly to lean in to it, convince myself that it could really be this easy – that I could redeem myself with this, earn back the right to look Christian in the eye. The potential of it bloomed on my tongue, sweet like a sugar rush.

'You think it'll really make a difference?' I asked. 'If we find the key, you think we can change things in Castello?'

'Of course,' Veronica said. 'I wouldn't have spent so many years planning for it otherwise.' She glanced at me sideways. 'But even if I wasn't certain, I would still fight. For just the tiniest chance to rid the city of the General. Stop the burnings in the square, end the hatred – build a future where the people I cared for didn't have to fear who they are.' A faint smile, and a challenge in Veronica's eyes. 'Would *you* fight for that, Lilly? For even the smallest chance to alter the course of that boy's life?'

When she said it like that, there was only one answer.

'Tell me what to do.'

The door to my apartment was ajar when I got home. The shameful, selfish part of me wanted to find Christian waiting inside, but of course he was gone. There was a place on the armchair in the living room where his jacket had disturbed the dust, and I stood staring at it for a long time, pain swirling through my body like ink in water. Then I realized that my father's boots weren't on the mat, either, and felt my guard rise. *Someone else is in the house.*

I squinted around, eyes burning from exhaustion and the rare burst of sunlight that had lit the apartment. It was late morning outside, a completely lovely day, and I hated every second of it. There was no one in the kitchen or the bathroom, and my father's bedroom was empty, too. I was starting to think that the front door might've been blown open by some kind of freak wind when I entered my bedroom and smelled it: incense and vanilla. Faint but unmistakable in the air.

'Liza?' I whispered.

My room looked exactly like I'd left it last night, bedsheets shaped by the imprint of Christian's body,

*Richard III* discarded on the floor. My mother's glass lions glinted innocently from my dresser. It was all I could do not to pick them up and smash them against the wall.

'Liza?' I said again.

I could sense her presence like an echo around me, but had no idea how to explain it. Maybe she'd been worried about me skipping school, had come over to check in. But then why not wait for me to get home? She hadn't left a note, either, and when I powered up my phone I had no new missed calls. I did another survey of the room, trying to force my deadened brain to solve this puzzle. It took a while, but finally it dawned on me, the one thing out of place.

My mother's map was missing.

I called her a dozen times. No answer, nothing at all. Normally, I would've blamed it on the terrible reception in Castello. But today I was sure she was ignoring me on purpose.

*Pick up*, I thought furiously. *Pick up the goddamn phone –*

Finally, *finally*, I heard the line click.

'Jesus,' Liza said. 'You're needy.'

'What did you do with it?' I demanded.

The connection was muffled and ribbed with static, and yet I swore I could hear the swivel of her desk chair –

imagined her lounging there and rolling her eyes, telling me not to take things so seriously.

'Liza, I know you were in my house,' I said. 'How did you even get in?'

'The door was unlocked,' she said matter-of-factly. 'And I wanted to make sure you were still alive. I mean, first you vanish from church, then you ignore my texts, and now you're not even showing up at school. Forgive me for being concerned –'

'So you came to look for me,' I said, trying to keep my voice even. 'But instead you stole my map.'

'*Borrowed* it, Lilly. And, honestly, I don't know what you're so upset about. I mean, I'm the one who should be raving. You've got the plan for the princelings' fire in your bedroom, and you didn't see fit to show me?'

'I only just found it,' I said. 'Sorry I didn't come rushing to you with the blueprint for a massacre.'

'Oh, please,' Liza said. 'Drop the Little Miss Perfect act. You're just as fascinated by this stuff as I am.' I imagined her leaning forward in her chair, map in one hand, daring me with her eyes. 'I'll even forgive you for hiding things if you help me figure out what all these notes mean. The princelings had a ton of ideas – I bet we could retrace their whole strategy if we try. And did you see the signature? It must be the girl's. So her name was Lecta. I've been wondering about that for so long. She was a *genius* –'

'Liza, stop it,' I said sharply, hating the admiration in her voice, gripped by a fierce spark of jealousy, despite everything else. *You're supposed to like me*, I thought.

*Want me. Not my mother.* All of a sudden, the urge to smash those lions was almost irresistible.

'She's not who you think she is,' I said. 'The princeling girl isn't some kind of misunderstood hero. I know you hate this town, but setting fire to things isn't the way out. You have to stop glorifying her. You're better than that.'

For a moment, Liza was silent, just a crackle of static on the line. Then she sighed. 'Don't tell me how to be, Lilly,' she said. 'I told you I'd take you with me, but you don't get to tell me to stop.'

There was another creak of her chair, like she was spinning absent-minded circles across her bedroom, with no idea how deep this was cutting me.

'Oh, we got homework, by the way,' Liza said. 'That's why I came to your house in the first place. I left yours on your couch. Christian's too.'

'What?' I said blankly. 'Why Christian's?'

'Because,' said Liza, 'he didn't come to school, either.'

The first thing Alex said to me was, 'Get out of my room.'

I crossed my arms and stayed exactly where I was, swinging my legs from his window sill. I'd been waiting ages for him to show up, mistakenly assuming that he'd be in his bedroom after school. But it was mid-afternoon by the time he appeared, carrying a satchel full of art supplies, which he promptly dropped at the sight of me, swearing.

'How did you even get in?' he demanded. 'The window locks from the inside.'

'I'm a witch, remember?' I said, wiggling my fingers around.

'Ugh,' Alex said and bent down to pick up his stuff.

I felt a little guilty about being here after my fight with Liza – what with the whole breaking-and-entering thing. But I hadn't come to steal from him. And I was afraid that if I'd tried to ring the bell he would've slammed the door in my face. So I'd taken a chance and come the back way, inching across the slanted rooftop outside my window, counting on finding Alex's bedroom on the other side. Christian had made it sound like we shared a wall, and he'd been right.

I'd only done minor damage to Alex's window when I'd forced the lock, trying to control my power properly this time. But it was harder than Veronica made it sound. It seemed to rush through me like a fiery flood, responding to every twitch and flare of my emotions. Demanding all of my attention to keep it in check. Alex's window lock hadn't merely snapped open when I'd touched it: it had been wrenched from its hinges completely. But I decided he didn't need to know that.

'Oh my God,' Alex said, when he'd tossed all his supplies into his wardrobe and turned around to find me unmoved on his window sill. 'You're still here? Can't you take a hint?'

'I need your help.'

'Nope,' Alex said. 'Good talk, go away now.'

'It's about Christian.'

Alex tensed a little, then covered it up with a shrug. 'What, are you bored of him already? Cos I'm not taking him back –'

'Will you just hear me out?' I snapped.

Alex threw me the dirtiest look he could manage. 'Fine,' he said, collapsing on his bed with his hands over his face. 'Make it quick, though. I have a whole bucket list of chores I'd rather be doing than talking to you.'

'I need your help,' I said again. 'Believe me, I wouldn't be here if I had any other options. But Christian trusts you, so I'm going to trust you, too.'

'How generous of you,' Alex said, voice muffled by his hands. 'Only you seem to have missed the part where Christian clearly doesn't trust me at *all* –'

'Of course he does,' I said. 'Just because he didn't tell you about the whole Saint thing –'

'Deluca, please. You've been in this town for five minutes. Don't pretend you have any idea what Christian's thinking.'

'I can read his mind,' I said, seeing no point in hiding it, although I regretted it a little when Alex flinched. 'Not all the time,' I said quickly. 'But enough to see what's really going on. He's ashamed. That's why he didn't tell you. It's not about trust: he just hates what he is. He thinks his power's a curse. And –' *He thought he'd lose you.*

But I couldn't say that part out loud. Christian had to tell him on his own.

Slowly, Alex slid his hands from his face and propped himself up on his elbows, considering me. 'I guess that makes sense,' he said grudgingly. 'About power, I mean.

You must've realized who his dad is by now, right? I've been freaked out by him since we were kids. He's got all these weird altars and demon traps in the house. And, with Christian, sometimes he –' Alex stopped short, unwilling to say it.

'I know,' I mumbled.

A bolt of pure shock flashed through his eyes, turning him momentarily vulnerable. He hadn't expected Christian to tell me this. It had always been their secret.

'Wow,' Alex said, sinking back on to the bed. 'I really have been replaced.'

'You haven't,' I insisted. 'That's why I'm here. What you said in the alley, about me messing him up – you were right, okay? I don't mean to, but I make his power stronger, and my mom –'

The words caught in my throat, knotted into a web of guilt. Roughly, I shook myself. 'The point is, he really needs you right now. To look out for him and make sure he doesn't do anything stupid. Because I'm scared he's going to get himself killed otherwise. He's addicted to those injections, and Liza said he didn't even come to school today –'

'So?' Alex said. 'He skips all the time. And maybe I'm sick of babysitting him. Maybe you should do it yourself.'

'Didn't you hear me?' I demanded. 'I only make him worse. And besides I don't have time. I have to break into the enforcer headquarters.'

'You *what*?'

Too late, I realized my error. Veronica would murder me if she found out I was broadcasting her rebellion plans all over town. 'Never mind,' I said quickly. 'Forget I said that.'

'You're *breaking into the enforcer* –'

'I *said* forget it.'

'Deluca, my mum's the head of security there. The alarm system is really good.'

'I'm sure I'll manage –'

'Yeah, manage to get *caught*.'

Heat surged inside me, a sudden wave of frustration, and the chest of drawers in the corner of Alex's bedroom overturned with a crash. Afterwards, I was out of breath and ashamed of myself for losing my temper so easily. Besides, my stunt hadn't had the effect I'd been hoping for. I thought Alex might be intimidated, but he seemed deeply unimpressed instead.

'What is that supposed to mean?' he demanded, toeing at the fallen chest with distaste. 'You're gonna throw furniture at the enforcers when they're chasing you? Good plan, very subtle. I look forward to seeing you burned at the stake –'

'Oh my God,' I said furiously. 'Do you have a better idea?'

Alex crossed his arms and glared at me. 'Of course I do.'

# CHAPTER TWENTY-SEVEN

The enforcer headquarters were directly behind Icarium, a towering building of brick and marble wrapped around an open courtyard. It reminded me of an armoury, with high barred windows and heavy iron doors on all sides. Like the church, the courtyard lay strategically across the boundary line, so that it could be entered from both Marconi and Paradiso sides of town. Each entrance was adorned with fluttering banners displaying the General's trinity symbol. Just for a change in decor.

Alex was pacing by the Marconi entrance, surveying the area. Enforcers criss-crossed the courtyard every so often, bursting in and out of doors, carrying boxes and paperwork. All of them had guns in their belts. All of them had power scanners.

'Please remind me how this is going to save Christian's life?' Alex asked. Once he'd decided to come along, I'd given up on secrecy and more or less laid the whole plan out.

'Veronica says they're doing research in here. Building new machinery to find the founding city key.'

Alex made a face. 'And you're sure Professor Marconi said to go to the fourth floor? Because it's just old offices up there. Not exactly cutting-edge.'

'How do you know?'

'I spent lots of time here when I was little,' Alex said. 'My mum thought it would build character if I got a gun in my face every time I wandered off.'

'That's not very nice of her.'

Alex shrugged. I shifted on my feet, watching him watch the courtyard – impatient to get on with it. He'd already delayed me by two days, claiming he needed the extra time to set up whatever genius strategy he had for breaking in. Which, incidentally, he hadn't bothered to share with me yet. 'So what's your great idea, exactly?'

'It's very simple,' Alex said. 'While I know how much you'd enjoy smashing through armed stairwells with your terrifying dark powers –' he held up a little metal square, like a hotel room key imprinted with a pattern of dips and ridges – 'I thought we could use my mum's security pass. And just take the lift.'

'Did you steal that?' I asked, impressed despite myself.

'Right out of her bag,' Alex said. 'But she has a backup.'

He sounded a little smug for my liking, but I had to admit that the elevator made sense. I could see it across the courtyard, a shaft of blackness sealed by an old metal grille. Simple and inconspicuous. None of the enforcers passing by had spared it a look.

'You don't have to tell me,' Alex said, following my gaze. 'I already know I'm brilliant.'

Then he stepped into the courtyard.

I caught my breath, power surging in my hands – instinctively wanting to yank him back to safety. But, of course, we had to get to the elevator somehow. And the courtyard was empty at the moment. Grimacing, I ran to catch up.

Alex was already at the elevator shaft when I reached him, fitting his mother's key into a slot in the wall. There was a thudding sound, like a mechanism punching into the metal, reading its pattern. Then, from deep underground, the elevator shuddered up to meet us. It was even more decrepit than it had looked from afar, red with rust, its cables worn to the point of fraying.

'This seems safe,' I muttered.

'We're about to steal from the General,' Alex said, tugging back the grille in the wall, 'and you think the lift's *unsafe* –'

I shoved him forward into the elevator just as a pair of enforcers burst into the courtyard, talking in low voices, cigarettes dangling from their lips. For a terrible moment, we stood pressed against the wall, both of us holding our breath. Power burned in my palms, feeding on my fear, pushing at my fingertips. Demanding to be free.

*Stop it*, I thought, imagining Veronica's judging eyes on my face. *You obey me. You listen.*

The enforcers passed dangerously close to us, their cigarette smoke curling around our faces. Then they were gone. Slowly, I let out my breath and shot a look at Alex.

'Tell me more about how brilliant you are?'

He rolled his eyes and slammed the elevator grille shut.

We moved skyward, the elevator rattling below our feet, making my teeth smash together. When it stopped on the fourth floor, it pitched us forward, through a broken gate into an open-air hall. For a moment, we were both reeling, shaking the vertigo off.

Then, 'My completely flawless plan ends here,' Alex murmured, voice gone quiet to fit the sudden silence. 'I haven't been to this part of the building in years.'

We were standing on a balcony of sorts, wrapped around the courtyard's highest tier. No enforcers here, just that heavy silence, like someone had covered the hall with a lead blanket. More iron doors spread out before us, but they looked dirtier than the ones downstairs, closer to abandonment. Like this was a place people had forgotten to clean. Not exactly a weapons lab.

'Veronica says it'll be the door without a handle,' I offered.

'Wow, cryptic,' Alex said.

We went slowly down the hall, soot-covered lanterns swinging above us in the wind. The first dozen doors we passed all had handles. I could hear my heartbeat echoing inside my head, growing in time with the way the lanterns moved, putting me on edge. It was too quiet up here; it wasn't normal. Something bad was going to happen. On cue, Alex grabbed my wrist, pulling me up short.

'There,' he whispered.

At first, I thought it was a man waiting for us up ahead. But after a second, I realized it was a statue. A hooded guard stood at the end of the balcony, his body sculpted from dull green copper, streaked with dirt and mould. In his outstretched arms he held a sharpened scythe. Directly behind the guard, there was a door with no handle.

'Bingo,' Alex said.

I stared at the statue, trying to figure out how we were meant to get around it. The guard's metal eyelids were closed, but I couldn't shake the feeling it was watching us anyway: anticipating our next move.

*It's a test*, I decided. *A mechanical riddle*. Familiar to me in some way that I couldn't quite place.

'Do you think your mom's key will work again?' I asked Alex, already knowing the answer.

'No way. This isn't normal security.'

And he was right. I frowned, taking a tentative step foward, ignoring Alex's whispered, 'Deluca, wait –'

But it was too late. The statue's eyes had already snapped open.

I gasped and lurched backwards, colliding with Alex's chest. Red lights blinked from the empty sockets of the guard's eyes, scanning my face, reading every panicky muscle twitch. And I knew somehow that if I'd just stood still – if I hadn't flinched and retreated – then it would've been all right.

But I *had* flinched. So I'd failed the test. I was an intruder.

The next thing I knew, the guard's arms were snapping down on a set of hidden hinges and swinging the scythe directly at my throat.

Power surged inside me, and this time I welcomed it – let it flood from my fingertips and warp the air with electric heat. The statue's head tore from its shoulders like I'd snapped its neck. Sparks and metal flew everywhere, the guard's arms jittering wildly as the electrical wires inside it came apart. The scythe cut a shimmery arc through the air and imbedded itself in the ground at my feet.

For a moment afterwards, I basked in the adrenaline: my blood burning, my heart hammering in my chest. Power coursing through me like it would never end. The statue's severed head lay in a twisted heap across the balcony, the floor around it studded with metal.

'Jesus,' Alex said, surveying the damage as he pulled a copper splinter from the arm of his jacket. 'Overkill much?'

'I'm still learning to control it. I can practise on you if you like.'

'Kinky,' Alex said, 'but I'll pass.'

I was turning to grin at him when I felt my head go light, the adrenaline fleeing my body in a rush. The drain kicking in. My muscles went slack, my head spinning like I'd been fighting the statue hand-to-hand. I slumped against the wall, too dizzy to stand all of a sudden. Alex gripped my shoulder to stop me from falling.

'Deluca, what's wrong? There's no way I can carry your dead body out of here.'

'It's nothing,' I said. Squeezing my eyes shut and trying to breathe. This was the price, I realized. For using power like that, sudden and instinctive. For using so much. This was why I was supposed to reel in my temper. Because I had a limit. And if I wasn't careful, I could drain myself. Like that first night, when I'd lifted all my furniture and had barely been able to move in the aftermath.

*Your power's not infinite. You can ruin yourself if you go too far.*

But then, with a bright spark of resentment, I thought, *Why? I want to be stronger than this. I want to do more –*

There was a clicking sound ahead of us, and I felt Alex's hand on my shoulder go tight. When I blinked my eyes open, I saw that the door behind the statue had come unlocked, its bolt sprung when the guard's head had fallen. Alex and I exchanged a look. Then, by unspoken agreement, we moved forward and stepped inside.

It was a storage closet. That was my first thought, until I noticed the desk in the corner. Then I realized it must've been an office. A cramped, filthy, windowless office. Alex had told me to expect this, but after what we'd been through to get in I felt massively let down.

An overhead light flickered to life when we stepped through the door, casting a dank yellow glow. There were splintered bookshelves against the far wall, piles of parchment rising in the corners, greasy machine parts strewn across the floor. A shabby desk, layered with drill bits and sheaves of water-stained paper. I didn't know if we were in a historian's study or a crude engineering workshop, but both struck me as inherently wrong. This couldn't be where the General kept his secrets.

'You really think they build power scanners in here?' Alex asked, glancing around.

I hesitated, uneasy all of a sudden, wondering if this was an elaborate and deadly mistake. 'I don't know. Just ... look for anything metallic. Like what Tiago has, minus the needle. And research, too. Maps or diagrams. Anything to do with power. Veronica said –'

'Veronica needs better leads,' Alex muttered. 'This place is a junkyard.'

'Ten minutes,' I insisted. 'If we can't find anything, we'll go.'

Alex wrinkled his nose, but went to rifle through a bookshelf, wincing when he moved his left arm, which was bleeding where he'd pulled the copper splinter out. I started my search at the desk, sorting through the papers there. Old notes in cramped writing, twisting symbols, sketches of a ruined castle. I grabbed a handful of random pages to show Veronica, but it was hard to see what any of them had to do with the city key. Still, there was something vaguely familiar about them that I couldn't quite put my finger on. Like the statue outside, I felt as if I should've understood what I was looking at.

Halfway through the pile of papers, I found an ancient-looking map of Castello, labelled in Latin. It showed a maze of tunnels snaking below the city, which made no sense to me, until I realized –

'Alex, are these the catacombs?'

He glanced up from a stack of books and shrugged. 'Probably. I've never seen them on a map. It's been decades since anyone went down there.'

'Why?'

'They got too full,' he said, coming over for a better look. 'During the clan wars, there were too many bodies, so.' He shrugged again.

I grimaced, setting the map back down, feeling my fingers brush against something metal underneath. It was a long object shaped like a pen flashlight, assembled from rusted machine parts. Not exactly the shiny scanner Tiago carried around. And yet ... there was some fundamental similarity that made my heart kick up a notch.

'Look at this,' I said, holding it out to Alex. 'Do you think –'

He took it from me curiously, frowning at the home-made quality, then pressed a button to power it up. A light began to glow at the front of the pen, casting a projection on the wall of the office. Tangled lines of red laser that swirled and distorted, creating shapes and then destroying them, as if there was a kaleidoscope turning inside the device.

'It's a scanner, isn't it?' I said, hardly daring to believe.

'I think so,' Alex murmured, frowning at the lines on the wall. 'But ... not for power. It's looking for a symbol of some kind.'

I followed his gaze, trying to make sense of the refracting light patterns and coming up blank. 'What symbol exactly?'

'I don't know,' Alex said, sounding miffed. 'It's encrypted, see? Every pattern that shows up has one line that's darker than the rest, which means it's part of the final design. But you never see the whole picture at once. So, if someone did get hold of the scanner, they wouldn't know what they were looking for. Unless they could keep track of all the lines at the same time, which is . . .'

*Impossible*, I expected him to say.

Instead, Alex said, 'Can you pass me a marker?'

I rummaged around in the desk and found him one. He clamped the scanner between his teeth to have both hands free. As the swirls of red light shifted on the wall, he used his good arm to copy a series of lines on to his palm. I watched, transfixed, as a smudged black image began to take shape on his skin.

After that, three things happened almost simultaneously. First: I heard a sound from the corridor outside, the rhythm of approaching footsteps. Second, the papers I'd been messing with tumbled off the desk, uncovering a chipped gold plaque, which showed the name of the person whose office we had broken into. It was someone I knew well.

The third thing that happened was that the door opened up.

I moved in an instant, grabbing the collar of Alex's jacket and shoving him down hard. His knees buckled and he slammed to the ground behind the desk, out of sight, but only just. The person at the door snapped their head around.

'Hi, Dad,' I said.

# CHAPTER TWENTY-EIGHT

'Lilly,' said my father. For an instant, his eyes were bright with a kind of shock so profound it almost looked like terror. 'What on earth are you doing here?'

'I'm visiting,' I heard myself say. 'You kept saying you were worried about me. So here I am.'

I could feel my heart in my throat, every muscle in my body tensed for a fight-or-flight response. I'd assumed that spotting Jack in church was the worst that things could get between us, but now I realized how wrong I'd been. Maybe I should've seen this coming, when he'd been hiding all those papers from me. When he'd been working endless hours, lying through his teeth, staying awake all night to help the General find a way to destroy the rest of us –

Betrayal rushed through me, setting my body alight.

'I'm glad to see you,' my father said, trying to keep his tone pleasant. His face told another story: he looked like he'd just seen a dangerous and unwelcome ghost. 'But can I ask how you got inside? This is a highly restricted area –'

'I took the elevator.'

'And the door guard – was it broken when you arrived?'

'No, I did that,' I said, not caring whether it was foolish to tell him. 'It wouldn't let me in.'

My father's eyes flashed. 'That's impossible. I rigged it myself. It's pure copper –'

'Oops,' I said. That explained why the statue had seemed so familiar: it was the same mechanism as my music box. Little metal eyes telling you to stay still. Only this time it was deadly. Jack looked at me hard, like he was trying to work something out very quickly in his head.

'Well,' he said slowly, 'while this has been a lovely surprise, I think you should go home now. We have a lot to talk about, but this is not the right moment –'

'Why not?' I asked. Shocked at how even my voice sounded, all my anger and betrayal coiled so tight it could almost pass for serenity. 'I came all this way. Surely you can make time for me. I am your daughter, after all. We could even play a game. Like twenty questions. I'll start.'

'Lilly –'

'Round one: how long have you been lying about your job?'

My father's jaw twitched. 'Excuse me?'

'I said, how long have you been lying –'

'I heard you the first time,' Jack said. 'I just don't know what you mean.'

'Don't you? When we moved to this town, you told me you were hired to modernize. But the power still cuts out, and there's no Wi-Fi. So I'm wondering if you were ever planning to be an engineer for this city. Or if you knew from the start that the General would have you looking for something instead?'

My father reeled back as if I'd punched him. For a moment, there was a spark in his eyes – a pulse of raw panic, before he got it under control. But that was all the confirmation I needed.

'It's an object, right?' I said, feeling the truth of it sink into my bones. 'Probably something old, and he's got you building scanners to find it –'

'Lilly,' my father whispered, 'how on earth do you know about that?'

I shrugged. 'The General's not exactly subtle, is he? He's had enforcers raiding houses all month. They're hurting people, and you're helping them. You're giving them the tools.'

Jack's forehead creased. 'That's not true.'

'Of course it is. I'm not blind. I saw you in church. I know how important you are to him. I know you're loyal –'

'You're wrong,' my father said sharply. 'This is much more complicated –'

'Then explain it to me.'

'I don't think –'

'*Explain*,' I snapped and felt power surge in my fingertips.

Books shuddered on the shelves, the lights flickering overhead, metallic parts rattling together on the floor. I wasn't sure if I meant it as a threat or a defence, but I liked the way it felt to not be so helpless in front of him – to not be that little kid any more, wounded and lonely, waiting for my father to remember I existed.

Jack glanced around, eyes wide, watching the room collapse a little at a time. I had no idea how far I would've gone if Alex hadn't nudged me, a painful jab under the desk that meant, *Calm down.*

I chanced a look at him, saw that he'd managed to keep the scanner in his teeth, the marker in his hand. He was shining the laser on the back of the desk, still copying the pattern. Reluctantly, I reeled in my power, fighting the part of myself that just wanted to make everything explode.

When my father faced me again, his face was drained of colour, a panicked question in his eyes. *What are you?* But I didn't give him time to ask.

'Explain,' I said. 'Tell me what you're looking for.'

Slowly, my father inclined his head. 'The General has an ... obsession.' His voice was more tense than I'd ever heard it, hounded and bitter at the edges. 'I didn't know about it before we moved here, but he's made it my main focus now. He's asked me to search for an heirloom. Something that was lost in this city. He says it's of sentimental value to him.'

'Sentimental value,' I scoffed. 'You don't actually believe that, do you?'

Darkness crossed my father's face. 'What I believe is unimportant.'

'Right, because you're such a good soldier.'

'Watch yourself, Lilly,' Jack hissed. 'If someone hears you –'

'Then what? You'd get fired? And we'd have to leave this town before you can finish your precious treasure hunt for the General?'

'I'm not doing it for him,' my father said furiously.

It was like a stone dropping into a deep dark well, sending ripples out all around. Shifting something that could never be put back into place. Fouling the water forever.

'What is that supposed to mean?' I whispered.

Jack removed his glasses slowly, pressed two fingers into the bridge of his nose, like he was working up to something. But I couldn't wait.

'Why did we come to this stupid town if not for the General? Why did you take this job halfway around the world? Why did you drag us to this horrible place where they burn people alive if not because of *him*?'

And then it hit me, making me sway on my feet and grip the desk for balance. 'Oh my God. We're here because of her.'

Briefly, my father closed his eyes. So that meant: *yes*.

'You knew Carly lived here,' I stammered. 'You knew this was her city. How? Did she *tell* you? Or was it in her diaries? Did you read about Castello, after she was gone, and think maybe if you showed up in her hometown she'd still be alive and waiting for you to save her –'

'I didn't know,' my father said. He seemed dazed, holding his hands out in front of himself like he was showing me he had nothing to hurt me with. As if the damage hadn't already been done. 'I wasn't sure it was her town. I only had a hunch –'

'Like that makes it any better –'

'I just needed to understand,' Jack said. 'I had to know *why*. You can't imagine what it was like for me, Lilly – to lose her like that. To watch her unravel. She was so paranoid by the end, convinced she was being hunted, asking me to fix things – and I thought it was just a delusion at the time, that we'd get through it somehow, but then ... after she was gone, I started to wonder if there was truth in what she'd been telling me. If I should've listened to her, after all.'

'So you decided to come to Castello and check? See if the town turned out to be as bad as her delusions? If we could get ourselves killed just like she did?'

'Of course not. It's much more complicated –'

'Stop saying that,' I breathed, feeling tears threaten at the corners of my eyes, my heart an aching lump in my chest. 'It's perfectly simple. It's just a choice you made, right? Her before me. Her before both of us. Same as always.'

'Lilly –'

'I was so afraid after she died. And I needed you. I've needed you for six years. I feel like I've missed you every single day. But whenever you look at me, it's like there's a wall in your eyes. Like you can't stand to be reminded that *I'm* the one who lived. That you'll never, ever get her back. It's been like that for so long that I don't think you know who I am any more. And I don't think I want you to.'

My father flinched, and for the first time ever, I wasn't sorry about it at all.

'Let me tell you something, though,' I said. 'Since you want to understand her so much – since you need to know her story. Whatever answers you think you found in this place, whatever explanation you've got for why she killed

257

herself, it's all backwards. It wasn't Castello that messed her up. She messed up the town. She made it like this. *She's the nightmare, not the city. She's the problem –*'

'Lilly, please –'

'She burned the church down, killed everybody. Do you get it now?' I wanted to laugh all of a sudden, to smile the way she used to smile. The way that had made her so irresistible. 'Your wife was a murderer. I don't know how you ever loved her.'

My father turned on his heel and walked out.

I couldn't remember leaving the enforcer headquarters, had no idea how I ended up back on Castello's streets. The outside world was a blur around me, my head full of static.

After a while, Alex said, 'Your house or mine?'

I turned, surprised to find him at my side. I'd forgotten that I wasn't alone. Alex was holding my arm tightly, guiding me down an alleyway, which explained how I'd gotten outside: he must've dragged me.

'I just thought we should debrief,' Alex said. 'Since I got the symbol.'

That made me focus as much as anything could. 'Really?'

Alex nodded, flashing me the smudged image on his palm. 'Bet you anything there's a pattern like this on the founding key.'

I appreciated that he had the decency not to ask me about what had just happened. Even though I probably owed him an explanation. I probably owed one to everyone. *So sorry that my mother wrecked your town!*

'Let's go to your house,' I said finally.

'Okay,' Alex said. 'But if my mum shows up, you have to pretend you're dating me. I need to see her face.'

He was smirking when I glanced over, and I was surprised to find my mood improved, if only a little.

When we reached his house, Alex fumbled with his key ring, his injured arm making his movements clumsy. 'Ow,' he said. 'Can you –'

As he handed the keys over, I got a proper look at the symbol he'd drawn on his palm. It was ridiculously simple: two vertical lines with an archway over the top. A door full of thorns. I recognized it immediately. Suddenly I was standing in a carnival tent with a boy and a rough gold coin. *Endings and beginnings*, the boy was saying. *Even life and death.* Then his fingers were closing around mine and tugging the coin away.

'Oh my God,' I said, dropping Alex's key ring to the ground. 'Sebastian Paradiso.'

# CHAPTER TWENTY-NINE

'No.'

'Yes.'

'*No*, Lilly.'

'I have to,' I said sharply.

'No, you don't,' Alex snapped.

We'd been having the same conversation for what felt like an eternity, me sitting cross-legged on Alex's bed while he paced back and forth, cradling his bloodied arm to his chest.

'Deluca, you can't cross the boundary line,' he was saying for the hundredth time. 'It's so illegal. Like, the most dangerous thing you could possibly do in this town. Besides, the kid has a coin, not a key. Coins don't open anything. That doesn't make sense.'

'But it's the same symbol,' I insisted, also for the hundredth time, pointing at his hand. 'It's exactly what the General has my dad looking for. And besides, I felt it myself.'

The memory washed over me – that exhilarating pulse of gold in my palm.

'Veronica said the key could be anything. All that matters is it can access the town's power. And there *was* something powerful about that coin. I'm positive.'

'Amazing,' Alex snapped, whirling around to aim a vicious kick at the bedpost. This, at least, was new. 'So first-class brat Sebastian Paradiso found the magical rebellion key everyone's looking for. Forget the General – we'll be bowing down to a spoiled little rich boy soon enough. That'll be *so* charming –'

'I don't think Sebastian knows what it is,' I said slowly. 'I'm pretty sure he thinks the coin's junk. But I bet he'll talk to me about it if I ask.'

'*Talk* to you?' Alex said incredulously. 'Are you mad? Have you forgotten the part where he's our *mortal enemy*?'

'He's a Paradiso,' I said, feeling like I was arguing with Liza. 'Not some kind of monster –'

'You really don't get how this town works, do you?' Alex said and turned his back on me. I frowned, considering for the first time how Sebastian appeared from the outside: stuck up and haughty. Probably if I'd never met him, I wouldn't be a fan, either.

'Look, you don't have to like him,' I conceded. 'But I don't think he's some kind of arch-villain. I just have to get to him before the General figures out what he's wearing around his neck.'

Over his shoulder, Alex shot me a glare. 'Why don't you ask your evil twin for help? She's half Paradiso, anyway.'

'My *what*?'

'Mezzi,' Alex said. 'You two are practically joined at the hip. In fact, I'm surprised you're not with her right now.'

'We're not joined at the hip,' I said sharply. Disliking the twin metaphor, thinking of her lips on my skin. 'And we're sort of . . . fighting at the moment.'

Alex snorted. 'Trouble in paradise?'

'Liza thinks my mother was right.'

The room got very quiet all of a sudden. 'She burned down the church, didn't she?'

I nodded.

Alex sighed. 'Christian has such excellent taste.'

I said nothing. I deserved that.

'Okay, look,' Alex said finally, 'if you want to go and pal around with the Paradisos, I can't stop you. But you have to understand the risks. No one crosses the boundary line. It's like . . . rule number one in the truce. If you're caught over there, it could be treason. No joke.'

There was something uncharacteristically earnest in his voice, which made me want to reassure him. But, before I had a chance, Alex said, 'And you'd better change your clothes. Or the Paradisos will arrest you for being un-pretty.'

I glanced down at my faded jeans and realized how out of place I'd look in a Paradiso crowd.

'This is the nicest thing I own,' Alex said, grabbing a long red cloak from his wardrobe and tossing it at my head. 'Don't you dare get blood on it.'

I slung it around my shoulders, surprised by how soft it felt. The fabric was velvety and decadent, lined with fur around the collar, so different from what I was used to seeing on our side of town. 'It's beautiful,' I murmured.

'I know,' Alex said testily, and flipped the hood up over my eyes. 'Shouldn't you tell Professor Marconi your plans before you go storming off in search of her precious city key?'

I hesitated, considering it – wondering if I owed her an explanation. Thinking of the hard edge in Alex's voice when he'd said *mortal enemy*. What if Veronica agreed that Sebastian was a threat? What would she do to him if she knew what he had?

Slowly, I shook my head.

'I'll tell her when it's done.'

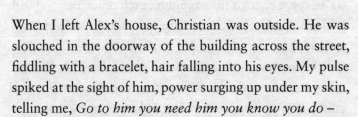

When I left Alex's house, Christian was outside. He was slouched in the doorway of the building across the street, fiddling with a bracelet, hair falling into his eyes. My pulse spiked at the sight of him, power surging up under my skin, telling me, *Go to him you need him you know you do –*

I took a sharp step back into the shadow of Alex's lobby, putting as much distance between us as possible. Ashamed of myself for wanting this still, when I knew I had no right.

'Finally,' Christian said, rising to his feet and crossing the street. 'I was starting to wonder if you and Alex were cheating on me.'

'You're okay,' I whispered.

He shrugged. 'Why wouldn't I be?'

*Because you don't go to school. And your dad rips you up, and you were stupid enough to kiss me when I rip you up, too –*

'No reason,' I muttered.

Christian frowned, like he could sense what was going through my mind, although I doubted he could see it. His power felt dulled to me, knocked out by an injection, just beginning to crawl back. He leaned against the door, watching me through the golden mess of his curls. His blue eyes, threatening to drag me under.

'You should go upstairs,' I said, looking away. 'Alex isn't mad at you any more. I mean, he is, but –'

'I didn't come to see him, Lilly. I was looking for you.'

'What?' I stammered. 'Why?'

'Because, the other night, you ran away. And I figured we've spent enough time avoiding each other. Being afraid. I think I'd rather just . . . be with you than try to fight it any longer.'

'Christian, stop,' I said, taking another step backwards. 'Do you hear yourself? My mother ruined your life, and you're here to tell me you want to *be* with me –'

'I don't care about your mother. I care about you. And you're not her. You're a different person.'

'You have no idea who I am,' I said sharply. 'Alex is right. You've known me for five minutes. And half the time all you feel around me is pain.'

'That's because the injections are running out,' Christian said. 'I just need to get more of them, then it'll be easier –'

'So you want to be with me, but only when you're high.'

His eyes flashed. 'I didn't say that.'

'Christian, you can't have it both ways.' I was still afraid to look at him properly: his body leaned against the door like a dream, too pretty to be real, too dangerous to touch.

'You can't want me and hate yourself. You said it that night – it doesn't make sense. If you kill your own power, why do you want to be around mine –'

'I don't know, okay?' Christian snapped. 'I just *do*.'

He stepped forward again, but I was quicker, springing the lock for the security gate, making him lurch back as the metal bars shot down in the doorway between us.

'It's because you think you deserve it,' I said. Feeling like I was breaking my own heart a little at a time, but knowing I had to get it out. 'You want me, even though I hurt you, because you think that's normal somehow. But it's not. And I can't be someone who makes things worse for you. I have to try to make them better.'

Slowly, Christian leaned forward and wrapped his hands around the bars of the gate, regarding me with those bottomless blue eyes. 'That night, you said you liked me. Did it ever occur to you that maybe I just like you back?'

Something burned at the back of my throat. It felt like hope. I was terrified of it. 'Then you'll have to wait. Until I can fix what my mother did to this town.'

'What do you mean?' Christian asked, and then seemed to realize. 'Oh God, don't tell me you let Professor Marconi talk you into some insane rebellion plot.'

'It's not insane,' I said. 'Just because you're convinced nothing can ever change here doesn't make it true.'

'Lilly, she's head of a clan,' Christian said. 'That's just as bad as the General in its own way. You can't believe a word she says.'

'Maybe. But I have to do something. I have to try. Otherwise, what's the point of having power at all? And I owe it to you. I owe it to everyone –'

'You don't owe me anything,' Christian said roughly. 'Stop being all guilt-ridden and just open the gate.'

'Why don't you do it yourself?'

'It's locked,' he said. 'I can't –'

'Of course you can. Your power's coming back, I can feel it. So why don't you use it for once?'

Christian seemed to freeze, a metallic bolt of fear cutting through his eyes. Panic surging in his mind, strong enough that I could sense it even through our weakened link. *You're a coward*, he was thinking. *You could do it, just this once. You could show her –*

But no. Some things were a step too far. His father had taught him: the only thing worse than having power in your blood was choosing to *use* it.

'I can't,' Christian said dizzily. 'You *know* I can't –'

'I know,' I whispered. 'That's why I owe you.'

Something in his face went cold. 'You're delusional about fixing the town,' he said. 'Whatever stupid ideas Professor Marconi has about a rebellion, it's all a sham. Nobody touches the General. No one ever will.'

'Have you got a better idea?' I asked. 'Or am I supposed to watch you hate yourself until you get burned alive?'

Christian's eyes flashed again, and this time I felt it like a physical blow: a desperate rush of pain and anger pouring from his mind into mine.

'Damn you, Lilly,' he said. Then he walked away.

I realized for some reason that I was crying.

# CHAPTER THIRTY

There was a storm brewing.

I stood in the middle of the town square in Alex's red cloak, the air heavy around me with the anticipation of rain. At my feet, the boundary line glinted in the marble like a winking eye. I'd chosen early afternoon to cross over, the time of day when Castello had always seemed most deserted. And yet I still felt like the empty square was full of watchers lurking behind the boarded-up windows, ready to strike at me.

I'd spent the day yesterday locked in my bedroom, poring over the map from my first day in Castello – examining the Paradiso side of town. Sometime around eleven p.m., I'd broken down and called Liza. Hearing Alex say *trouble in paradise* had sparked something inside me, made me feel itchy and hollow, bitterly aware of how wrong my days were without her. Hating myself a little for how easily I was willing to give in. It was like picking at a scab, digging my fingers into an open wound. Telling myself that I could change her mind, make her see reason about the princelings, even though deep down I sensed it was futile.

In the end, though, none of it mattered. Because Liza refused to answer the phone.

I spent the rest of the night dully furious: with her, with Christian and with my father, who kept banging on my bedroom door and demanding to talk. As if we had anything left to say to each other.

Instead, I'd focused on the map. My destination on the Paradiso side of town was a place that Alex had referred to as *the fortress*, buried deep in northern territory. During the clan wars, he'd told me, the Paradiso family had built a kind of fortified mansion in the woods. It wasn't plotted on the map, but I knew where it was, anyway: in the vast blank space at the edge of the paper, where all the streets suddenly stopped short. Uncharted territory.

I was confident enough of the route I'd planned to get there, but I had to deal with the boundary line first.

Up close, it was much bigger than I'd realized, two feet wide and strange to look at, as if someone had carved a canal in the square and filled it with rusty spikes. I thought of the video we'd watched in class, where the spikes had been a real wall, twenty feet high and made of sheet metal, and tried to imagine that embedded below me in the ground. Then I wished I hadn't, because I was suddenly having paranoid fantasies of the wall shooting up and impaling me as soon as I tried to step across.

*You could turn back*, I thought uneasily. *You could find another way –*

But that was a lie. There was no other way.

Holding my breath, I stepped across the boundary line.

I was sure that something would happen: that I'd set off an alarm, like when I'd broken curfew; that the watchers behind the boarded windows would spring to life and shoot me down. But there was nothing. The square stayed silent around me, completely unchanged. It was as if this crime was so big that the General hadn't even bothered to rig any traps.

*Because honestly*, said Alex's voice in my head, *who would be stupid enough to commit it?*

Still holding my breath, I pushed forward across the square, refusing to stop until I reached the Paradiso buildings on the other side. When I chanced a glance over my shoulder, I saw the Marconi skyline like a desert mirage, shimmering and terribly distant on the horizon.

Turning my back on it, I faced the Paradiso side of town.

I was standing in the mouth of an alleyway, dank and abandoned, just like our own streets. But when I got to the end, I stopped short, wide-eyed at the sight before me.

Because, of course, the Paradisos were rich.

It wasn't that I'd forgotten – just that knowing it in my head was so different from seeing it in real life. The fundamentals of Castello were the same: the ancient buildings, the pitted cobblestones. But the Paradisos had glossed over it all with a kind of frigid luxury, polished the streets to a shine, planted statues and flowery shrines where old bullets had left dents in plaster walls. I could see signs of their industry in the intricate marble fountains and carved door frames, in the lavish shop displays, piled high with gems and sweets and golden trinkets. For a moment,

I stood still in the middle of the street, drinking it in: feeling almost starved for beauty.

Laughter echoed around a corner, and I stepped backwards as two young girls skipped by me with their arms linked, wearing matching dresses, their shiny leather shoes pattering on the ground. One of them had long blondish hair, reminding me vividly of Liza in another life. I watched them vanish into a pastry shop, feeling my awe at all the beauty give way to resentment. *They don't deserve this*, I thought, *not when we're stuck on the other side*.

Gathering Alex's cloak around me, I pushed into Paradiso territory, keeping my head down.

The streets remained mostly empty as I walked, and by the time I reached the blank space on my map, there was absolutely no one around. I had a feeling this was because of the storm, Castello's slate-grey sky darkening above me with thunderheads. Around the next bend, the buildings stopped abruptly, and I found myself face to face with a huge hole that had been blasted in the city wall. No Paradiso wealth to be found here – it was a war ruin, plain and simple.

Lumps of stone littered the ground, collapsed statues and pillars overgrown with weeds. And beyond it all: the woods. Just as Alex had said.

I clambered through the breach in the wall and ended up before a gnarled forest. The trees were thick and bent together, branches like interlocked hands, cut through by a trampled dirt path. Somewhere deep in the woods, just barely visible above the trees, I saw the outline of a stony grey tower. The Paradiso fortress.

I approached the path slowly, on the lookout for some kind of security system, unwilling to believe that Paradisos would make it so easy for someone to enter their home. But then I wondered if this might be like the boundary line – if breaking into a clan stronghold was such an absurd idea that no one had bothered to ward against it.

*Well, good luck then, Deluca*, said the Alex-voice in my mind. *If you die, I still want my cloak back.*

Gritting my teeth, I stepped into the woods.

The path was damp and shadowy, hemmed in by misshapen trees. I walked carefully, feeling burdened by the silence, as if the woods were pressing down and trying to keep me there. Even my footsteps were hushed, drowned in a bed of decaying leaves. And I found myself thinking unwillingly of fairy tales: the twisted kind, where the forest blocks out the sky, and the little girl in the red cloak never finds her way home.

Just when I was starting to make myself uneasy, the path ended, spitting me out of the woods and on to a vast lawn of rough grass. In front of me, the fortress loomed.

It was a sprawling building of weather-stained stone, cracked towers rising up at uneven intervals against the sky. Half palace, half rubble, like something that had been built too big to care for and was falling apart a little at a time. Ivy crawled up the walls, spreading spidery tendrils into empty window frames. The huge front steps were split down the middle as if a missile had been dropped there.

I hesitated at the edge of the woods, scanning the fortress for signs of life – wondering suddenly if Alex had made a mistake, and the Paradiso family had actually moved away. If that was why the woods had been unguarded. I couldn't imagine anyone choosing to live in a place like this.

But then I heard the music.

It was a lone piano, the notes carried across the overgrown lawn on the rising wind. The melody was dark and familiar, a waltz of some sort. Maybe another one I'd heard from my mother. I moved towards it automatically, mesmerized and wanting to know its source.

The entrance to the fortress had mostly caved in, leaving only an empty archway to duck through. Behind me, I could sense the weather changing, the storm closing in, infusing the air with static. Ahead: the darkness of the house and the tantalizing piano. Beckoning me inside.

*Get in, find Sebastian, get out,* I thought, and stepped into the Paradiso fortress.

I was greeted by a shadowy hall with towering ceilings and a wide flagstone floor. A series of narrow passageways opened up on either side, like the twisting branches of a maze. And somewhere far ahead, the music was playing.

*Get in, find Sebastian, get out.*

I moved down the hallway in what felt like a trance, careful not to disturb the debris on the floor: shattered lanterns and rusting pieces of armour. The music swelled in the dark before me, and I knew it was foolish to walk towards it, but I couldn't seem to stop. It was as if I was being pied-pipered, like the hallway itself was propelling me forward, widening with each step, leading to a final reveal. The throne room.

It was massive, dirt-streaked and completely empty except for a grand piano. Seated on the stool, bent fingers dancing flawlessly over the keys, was Enrico Paradiso.

He was facing the hallway, and if his eyes had been open he would've been staring right at me. But they were closed. He wore a long black trench coat, his stringy silver hair framing his face, ebony cane resting against his knee. Directly above him, mounted on the wall of the throne room, there was a giant painting, almost too dark to make out. I thought it was the silhouette of Castello, wrapped in angel wings. But everything below the skyline had been painted as a cascade of blood.

I stood in the hallway, still feeling like I was in a trance, lulled by the haunting piano. Impressed that someone as grizzled as Enrico Paradiso could make it sound that way.

Then, all at once, the music stopped.

I blinked slowly, mourning the loss, and noticed that Enrico Paradiso's eyes had opened. He was looking at me now.

For a moment, I felt nothing – not panic or fear, just vague curiosity – staring into his sunken green eyes and thinking he was just another version of Liza.

Then I came to my senses.

I lurched backwards through the nearest doorway, stumbling into one of those maze-like passages and catching myself on a wall. Standing perfectly still, heart in my throat – willing myself not to breathe, or move, or exist at all.

*Maybe he didn't see me*, I thought. *He was in the light, but I was in the dark. So maybe he didn't notice –*

But then there was a thud. Enrico Paradiso's cane on the flagstone floor. His slow, shuffling footsteps coming my way.

I retreated deeper into the passage, afraid to run because of the noise it would make – equally afraid not to. Around a bend, there were two choices: the passage splitting off to left and right. I choose right at random, then took left at the next fork, trying to even it out. My breath coming in quick bursts, the daze I'd felt before replaced by the bright sting of terror. Doors flashed by, some sealed with dozens of padlocks, some cracked open to show racks of guns and blackened test tubes, like an old medical lab.

Behind me, Enrico Paradiso's footsteps kept shuffling along, amplified by the hollow passageway so I could no longer tell if he was just around the corner or a mile away.

*He's old*, I told myself, *and you're so much faster –*

But I was also lost. I'd been lost the moment I turned off the main hall. And this was his fortress.

*Get in, find Sebastian, get out*, I thought, and cursed myself for how quickly I'd let that plan fall apart.

Another random turn, another twist in the maze – panic beginning to close over my throat. I could see light up ahead, a room at the end of the passageway: circular and roofless, opening up straight to the sky. It was a ruined tower, pavement cracking with weeds, walls coated thick with ivy. I spun in a circle, searching for another door, somewhere to go from here. But the ivy was like a curtain, sealing over everything. There was nowhere to hide, and I could see no way out. And the footsteps were still coming. They sounded like they were just outside the tower now.

Halfway around the room, looking for an escape, I realized it was pointless, and turned back to face him. I felt delirious, gathering power in my fingers, not knowing what I'd do with it – just thinking that at least I would fight.

His shadow reached me first, bent and stretching around the corner. Slowly, I raised my hands.

A split-second before Enrico Paradiso entered the tower, someone grabbed me from behind and dragged me backwards into the dark.

# CHAPTER THIRTY-ONE

There was a hand over my mouth and another on my waist, holding me so close and tight that I could hardly breathe. I knew it was a boy from the size of the hands, and from the heat of his chest pressing against my back. I also knew which boy it was, because he'd held me before. Not by choice, and not quite this hard, but still – the feeling was familiar. *Except*, I told myself, *that's impossible*. Because there was no way *he* could be here.

We were standing behind a curtain of ivy, in the arch of that elusive doorway I hadn't been able to spot on my own. I could see glimpses of the tower before me: Enrico Paradiso limping slowly inside – the hand on my mouth tightening with almost unbearable pressure as he passed us. Cigarette smoke seemed to leak from his clothing, along with the blackened, metal scent of dirt or iron. Then he was gone, weaving through a different patch of ivy, disappearing out of another hidden door across the tower. Abruptly, the hand on my mouth let go.

I twisted around, feeling the hand on my waist loosen in response, letting me see –

'No way,' I whispered.

Nico Carenza was standing in front of me, body lit by the faint glow of a passageway at his back. He was wearing a white button-up, open halfway down his chest, his bruised eyes wide and furious on mine. My first thought was, *I'm hallucinating. He can't be here. They'd kill him faster than me.*

But then I noticed a circle of scarred skin on his left pectoral, peeking out from inside his shirt. Like someone had burned the General's trinity symbol into his chest. *Branded*, Liza had said once. *For disturbing the peace.* The burn was much too detailed to be a figment of my imagination. So maybe Nico was real, after all.

'What are you doing here?' we both said at exactly the same time.

Nico's eyes flashed. He didn't answer, though. So neither did I. For a long moment, we stared at each other, each daring the other to speak again first. Nico broke before me, which was a surprise.

'You need to leave,' he whispered. 'Right now.'

'I can't,' I said automatically. 'I'm looking for someone.'

'Are you mad?' he hissed. 'You can't be here. They'll string you up –'

'What about you? I thought no one was allowed to cross the boundary.'

'Oh, for God's sake,' Nico said, and then he was grabbing my arm, pulling me roughly towards the passageway behind him.

'Let me go,' I said furiously. 'Worry about yourself –'

'I am,' Nico snapped.

We came out into a bright hallway with high windows and elegant furniture, a sharp contrast to the parts of the fortress I'd seen so far. This must be the wing that the Paradisos actually lived in. I saw a white-tiled washroom, a walk-in closet, a raised marble platform with a king-sized bed. Nico's fingers had a vice-grip on my arm, his body tensed up and defensive, so different from his usual easy grace.

'Here,' he whispered, shoving me towards another passageway, which branched off the hall and into darkness again. 'This leads to a kitchen. There's a door at the end. You'll be back on the front lawn –'

'How do you know that?'

'It doesn't matter,' Nico said, pushing me harder. 'Just get out of here.'

'I have to find Sebastian.'

It was a stupid thing to say, but I had to remind myself what the point of all this was. I had to focus.

'Forget him,' Nico said, and he sounded really angry now, worse than I'd ever seen him. Like he was hiding fear underneath. 'Don't you understand where you are? Don't you know what she'll do if she finds you?'

*She.* The word pierced me like a needlepoint. My eyes flicked around the hall again, taking in the details now: the clues to whose rooms these really were. The black stilettos on the floor, the expensive jewellery slung over a mannequin in the corner. *She.*

'What's going on?' I asked Nico, trying to put the pieces together – what it meant to find him in the Paradiso fortress, alone and unguarded, knowing the hallways by heart. 'These people want you dead. So why are you just hanging around?'

'Because of me.'

The voice came from behind us. Nico stepped away from me so fast I might've caught fire. Slowly, dreading it, I turned around.

Chrissy Paradiso was standing in a doorway across the hall, leaning against the frame. She wore an oversized T-shirt like a dress, red knee-stockings to match her cherry lips. Blonde hair tumbling everywhere, that thoughtless perfection that made me feel like a fraud. I bit my tongue, hating her without even meaning to, without trying at all.

'This is a surprise,' Chrissy said coolly, glancing at Nico. 'Weren't you going to tell me we had a guest?'

Nico didn't answer. He had his back to her, standing very still, his eyes squeezed shut. Chrissy's gaze fell on me and stayed.

'Lilly Deluca,' she said. 'I have to admit, I wasn't expecting you. When I heard a whiny little girl in here, I thought it was Sebastian. Not an actual whiny little girl.'

She crossed the hall with smooth, decisive steps. I shot another look at Nico, hoping for guidance. His eyes were open again, but there was no expression on his face. All his emotion had been wiped clean. I was on my own.

Chrissy laughed at me. 'What did you do, follow him here? Did you think he'd be impressed? God, you must be really desperate, breaking into my house for a boy who won't even look you in the eye.'

She stopped just behind Nico, stood on tiptoe and threw both arms around his neck. Nestled her chin comfortably into the hollow of his shoulder.

'You shouldn't have risked it, *cara*,' she said. 'He's taken already.'

For a moment, I just stared at her. Hearing what she was saying, but refusing to process it, because it was too awful to be true.

'You're not,' I said numbly, looking between the two of them like a kid seeing monsters for the first time. 'You're not *together*, you can't be.'

'Except we are,' said Chrissy.

'But you hate him,' I stammered. 'You tried to kill him at the carnival. You wrecked his face –'

'He looks better with bruises,' said Chrissy dismissively. 'Don't you agree?' She ran her finger over one of them, a splotch of angry blue on his cheek. 'We have our differences, but in the end it's a law of nature. Pretty things attract. Of course you wouldn't know about that.'

Humiliation cut through me, sharp like a blade. *God, why her?* I thought, turning to Nico, gripped by the sudden urge to scream. *You could have anyone in this stupid town – why would you choose her?*

But Nico was staring straight ahead, eyes blank, as if he'd tuned out of what was happening. Like it didn't matter at all.

'Don't fret, *cara*,' Chrissy said. 'You mustn't be jealous. This is how it works. I tried to tell you before: there are people like you, and there are people like me. And nobody ever wants the people like you.'

I nodded automatically, moving backwards towards the door, knowing that I needed to leave right now, before I did something awful, like start to cry. But then Chrissy reached out, seized the neck of my sweater and yanked me forward again.

'Where do you think you're going?' she said sweetly. 'We haven't had any fun yet. Or did you really think you could stalk him to my house and get away with it?'

'I wasn't stalking him,' I hissed, twisting against her grip. 'Get off me –'

'I could gut you for breaking in, you know,' Chrissy said. 'Legally. It's in the truce. But I'll be generous. Leave you with a warning this time.' She reached out her free hand and smoothed it down my forehead. 'Your face isn't much to look at, anyway. I doubt people will notice the change.' She glanced over her shoulder at Nico and said, 'Give me your knife.'

Fear shot through me, a sudden adrenaline rush, making my power spike. Nico blinked once, dark and disinterested, looking between us. He didn't move.

'Give me your *knife*,' Chrissy said again.

Slowly, Nico shook his head.

Chrissy laughed, like she thought he was joking, and, for a second, her grip on my sweater loosened.

I wrenched away, trying for the door again, but she was faster, slamming my head sideways into one of the mirrors on the wall. Glass shattered, and I felt blood splash down the side of my face, my vision swimming with pain. Power thudding wildly through me, sending hairline cracks spinning across the window in the far wall.

*No*, I thought, trying to reel it in – praying that Chrissy hadn't seen. She was too busy trying to choke me, her fingers curled in my collar so hard I was starting to see black.

I swung a hand out and raked my nails across her cheek, the only defence I had without power, making her scream and jerk backwards, relinquishing her hold on my throat. I stumbled away, gasping for breath, my lungs burning, but then she was coming for me again, a shard of the broken mirror in her hand like a better, deadlier knife, and I was lurching sideways, trying to dodge her, before –

Chrissy slashed the glass at my throat, hard and with perfect aim, but I wasn't hit. Nico stepped forward at the last second and caught her wrist, stopping her mid-swing, wrenching her around to face him. Their eyes locked, and I saw something pass between them, a current of rage or warning that I couldn't understand.

'Enough,' Nico said. 'That's enough now.'

Chrissy curled her lips back, green eyes burning. 'Why do you care?'

I didn't wait around to hear Nico's answer. I wiped the blood out of my eyes and ran.

# CHAPTER THIRTY-TWO

I tumbled out of the passageway and into the kitchen that Nico had mentioned, a boarded-up doorway in the corner promising freedom. Power was coursing through my body, furious and desperate to hurt. I let it out now, thinking of all the things I hadn't been able to do to Chrissy – all the ways I couldn't protect myself. The kitchen exploded around me, pots and pans smashing against the walls, meat cleavers spinning frantically through the air. It was so infuriating to have this strength inside me but not be able to use it when it counted most.

*She would fear me if she knew*, I thought viciously. *I'd have her at my mercy.*

I aimed a hand at the doorway and made the boards splinter open, showering wood on to the lawn outside. Icy wind rushed through the kitchen, making me stagger, cooling the wild power in my veins. Bringing me slowly back to earth.

*I don't want anyone at my mercy*, I told myself. *I just want to be left alone.*

Outside, the sky was darkening so fast it was like watching a time-lapse: huge thunderheads pulling together to block out the sun. Lightning flashed from deep inside the clouds, illuminating them like veins below translucent skin. The storm had come.

Pots were clanging behind me, not from power now but from the wind, and the noise was like a beacon, telling Chrissy or her father or anyone else exactly where to find me.

*Get in, find Sebastian, get out.*

*No*, I thought. *Now you just get out.*

I fled down the steps on to the Paradiso lawn, blood congealing down the side of my face. Lightning flashed again, and the echoing thunder was close behind it, reverberating through the ground. The woods swayed in the wind ahead of me, trees bending together over the dirt path like they wanted to devour it. I ran towards them anyway, knowing I had no other choice. When I glanced over my shoulder, the Paradiso fortress was backlit by the flickering sky, a silhouette of cracked towers and broken walls like a house of horror. It made sense, considering what I'd discovered inside.

I plunged into the woods, racing through spirals of dead leaves, branches that scratched and snapped at me like whip-sharp claws. I was so busy trying to dodge them that I didn't notice where I was going until it was too late. I only had time to register a white blur streaking across the path before I was tripping over it, falling hard to the ground. The white blur came down with me in a mess of fur, and when I got my bearings I was lying flat on the ground with Cat standing on my chest.

'Hi,' I mumbled, head spinning. Cat hissed.

Then, from the woods, I heard a noise: a metallic click, like the safety of a weapon being flicked off.

'Stand up,' said a low voice. 'Turn round.'

I obeyed slowly, thinking, *This day will never end.*

The person behind me drew in a breath. 'New girl,' said Sebastian.

He was standing a few feet away on the path, pointing a gun at my chest. I almost laughed at the sight because it was so absurd – finding him now, after everything else had gone wrong. Finding him with a gun. Cat shot me one last suspicious look and then slunk over to Sebastian, winding a fluffy tail around his trainers.

It felt like dusk in the forest, the canopy of trees blocking out what little light the sky had left, but I could see Sebastian clearly whenever the lightning flashed. He was wearing a T-shirt that looked like it had been expensive once – now ripped at the sleeves and folded into cuffs. His shaggy blonde hair was wild, cheeks and bare arms streaked with dirt. It was strange to see him like this, stripped of all the Paradiso wealth and decadence. Only the thick line of gold rings on his fingers gave away his origin.

My gaze went immediately to his neck, searching for the chains I'd seen at the carnival. He was wearing fewer of them now, but they were still there, tangled up and glinting. I just didn't know if he had the one I needed.

'God, your face,' Sebastian said, examining me as I was doing to him. 'My sister already caught you, didn't she?'

I nodded, very aware of the gun still pointed at my chest. The air was tense between us, like something might snap at any second. I glanced again at the necklaces, and this time Sebastian followed my gaze. His body seemed to stiffen when he realized what I was looking at.

'Oh,' he said. 'You're here about the gateway.'

'I – what?'

'That necklace I had,' Sebastian said. 'The Janus coin with the gateway on it. You touched it at the carnival, and now you're back for more.'

'How could you possibly know that?' I said uneasily.

'Because it recognized you,' Sebastian said. 'And you recognized it, too.'

He was lowering the gun, clicking on the safety and tucking it into the back of his jeans. I watched him do it, muscles strung tight, afraid without being able to explain why. Maybe it was the storm, the memory of Chrissy's hand at my throat. The gold-green haze of Sebastian's eyes, almost supernaturally bright.

'Do you know what it is?' I found myself asking. 'Do you know what that coin can do?'

At the carnival, he'd acted like it was just another necklace. But it seemed that he understood a lot more than I'd given him credit for.

Slowly, Sebastian shrugged. 'It's like a trap,' he said. 'For people who think they can make the universe obey them. But then they realize.'

'Realize what?'

'That they can't.'

Lightning burst through the trees above us, illuminating the woods like a camera flash, burning the negative image of him on to the back of my eyes.

'I thought the coin might access power,' I murmured.

Sebastian looked at me like I was very stupid. 'And what did I say?'

Rain had begun to sputter through the canopy in thick, heavy drops, slicking my clothing against me and making the wound from Chrissy streak watery red down my face. Sebastian's eyes narrowed at the sight of it, tracing the progress of the blood.

'She's not done with you, you know. She doesn't like half-finished things. I think you should go.'

But I didn't move. 'Would you give that coin to me, if I asked?'

A spark of surprise on Sebastian's face, like he hadn't expected me to say it outright. I hadn't expected to, either. But nothing today was going as planned. This whole conversation was making me dizzy, like something not quite real. I felt like one of those fraudulent hypnotists, who had come to trick their victim out of a fortune and ended up being hypnotized by them instead.

'No,' Sebastian said. 'I can't give it to you. I haven't got it any more.'

For a terrible moment, I was sure he would tell me it was with the General. But then he said, 'I put it back.'

'What?'

'I put it back where it came from.'

Lightning flashed again, and I realized that one of us had stepped closer to the other because I could see the details of his face now, the freckles spotting his nose, the dirt on his cheeks smudging in the rain like mascara. The strange flicker in his eyes, like gold buried below the green. *He's just a kid*, I thought, unnerved. *But his eyes are different*.

'Where did it come from?' I whispered.

'The tombs,' Sebastian said. Then, when I didn't react, 'The tunnels. The *catacombs*, Lilly.'

I did a double take. 'I heard they were closed off.'

Sebastian just laughed at that. Thunder broke out overhead, so loud that I couldn't stop myself from flinching. Something rustled in the woods, and he cast a glance around, as if he was expecting his sister to burst through at any second.

'You really should go now,' Sebastian said. 'It won't be nice for either one of us if she finds you.'

'I need that coin.'

A cold flare in Sebastian's eyes. 'You too?' he said. 'Isn't it enough that everyone else wants it? Don't you realize that's the problem with this town?'

'It's not for me. It's for someone else. I owe them a debt. I need to fix things –' I stopped short, heart clenching, struggling to explain it. 'Please,' I said. 'Just – tell me where to look for it.'

'No,' Sebastian said. 'I hid it. You'd never be able to find it on your own.'

'Then find it for me.'

Shock on Sebastian's face again, and below that, something new, like outrage. 'What are you going to do with it?' he demanded. 'Why do you want it so bad?'

'It's a gateway, right?' I said. 'Beginnings and endings. Life and death.' I met his eyes straight on, soaked to the bone and wounded, past caring now. 'So I'm going to use it on the General.'

# CHAPTER THIRTY-THREE

I barely slept that night. The storm was still raging outside, thunder shaking the walls of my building, trinkets rattling on my dresser. My hair was damp and knotted, and the cut on my forehead pulsed like fire. Alex's cloak had been ruined on my little excursion, which was going to be thrilling to explain to him. I'd tried to scrub it clean as best I could, but my hopes were not high. Afterwards, I'd stepped into the shower and sat there until the water ran cold.

All night, I tossed and turned, slipping in and out of feverish dreamscapes: Christian trapped in the dark place where my mother used to hide me. Me, standing outside, pulling desperately at the door. Needing to get him out of there, but knowing I would never manage in time. And over my shoulder, Chrissy and Nico were laughing.

In the morning, I lay exhausted and half comatose in bed, feeling sorry for myself, until there was a sharp knock on my door.

'We need to talk,' my father said.

I tensed immediately.

'Lilly,' Jack said, knocking harder.

He must've learned his lesson from all the other times I'd locked him out of my room, because the next thing I knew there was the scrape of a skeleton key, and the door was swinging open. I sat up in a rush, shocked. My father looked harried and sleepless, his dark hair awry. I wondered if he'd been up all night.

'We need to talk,' he said again.

'Are you sure? It didn't go so well last time.'

My father ignored that. 'I have twenty-five minutes before work,' he said. 'Meet me in the kitchen.'

It was so rare for him to give me orders that I found myself obeying out of sheer surprise, pulling on a sweater and jeans, wrapping my head wound in the black bandana Liza had given me – following my father down the hall. There were work papers all over the kitchen table, which looked like the same ones he'd kept hidden from me before. And in the middle of it all: the leather-bound pages of my mother's diary.

'What's going on?' I asked. Wanting to sound angry, but finding the facade impossible to maintain. My body and mind felt drained and docile after last night. I couldn't muster the energy for another fight.

Jack watched me from across the table, his face grave. 'When you came to my office, what did you see?'

'You know what I saw,' I muttered. 'Your little quest for the General –'

'Yes, but what *exactly* did you see?'

*He means the scanner. He means the symbol for the key.*

I shrugged. 'Does it matter?'

'Lilly, I know you think you understand what's happening here,' Jack said, 'but I promise it's not as simple as that. Maybe I should've explained it to you sooner, but it took me some time to properly work it out.' He paused, rubbing a hand through his hair, his eyes urgent and honest in a way I hadn't seen for years. 'What your mother wrote in her diaries about this town – it tells a different story than the one you think you know. And she didn't just write about herself. There were things about you –'

Abruptly, Jack stopped. Someone was banging on our front door. I glanced at my father, wondering if he was expecting company. He shook his head.

'Stay here,' he said, and motioned to the papers on the table. 'Hide them.'

I picked them up as fast as I could, shoved them into the breadbox on the counter. In the hallway, I heard my father answering the door.

'Hello, Jack,' said Tiago pleasantly. 'Lovely home. I'm looking for your daughter.'

I froze.

'What on earth for?' said Jack.

'Well,' said Tiago, 'it seems she's got herself put on trial.'

I took a tentative step out of the kitchen, unable to help myself – saw Tiago standing in the door of my apartment with a dozen enforcers behind him. Just like a raid.

'I'm sure there's been a mistake,' my father was saying coolly. 'You must have the wrong house –'

'By order of the General,' Tiago said, reading from a piece of parchment in his hand. 'Lilliana Deluca is

293

summoned to trial for trespassing, violent assault and violation of the truce. She will stand before the city in the arena and defend her crimes.' Tiago glanced up and spotted me in the hall. 'You've been very bad, haven't you?'

Jack snapped his head around, gave me a quick, hard look that seemed to say *what have you done*, and *get back in the kitchen* at the same time. 'Those charges are obscene,' he told Tiago. 'I can assure you my daughter has been home sick all week.'

'Well,' Tiago said, glancing down at the paper again, 'Christina Paradiso thinks differently. Now, if you'll excuse us –'

A sudden blur of movement: the enforcers swarming in and seizing me by the arms, dragging me out the doorway. I could hear my father's voice, bright with rage, but I couldn't see him any more because we were already halfway down the stairs. My wrists were pinned behind my back, something metallic against my neck. A gun muzzle. I kept waiting for the fear to hit me, but felt a numb kind of acceptance instead. I should've seen this coming a mile off. Sebastian had tried to warn me, after all: there was no way Chrissy would just let me go.

When we reached the streets, there was already a crowd – faces pressed to grimy windowpanes, people crowded into alleyways, watching the enforcers march me past. It seemed as if word was spreading ahead of us, driving people out of their houses before we even showed up.

*Walk of shame*, I thought, trying not to squirm under their gazes. Then the enforcers turned into the town square, and I felt a rush of dread. *Please don't take me past school.* Strangers could stare at me all they liked, but I'd die of humiliation if my classmates saw.

Except, of course, we were heading straight for Lafolia.

They were all waiting for me when I came around the corner, packed tight in the doorway, penned by a row of enforcers. I saw Liza first, windswept hair and narrow eyes, watching me like I was a madwoman heading for the asylum, who she was glad she didn't know. *But you do know me,* I thought angrily. *And you're supposed to be on my side.*

Alex was next, looking murderous. *You idiot,* he was saying. *I told you so.*

Then there was Christian. My heart skipped at the sight of him, his tangled hair and unflinching blue eyes, like the one good thing in a sea of nightmares. Our gazes met, and I felt that white-hot ache burn through me, saw him press forward, shoving against the enforcers – trying to reach me.

*Don't,* I thought sharply, wishing I could force the words into his mind, even though I knew his power was locked up, and he couldn't hear. *This is my mess. Stay out of it.*

Then someone jabbed the gun into my neck again, and I was forced to bow my head.

We turned a corner, down a narrow alleyway, only to stop a moment later, the enforcers tugging suddenly on my wrists like they'd been caught by surprise.

I stared down at the grimy cobblestones, unwilling to risk looking up, wondering what was wrong. Tiago had taken the lead in the procession, and I could see his boots in front of me, and another set of boots in front of his. Someone was in our way.

'Step aside,' Tiago said.

The boots didn't move.

'Are you really going to make me say it twice?'

The boots seemed to consider this, rocking slightly on the toes. But still: they remained. Silence for a while, a stand-off happening beyond my sight.

'What did she do?' Nico said finally.

My head shot up. He was standing in front of Tiago in the street, wearing a ratty white jumper, with his book bag slung over one shoulder. Late to school, like Christian usually was. Sunlight caught on the studs of his earrings and reflected in my eyes.

'Do you have a warrant?' Nico asked.

'Carenza,' Tiago said. 'Last chance. Step *aside*.'

'Do you have a warrant or not?'

Tiago didn't deign to answer. He just shoved Nico into a wall so hard the plaster cracked. We were moving a second later, the enforcers pushing me forward, but Nico got in front of us again, cutting off Tiago's path.

'Who called it in?' Nico demanded.

For a moment, Tiago seemed truly surprised, like he couldn't believe Nico was asking for it this much. Then, slowly, he reached for his gun.

Nico didn't seem to notice. 'Who called it in?' he said again. 'Who reported her?'

'Who do you think?' I snapped.

It was stupid, made the gun press harder into my neck, but I couldn't help myself. I didn't understand why Nico was pretending not to know what Chrissy had done.

Except, for some reason, he looked stunned. His dark eyes flooded with confusion, lips parting on another question, but this time Tiago had had enough. He raised his gun and brought it down crisply across Nico's face, reopening the split in his lip and sending him crashing into the ranks of waiting enforcers.

'Bring him in,' Tiago said. 'Let them rot together.'

# CHAPTER THIRTY-FOUR

They put us in a dungeon. It was underground, down so many stone stairways that I lost track of time getting there. Then, finally: a mouldy, dripping passage with iron-barred cells on either side. The enforcers shoved us into one of them, snapped cold metal chains on our wrists and tethered us to the walls. Then the iron door clanged shut, and we were alone.

I stared around the cell – a cavernous space drenched in dirt. There was no ceiling in sight, just endless walls stretching up into darkness. Old ropes hung down in the corner, a wooden platform suspended by a network of pulleys. Like an elevator. I wondered where it was meant to take you.

Nico and I were locked to opposite walls by rusty coils of chain that pooled on the floor around us like bridal trains. The only light was what filtered in from the weak lanterns beyond the barred door. I fiddled with my handcuffs, wondering if I could slide out of them without using power. But they were too tight. Opposite me, Nico was doing the same thing: testing the strength of his chains, tugging hard at the wall.

After a while, he stopped struggling and slumped on the floor. I hesitated a moment, then mirrored his position, drawing my knees to my chest. I could see blood on his face from Tiago's gun, slicking over his bruises. I was dying to ask him what he was playing at – what had possessed him to argue with the enforcers like that. But I refused to be the one to break the silence.

Then, 'She told me she wouldn't report you,' Nico said.

I did a double take, shocked that he'd spoken first. That was twice in twenty-four hours. I was starting to think there was something wrong with him.

'Yesterday, when you left, she was going to call the enforcers, but then she changed her mind. She said she wouldn't report you.'

'Wow,' I breathed. 'Are you saying Chrissy Paradiso *lied* to you? But she seems so honest and sweet –'

'You don't understand,' Nico said sharply. 'She can't just – she's not allowed to *do* that.'

He kicked a leg out angrily, rattling his chains. I frowned, wondering what I was missing. Still unwilling to believe Nico could be this shocked by Chrissy's choices.

'No offence,' I said, 'but your girlfriend's evil. You should've figured that out before you chose her.'

'I didn't choose her,' Nico muttered.

'What is that supposed to mean?'

'Nothing. Just – we have an agreement. But I didn't *choose* –' He stopped again, knocked his head back against the wall of the dungeon. 'Forget it.'

'What are you –'

'I said forget it,' Nico snapped, and then flinched, like he was hearing how harsh his voice was for the first time. He hit his head against the wall again, hard enough that he must've wanted it to hurt. I shifted uneasily, feeling like I was seeing him unravel – not sure if I should avert my eyes.

'Are you okay?' I asked.

Slowly, Nico lowered his gaze to my face. 'Do you think I killed my father?'

I gaped at him. 'Do I *what*?'

He shrugged, like this was the most natural conversation in the world. 'I know you've heard the rumours. Everyone has. Some old man chokes to death. He wasn't very nice, but he was important. People riot. They decide it was murder.' Nico's lips twitched, an imitation smile. 'So did I do it or not?'

I shook my head, at a loss for answers – hardly able to believe we were talking about this. When Liza had told me Nico's story at the carnival, I hadn't stopped to question whether it was true or not. But . . . she had said herself that there was no real proof.

'I don't know,' I said.

Nico nodded. 'But Chrissy does. She was there when it happened. She was the only person who could've proved it. So she offered me a deal. She said she wouldn't tell them what she knew. In exchange, I have to . . . whatever.'

'Have to what?'

Nico made a sharp gesture with his hand, like he wanted to erase the words before they were out of his mouth. 'What do you think?' he asked. 'Be around her. Play house.

Let her believe it might actually end up as something more –'

He tilted his head back again, talking to the walls of the dungeon, no longer meeting my eyes. 'She's always wanted me like that. When we were kids, she told me we were going to get married one day. But I never wanted her back. So I guess, after what happened with my dad . . . she saw an opportunity. To keep me close by. To try to make me . . .'

He let it hang, shrugging a second time, unwilling to say it. 'I didn't *choose* her, though,' Nico said. 'I never would have. I just do what I have to do. To stop her from telling the truth.'

I thought abruptly of yesterday: Chrissy's hands on his body, her chin tucked into his shoulder, saying *pretty things attract*. The way Nico had just stood there. Not stopping her, but not reacting, either. Like he was sleepwalking. Like he *had* to let her do it.

And all of a sudden, I was terrified of how far she might go. How much she'd demand of him if she had the chance. Anger tangled inside me, tight like a vine, the hatred I'd always felt for Chrissy Paradiso threatening to swallow me whole.

'What about the rumours?' I found myself asking. 'People think you killed your dad even without her proving it.'

'Yeah, that's the point,' Nico said. 'People think it was me. The thing is, it was my brother. He was ten. He would've been executed. I couldn't let that happen.'

For a long moment, I was silent, letting it sink into me: the weight of what he had done, what had been done to him. 'Why are you telling me all this?' I whispered, at last.

'Because it doesn't make sense,' Nico said. 'A deal only works if both people keep their side of the bargain. I give her what she wants, but I know how to get things in return. And, last night, I made her promise she wouldn't report you. She's not allowed to just break the rules.'

He made it sound dangerous, like he was really saying, *There's something wrong*. But I was stuck on the other part.

'You made her promise,' I repeated. 'Why would you do that?'

Nico didn't answer, acted like he hadn't heard. Instead, he climbed to his feet and started to pace back and forth, the chains trailing behind him on the dungeon floor.

'I mean, we all know you hate me.'

That stopped him short. I bit my tongue, wondering if I shouldn't have pushed him. But I felt it was unavoidable. We'd gone on like this long enough, staring daggers at each other for no discernible reason. I wanted an explanation.

'I don't hate you,' Nico said. 'I never have. You remind me of someone, that's all.'

'Who?'

'You remind me of myself, before I knew better.'

He was pacing again, slower now, boots scuffing at the floor. I stayed silent, feeling like a priest in a confessional: waiting for the truth to come out.

'Because I was supposed to do it,' Nico said. 'I mean, I was supposed to kill him. My dad had it coming. And I wanted to. I just – couldn't. I'd go into his room when he was sleeping and hold a knife to his throat, but I couldn't press it in. I loved him, somehow. I thought things would get better. That he'd change. But he didn't. He got worse. Then my brother killed him. And I finally understood.'

'Understood what?'

'That it doesn't work,' Nico said, turning to face me. 'Pity, or whatever you want to call it. Love. However you learned to be, where you came from. You can't be like that here. It ruins everything. It makes you –'

'Weak,' I said. Our eyes were locked across the dungeon, and I found myself rising to my feet, moving towards him as if his gaze commanded it. Like this was the trial and the judgment I had been waiting for all along.

Nico nodded. 'That first day, when you walked into class, I could read you so easily. You looked wounded. And angry and scared, and I could see it so clearly, I could see *myself*, and I couldn't start thinking that way, not again.'

'So Chrissy was right,' I said, with a breathless laugh – maddened by the irony of it. 'This whole time, she knew why you didn't want to touch me. You think I'm weak, and if you get too close then I'll poison you –'

'I think you feel too much,' Nico said, 'and it's suicide. You can't survive in this town like that. I tried.'

We had gotten very close together somehow, the chains unravelling at our backs, the shadowed angles of Nico's face inches from mine. His eyes were impossibly dark, the swollen curve of his bloody lip glistening in the torchlight.

*You don't know me*, I wanted to say. *You have no idea what I'm capable of.*

'I have to survive,' I said instead.

303

'Then care less,' Nico said. 'It's how they hurt you. When they know you have something to lose.'

Then he did something strange – raised a hand and pressed his thumb against my mouth, the denim, bloodstained taste of him ripping through me like a drug.

'For the record, though,' Nico said, 'I always wanted to touch you.'

We were still standing like that when the enforcers came.

# CHAPTER THIRTY-FIVE

They unchained me from the wall and herded me towards the corner of the cell, snapping new manacles on as I went – big iron handcuffs this time. Nico was set free.

'They're letting you off,' one of the enforcers told him. 'The General can't be bothered to put you on trial a second time.'

I twisted to face him as the enforcers pulled me away, wishing I'd thought to question him sooner about what was going to happen to me. He'd been through this himself, after all.

'Do I get a lawyer?' I asked. 'Can I talk to my dad?'

One of the enforcers laughed unpleasantly. They were loading me on to the swaying elevator platform, making me grip the ropes for balance.

'No lawyer,' Nico said. 'And family's not allowed in the arena. It's a conflict of interest.' He was still standing in the middle of the dungeon, ignoring the enforcers trying to herd him towards the door. 'You have to defend yourself on your own. And then there's a punishment.'

'Like jail time?'

Nico shook his head. 'We do more of an eye for an eye in Castello.'

The platform jolted below me and I tightened my grip on the ropes, feeling the elevator begin to climb. Nico kept his eyes on mine, still resisting the enforcers, now tugging at him from all sides.

'You'll be fine,' he said. 'You can say it was an accident. That you're new in town, and you didn't know. Just don't get convicted of treason.'

'Why?' I said. 'What happens if it's treason?'

But the enforcers had finally dragged him away.

I turned my back on the dungeon, the rapidly vanishing floor, and faced the wall instead, watching the grimy stone slip past as I rose from underground. My heart was starting to pound, the first jolt of real fear lacing through me. I could hear chatter overhead, hushed but undeniable, like dozens of people all whispering at once. The howl of the wind and a man's voice calling for order.

Tiago.

'City of Castello! This is a civilian trial. Let the charges be known.'

There was light in the darkness above me, a doorway to the outside. Tiago was listing off my offences to whoever was waiting beyond: *trespassing*, *violent assault*, *violation of the truce*. His voice was full of echoes, like he was speaking in a huge empty space.

*Arena*, Nico had said.

'The accused will stand before the General and defend her crimes. Enter, Lilliana Deluca.'

The elevator stopped abruptly, swaying in mid-air. There was an arched doorway in the wall in front of me, bathed in hazy daylight. Cold air swept in, tugging at my clothing. I allowed myself a brief fantasy of cutting the elevator ropes, careening to the ground, smashing my way through the waiting enforcers with power –

But that only ended in burning.

Steeling myself, I stepped through the door.

After the darkness of the dungeon, the daylight was blinding, and I had to blink hard to get my vision back. Then I almost wished I hadn't. Because I was in the arena.

I thought of gladiators, death matches, Rome before the fall. I was standing on a wide dirt floor, surrounded by a massive oval of stone benches tiered sharply towards the sky. A swell of whispers hit me instantly: hundreds of townspeople staring down from the stands. I turned a dizzy circle before them, feeling tiny and crushable, alone on the vast arena floor.

'Come forward, girl,' Tiago called, beckoning to me from a distant podium. 'Face your judges. Kneel before your judgment.'

That was when I spotted the General: seated on a platform high in the stands, shrouded in his monk's hood. The clan leaders were perched on stone thrones on either side of him, Enrico Paradiso hunched over his cane, Veronica Marconi ramrod straight in a blood-red coat. A giant trinity banner hung down below them, unfurling towards the arena floor in black and gold.

Numbly, I crossed the distance and sank to my knees before the General's platform, my manacles clattering against the dirt floor.

'Now rise,' Tiago said. 'We'll begin.'

The shape of the arena seemed to amplify his voice, making it loud enough to reach the whole crowd. It seemed like everyone in Castello had turned out for this occasion – I swore the stands were more packed than the carnival had been. Far above me, I could see a familiar blur: a group of my classmates clustered together on a bench, but I didn't dare to look closer.

'Lilly Deluca,' Tiago said, 'you belong to the south side of our town. Charges have been brought against you by a resident of the north. Cross-boundary offences are an affront to the fabric of our unity. If the charges prove true, the punishment will be swift and fitting. We will now hear from the victim of your crimes. From the north side of Castello: Christina Paradiso.'

I snapped my head around, saw her descending from her seat and stepping out on to the arena floor. She was dressed like a schoolgirl in a white skirt and blouse, her blonde hair tied behind her head in gentle pleats. None of that cold entitlement I was used to – instead, she looked harmless, soft and easy to relate to. I could see the marks on her cheek where I'd scratched her, so red I was sure she'd painted them bigger.

'Yesterday, I was attacked,' Chrissy said. 'A girl from the south crossed the boundary line and broke into my home. I believe she meant to steal from me. When I confronted her about it, she turned violent.' Chrissy gestured to her wounds. 'As you can see. Now I seek justice for the harm I suffered. And to prevent what was done to me from happening to anyone else.'

'That's very noble of you, *signorina*,' Tiago said. 'Tell me, was the girl who attacked you the same one standing in this arena today?'

Slowly, Chrissy turned to face me. For an instant, when her back was to the crowd and no one else could see, she dropped the schoolgirl routine and grinned at me. Bared her teeth and snapped them together, white and sharp and wolf-like.

'It was.'

A ripple ran through the arena. Veronica Marconi shifted slightly on her throne.

'Very good, Ms Paradiso,' Tiago said. 'Thank you for your bravery.'

Chrissy curtseyed and retreated to the stands.

'Deluca,' Tiago said, 'you've heard the victim's account. Do you deny the charges against you?'

I froze, aware of the attention shift: the crowd turning as one to face me. I was suddenly conscious of what I must look like to them, in an old sweater, chained up and covered in dungeon grime. How impossible it would be to convince them that I was the innocent one in this scenario. Besides, I *wasn't* innocent. I'd just been stupid enough to get caught. Suddenly all I wanted was for this to be over as fast as possible, come what may.

'No,' I said. 'I don't deny the charges.' Then, to make Nico happy, 'But I didn't do it on purpose. I haven't lived in this town very long, so I'm not familiar with all the rules. There's a lot of them, as you know.' Someone in the stands tittered, and was abruptly shushed. 'I realize I made a mistake, but I never meant to hurt anyone.' I frowned, remembering the lie in Chrissy's speech. 'And I didn't steal anything. I swear.'

I chanced a look at the General, gazing into the darkness of his hood. Maybe it was my imagination, but for a second, I swore I saw the twitch of a smile. Like I'd amused him somehow.

'Deluca has confessed,' Tiago said. 'She admits to her crimes, but claims they were committed *mistakenly*.' His lip curled. 'However, we would do well to remember that crossing the boundary line even in error is our most grievous offence. The citizen leaders should propose a punishment accordingly.' He nodded to the judge's platform. 'The south speaks first.'

So it was Veronica. I gazed up at her, hoping I might find some reassurance. But no: her eyes were quite hard. I could almost hear her voice in my head, saying, *I suppose I'll be needing to save you again, Lilly?*

I scowled.

'Clearly,' Veronica said, 'the girl has done wrong. But I believe we should look kindly on her honesty in confession. And she speaks true when she says she is new to our city. She has not yet had the privilege of learning the intricacies of our customs. As such, I propose that Ms Deluca be schooled today, rather than punished. Perhaps I myself could be of service in teaching her about the truce –'

'The south proposes an *education*,' Tiago said disdainfully. 'I'd almost forgotten how much he hated Veronica. 'How does the north respond?'

All eyes turned to the bent silhouette of Enrico Paradiso on his throne. He'd been very still for the whole trial – that unnatural snake-in-the-box tension, hiding some terrible violence below the surface. It occurred to me that I'd never heard him speak before, and I was suddenly dreading it more than I could believe. But, as it turned out, he didn't open his mouth. Instead, he leaned forward on his cane and crooked a withered finger at Chrissy on the benches below.

She rose from her seat and darted up the staircase, crossed the platform to her father's throne and knelt at his side. There was an eerie, almost fairytale quality to the image: Chrissy's sharp, elven profile gazing up at the grizzled man in black. Her blonde hair mixing with his silver grey as Enrico Paradiso bent to whisper in her ear.

After a moment, Chrissy nodded, climbed to her feet and faced the arena. 'My father proposes a treason charge.'

# CHAPTER THIRTY-SIX

A wave of shock ran through the crowd. Veronica's fingers tightened on the arms of her throne. Distantly, I was aware of my heart beating very fast, but the rest of my body felt numb, unable to process what was happening.

'My father believes a treason charge is necessary,' Chrissy said. 'To discourage the girl from committing similar crimes against other people. And I believe he's right.'

She left the judge's platform and began to descend the steps again, but she didn't stop talking. Behind her, Enrico Paradiso leaned back on his seat. He'd done his job, set all this in motion. Chrissy would finish it for him, I had no doubt.

'If the girl isn't punished properly,' she said, 'what's to stop her from harming someone else? She could turn on anybody here the same way she turned on me. If we let her off for breaking the truce, what kind of example do we set? That our laws don't matter any more? That we can all just do as we please –'

'Objection,' Veronica Marconi said sharply, knocking her knuckles against the arm of her throne. 'Why on earth is the victim monologuing?'

'*La signorina* is merely ... expanding on her father's opinion,' Tiago said. 'She may finish.'

Chrissy reached the arena floor and stepped out in front of me. I could feel the eyes of the townspeople glued to her, eager for the drama.

'Ever since I was little, I've believed there's nothing more important than the truce. It's what protects us from violence – what allows us to live peaceful, happy lives. My family and all our citizens have made countless sacrifices to preserve it. And I would make those sacrifices over and over again a thousand times. Because what happened yesterday is proof that we can never let our guard down. We can never be too careful. A southern girl came across the boundary line and broke into my house. She claims it was a mistake, but she's lying. She did it on purpose. She *wanted* to hurt me. Because she has a grudge, a personal dislike. A kind of jealousy. So she ignored the truce. She ignored our values. She walked through two miles of backstreets to get into my bedroom and *steal* from me –'

'Objection,' Veronica said again. 'You're speculating wildly on Ms Deluca's motives. And I don't recall theft being one of the crimes she was charged with –'

'Just because she wasn't charged doesn't mean she didn't do it,' Chrissy snapped.

'What are you talking about?' I asked, genuinely baffled. 'I've never taken anything from you.'

'But you tried,' Chrissy said. 'Didn't you?' She turned to face me again, voice sweet like honey, eyes glittery with disdain. 'Unfortunately, he wasn't interested.'

For a moment, I just stared at her, not understanding. Then it dawned on me, a realization so absurd I almost laughed out loud. The real reason we were all standing in this arena in the first place. It wasn't because of trespassing or the truce; it was because of Nico. Chrissy had put me on trial for Nico Carenza.

'You're mad,' I breathed. 'This is mad. I had no *idea* he was even going to be there –'

But she was long past listening to me.

'On behalf of all the north,' Chrissy said, 'and all of Castello – I demand that Lilly Deluca be punished for treason.'

The crowd was buzzing when she finished, gripped by a nervous kind of expectation. As if the townspeople were starting to think that maybe a treason punishment might be entertaining to see. Clearly, they all knew what to expect. I was the only one who had no idea what was going on.

But then I realized that I *did* know. Because Liza had told me on my very first day in town. She'd tossed it off as we'd walked past the boundary line, warning me not to cross. *The last person who tried got executed for treason.*

*Oh. Executed.*

For some reason, all I could think right then was, *Nico's going to kill me.*

'This is absurd,' Veronica Marconi snapped. She was leaning forward on her throne, looking magnificent in her red coat, body thrumming with anger. 'Need I remind you all that we are dealing with children? Children fight. Children are cruel to each other. Treason is a conviction for

314

adults with no redemptive path. Not for little girls and their playground bickering.'

'But Deluca broke the truce,' Chrissy said furiously. 'That's treason; it has to be –'

'Order,' Tiago said. '*Order!*'

Out of the corner of my eye, I saw the General move. It wasn't much, just one skeletal hand held up for attention. But silence fell around the arena as if everyone's tongues had been cut. Veronica's posture went lax; Chrissy dropped instantly into a curtsey. I stared up at the judge's platform, thinking of the fleeting smile I'd seen below that hood before – wondering if I'd made the whole thing up.

'Hail the General,' Tiago said, and the crowd bowed their heads as one.

'Citizens,' the General said, 'we have argued long enough. Let us not prolong our strife and differences.'

I'd managed to forget how irresistible his voice was until he spoke: that silky warmth spreading over the arena like a blanket, gathering us all in its folds.

'Twenty years ago, we united our city in the light. Side by side, we battled against a great evil, and we triumphed. Through our peace, we gained salvation and reaped the rewards of blessed and prosperous lives. But, citizens – we must remain vigilant! For the victories of the past do not guarantee our future safety. It is up to us to fight every day to preserve the gains we have made. Our truce is the sacred heart of our unity. It is our pledge to each other to keep the demons at bay.

'And yet,' said the General, 'even in our strict order, there is room for mercy.'

He rose from his throne and came to stand at the platform edge, face still hidden by his hood.

'I see before me a child newly born into our way of life. She has crawled, but not yet learned to walk among us. She must be punished, but I would not see her irreparably harmed. I would consider this day her baptism; her initiation into our fine ranks of citizens. We will not cull her from our union – rather, we will bind her to our city with a seal, which she will carry as a reminder of the loyalty she owes us. This is a solution that can satisfy both the north and south, that punishes those who affront our peace, but embraces their repentance with open arms. This is merciful. This is just.'

The General finished speaking, with one hand in the air, a conductor standing over an invisible orchestra. Around the arena, the crowd burst into spontaneous applause. I stood at the centre of it, trying to understand what he'd sentenced me to. *Mercy*, the General had said. Not execution. So maybe Nico wouldn't kill me, after all.

'The judge has ruled,' said Tiago. 'Deluca will be branded with Castello's seal. Bring out the iron and the trial log.'

There was a sudden bustle of enforcers around me, emerging from hidden doorways and striding briskly across the arena floor. One of them had a wheelbarrow filled with glowing orange coals; another a long iron poker. The General's trinity symbol was carved into the end of it like a huge stamp. And just like that, Tiago's words made sense.

*Branded.* That iron was going on my skin.

All of my emotions seemed to catch up to me at once, and I felt sick, had to turn away from the wheelbarrow of coals to stop myself from panicking. Tiago was busy flicking through an old book stuffed with thick parchment. I assumed this was the trial log.

'As is customary,' he told the crowd, 'the punishment will be handed down by the last citizen who received it.'

'I wonder who it will be?' Chrissy said, to no one in particular. There was a glint of triumphant anticipation in her eyes that I didn't like at all. 'We've had so many insignificant crimes recently. Bread theft and such. I think we'll have to go quite a few years back to find anything punishable by branding.'

And it suddenly occurred to me that she hadn't been the least bit upset when the General had commuted my execution. Quite the opposite. It seemed like she was looking forward to this.

'If I'm not mistaken,' Chrissy said, 'the last person to take the seal was –'

'Nico Carenza,' said Tiago, finding it in the log. 'Branded and exiled for disturbing the peace.'

'That's what I thought,' Chrissy said and smiled.

It hit me like a rush of exhaustion, making me feel useless and outwitted a thousand times over. Ready to sit down on the arena floor and just give up. This was brilliant of her, really clever. She'd put me on trial for looking at Nico, and now she was going to make him punish me. Just in case I had any bright ideas about looking at him again.

'Excellent,' Tiago said, snapping the trial log shut. 'Nico Carenza will carry out the branding. Bring the boy.'

A door opened on the far side of the arena, and I turned to see Nico being marched forward, flanked by half a dozen enforcers as if he was the one on trial. The crowd broke out instantly into jeers, the Paradiso side of the arena raining their hatred down on him.

'Now, now,' Tiago admonished. 'Carenza is our avenger today. He is blessed with the sacred duty of administering justice. As the last citizen to receive a branding, he is responsible for passing on his lesson of obedience to the new wrongdoer.'

I tried to catch Nico's eye as the enforcers marched him past, but he wasn't paying attention to me. All his anger was aimed at Chrissy.

'What the hell are you playing at?' he hissed.

'Aw,' Chrissy said. 'Did you not realize you were the last one in the log?'

Things started happening quickly after that: the enforcers seizing me from behind and forcing me to my knees, Tiago pressing the branding iron into the hot coals. It flared orange at the end, the trinity symbol sizzling as it heated up. Nico had been positioned nearby, his body tight with suppressed outrage, making the enforcers circle him nervously.

'Behold the seal of the city,' Tiago called, showing the iron to the crowd.

'Behold,' they called back.

Someone reached down and ripped open the front of my sweater, exposing my chest to the wintry air. They kept their hands on me afterwards, clamped unforgivingly on my shoulders. Locking me in place.

'Lilly Deluca,' Tiago said, 'you went to your knees as one who dabbled in treason, but you will rise again as one of the redeemed. Count the General's mercies today. See how blessed you are to live within his grace! This brand will transform you from a lost child to a living symbol of loyalty to our town.' He handed the iron to Nico. 'Go on.'

Nico didn't move. I was scared to look at his eyes right then, so I focused on his hands instead, the flex of his fingers around the iron. Trying to remember what it had felt like, those times he'd held me, so I could have something good to think about when the pain hit.

'*Now*, Carenza,' Tiago said.

Slowly, Nico stepped forward and raised the iron to my chest. I chanced a look at him, saw him hesitate a beat, glancing from Chrissy to me and back again. For a moment, the rest of the world seemed to fade out, and it was just the three of us: a twisted trinity like the one on the stamp.

'Why did you turn her in?' Nico asked.

Chrissy shrugged. 'Why did you tell me not to?'

It was the same question I'd asked him in the dungeon, but he hadn't answered me then, and he wasn't answering Chrissy now, either. Instead, he stood there, iron swaying in his grip, weaving closer to my chest and then pulling away. I could feel his eyes on my face, and, when I allowed myself to meet them, I was stunned by what I found.

All his poise, his perfect mask of disinterest – it was gone now. Instead, I saw doubt, anger, the dark curl of something panicked and desperate. Almost like desire. And the fear. Nico Carenza was afraid. It was such an alien thing on his face that I almost turned away.

*Care less*, I found myself thinking. *It's how they hurt you.*

'Do it,' I said, understanding all of a sudden how important this was – how badly he needed to press the iron to my chest. 'It's okay. I don't care.'

'No,' Nico said and let the iron drop.

It hit the ground hard, crackling viciously in the dirt. Around me, the crowd seemed to draw breath as one. I felt lightheaded with shock, staring up at Nico but unable to comprehend what I was seeing.

*You told me not to be weak*, I thought dizzily. *Why did you say that if you're just going to be weak yourself?*

'Are you out of your mind?' Chrissy breathed. 'I *own* you.'

'No, you don't,' Nico said.

Then he turned his back: on her, on me, on all of it. Walked away across the arena floor. Chrissy watched him go, stunned, her anger like a physical thing in the air. When she reached sideways and snatched one of the enforcer's guns, I think it was mostly just to make him pay attention to her again.

The shot rang out through the arena like a thunderclap. Nico stumbled forward, clutching at his right shoulder. A flower of blood was spreading across his back, staining his white sweater wine-red. The crowd gasped in surprise, even Chrissy – as if she hadn't really meant to do it, had expected the gun to be full of blanks instead of bullets, hadn't planned to leave a wound. Except that now it was real, and she had shot him, and somehow no one had thought to take the gun away from her yet.

Nico turned around slowly, still clutching his shoulder. There was more blood on his chest where the bullet had passed through, seeping over his fingers and leaving a trail down his front. He was the only one in the arena who didn't seem remotely surprised by what had happened. It terrified me when I realized – he seemed almost relieved.

'Good,' Nico said. Nodding at Chrissy, baiting her like he'd done to me a dozen times. Daring me to come closer or back away. Daring her to shoot again.

*But the enforcers will stop it now. They won't let it get any worse –*

Except then I remembered that this was Nico Carenza. And no one seemed inclined to care what happened to him either way.

For a moment, Chrissy just watched him, like she couldn't quite believe it had come to this. The crowd was on the edge of their seats, the violence they'd been craving this whole time finally playing out in front of their faces. Nico's eyes were very dark, his bruised lips set together.

'I'm done,' he told Chrissy. 'Do you understand? I can't any more. So just finish it.'

Chrissy's eyes sparked. In that moment, she reminded me of a tantrumming child: destroying their most prized possession to prove a point.

'You should've just let me slit her throat,' she said, and raised the gun. I didn't wait around to see where she was aiming this time.

Power exploded inside me, all my fear and rage coiling into a deadly wave of heat. I wanted to kill her in that moment, take her heart out, just to see if it was there at all. I got far enough to snap apart my manacles – but then the power stopped.

Something was blocking it at the end of my fingertips, preventing it from leaving my body. Like a trapdoor slamming inside my head, a crippling pain that made me double over, unable to move or breathe or think straight. I felt like I was pushing all my muscles in one direction while someone else was tearing them back.

*Lilly, don't.*

It was Christian.

His voice swirled through me, flawless and all-consuming, coming from somewhere in the stands above my head. *Don't you dare.*

*Let me go,* I thought desperately, bent forward and sick to my stomach; trying to raise my hands but feeling like my body was being ripped apart. Feeling like that was what Castello had done: dragged me in a hundred different directions, made me want more things than I could stand. *Let me go, please, it's Nico –*

*I know,* Christian said.

A deafening crash echoed through the arena, shaking it to the core. It was like an earthquake: a wave of pure energy that threw me sideways, splintered the ground under my knees. Cracked open the benches and sent the crowd sprawling. It couldn't have lasted more than a few seconds, but when it stopped everything was different.

I dragged myself upright, aware that the pain in my body had gone, and tried to make sense of what I was looking at.

There was a bomb crater in the centre of the arena. Rubble littered the floor around it: collapsed chunks of stone, the overturned wheelbarrow of coals smoking in the dirt, the trial log blasted to smithereens. Chrissy had been knocked to the side like I was, and the gun was gone, buried somewhere in the debris. Nico was slumped in the middle of the crater, one hand still pressed against the wound in his shoulder. Otherwise, he was completely unharmed.

'Christian,' I said.

He stood alone on a bench, more beautiful than he'd ever been. Hair swirling in the wind, blue eyes laced with gold, lips flushed a deadly red. His whole body seemed to radiate power, veins glowing below his skin, sparks curling at his fingertips, and he was so tired, so angry, so sick of this, but I'd dared him to use it, and finally he had.

*See, Lilly, are you proud of me?*

And now it would be over. Now it would end.

I thought, *Why?*

*Why why WHY WHY WHY –*

The whole crowd was staring at him, and I had a moment of wild jealousy, because these people had seen something they didn't deserve – real power, something he'd had to fight for, and I'd missed it all.

*And he's strong*, I realized. *He's so much stronger than me, I can feel it –*

'Oh my God,' someone said. It was Chrissy, dirt-streaked and glorious, rising to her feet in the destruction of the arena floor. 'He's a *Saint*.' And she laughed.

The chant spread slowly at first, like the crowd was too stunned to process what it meant, until all of a sudden it was everywhere, and they were shouting it at him like a curse, like the end of the universe.

*Saint! Saint! Saint! Saint!*

The enforcers were on him in seconds, pinning him to the bench and jamming injections into his arms. The link between our minds collapsed instantly, shredded to pieces by the drug and the way he was losing consciousness from how many they'd given him. I stumbled to my feet, needing to reach him, but then someone was hitting me from the side and slamming me into the ground again.

'You idiot,' Alex said furiously. 'Do you want to die, too?'

The last thing I saw was Veronica Marconi. She was coming towards me, moving through the frenzied crowd in her blood-red coat. Arms outstretched, as if she wanted to embrace me.

Then there was a terrible pain in my head, and everything went black.

# CHAPTER THIRTY-SEVEN

I woke to gloom and faint torchlight. I was lying on a damp flagstone floor, staring up at a dirt ceiling. The air was heavy around me, that sweet dying-flower smell. A metallic rattling noise came from somewhere to my left. Slowly, I sat up and tried to blink my vision into focus.

I was surrounded by rows of iron cages, big enough to fit wild animals inside. Another prison, then. The flagstones where I'd been dumped were like a hallway, and the iron cages were the blocks of cells. They were all empty, except for the one closest to me. Alex was in it. He was slumped in the back corner, kicking out at the bars with rhythmic despondency. When he saw me sit up, he scowled and delivered a particularly hard jolt to the bars.

'About time,' he said. He was sweaty and covered in scrapes, his black hair thick with grime.

'What's going on?' I asked, forcing myself to stand a little at a time. The world felt tilted and blurry, my head throbbing like when I'd smashed out of a tree in Gracie's backyard and had to stay overnight at the hospital. I had a feeling it was a concussion.

'Well, for starters, I'm in a cage,' Alex said.

'I'll get you out.'

I lifted a filthy hand and focused on the padlocked door, summoning the heat from inside me. Nothing happened. My palms were numb where my power should've been, useless and vacant like my mind. Panic slammed through me, making my heart pound.

'Where is it?' I demanded, stalking towards Alex like he'd stolen it from me. 'What did you do to my power?'

'Don't look at me,' he said coolly. Pulling himself up by the cage bars and coming forward to meet me. 'It was Professor Marconi. She gave you an injection in the arena. Right after she knocked you out.'

'She did *what*?'

'It was hysteria,' Alex said. 'After Christian ... you know. People started to panic. The General made everyone get tested for power right then, and Professor Marconi thought you'd be less threatening in a dead faint.'

I winced, feeling dizzy, willing my heart to slow down. 'Where are we now?'

'Dungeons,' Alex said. 'Below the Marconi safe house.'

'Why are you locked up?'

Alex shrugged, wrapping his hands around the bars, leaning towards me. 'I asked her how we were going to get Christian back. She said there was nothing we could do. I said I was going to kill her, and she put me in a cage.'

'That was stupid of you.' I grabbed the padlock and fiddled with it, infuriated by how helpless I was without power. Glancing around the cell for another way to break through.

'How long have we been here?'

'Ages,' Alex said. 'Hours, days, I don't know. I'm losing track. I have to get out of here. Before –'

'What?'

'The General announced it in the arena,' he said. 'After the rest of the city tested clean. It's November the first this week. There's always a big celebration, to honour the anniversary of the fire, and now it has a grand opening. They're going to burn Christian at midnight. As a tribute, you know? To show how far we've all come. On the day the Saints destroyed us, we get to destroy one of them.'

He flicked his eyes up to my face, and I saw for the first time how dead they were, how very hollow. 'The thing is, Lilly, it should be you.'

Something rose inside me: a wall of pain so fierce I believed it would split me in two. 'I know,' I said. Snatching up an old brick from the ground and bringing it down over the padlock, hoping it might break. Nothing. Just a cloud of dust in our faces.

'You asked for my help because you wanted to save him,' Alex said. 'You told me you knew what to do, but you messed it up, and now he's going to *die* because of you –'

'You're the one who stopped me.' I smashed the brick down again, harder now, making Alex jerk away. 'In the arena, I could've gotten their attention, but you held me back –'

'Only because he told me to,' Alex said furiously. 'He's been like this ever since you moved here. All, *be nice to Lilly*, *watch out for Lilly*, *keep Lilly safe*.' He threw me a disgusted look. 'Because, for some reason, he still cares about you, even after everything you've done –'

'It's not his choice,' I snapped, feeling tears burn at the corners of my eyes. Smashing the brick down one last time and then giving up, hurling it at the wall.

It was useless. I was useless. All of this was useless. And Christian was gone.

'He only cares about me because of his power. He only cares because it tells him what to feel –'

'You're wrong,' Alex snapped back, and then squeezed his eyes shut, like he couldn't believe I was making him voice this out loud. 'Believe me, I wish you weren't. But you are. It's more than that.'

'How do you know?' I demanded.

'Because Christian's not stupid. He knows what he wants. And because I know what it looks like on him. When it's real.'

For a moment I stared at him, out of breath from arguing, my fingers aching from smashing the brick so hard. Trying to work through what he'd said, between the hazy tremors of pain in my skull. *I know what it looks like on him. When it's real.*

'Alex,' I said slowly, 'what exactly is there between the two of you?'

He glanced up at me through his lashes, a bitter, haunted thing. 'Isn't that the question?'

I thought suddenly of how I'd seen them that day, bent towards each other in the empty washroom. Alex's hand on Christian's jaw; Christian leaning in to him so effortlessly, like he'd done it a hundred times. Like he belonged there. Realizing in a rush just how little I really knew about Christian's life.

'He's not all good, you know,' Alex said, as if he was the one who could read my mind. 'You treat him like a china doll, some perfect broken thing you can piece together if you try hard enough. But it won't work. Trust me, I tried. He just takes what he needs from you and then destroys himself anyway. But the problem is, I don't even mind. I still want to give him everything. And I *have*. I've been there, right from the beginning. I stopped the bleeding. I made him forget. It used to be that he could only ever sleep if it was in my bed. For my whole life, it's been the two of us. No one else mattered. Then you came along.'

Alex flicked his eyes to my face again, pinning me in place with the force of his gaze. 'You're the one he wants right now. And that's fine. You can have him. You can have anything. But I swear to God, Deluca –' his fingers flexed on the bars of the cage and for a moment I thought he was going to do something bad: reach out and seal his hand around my throat – 'I'll destroy you if you let him burn.'

There was a dirty staircase at the end of the dungeon, with a metal door at the top. I came out behind heavy curtains, pushed them roughly to the side and found myself standing in the flickering candlelight of Veronica's ruined palace. Veronica herself stood at her desk with her back to me, staring up at the painting of the dark-haired man holding Castello's original coat of arms. He looked very alive in the soft light, young and bold and dangerous.

'Who is that?' I heard myself say. Veronica glanced over. If she was surprised by my sudden appearance, she didn't let it show.

'It's my ancestor,' she said. 'Vittorio of the House Marconi. The first of our name.'

The name rang a bell, distantly. 'The one who started the clan war,' I said. 'Who fought his brother for the founding key.'

'It should have been his all those years ago,' Veronica murmured. 'It should've been easy. But he let the war drag him under. Both of them did. Foolish boys: they relished the fight so much they began to forget why they'd started it in the first place. They lost the key. And now we're all trapped here in this cage they left us.' Her eyes skated across the ballroom, with its metallic gun pile, its broken remnants of glory. 'Sometimes I wonder if that's all our lives are good for: trying to remedy the sins of our predecessors. Proving we can be better than they were.'

Veronica turned to face me properly, her eyes cooling as they settled on my face.

'For your head,' she said, pointing at two white pills on the banqueting table.

I went over and took them gratefully, hoping they'd stop the pain. When I looked up again, she was still watching me, the anger from the arena a low simmer in her gaze. I suppose I couldn't blame her. I hadn't exactly been a model student lately.

'Your father has been calling me endlessly,' she said. 'He's taken quite a sudden interest in you. He's got the noble idea that you should both be leaving town right about now. I told him you were unfortunately detained with me.'

'What does that mean?'

Veronica gave me a sad smile. 'It means you've become incapable of acting sensibly. And if you can't protect yourself, I will simply have to do it for you.'

I didn't understand until I crossed the room and tugged on the bank-vault door in the wall. It was locked.

'Let me out,' I said. 'You can't keep me here. I have to get Christian.'

'I'm afraid that won't be possible. He's being held in the enforcer headquarters until the burning starts. Surrounded by guards twenty-four hours a day –'

'So I'll break in. I'll fight them. I did it once, I can do it again –'

'For God's sake, Lilly,' Veronica snapped. 'It's all different now. The city is on high alert. Do you think the purges would've worked if the General had allowed the Saints to run around freeing each other? You'd be dead the moment you approached. And I will not be responsible for sacrificing both of you in one night.'

'I don't care what you want to be responsible for,' I said furiously, pulling at the door, feeling anger grow inside me where the power was meant to be, filling me to the brim with no outlet. 'Let me out of here right *now* –'

'What on earth were you thinking,' Veronica said, ignoring me completely. 'Going to the north? Hasn't anyone ever explained the truce to you? And what was so difficult about simply following the instructions I gave?'

'Your instructions were bad,' I said. 'There were no power scanners in my dad's office, and it's pure luck I got any clues about the key at all.'

Veronica's eyes flashed. 'And did it ever occur to you to bring that information to me? To ask for advice, before rushing across the city and nearly dying?'

'I'm sorry,' I said, not meaning it at all. 'I'll do better next time. Now let me *out* –'

'Don't apologize to me,' Veronica said. 'It's Christian they're burning.'

I recoiled sharply, gripped at the wall for balance. Veronica watched me struggle, looking mildly surprised, as if she hadn't realized the impact her words would have.

'He chose to give himself up, you know,' she said, as if that made it better. 'He went willingly.'

'No, he went for me. I was supposed to fix him, make it right – what my mother did – but instead he's going to die because of what *I* did –'

'Sometimes,' Veronica said, 'people don't want to be fixed.'

'I don't care what he wants,' I said. 'I'm not going to lose him.' It settled into me like a vow, a steely, molten weight in my bones. Telling me exactly what I had to do next. 'I can get the city key,' I said. 'I can bring it here, and we can use it to stop the burning.'

Veronica shrugged, like she thought I'd been asking her a question. But I hadn't been.

'You told me it could overthrow the General. That it's the strongest weapon in town. So it has to be enough to save Christian –'

'In theory,' Veronica said, 'the key could do any number of things. But until I see it in front of me, there's no point in speculating. Christian will burn on the eve of November first. That's two days from now, Lilly. And the key has been gone for centuries. Forgive me if I don't believe we'll be able to get our hands on it in time.'

'But we *can*,' I said, refusing to let any shred of doubt enter my mind. Refusing to think about how long I'd been lying in that dungeon, letting hours slip by. 'I know where it is now.'

'You know where it is,' Veronica repeated, and looked at me hard. 'I suppose this is going to explain why you crossed the boundary line?'

I nodded. 'There's a coin,' I said. 'It's gold, and it has a symbol on it. I think it's what the General's been searching for.'

'What kind of symbol?' Veronica asked.

'Sebastian calls it the gateway to life and death –'

'Sebastian?' Veronica said sharply. 'Sebastian Paradiso?'

I froze, realizing a second too late that I should never have said his name – that I should've left him out of this completely. Veronica leaned forward, her eyes gone cold, hands braced on the desk. 'Are you telling me that after all these years, all these centuries of searching, the runt of the Paradiso litter managed to get his hands on Castello's founding key?'

'Why does everyone hate Sebastian so much?' I demanded.

Veronica ignored me a second time. 'Why didn't you take it from him?'

'Well, I tried. I mean, I asked him, but –'

'As long as you *asked* him,' said Veronica disdainfully, 'no one can fault you for anything.'

'Sebastian didn't have it any longer,' I snapped. 'But he said he could get it back. And I know how to reach him without being caught this time. You just have to let me out of here. You have to let me try.' I took a step towards her, leaning across the desk, ready to beg, ready to do anything. 'Please,' I said. 'Let me get the key. And then let me get Christian.'

For a long time, Veronica watched me, like she was making a calculation with her eyes – racking up numbers and figures in her mind. Trying to decide if I was reliable after the messes I'd made. Settling on something that surprised me, because it looked a lot like pity.

'Poor child,' she said. 'You'd destroy yourself for him, wouldn't you? I remember the feeling.'

She reached across the desk and brushed a filthy strand of hair off my face, let her palm linger against my cheekbone. It was an unexpected gesture, warm and strangely gentle, and it triggered some kind of flashback: the childhood memory of a beautiful woman who I desperately wanted to love me back. For the first time in years, I realized that I missed my mother.

'Very well,' said Veronica Marconi. 'Bring me the key, and we'll get your boy out alive.'

# CHAPTER THIRTY-EIGHT

I reached Liza's house just before curfew, the broken bottles on the pavement glinting in the moonlight. When I pressed her buzzer, it sounded like a funeral bell. At first, nothing happened. Then the door opened, and she was standing before me, hair loose down her shoulders, one arm wrapped across her chest like a shield. I felt a sharp pang of relief at the sight of her, despite what had happened between us. Seeing her in person, I had to believe that everything would work out somehow.

Then Liza said, 'Get away from my house,' and tried to swing the door shut in my face.

I lurched forward and wedged my body in the doorway just before it closed, stumbling out into her entry hall. It was very dark in here, and Liza was suddenly very close to me. For a moment, we just stared at each other, my breath coming a little too fast. I tried to read her eyes, but they were blank, devoid of all her usual charm. It made me feel out of kilter, unsure how to behave. *I* was meant to set the tone here. *I* was the one who was allowed to be mad.

'Have you come to take your precious map back?' Liza asked finally.

'No,' I said. 'You can keep it. I know you like to be surrounded by murder scenes.'

Liza gave a tight little laugh. 'So it's one of those days again. Where you pretend to be better than me.'

She was turning away the next second, heading up the mouldy staircase towards her apartment.

'Liza, wait,' I said, but she didn't look back. I hesitated a moment, then decided I had no choice but to follow.

When I came out into the apartment, the lights were low, and Liza was a dark silhouette down the hallway. I could hear music playing from a scratchy record in a nearby room. It sounded like an opera, huge and tragic: a man and a woman singing together in tangled harmony.

'What is this?' I asked, curious despite myself.

'*Carmen*,' Liza said. 'It's almost the end.'

'What's happening?'

'There's this girl. She's really beautiful, but she's careless. She makes a boy fall in love with her, and then she leaves him. So he kills her. He's doing it now.'

Liza turned away again, disappearing through a door at the end of the hall. I swallowed hard, breath still coming too fast – all the conviction I'd felt on her front stoop vanishing in an instant. Now I just felt stuck, caught between the urge to get closer to her and the urge to back away. In the end, getting closer won out, even though my brain was screaming at me that this felt like a trap.

I found her in a chipped-tile bathroom, filling up a massive porcelain tub. The music was louder here, the woman's voice climbing high and then crashing fast.

'The hot water is almost out,' Liza said, without looking at me. 'So you'll have to make do with cold.'

'What?'

'The bath is for you,' she said. 'You're filthy. You've tracked dirt all through my home.'

I glanced down, registering for the first time the layers of blood and grime on my clothes.

'I'll even tell you a story while you clean yourself,' Liza said. 'About how the princelings started the fire. I figured it out from the map: they put gasoline in the holy water. So every single person who came into church spread the blaze –'

'Liza, stop,' I said. 'You know I don't want to talk about them.'

'No, I *don't* know,' she said, turning to face me. 'It turns out I don't know anything about you. Well, except that you're a liar. And a thief.'

I did a double take. 'You stole *my* map –'

'Sure,' Liza said. 'But you stole my power.'

It was like the ground had tilted below me, my head spinning, my stomach sick with sudden understanding. So this was why she was looking at me like she wanted me dead. This was the trap.

'You seem stunned,' Liza said coldly, reaching down to turn off the taps. 'Did you not expect me to figure it out? Honestly, Lilly, how stupid do you think I am? I'm just

337

surprised no one else noticed in the arena. Your handcuffs broke like that.' She snapped her fingers. 'A miracle. It was so obvious.'

She took a quick step towards me, green eyes burning black. 'It was the only thing I ever wanted. Nothing else: just power. And then you come here, pretending to be all sweet and innocent, and you *take* it from me –' Her voice twisted like a whip. 'Your bath is ready,' Liza said. 'In you go.'

It was a bad idea, the worst idea, but somehow I couldn't bring myself to disobey.

'I'm sorry,' I whispered, stripping off my jeans and sweater and sinking into the tub. 'Liza, I swear I didn't mean to –'

'Shut up, Lilly,' she said. 'And show me what you can do.' She stepped into the bath and stood over me like a vengeful god. 'I mean, breaking handcuffs is nothing. I want to see you smash something real.'

'No,' I mumbled. 'I'm not going to do that.'

'Why not?' Liza said. Dropping abruptly to her knees, splashing icy water everywhere. 'Don't tell me you're scared of it? Afraid you might like power a little too much? Afraid you'll have to stop with the good-girl routine once you admit how much you want to mess things up?'

'Why do you do this?' I demanded, leaning towards her, meeting the fury in her eyes with my own. 'Want me to be bad so much?'

'I just want you to be honest,' Liza said. Her lips were curved into one of those vicious smiles, telling me she knew me better than I knew myself. 'I want you to be *interesting*. To admit that you're angry, that you're desperate to lash out. I'm so sick of watching you pretend you're happy with your narrow little life –'

The bathroom mirror behind Liza's head shattered into a million tiny shards. Glass rained down on us, shimmering in the bathwater, sprinkling her hair like falling snow. I felt dizzy in the aftermath, unable to explain why I'd done it – risen to her bait, when my logical brain had been screaming *no*. Maybe it was because some secret, deadly part of me agreed with her. Or because I knew it would make her look at me like this: her eyes gone wide and hungry, raw with desire at the electric feeling of power in the air. Our knees pressed together below the waterline, my body wanting to bend towards her like a flower to the sun.

'That's better,' Liza said, running her tongue over her lip, feeling for glass. 'I hate it when you act all docile. Deep down, you know you're just like me.'

She pulled back then, a cruel thing in her eyes when I tried to follow her instinctively. 'Why did you come here, Lilly? What do you want from me?'

I took a moment to remind myself, trying to unglaze my mind. 'Sebastian,' I said finally. 'He said he'd find something for me, but I'm out of time. So I need you to tell me how to meet him again without crossing the boundary.'

Liza arched an eyebrow. 'And why exactly would I do that?'

'Because you're my friend. Because I'm asking. Because, no matter how angry you are right now, I know you care about me.'

'I *care* about you,' Liza repeated and smirked. 'Is that what you think?'

I said nothing, refusing to react.

'Didn't you listen to Chrissy?' Liza said. 'You're just a toy. It was fun playing with you for a while, but now I'm bored.'

'I don't believe you,' I whispered. 'I don't believe you at all.'

'Well, you should. Because it's been a game, don't you see? A laugh for me. And you made it so *easy*.'

Her voice was dripping with scorn, and I recoiled from it instinctively, my hands curling around my knees.

'I saw how you looked at me when you came to town. At Nico. At Christian – at all of us. Like a lovesick puppy. Desperate for someone to want you. For someone to accept you the way you are.'

'Maybe I looked at you that way,' I said, 'but you looked back.'

'Did I?' said Liza and shrugged. 'It's funny – I can't recall.'

'You're a hypocrite,' I said suddenly. 'Talking about being honest, about taking the things you want. About how you admire the princelings for being brave, when the truth is you're nothing like them at all. You're just as small and terrified as the rest of us. You can't even admit that you feel something for me. This whole time, you've been too scared to acknowledge that you want –'

'What, Lilly?' Liza demanded. Leaning forward again, eyes dark and furious, but also guarded now, holding something tightly inside. 'What exactly do you think I want from you?'

'This,' I said and kissed her.

My mouth was slick with water, and Liza tensed for a second, hands on my chest, on the verge of shoving me away. But then I felt her lips part below mine, and suddenly it was real. A wave of relief crashed through me, my heart beating like a frantic thing in my chest. She was different from Christian in every way: sweeter, sharper, her jagged edges scraping at my bones. But it still felt right. It felt like I needed her, too.

'You see?' I said breathlessly, pulling back a little. 'This is good.'

Liza didn't answer, just threaded a hand through my hair and pushed me down hard, sending water splashing over the edges of the tub. I let her hold me there, curving my neck up to meet her, feeling glass shards cut into my skin and not caring one bit. Our mouths slipping together, half in and half out of the water, her teeth tugging at my bottom lip, filling me up with incense and vanilla and blood.

When she finally let me go, I slid underwater all the way, eyes sealed shut, lips burning. Below the surface, everything was silent and still, and when I blinked my eyes open I could see her watching me from above.

*She kissed me back*, I thought, feeling giddy relief sweep through me again – convinced for the second time that things would be all right. *She kissed me back.*

Abruptly, Liza rose to her feet and stepped out of the bathtub. I surfaced from the water, gasping a little, watching her cross the room to the window sill and swipe up her phone. Her sweater was glued to her body, water trailing from the sleeves. Tension in the set of her shoulders, her back turned towards me, and I didn't want that, couldn't accept that at all.

'Liza,' I said, touching a finger to my swollen lips, relishing the heat that her mouth had left. 'Liza, can we talk about this?'

'It's done,' she said.

I stared at her blankly.

'Sebastian,' Liza said, and I realized I'd forgotten about him again. 'Tomorrow at dawn. He'll meet you in the catacombs.'

# CHAPTER THIRTY-NINE

In the end, the entrance was obvious. For all I'd been told that the catacombs were sealed off, the doorway was perfectly intact. It was nestled inside an ancient stone mausoleum, with a padlocked gate that had been smashed open. Beyond the gate, in the mouth of the tomb, I saw a stone staircase plummeting down into the ground.

It was still mostly dark out, the glow of dawn barely tinting the sky, and the inside of the mausoleum was even darker. I flipped on the flashlight Liza had given me and let it glance off the walls, revealing spray-painted murals, overturned candles and smashed-up glass, like kids had once gathered here to bait ghosts. There was a biblical carving in the floor at the top of the stairs, coming into focus when I ran the flashlight across it. Two skulls with roses blooming in their mouths.

DRY BONES, YOU WILL COME TO LIFE.

*Cheery*, I thought, and started down the stairs.

The ceiling closed in almost immediately, narrowing above me, curved like the inside of a pipe. When I chanced a look at the walls, I found them still paint-smeared, with childish drawings of twisted bodies and figures in flames. Below my feet, the ancient stone steps descended into the earth like a mineshaft.

I tried to maintain a sense of direction as I walked, but the angles kept shifting, the staircase cutting one way and then another, making me feel like I was moving in spirals, deeper and deeper underground. The air turned colder the further I went, the walls now damp around me, covered in slime. When the stairs finally ended, I felt like I'd been climbing down for miles.

I stepped tentatively forward, then leaned against the wall to get my balance back after the vertigo of the staircase. The dark was extreme now, cut through with ice. I shivered, wrapped my arms around myself – shifted my feet uncertainly and felt something snap below me. Slowly, unwillingly, pointed the flashlight down.

It was bones. Dry bones. I was in the tunnels now.

I panned the flashlight in a reluctant circle, taking it in: the huge banks of dismembered skeletons piled up around me, coating the floor in glittering white. Alex had told me that the catacombs were too full to use, but I'd never imagined them looking this way. I felt like the bodies were going to drown me.

I started to walk in a rush, ignoring the snap and crunch of bones below my feet. Skeletons pressed in from all sides, masses of grinning skulls and body parts I didn't know how to recognize. Just when I thought I couldn't take it any longer, the passage began to broaden, spilling me out into a cave. It was like a crossroads, a wide cavern with a new range of tunnels branching off in different directions. I stopped short where I was, afraid I'd never find my way back to the stairs if I lost track of the tunnel I'd come from. And I didn't need to move, anyway. Sebastian was already waiting.

I sensed him before I saw him, a faint ripple in the dark that made me sweep the flashlight around.

'Here,' he said, and then there was a flicker of light to my left, a match being struck.

Sebastian's face came into fleeting view across the cavern. I thought he looked much taller than normal. The match went out, but he lit a second one, reached up towards the cave wall and seemed to set a pile of crooked skulls on fire. After a moment, I realized it was a nest of half-burnt candles in the bones, lighting the cavern with a fierce orange glow.

Sebastian was perched high up on the rim of a towering coffin. The coffin was open, dripping bones from all sides, but he seemed completely at ease with that. He was wearing a crisp green and grey school uniform with a tie that reminded me of Christian's, only a hundred times newer. I expected Cat to be with him, curled on his shoulder or investigating nearby. But Sebastian was alone.

We took a moment in the silence to size each other up. I hadn't noticed him at my trial in the arena, assumed he'd been excluded, the same way my father had. But I knew he must've heard what Chrissy had done.

'I told you she wasn't finished,' Sebastian said, right on cue.

I shrugged. Chrissy's vendettas felt light years away now, but Sebastian seemed to disagree.

'People are making her a hero for it,' he said. 'Smoking out a Saint.' His eyes narrowed. 'It's dangerous to let my sister think she's got that much power. You cause an awful lot of trouble for someone who just moved to this town.'

'Yeah, well,' I muttered. 'Apparently it runs in my family.'

Frowning, Sebastian slid down from the coffin. He landed lightly on his feet and came towards me. There was a gun tucked into his belt, a strange contrast with his school uniform. The thick line of rings on his fingers glinted in the firelight.

'I brought that stupid coin,' Sebastian said. 'Just like you wanted. I wouldn't have done it, except that it's been waiting for you. It's already tasted your blood. So I figured I couldn't stop you getting it eventually.'

'What are you talking about?' I whispered, unnerved, watching him reach into his pocket and draw out the necklace on its gold chain. 'Why do you keep saying the key knows me?'

Sebastian didn't reply. The chain unfurled from his fingers, the coin on the end of it swinging like the hypnotic pendulum of a clock. The sight of it made my heart skip, an exhilarating pulse of power fluttering below my skin. Wanting to touch. Maybe it was the quality of the light, or maybe Sebastian had cleaned it, but I found I could see details on the coin much more clearly than before: the savage cut of the thorned doorway, the Latin words scrawled across the top. *Per me omnia.*

'Do you know what it means?' I asked.

'Through me, everything,' Sebastian said instantly, and then wrinkled his nose, correcting his grammar. 'Everything through me.'

'That sounds like a promise.'

'Or a warning,' he said.

'Did you ever think about keeping it?' I murmured, tracing the gold with my eyes, resisting the greedy urge to snake a hand out and simply snatch it away from him. 'If the legends are true, and it controls the city's power, then your family could rule this place –'

A flicker of rage crossed Sebastian's face, so vivid it almost felt like a blow to me.

'New girl,' Sebastian said coldly, tensing his fingers below his rings, 'what makes you think I want my family to rule anything?'

He thrust the key towards me, eyes hard. 'Take it,' he said. 'But watch out. Some doors are better when they stay shut.'

That was when the skeleton banks around us shattered apart, and the enforcers closed in.

Sebastian aimed his gun at the same time as I loosed my power – took three shots before the enforcers caught him from behind and shoved him to his knees. I swiped a hand out and made them crumple, falling away like paper dolls.

347

But then there was a bone-deep pain in my wrist and everything went numb. It was a sudden, nauseating cold, like I was sinking through layers of black water. My power was gone.

Tiago's silhouette loomed in front of me, holding a cluster of syringes in one hand. He'd given me more than the normal amount, enough to make my head spin, limbs weakening in an instant.

'Deluca again,' he said pleasantly, pulling me to his chest. 'I knew we hadn't seen the last of you.' He was smiling, but it looked blurry, a suspended white gash in the air. 'Two Saints in one week. Before you know it, we'll have a full-blown purge on our hands.'

Tiago reached down to where the enforcers had pinned Sebastian and swiped the key from his hand.

'I see you've found the General's lost heirloom, too. He's been waiting a very long time for this to turn up. I'm sure he'll be most grateful.'

My vision was failing for real now, smudging the outline of Sebastian's body as the enforcers dragged him backwards into a tunnel. Vaguely, I was aware of thoughts trying to break through the haze in my brain: *How did they find us here? How could they have known?*

Then the full force of the injections kicked in, and the world disappeared. I felt myself slip in Tiago's arms. I don't think he bothered to catch me.

# CHAPTER FORTY

I woke up on a cold surface in the half-dark, déjà vu from Veronica's dungeon, only this time I was in chains. My wrist throbbed from the injections, my body numb and craving power.

'Christian,' I said, desperate for a response, thinking that if we were both dying, then at least it could be together.

But there was no answer.

I was chained to some kind of stone column at the foot of a wide staircase, illuminated in patches by light filtering down from windows at my back. An arched ceiling formed a dome far above my head, but I already had the sensation of being high up, as if there was a long drop in the dark on either side of me.

'Christian,' I said again. *Answer me, come on –*

'He's not here,' said a voice. It was a smooth sound, instantly recognizable even to my half-dazed mind. I shrank back against the thing I was chained to. The voice stretched like a smile.

'Are you afraid of me?'

'Yes,' I whispered.

'Good,' said the General and stepped into the light.

He was moving down the staircase in front of me, a hooded figure in a burlap robe. Almost gliding across the stone. When he reached the landing where I was chained, I recoiled even further, dreading his approach, but he turned away instead, weaving through the darkness around me, in and out of sight.

'Where's Christian?' I demanded, trying to fight my fear, the wicked pounding of my heart.

'In a prison cell,' the General said. 'Waiting for the festivities to begin.'

*Festivities.*

'Why aren't I with him?'

'Because I am merciful,' said the General, coming to stand in front of me at last. 'And I need you for something else.'

I stared up at him almost unwillingly, not wanting to look, but unable to tear my eyes away. I could feel him watching me in return, the bruising weight of his gaze on mine.

'Remarkable,' the General said. 'You look just like her.'

Slowly, he reached up and pushed his hood back. I'd seen his face before, but it still managed to stun me – his cruel beauty, so different from the phantom silhouette of his robe. Up close, everything about him was brutal: the military undercut of his hair, the black tattoos curling from his neck to his temples. The crown of thorns inked on to his forehead, sharp enough that I believed it could wound me.

'You look just like your mother,' the General said.

Something in my chest went cold.

'Lilliana Deluca. A meaningless name on paper. I never imagined you were hers. She was prettier than you, of course. More charming, too. But you have her blood in your veins. That's all that counts.'

He stepped out of sight again, moving behind me, speaking from the dark.

'You hid yourself well, I admit. Blending into the crowd – I had overlooked you completely. But the trial showed me. You were like a ghost in that arena: the little princess resurrected. The burning queen come back to haunt me.' The General reappeared by the stairs, mocking now. 'Your mother set the fire of the century. What a legacy to live up to.'

'How do you know it was her?' I whispered. Then, thinking of Veronica, 'Oh God, don't tell me you were friends with her, too –'

'Friends?' said the General. 'Do you really think so little of me? No. Your mother made it her mission to rip my life apart. And that was *before* she set her fire.'

'She must've been pretty smart, then,' I said, surprised to find myself defending her. 'To escape this town when so many people seemed to know exactly what she did.'

'Smart,' said the General, 'perhaps. Or simply heartless. After all, they were breaking my brother apart in the square, waiting for her to show herself. But she chose to run instead.'

There was silence, a moment when his eyes reflected contempt so profound I was afraid it would drown me.

'Your mother was very special,' the General said. 'She did not seem to feel.'

I was silent, curled in on myself – wanting to argue with him, but not knowing how.

The General walked away again, and this time I chanced a look around the column to see where he'd gone. The marble floor branched out into walkways behind me, a suspended maze of balconies criss-crossing through the air. The widest balcony led to a wall of stained-glass windows, glowing with fading light from outside. Played out across the glass, I saw the Icarus myth, huge panels of boy and wings and devastation. So we were in the church.

The General stood before the central panel: Icarus in flight, wings brushing against the sun. Flames were just beginning to spread across the feathers in sharp slivers of golden glass. Castello's square stretched out beyond the window, a sheet of marble that should've been tiny from this height, but looked massive instead. I could see details on the pavement: a discarded paper streamer, a child's hair ribbon fluttering in the wind. The glass was magnifying, I realized. The General could see the whole square from up here as clearly as if he was standing on the ground.

'I've come a long way,' he said softly. 'From nothing, I've come a very long way indeed. I taught this city to worship me. No merit, no wealth, no title, but they worship me all the same.' The General nodded at the glass. 'I've come a long way, but I could go further.'

He glanced over his shoulder, seemed unsurprised to find I was watching him. 'Do you know what your mother used to say? When we were children, she told me the Saints were the chosen ones, and it was the mortals who were cursed. She used to torture me for it – for being so *human*. And I was. I am. But nothing is permanent. There's more to the world than people born with power and people who go without. You can take it, too. You can just reach out and take it for yourself.'

He came to stand before me again, his cloak whispering on the marble floor. 'The people of this city believe I saved them. They call me a prophet, and why shouldn't I be? You're going to make it happen.'

'What are you talking about?' I said.

'You brought me the founding key to Castello,' said the General. 'And I thank you for that. I've been searching for it for a very long time. The gateway to the city's power – the iron fist to rule this town. I've always wanted to have that right. To do what your mother did: to shatter people without needing to try.'

'But you hate it,' I said. 'You hate power – you want to destroy it.'

The General laughed, clear and uninhibited, like a boy. 'What on earth gave you that idea?'

I stared up at him, convinced I was being tricked. 'Everything about this town,' I snapped. 'The blood tests, the enforcers, the sermons you preach, saying that power comes from the devil, that the Saints are cursed –'

'Come, child,' the General said carelessly. 'Those are just the stories I tell to make the people love me. You should know better.'

But I didn't know. I didn't understand.

'It's very simple,' the General said. 'Once upon a time, your mother tried to burn this city to the ground. I decided to build it up again. I had no power to do it with. Just words. An idea. Give them something to hate. Something to fear. People will do anything if you make them fear enough. So I made them fear *you*. I told them the Saints were witches, and they begged me to redeem them. I said your blood was corrupt, and they prayed to me like a deity. They slaughtered you because I told them it would end their pain. Words are strong like that. Words make people believe. Words bought me this city.'

The General smiled. 'But power is better.'

I watched him pace before the staircase, feeling as if things were dissolving around me, like someone was trying to turn the world upside down.

'Words can still be doubted. There will always be someone who chooses not to believe. But no one doubts power. Power obliterates. Power makes people bow down whether they choose to or not. It bends their limbs. It alters their minds. Power is inescapable.'

The General turned to face me, caging me in with the easy honesty in his voice, the feral grey of his eyes. 'I'm tired of words,' he said. 'I want to shape the universe in my image, and I don't want it to fight back. That's what the key is for.'

'So you made it up,' I breathed. 'Everything bad about the Saints, you just ... created it. You told a story about darkness and light, and people listened. They turned on each other. They killed for you –'

'Don't be silly,' the General said coolly. 'The people in this town have been killing for centuries. All I did was give them a better target.' He shrugged. 'They say the founding key has the power of a god inside. I'm the only god this wretched city has ever deserved.'

I sank back against the stone column, dizzy from the weight of understanding. 'You're a fraud.'

'No,' the General said, 'I'm a ruler. With that key, I'll be ruling for a very long time.'

He walked away again, and I found myself thinking of eternity, of a man in a hood with a deadly voice handling puppets on strings.

'What are you waiting for, then?' I asked. 'You have the key. Why aren't you using it?'

'Didn't she tell you? Veronica Marconi, sending her little soldiers out on missions with a pack of lies. Shame on her.'

I shifted in place, unnerved that he knew about Veronica's plans.

'The gateway in the key has been locked,' said the General. 'Someone paid a very high price to do it. They made a blood sacrifice, gave over their power to the city in exchange for sealing the city's power off from the rest of us. Because they were greedy and hateful, and they couldn't bear the idea of anyone else being allowed to reign –'

'Who would do something like that?'

The General looked at me strangely. 'Who do you think? It was your mother.'

It was happening again: that tilting sensation, everything turning out crooked and wrong.

'No, that's impossible,' I stammered. 'The key's been lost for ages. It's been a thousand years since anyone's been able to find it at all –'

'Another lie from the Marconi clan, I see. Did Veronica really pretend that the key had never been found? When it was her idea to dig it up in the first place . . .' The General made a *tsk-tsk* sound, like he was admonishing a child. 'It was always the four of us when we were young – me and Val, your mother and Veronica. Sneaking across the boundary line, meeting outside the walls. Playing rebels in the warzone all around us. The girls despised me, of course, and I despised them, but Val managed to convince us all to get along. He was in love with your mother, and he believed we could be a kind of family somehow.'

The General's eyes darkened suddenly, a gathering storm. 'My brother was all I had, and your mother took him from me. She forced me to destroy him. Of all her sins, that's the one I will never forgive.

'It was Veronica who suggested we look for the key. Her family had kept alive stories that everyone else had forgotten about – how Castello's founding key could open the gateway to the city's power. How we could use it to become kings and queens. At the time, we had nothing better to do than seek it out. Stupid children, lost and looking for purpose. But there was a catch, you see. Two of us already *had* power. And that was Veronica's mistake: believing that someone like your mother would ever be willing to share.'

The General had vanished behind me again, voice drifting

in from the shadows. 'It took a very short while for your mother to locate the key. She could sense it, I presume, and she took my brother with her to dig it out. They wouldn't show it to us, afterwards – wouldn't let us touch. All we knew was that suddenly they were unstoppable. *That* was when the two of them changed: not when they became Saints, but when they opened the gateway. When they had Castello's power in their hands. They shut everyone else out, built their own little world together. Drunk on power, demanding everything. Like true princelings, leaving the rest of us in the dust.

'I suppose that's why your mother locked the key in the end. After the fire, when all her plans had gone wrong, she simply couldn't bear the idea of someone else using the city's power like she had. She'd coveted it too much, worked too hard to keep it hers. So she made a sacrifice – offered her own power up to the key in order to seal the gateway off. And then she hid it. Because, no matter what happened, the truth she held most dear in life was that only she deserved to rule.'

The General circled back to stand before me, eyes glinting with amusement. 'I never imagined she'd have children. It makes it much too easy to reverse her sacrifice. Your blood is the same as hers, just like your power. You're the only person on earth who can undo what she did. I suppose she'd be very disappointed in you right now.'

I couldn't move when he'd finished, my mind turning over and over like a broken wheel. Thinking of Sebastian in the tunnels saying, *It's already tasted your blood*. Of my mother's anger all those years; the locked doors and the way she was always so ashamed to look at me.

*She didn't just hate me because she knew I'd end up like her*, I thought, with a thick, sinking understanding. *She hated me because I wasn't meant to exist at all. Because she knew I could ruin everything.*

'I won't do it,' I whispered. 'I won't open the key. You can't have my blood.'

'Of course I can,' said the General. 'I could force you if I chose. But that would be terribly boring. I'll have it, anyway, though.' He gestured towards the stained-glass window, one bony finger pointing at the square below. 'They're building his pyre now. The boy will burn at midnight unless I give the order to stop.'

My heart was pounding, driving me to my feet despite myself, desperate for a proper look outside. The General moved ahead of me, beckoning me to follow. 'Come, child,' he said. 'Stand with me. See what I see.'

I went slowly, finding that the chains allowed me leeway to walk, trailing behind me from my waist and arms. Through the glass, I could see dusk beginning to fall, a crowd forming in the plaza. Castello's citizens, dressed in their best clothes – come out to pay their respects on the anniversary of my mother's fire. It was half memorial, half celebration, like Alex had said. *On the day the Saints destroyed us, we get to destroy one of them.*

Men in tunics lined the edges of the square, drums strapped to their chests, readying for a performance. Red flags with the General's trinity symbol unfurled from windows like bloody tongues. And at the centre of it all, on a high platform by the church, I saw Christian's pyre. It was a massive pile of wood with a stake rising up in the middle, circled by enforcers hammering nails and ropes into place.

'This is my city,' the General said. He'd become a preacher again, that hypnotic charm even I couldn't resist. 'My people. They'll tie your boy up and cheer when the flames catch. If you unlock the key for me, I'll spare his life.'

I was silent, imagining what Christian would say if he knew about this: how furious he'd be.

'Hesitation,' the General said curiously. 'You really are your mother's daughter.'

'I want to see him first,' I said. 'Bring him here, where they can't touch him. After that –'

'Hush, child,' the General said. 'You're in no position to make demands. Break the lock, save the boy. That's my final offer.'

'But you're a liar,' I said coldly. 'You've been lying to this city for twenty years. Why would I trust you to spare him when it's over?'

The General smiled, amused again. Taunting me. 'Why would you trust anyone? You've been lied to from the start in this town. Haven't I already made that clear? I'm no more treacherous than anyone else you've met here. Take the girl who sold you out to me, for example.'

'What girl?' I said.

'Do you really think it was an accident that my men came upon you in the catacombs? And not just you, but the key to the city, too. Such good fortune after so many years of failure. It would've been unthinkable if *signorina* Elisabetta hadn't told us where to look.'

I stared at him blankly, certain I didn't know anyone by that name. But then it dawned on me in a horrible rush: *Liza. He's talking about Liza.*

'No,' I breathed. 'That's not true, I don't believe you –'

'The south-west catacombs at dawn,' said the General. 'She led my enforcers down the steps herself.'

I shook my head, refusing to accept it. 'You're lying again. It wasn't Liza. She wouldn't do that to me –'

'Don't be hurt,' said the General. 'She's just a jealous child. Hardly your worst betrayer.' Something bright flickered in his eyes. 'Or didn't you ever wonder how you came to live in this hellish city in the first place?'

I was backing away from him with my hands outstretched, thinking, *No more. Stop, please. I don't want to know.*

'It was my father,' I heard myself say. 'You offered him a job –'

'Me?' The General sounded delighted now. 'Is that what you really think? That I sought him out on my own? That I called him to my city, a strange man named Jack Deluca, to meddle in my affairs? No, child. Someone else brought us together. Someone who wanted *you*. Who schemed and lied and bargained to get you here, knowing your bloodline, knowing how valuable you would be . . .'

The General took a lazy step forward, the sunset colouring his face in streaks of red and gold. Turning him

360

glorious, godlike already, even without the key. He pulled something from the folds of his robe, a slip of parchment, and pressed it into my hands. When I looked down, I was staring at my father's job contract. Home address, previous employment, family members, living and deceased. And at the bottom, in neat cursive, the written note:

*Jack Deluca: engineer – recommended to the General by Veronica Marconi*

For a moment, I couldn't breathe at all.

'You were safe,' the General said. 'An ocean away, invisible to me until she whispered your father's name in my ear. She insisted I needed an engineer, a new talent in my ranks, so I took a chance – invited your father to town, and his daughter came along, just like she'd planned it. Clever woman: she had us both fooled.'

'But it doesn't make sense,' I stammered. 'Veronica was surprised to see me. She said she couldn't believe it when I showed up in school –'

'And who made Veronica Marconi the sworn truth-teller in Castello? She's just as tainted as the rest of us. She has her own grudges to bear. How do you think it felt growing up like she did, heir to the Marconi throne, expecting the world at her feet, only to watch your mother's power grow and grow? Veronica wanted to be special, too. She wanted to keep pace with your mother's talents. She'd been hearing stories of the founding key since the cradle. Imagine her rage when your mother stole it from right under her nose.

And then *sealed* it off. Locked the gateway from the rest of us and hid it away . . . Not to mention the fire. That was the ultimate disgrace.

'What the princelings did in this church wrecked Veronica's future. It destroyed her family dynasty and her chance to rule the town. How could she let that go? More than ever, she needed the key. She wanted her inheritance back, and this time she planned to claim it with power. So, when your mother vanished, Veronica tracked her down. It took her years, but eventually she found a woman named Carly Deluca. And then she found you.'

The General sounded almost impressed now, but his voice was tinged with mockery. 'The last person on earth carrying the princeling queen's blood. The only one who might have a chance of finding the key and opening the gateway again. So she brought you to Castello and waited patiently. Took you under her wing, stroked your hair, dried your tears, and in return you risked your life to get that key. She would've asked for your blood when you handed it over, and you'd have given it without a second thought.'

'For the city,' I said helplessly. 'Because she wants to protect Castello from *you*.'

'A noble cause,' the General said. 'But Veronica Marconi wanted power a long time before she wanted to destroy me. You were her perfect solution.'

I let it sink into me, standing numbly by the window, mind clouded over with everything I was afraid of in this town: Christian in flames; Liza's fury; Nico with a bullet in his shoulder. All of Castello's shadows twisting together into one crushing truth.

*She did this to you. Veronica Marconi wanted her city back so she dragged you here. She used you. She didn't care what it cost.*

I felt sick all of a sudden, stunned by how blind I'd been, swallowing her lies about the key, how it was the only way to fix the city. Believing her when she told me I could save Christian – as if she'd ever cared whether he lived or died.

*I'm alone*, I realized. *I've always been alone. They never love you – they only want you while it's easy, and when they're done they slit their wrists and you are ALONE –*

'So you see,' the General said softly, 'trust is an illusion in this city. Our hatreds run too deep. We're all just skeleton keepers here. Carrying the bones of the past, damned by their memory, desperate to overcome. But the past is vicious. It doesn't die so easily. You have to kill it yourself.'

He put his hand against the window, where Christian's pyre loomed in the dusk. 'This is your choice. Twenty years ago, your mother stood in the shadows and watched them tear my brother apart. Are you going to do the same to him?'

'No,' I said. The word seemed to cut the air, cracking something that could never be made whole again.

'Good girl,' the General said. 'Your injections will wear off before midnight. Then the sacrifice can begin.'

# CHAPTER FORTY-ONE

It was hard to keep track of time in the church after night closed in. Seconds became minutes became hours of hazy dark, broken only by the noises from outside: high laughter in the square, the voices of the gathering crowd. Once in a while, the darkness was lit up by a flicker of firelight from the stained-glass window – enforcers with torches crossing the square below. Preparing for the burning.

I was curled on my knees at the foot of the stairs, the chains thick around my arms and stomach. They hardly felt like restraints any more, just sheer weight to carry, a burden I'd never be able to shake. My lips were very dry, my body feverish.

I saw my mother standing at the top of the steps with gashes on both wrists, her skin white and bloodless in the dark. Then Veronica was there, a shimmering figure who coaxed and whispered and fed me poison as sincere advice. Eventually, she faded out, and it was Liza on the staircase. She wore a black velvet cloak, held a kerosene lantern in one hand, casting shadows on the marble as she came towards me. I assumed she was a fantasy, too, until I felt the warmth of her lantern on my face, and even then I couldn't be sure.

'You're looking glum,' Liza said. 'It doesn't suit you.'

'What are you doing here?' I whispered.

'He sent me to get you ready. Blood sacrifice and all that – you should look the part.'

'So you're running errands for the General now?'

'Hardly,' Liza said. 'I'm here for my own entertainment. I like watching things fall apart.'

'You turned me in,' I said, willing my voice not to bend. 'I trusted you, how could you –'

'I told you once,' Liza said. 'You can't rely on anyone but yourself. That was your mistake.'

'What a lonely way to live your life.'

Liza shrugged. 'I gave you a chance,' she said. 'I told you we could be different together. But then you had to go and ruin everything –'

'I don't *want* to be different,' I said. 'I never have. I want to be normal. I want to talk about normal things with you. I want us to like each other the way normal people do. Without all the anger and the hurting –'

'You want to be normal?' Liza repeated and laughed at me. 'You really should've thought about that before you took my power.'

'You act like I did it on purpose,' I said furiously. 'Don't you know I can't control it? I didn't ask for any of this to happen. And I'd give it to you if I could. I'd let you cut my power out of me if it would make you happy. But I don't think it would. I don't think you'd ever stop wanting, no matter what I gave.'

Liza's face hardened, and she bent suddenly, meeting me at eye-level. Green burning in the dark. I felt my breath catch, face to face with her raw ferocity. The cruelty she was capable of, and the rage – all a part of her. All something I had tried to deny. All of it ready to destroy me.

'I should never have fallen for you,' I whispered. 'I should've fallen for Giorgia. God, even Susi. Someone who wouldn't ruin me. Someone who doesn't want to burn us all down.'

Liza smiled at that, leaned in close and ghosted the words across my lips. 'Don't be stupid, Lilly,' she said. 'Maybe I'll burn the rest of them. But I'm going to keep you.'

There was a sudden noise from above us, the distant scrape of a door in the dark. My body tensed with anticipation. He was coming.

'It's starting now,' Liza said, straightening up and stepping away from me. 'Do what he tells you and don't ask questions. Trust me.'

She sounded very sure about it, as if she knew exactly what the General was planning and had decided it should be of no concern to either of us. I watched her climb the staircase, pausing halfway up – raising her lantern high and smashing it down on the marble bannister to release the kerosene flame inside. Fire shot through the air, a jet of breathtaking light, blinding me after the hours of darkness. When I finally got my vision back, the whole church had come into view, illuminated by a massive line of flame running up the bannister.

Icarium was glowing around me, the towering walls and arched ceilings turned suddenly bright as daylight. I was on a balcony suspended high over the altar, directly under the curve of the church's titanic dome. I could see the blur of pews on the ground below me, tiny like dollhouse furniture. In front of me, the staircase seemed to rise for ages: sloping marble with a wooden throne at the top. The General sat there, leaning forward on his knees. His hood was still down, face painted in firelight, his robe creased by the strap of a shotgun slung across his shoulder.

Halfway up the stairs, on a dais between him and me, there were two ancient statues. They looked agonized and unfinished, as if live bodies were caught within the stone. Each of them was reaching one arm up and over towards the other figure, their marble fingertips nearly brushing at the top of the arch. Like a gateway.

The statue on the left had his head thrown back, a silver dagger clutched in his free hand. Around his neck, the city key hung from its dirty chain.

Liza took a seat on the edge of the bannister behind the statues. She seemed perfectly calm, like this was really just entertainment to her – as if she was in complete control. For his part, the General didn't seem to notice her. His eyes were fixed on me. He swung the shotgun off his shoulder and aimed it at my chest.

'Release yourself,' he said.

I did it automatically, using the first traces of power to break the chains around my arms and body. When they clattered to the floor, the General pumped a cartridge into the shotgun's barrel.

'Rise, child,' he said. 'Fulfil your duty.'

I staggered to my feet, off balance for a moment without the pull of the chains as a counterweight. In the distance, there was something pounding: a hollow thud, like the beat of a monstrous heart. It took me a moment to realize that they were drumming outside. The men in the square had started to play an execution march.

Climbing the steps to the dais felt like wading through quicksand. The drums throbbed around me, rising and falling along with my pulse. The marble floor swam in circles before my eyes. Only the key seemed real, a flicker of gold beckoning me closer. It looked harmless from here, hanging snugly against the statue's chest, but my instincts told me otherwise. Every nerve in my body wanted to touch the key, and every ounce of reason told me to back away.

When I reached the edge of the dais, I hesitated, wary of the General's gun and the half curve of his smile – a phantom thing that always seemed to be mocking me.

'The knife,' he said.

I took the dagger from the statue's outstretched hand. The handle was cold, but my skin was on fire, power twitching under the surface, responding to the pull of the key. *It's been waiting for you*, I thought. *All these years, it's been waiting for you to find it –*

368

The drums swelled, and I glanced instinctively over my shoulder, through the stained-glass window to the square beyond. The crowd was massive now, thousands of people pressed together for a view of the pyre. They had brought Christian out.

He was surrounded by a knot of enforcers, an angelic vision in the moonlight, like something too ephemeral to hurt. Then the enforcers led him closer, forced him up the pyre steps, and I saw the gruesome details: the ropes trailing from his wrists and neck, the tatters of his clothing. His skin was flushed, curls smeared on to his forehead with sweat and bruises. There was no focus in his eyes, just a white, glassy sheen from the injections.

*They're going to take him from you*, I thought, watching the enforcers tie him into place. *They're going to take him, and there will be nothing left.*

I raised the knife over my palm and slashed down. Pain came first, and then the blood, pooling between my fingers, sticky and hot. I stepped forward into the shadow of the statue and pressed my hand to the key on his chest.

The response was immediate, a gut-wrenching pull inside my body, like my organs were being turned inside out. Power surged up, bigger than anything I'd felt on my own before, as if the key had found the deepest well of strength I had and was dragging it all out. The gold began to burn under my palm, and I tried to snatch my hand back, but realized that I couldn't move. The key had me in a death grip, an invisible lock on my power, funnelling it from my body into the coin.

I fell to my knees on the dais, gasping for breath, head spinning like I'd just stepped off a frantic merry-go-round. My hand on fire, skin sizzling where it was melded to the gold. The church was shaking wildly around me, plaster crumbling from the walls, balconies swaying, jewelled crucifixes twisting through the air. A sudden rush of images flashed through my mind, foreign and familiar at the same time.

*Running desperately down a hallway, injured and knowing I was being chased. A beautiful boy holding me in his arms, me knowing I never wanted to leave him. Veronica Marconi as a young girl, slapping me across the face.*

And all the while, as the slideshow played out, my power was slipping away. Just like hers had when she'd made her sacrifice.

*Mom, help me,* I thought, reaching out to the girl in the memories, begging her to listen. *Mom, please, I don't want to do this –*

Because the key was taking everything from me. I could sense the gateway beyond it, waking to the world after a long slumber. In my mind's eye, I saw it as that crumbling, thorn-crusted door, filled with blood and darkness: the lock my mother had woven across the city's power. On the other side of the door lay the infinite depths of the town. Castello's beating heart, warped and bulging, an abyss of power I was almost afraid to look at. All that was stopping someone from using it was the lock, and that was melting away fast. Thanks to my blood. Thanks to my sacrifice – the key stealing every ounce of power I had.

*No*, I thought frantically, and tore my hand away as hard as I could, feeling my skin rip open as it separated from the gold. *No, it's mine, it's part of me, you can't have it all –*

Stumbling backwards off the dais, realizing that I'd been lying to Liza before. I wanted my power. I *needed* it. I refused to give it up. And I wondered if this was what had destroyed my mother: to lose something so big. To have your soul ripped out.

Somewhere above me, I heard the General say, 'Put your hand back on the key, child. Or the boy will die.'

But I couldn't move. I was curled at the foot of the dais, cradling my ruined palm, shaking all over. 'No more,' I said. 'Please, no more, I can't.'

'*Now*,' the General snapped, and then he was there: standing over me and pointing the shotgun at my head.

'But it's enough,' I said. 'Don't you feel it? The lock's unravelling. The gateway's open most of the way. You can take the key now, you can use it –'

'I don't want *most* of this city's power,' said the General viciously, 'I want it all. Hand on the key now, or we'll be finishing this night the hard way.' He pressed the barrel of the gun to my forehead. 'Surely you realize that your blood will spill just as easily once you're dead?'

'NO,' someone snapped. It was Liza, risen to her feet on the staircase, eyes blazing. 'She gets to live. That was my condition.'

The General said nothing. He just lifted the gun and shot her instead.

It seemed to happen in slow motion, her body slamming backwards, bent in half and tumbling down the steps, leaving a trail of red. Blonde hair fanning out over the marble like a crown. I felt something inside me shatter, my head filling with static, body lurching forward, desperate to reach her. The toe of the General's boot smashed down on the side of my ribcage and pinned me to the ground.

'Silly girl,' he said, pressing the shotgun against my cheek. 'Do you see the stakes now? Do you understand what I can do?'

I shook my head, feeling the gun slide through the tears on my skin, no longer caring where it landed. 'Give her back,' I said, wanting to scream at him, but reduced to begging instead. 'Give her back to me –'

'No,' the General said. 'And the boy will be next to go. You could have saved them both if you'd done what I asked. It's such a waste.'

He sounded so casual, so smug, that I felt a wave of fury rise in my chest, blacking my vision out. Suddenly, no matter how exhausted I was, no matter how sick inside, I knew what I had to do. I knew how to end this. I just had to find the strength to move.

'You really are like her, you know,' said the General. 'Letting everyone else die in your place. But I've had quite enough of that.' He moved his shotgun to my forehead, slow like a caress, but quite definitive this time. 'When you see your mother, tell her that I won.'

'Tell her yourself,' I said. And thrust my good hand up, still clutching the dagger from the sacrifice. Driving the blade straight into the General's leg.

He reeled back, momentarily stunned: blood pouring down his robe, making me pray I'd hit a vein. The gun lost its purchase on my forehead, and I scrambled away, using every ounce of energy I had left to make my way up the dais. Stumbling and desperate, leaving red handprints on the floor. Heading for the city key.

I heard the shot behind me a second later, felt the slug explode next to my head, shattering one of the marble bannisters and making me trip and skid on the ground. The balconies shuddered with the force of it, swaying like hammocks in the wind.

'Fool,' the General said. Shooting again, shattering another bannister, scraps of shrapnel embedding in my side. 'Do you really think you can escape me like this?'

But I didn't want to escape. I just wanted to make it stop.

*I won't lose anyone else to you*, I thought. *I refuse. You will not have Christian, too.*

Lunging for the key, hand closing on the chain just as the General shot the statue it was hanging from. The head exploded in a marble cloud, and I couldn't see for a moment, couldn't breathe – throat thick with dust, eyes coated white. When I came to my senses, I was standing on the dais, clutching the key by its ruined chain, the golden coin swaying in front of me. The pavement cracked below my feet, the balconies trembling. The General a few steps away with his shotgun aimed.

I don't know how long we stayed like that, watching each other, the key hanging between us and humming with anticipation. Asking for more, always more – of my blood, of my soul. Of my power. I could sense it more clearly than ever: the wet heart of the city, lurking just beyond the gateway. Glistening and dangerous, but beautiful, too. So very beautiful. So very deadly.

Centuries of war and ruin and ravaged kingdoms: all for this. A tiny gold coin. What everyone who had ever lived on Castello's soil had died for – held in my hand. Promising me multitudes in exchange for one final sacrifice.

*Through me, everything*, I thought hazily. *Everything through me.*

*Fine*, I decided. *Take my power. Take my blood. I'll give you all I have. But then give me something in return. Help me make this end.*

'I see,' the General said softly, reading it in my eyes. 'You think you can use it against me. That if you offer yourself to it completely, it will obey you.' A slow shake of his head, almost pitying. Pumping a cartridge into the gun and pointing it straight at my chest. '*Tesoro*,' he said. 'Don't be naïve. Look how that worked out for your mother.'

But I had no other choice. I never had.

'Stop hurting my friends,' I said. And reached my bloody hand towards the key.

A shot rang out. The key exploded in a flash of gold.

The balconies fell.

# CHAPTER FORTY-TWO

When I opened my eyes, there was orange. The world was glowing around me, sharp edges turned soft in the flickering light.

*Fire*, I thought. *You're dead, so there's fire.* Then something slammed into the ground nearby, showering me with plaster dust, and I coughed until my bones ached. The pain brought me back to my senses. *Not dead, then. Not yet.*

I was lying in a pile of rubble on the floor of Icarium, staring up at the jagged remains of the balconies far, far overhead. A sick feeling rose inside me, like delayed vertigo – the understanding that I'd been up there before and had fallen all the way down.

I closed my eyes, unwilling to think about the staggering height. Trying to make sense of what had happened. My brain was thick and dull, like I was waking from a trance or a coma. Memories flickered in and out, barely lasting long enough to grab on to. Liza's body on the ground; Christian's glassy eyes. The General's shotgun bullet heading straight for me.

I sat up in a rush, pawing desperately at my chest, expecting to feel blood pouring out of me, but finding nothing there. Just my hands, raw and burnt from clutching at the key.

*The key.*

It had taken the bullet.

Fragments of gold littered the ground around me, like an explosion of fairy-dust: twisted fragments of the coin. I ran a shaky hand over the gold pieces, feeling for something familiar – the delirious pulse of power I'd sensed when I'd held the key. The awareness of that dark heart, swirling beyond the gateway. But it was gone.

The key was ruined. The General had tried to shoot me, but he'd hit the gold instead. He'd destroyed it. And he'd almost brought the whole church down in the process.

I scanned the ruins, the pieces of balcony still collapsing here and there like giant hailstones. What had once been the dais had fallen upright on the church altar. It looked like the deck of a sinking ship. That was where the General had been standing when he'd taken the shot.

A current of fear ran through me, forcing me to my feet, no matter how painful it was. Needing to be on my guard. *What if he's still here? What if he survived like I did? What if he has the gun?*

Folds of black silk unravelled from my waist as I moved, and I looked down to find one of the General's trinity banners wrapped around me like a cocoon. It must've been torn from the walls of the church during the collapse, tangled with my body – cushioned me when I fell.

I couldn't see another banner in sight. Just rubble and more rubble.

*Then he has to be dead*, I told myself. *There's no way he could live through a fall like that.*

Realization came slowly, hints of sunlight breaking through the fog in my mind. *That means I won.*

I waited for the victory rush, for the satisfaction to come. But there was nothing. Because nothing had really changed. Liza was still gone. And Christian was still on that pyre.

I turned desperately towards the church doors, remembering what I'd seen through the stained glass before: his body lashed to the stake with the enforcers circling. *How long has it been since then?* I thought, glancing around, searching for some indication of the time. *If it's midnight, if it's past –*

For a moment, the panic was so intense I had to shut my eyes against it. In the darkness, the world seemed to shrink, narrowing down to nothing but sounds from the square outside. They were faint at first, drowned out by the veil of hazy air in the church. But, when I concentrated hard, I could hear the drums. They were playing the same march, faster now, building to the climax. I didn't know much about executions, only that the drums would stop when he was dead. *So there's still time.*

My eyes flew open. The doors to Icarium loomed in front of me, monster panels of wood above the wreckage. I tried to visualize the scene outside: the marble terrace where I'd found Christian after mass that day. And below it the square, packed tight with Castello's citizens, all straining for a view of the pyre. All listening to the voice that was rising above the drums: Tiago speaking to the crowd.

I couldn't make out his words, but there was thunderous applause in between them, the townspeople responding like they had in the arena, hungry for someone to hurt. I saw a flash of the General in my mind, a black shadow against stained glass. *They'll tie your boy up and cheer when the flames catch.*

Tentatively, I flexed my fingers, trying to summon my power. Nothing came. It was a well inside my body that had been scraped dry, devoured by the key.

*Please*, I thought, praying to whatever god would listen. *Please let it not be gone completely.*

I knew I'd offered up the whole of my power in the end, but the General's shot had come before I could complete the sacrifice. So there had to be power left in me. There *had* to be.

Something cut through my thoughts, an out-of-place noise: a steady pitter-patter by the church doors. I narrowed my eyes, focusing on the marble holy-water fonts. They had been hit by falling balconies, cracked open, and they were dripping now, sending little streams of water towards the floor. Only it didn't smell like water. It smelled like gasoline.

For a second, I just stared, trying to work through it with my half-speed brain. Thinking of Liza in her frigid bathroom, telling me she knew how the princelings had started their fire. Her breath on my lips, saying: *Don't be stupid ... I'm going to keep you.* The way she'd been so unfazed by what the General was doing.

Because she'd had a plan of her own. She'd done something to the church. She'd set up an escape route for us. She just hadn't been able to see it through.

Slowly, like a daydream, I began to walk towards the fonts. There was wreckage all around me, low fires simmering in the smashed pews, and I reached down for a piece of burning wood, carrying it before me like a weapon. The gasoline was spreading faster across the floor, soaking the cracked furniture, forming shimmery pools on the marble. If it caught fire, it wouldn't die out like the rest of the rubble. It would spread. And spread. Unstoppably. Just like Liza would've wanted.

Without a second thought, I tossed the burning wood into a pool of gasoline and ran for the church doors.

I was hit by an icy rush of night air, the terrace slippery beneath my feet. My vision was useless in the sudden dark, the square swimming like a black hole before me. But I could sense the crowd from the silence that had fallen, the crawl of hundreds of eyes across my body. The drums had cut off abruptly, and Tiago's speech had stopped. The shock of the church doors crashing open must've caught everyone's attention. I wondered if people were expecting the General to appear now to give a rousing speech.

Instead, through the gaping doorway of Icarium, they saw fire.

There was a moment of collective disbelief, like the crowd couldn't understand what they were looking at. Then,

379

somewhere in the night, a woman screamed. Her voice pierced the silence like a needle, spreading panic instantly.

*Good*, I thought. *Let them panic. Let them fear.* As long as they were distracted, they couldn't burn Christian.

I took two steps towards the railing, needing to see him, but found myself unsteady on my feet, all the blood I'd lost suddenly catching up with me. I fell to the ground, afraid I was going to pass out, and felt someone grab me at the last second.

'Hey. Look at me.'

It was Nico, kneeling in front of me, holding me upright with a firm grip on my arms. I didn't know where he'd come from because the terrace had been empty a second ago, and the last time I'd seen him he'd been half dead on the floor of the arena with a bullet hole in his shoulder. Not for the first time, I had to wonder if he was a hallucination.

'Don't move,' he said, when I tried to reach out and feel for his skin. 'Just tell me where you're hurt.'

'It doesn't matter,' I said. Unable to explain that the worst wounds were inside me, where they couldn't be mended. In front of us, I could hear the clamour of the panicking crowd; behind us, the flames rising higher and higher. A whole world collapsing, just like that.

'Lilly, where's the General?' Nico asked. 'What did he do to you?'

'The General's dead,' I said, and pulled away from him, clutching the railing to force myself to my feet. Pushing past the pain and the exhaustion, knowing I had to get this out.

'The General is dead!'

When I spoke this time, it was to the crowd, raising my voice to carry above the noise in the square below. I felt possessed, overcome by the desperate urge to make them hear me. Suddenly their panic wasn't enough. I needed them to feel what I felt: all the hurt and the emptiness. I needed them to know that it was over.

'He's burning in that fire. He said he was a prophet, but he lied. He lied about everything. He's no different from anyone else. He's not saved. And he can't save you.'

I paused for breath and realized that silence had fallen. My voice was echoing through the square, saying things I didn't know I understood until they were out of my mouth. And the crowd was watching me. They were listening.

'The laws the General taught were false. And he knew it. He told me. Power isn't the curse he said it was. Saints aren't the enemy. We're not demons; we're people like the rest of you. Good and bad and stupid and scared.'

My eyes found the pyre for the first time: the stake where Christian was tied, his skin glowing in the firelight. His head was bowed, muscles slack under the coils of rope, but when I spoke he seemed to come out of a daze. Lifted his head like it was the most difficult movement in the world, and looked at me.

'I know that something awful happened in this town,' I said, feeling the ache of tears in my throat. 'I know it hurt all of you. That was my mother's fault, and it was unforgivable. And I'm sorry. But you can't make it better by hurting us in return. There's only hate like that. Hate and fear. It doesn't solve anything. You have to let it go.'

The crowd was motionless when I finished, their glittering eyes staring up at me like a frozen landscape. I scanned their faces, looking for sympathy or rage, something I could recognize. Mostly they seemed shocked, at a loss without a leader to tell them what to think.

Then someone said, 'Blasphemy.'

It was Tiago, of course. He was standing on a wooden platform in front of Christian's pyre, holding a torch in one hand.

'The girl's a witch,' he told the crowd. 'When she speaks, she damns us all. Stop her.'

The enforcers obeyed him instantly, marching in formation up the Paradiso staircase to the church terrace. Nico grabbed my arm again, and together we stumbled away from them towards the Marconi steps. Icarium's facade was glowing orange at our backs, flames pushing upward and out, making the roof sag. Plumes of smoke rose to darken the moon. The air was sizzling with heat.

We'd reached the top of the staircase when someone snagged me by the waist, halting my escape. Spinning me around so I couldn't see Nico any longer. It was Veronica Marconi.

She had climbed the stairs to meet me, her hair coiled in a knot behind her head, warrior-like. The fabric of her wool coat scratched against my cheek.

'You can't outrun them, *amore*,' Veronica said. 'But I've got you.'

I twisted out of her grip, not wanting to be near her – only to find myself face to face with a line of enforcers,

Tiago in the lead. Dazed, I let Veronica pull me back to her. Tiago levelled his gun at my head.

'Deluca,' he said, with a crooked smile. 'I knew you looked familiar. Who can forget the first girl who turns them down?' His eyes flashed to Veronica. 'Give her to me, Vee. She owes me for her mother.'

'Don't make a fool of yourself,' said Veronica quietly. 'Have the threats ever worked on me?'

'She's a Saint,' Tiago said. 'If I tell the crowd to burn her, they'll do it.'

'The crowd isn't yours any more,' Veronica said. 'Half of them belong to me.' She raised her voice, then, made sure it carried over the square. 'You heard what the girl said: the General is dead. So the truce is over. And you're standing on my territory.'

Something rippled through the crowd, a pulse of uncertainty. Tiago's lip curled, manic and furious.

'That's treason,' he hissed. 'You swore loyalty. You took an oath –'

'You always said I had my fingers crossed,' Veronica said. 'And I believe that's the only thing you've been right about in your whole life.' She took a step towards him, tall and hypnotic in the glow of the fire. 'Did you really think I'd let people like you take my city from me? The lowest, most base among us – did you think I'd let you rule?' She smiled disdainfully. 'Please. The General was just a sideshow. A brief interlude between rightful heirs. He's finished now. I'm reclaiming my inheritance.'

'No,' said Tiago. Something dangerous in his face, the

beginnings of real violence. 'I want the witch. You won't be keeping another Tale girl from me.'

'Let me tell you a story,' Veronica said, raising her voice again, speaking to the crowd. 'Once upon a time, there was a family who spilled their blood for this town until the streets were paved in red. That was the Marconi clan. We had principles then. We protected our own. We did not turn against each other. We will not turn against each other now.'

The crowd seemed to stir below her, like Veronica was waking them from a dream – reminding them of forgotten things.

'The girl is innocent,' she said to Tiago. 'You can't have her. And you're *still* standing on my territory.'

There was a whole lifetime of fury in Tiago's eyes, layers of betrayal and hatred I couldn't begin to understand. Slowly, he shook his head.

'You asked for this,' he told Veronica. 'Don't forget that you asked.'

Then he turned to the crowd.

'Citizens of Castello,' he said, 'the Marconi clan has committed treason against our town.' He raised his arms high, embracing the square, a perfect shadow of the General.

'Kill them,' Tiago said. 'Kill them all.'

# CHAPTER FORTY-THREE

It started slow.

Someone in the Paradiso crowd reached out, grabbed a piece of timber at the base of Christian's pyre and threw it across the square. The wood made a clean, breathtaking arc through the air and slammed down into the middle of a group of Marconis. A body fell. Tiago laughed. Veronica shoved me roughly towards the steps and said, 'Go.'

After that: pure chaos.

The square exploded into a frenzy, a stampede of bodies rushing to fight or flee. Most of the crowd was running for the streets on either side of town, parents dragging their children by the hand. But some people were pushing towards the boundary line instead, fists out, itching for a fight. It was like a fuse had been lit under the clans, and now it was irreversible – twenty years of pent-up anger pouring out like wildfire, creating a deadly free-for-all.

I raced down the stairs and plunged into the middle of it all, trying to keep my eyes on the pyre. It looked just like in my dreams, shrouded in a layer of smoke, only this time the boy who I'd believed could save me was the one set to die. The crowd raged around me, bloody fingers grabbing at my sweater as I shoved through. I heard someone call after me, telling me to wait, but I couldn't listen. A hand shot out and hit me in the shoulder, and I stumbled, fell, forced my way to my feet again.

To the left, Icarium's roof was caving in, that mile-high dome of bronze raining fiery debris on to the square. There were sparks everywhere, chunks of blazing wood that crashed into the ground like falling stars. A man lunged at me from the side, wielding a broken flagpole as a spear, and I moved a little too late, felt bright pain pierce my side, making me stumble again.

Then the church's foundations cracked.

It was like a glass lantern dashed to the ground: a sudden blast of heat and flame and shattered marble exploding into the plaza. The pavement shuddering hard, unbalancing the whole crowd. I hit the ground again, losing sight of Christian's pyre, and, by the time I was back on my feet, everything had changed. It was on fire.

For a moment, I couldn't breathe, couldn't think, couldn't move at all. A piece of the church's flaming roof had landed at the base of the pyre, and now there were flames snaking around it like bright orange fingers, climbing slowly up. Christian was a black silhouette on the stake, twisting uselessly against the ropes. The enforcers had tied him so tight he might as well have been chained.

I pushed forward in a kind of savage delirium, grasping at the arms of the people around me to stay upright. I was too dizzy, and Christian was too far away. I wanted him too much, so I was going to lose him. The pain in my side was worse, sending a wet flush down my sweater, telling me I was losing blood again. After what I'd given to the key, I didn't think I could afford that. A wave of nausea gripped me, and I had to pause to catch my breath, head pounding with the futility of it all. I needed to move, but I couldn't, and so Christian was going to burn alive.

'Lilly,' someone said, 'stop running away. I'm trying to help.'

Nico again, catching my wrist and turning me towards him. His skin was glowing in the firelight and he held his pocketknife in one hand, blood-soaked like he'd been cutting his way through the crowd. I swayed into him, grateful for something to lean against: trying to clear my mind.

'The pyre,' I said. 'We have to get to the pyre.'

Nico shot a glance at it, the flames working their way towards Christian's body, and flinched. 'Can't you stop it? You're a Saint, right? Can't you put it out?'

'I gave away my power,' I said, feeling the panic of it flush through me all over again. 'I don't know if I have any left.'

Nico's face set. 'Okay,' he said. 'Then I'll get him down. All you have to do is hold the flames back.'

I shook my head, wanting to tell him that it was impossible – that I couldn't do anything useful right now. But it was too late. He was already pushing his way into the crowd.

I stumbled a little without him, biting my tongue, using the sting of it to focus me. The steps to the pyre were all ablaze, so Nico was heading for the side – jumping a lower bank of flames and scrambling up the pyramid of wood to the top. It took Christian a moment to notice someone was there with him, even after Nico started hacking at the ropes with his pocketknife. His head hung low, body slumped in near-unconsciousness, all the fight drained out of him. But I saw his lips move anyway, something like, *Carenza, go away.*

Nico just kept hacking.

I used my nails to part the crowd in front of me, trying to ignore the pain in my side, how every breath felt like it was going to be the last one. By the time I reached the side of the pyre, the flames were too high to jump and rising steadily.

I limped a few feet in each direction, trying to find a place where the fire looked weaker, low enough for me to be able to hold it down. I could see every detail of the scene above me, so close but completely out of my reach: Christian drenched in sweat, blue eyes dancing with a feverish light. Trying to push Nico away before it was too late.

'Get down, Carenza,' Christian kept saying. 'Just go away –'

Flames were licking up the back of their jeans, the heels of their boots, like the fire was teasing them, having a taste before the real burning began.

'Shut up, Asaro,' Nico said, and swiped the knife hard, cutting the last of the bonds away from Christian's body.

Christian's knees buckled, and Nico caught him by the shoulders, dragged him away from the stake. The fire was everywhere now, an unbreakable barrier around them, singeing their hair and clothing. Nico turned an unsteady circle, with Christian at his side, waiting for me to do something: curl the flames back and make a path to let them out.

*But you don't understand*, I thought furiously. *It's over for me. I have nothing. I am nothing –*

Through the bank of flames, Nico met my gaze. He looked other-worldly, backlit by fire, dark eyes drilling into mine. I saw no uncertainty there, no panic. Like he was absolutely convinced I could do this. He'd staked his life on it, after all. Which was stupid, I decided. Because he was the one who had called me weak.

Slowly, I took a breath. Closed my eyes. Stood very still before the pyre with my hands outstretched, and tried to summon my power. *Come on*, I thought. *Come on, come on –*

Thinking of my blood on the key: the swirling door of darkness that had sucked the power out of me. Feeling my hope shrivel and die.

But then I thought of Nico, holding Christian upright, trusting me. Of the bright flutter of heat in my blood. Of being made whole again.

*Power is who I am*, I thought. Reaching down deep inside my body, feeling the skeleton of something very small and fragile stir in my chest. *It's part of me. No one can take it away, not completely.*

*So come on. Come on, and listen to me.* The fragile thing growing a little at a time; my breath stuck in my throat, my hands shaking. I'd never needed anything the way I needed this now, with a desire so intense I felt I could tear worlds open, raze cities to the ground. If I'd had any breath to spare, I would've been screaming.

*Fight for me. No one else can. Only me.*

*Only me.*

*So please.*

*PLEASE.*

And then I felt it.

The tiniest spark. Barely a scrap, enough to light a candle, maybe open a door. But still. The power was there. It hadn't left me. It was mine. And I could use it.

When I opened my eyes, I found Nico, still watching me from the pyre, Christian slumped unconscious against him, almost obscured by a bank of flames. Our gazes met again, and he nodded once. *Ready.*

I raised my hands and dragged my power out.

It was a different kind of agony than when the key had tried to drain me, because at least this time I was choosing it. But still – the *pain*.

I was tugging on that tiny spark of heat, amplifying and distorting it, forcing it out through my fingers. Aiming it at the pyre. Pushing my body past every limit, scraping away at lost and forgotten corners inside me, leaving blood behind. Throwing every ounce of my life force into those flames.

And it was worth it. Because, just for a second, they faltered. Rippled sideways and created a gap in the fire. Nico saw it. He shoved Christian in front of him and jumped. Together, they tumbled through the breach and into the square.

I keeled over instantly, the world sliding sideways, tears streaming down my cheeks. Retching on to the pavement, my heart pounding sick and furious, my vision spliced with black. But I was alive. And they were alive, too.

Christian was sprawled out next to me, Nico at his side. Nico sat up first, knees bleeding from the fall, the heels of his boots burnt clean off. He wiped ash from his mouth and put one arm around Christian's shoulders, trying to lift him. But Christian was dead weight. I crawled forward, shaky on my hands and knees, and reached for his body myself, feeling the perfect heat of his skin against me. His eyes fluttered once, a flicker of murky blue, then slid closed again. Dirt coated his lashes, painted stripes down his cheeks.

'You didn't have to,' he said, to me or Nico, I couldn't be sure. 'You shouldn't have.'

Then he was gone again. Nico glanced at me over Christian's body, something pained in his eyes. 'We need to get him out of here.'

'How?' I whispered.

The square was apocalyptic around us, thick with flame and shadows. We'd ended up on the Paradiso side of town, a little way north of the boundary line. The clans were still fighting around us, bodies swirling in the smoky air, but there had been a change in the tide of the battle, a new order beginning to form. The enforcers had left the church terrace when the foundations cracked, and now they were joining ranks with the Paradisos, aiming their guns at the Marconis in the crowd. The Marconis splintered under the attack, scrambling to retreat. And the Paradisos advanced. They rallied themselves into a unit, a knot of men with torches, women swinging their jewellery like whips, and marched towards the boundary line. At the front, leading them all, was Chrissy Paradiso in a beautiful red dress.

'Can you share the weight?' Nico asked me. His chin was slick with blood, soot-stained fingers clutching the neck of Christian's ruined T-shirt. 'I don't think I can carry him on my own.'

I nodded, not knowing how I'd manage, only knowing that I had to. Hooking an elbow around Christian's waist while Nico slid an arm under his shoulders. Together we raised him off the ground, staggering upright. We were caught in the most exposed area of the square, with the tide of Paradisos approaching from behind us, the safety of the Marconi streets a blur up ahead. It seemed impossible that we would make it that far. The enforcers were shooting with abandon, and people were dropping all around us, falling down and not getting up again. Only Veronica Marconi seemed unaffected by the danger. I could see her through the smoke, walking easily, head held high. She didn't care about the bullets, or the mob of Paradisos closing in, because she had a weapon of her own. She was raising the boundary.

I felt it before I saw it, a low rumble in the ground, like something was moving below our feet. Then, in the exact centre of the square, a wall began to emerge. Huge iron spikes rose out of the pavement ahead of us, rusted red in places, sharpened like the points of infected needles. Veronica was standing by the ruins of the flaming church steps, manoeuvring a system of coiled chains that had been hidden inside Icarium's foundations. She had done something to set the system in motion, and now the chains were unspooling, dragging up the boundary as they went. First came the iron spikes, rising one inch, two inches, three inches at a time, and then suddenly they were knee-high, and I was screaming at Nico to run, *RUN*, because below the spikes was a solid wall, twisted panels of metal and thick wire mesh, ready to divide the town for good. And we were still on the Paradiso side.

Time seemed to distort as we stumbled for the boundary line, like my brain was skipping, too fast and too slow, taking in a hundred things at once. The thick, burning air; the pain in my side and chest. Christian's unconscious body knocking hard against mine. The last of the Marconi fighters fleeing around us, flowing over the wall like a retreating tide. And, ringing out above it all, I heard a strange new sound, metal on metal: the church bells tolling.

They echoed from somewhere in the blazing ruin of Icarium, buffeted by the fire, pounding a dark rhythm over the square. It was like a giant clock, measuring out the seconds we had left to keep living. When we finally reached the boundary wall, it was already up to my waist. Shards of broken glass were woven into the barbed wire on the top. Every edge looked like poison.

'I'll take him,' Nico said, tugging Christian away from me before I could protest. He gripped the spikes on the wall with one hand and hauled himself over, dragging Christian behind him. Their jeans shredded on the iron, Christian's soot-streaked curls catching in the barbed wire. Then they fell to the ground on the Marconi side, out of my sight. Suddenly I was alone.

I turned to face the square, my vision fading in and out with the tolling of the bells. My body felt liquid, weak from blood loss and from the damage I'd done, forcing the power. Tendrils of darkness curled at the edges of my mind.

'Hey,' Nico said. He had risen to his feet behind the boundary line and was reaching for my hand through the iron spikes. 'Come on.'

I blinked, unmoving. My head suddenly flooded with the image of Liza's twisted body on the ground. With the way Christian had looked at me that night when he'd realized who my mother was. With the understanding of what I had left and what I didn't.

'Lilly, come *on*,' Nico said again.

The Paradisos were very close now, rushing at the boundary, but they hardly seemed dangerous to me, their figures soft and hypnotic in the firelight. Then Nico reached out and grabbed the collar of my sweater, yanked me viciously backwards. I whirled around to face him, furious, and noticed that the boundary wall had already risen up to my chest.

'What are you doing?' Nico demanded, watching me through the barbed wire. 'Why did you stop?'

394

I shrugged. It just seemed pointless all of a sudden – to keep going when I didn't even know what I was going towards.

Nico's eyes sparked. 'God, the two of you,' he said. 'Why do you want to punish yourselves so much?'

And then he was leaning towards me, fingers tight in my collar, careless of the wire cutting his face.

'Climb the wall, Lilly,' Nico Carenza said. 'Please. I'm tired of losing things.'

I did what he asked, then. Because I never thought I'd hear this boy beg me for anything.

I grabbed on to the boundary as it passed my shoulders, gripped the iron spikes with both hands and let it lift me off the ground. Nico reached up and took hold of my arms, pulled me up and over on to the other side. I fell hard, hit the ground and went down on the marble. Christian was there, laid out on his side, still unconscious. I knotted my hands in his T-shirt and tugged him towards me, unwilling to let him go, now or ever.

A moment later, the Paradisos collided with the boundary. Their hands punched gaps in the wire mesh, reaching for our clothing, laughing like hyenas. Spraying bullets through the holes. I stayed crouched on the ground, Christian in my arms, shielding him with my body.

The Paradisos gripped at fragments of the wall and tried to climb, but it kept rising, barbed wire giving way to solid sheets of metal that were impossible to scale. Distantly, I remembered what Liza had told me about bells in Castello: how the General had forbidden them because they were a symbol of war. *Before the truce, they would ring all day long.*

Above us, the boundary wall snapped into place: twenty feet of sheet metal, graffiti and rust. Blocking out the Paradiso side of the square and everything beyond it.

And the bells rang on and on.

# CHAPTER FORTY-FOUR

There was light around me. Real light, not the smoky orange haze of fire. Sunlight. I could sense the warmth of it on my face even before I opened my eyes. It felt like safety.

I came awake slowly, blinking in the glow. I was lying in a familiar bed, surrounded by walls I recognized. Bloody knights in scuffed-up armour: my most reliable friends. My bedroom was bathed in daylight, transformed to a state of almost-beauty. It was the first time in ages that I'd woken up unafraid. Then I remembered.

I sat bolt upright in bed, scrabbling at the sheets to get out. A hand caught my shoulder and pushed me back against the pillow.

'Don't,' said Nico. He was sitting in a dusty armchair next to my bed, wearing a fresh white T-shirt and sooty jeans. His hair was matted with grime, but his skin had been scrubbed clean. The silver studs in his ears glittered hypnotically.

'What are you doing here?' I stammered. 'Where's Christian?'

'He's okay,' said Nico. 'Everything's okay now.'

I stared at the light from outside, understanding for the first time what it really meant. Morning. A new day. We weren't in the square any more. We weren't burning. There was a black hole in my mind where the interim time should've been. My last memory was of falling on marble, Christian's body in my arms. The bells tolling.

'What happened to us?' I whispered.

'The square was evacuated after the boundary went up. You weren't really conscious. I don't think I was, either. There was just so much smoke –'

'And Christian?'

'He's okay,' said Nico again. 'Alex took him.'

'Alex is in jail.'

Nico shrugged. 'Not any more.'

I glanced at the wall behind my head, thinking of Alex's bedroom on the other side – realizing that Christian was probably there right now. The urge to see him was so strong it made my vision short out. I counted to five and waited for it to pass.

'How long was I asleep?' I asked Nico.

He glanced out the window, gauging sunlight. 'Twelve hours, give or take.'

'Did my dad take me home?'

'No,' said Nico. 'I haven't seen him, actually.'

'Then how did I get here?'

'I brought you,' Nico said. Leaning forward in the armchair, elbows resting on his knees. Eyes flickering to mine and then away again, like he didn't want to look for too long. 'Alex told me where you live. I just thought . . . you shouldn't wake up alone.'

Something warm bloomed inside my chest. 'Thank you,' I said. 'For saving Christian. I could never have done it by myself.'

'He did the same for me,' Nico said. 'In the arena, when he made Chrissy stop – I knew it was power that did it. But I never expected it to be *him*. Not in that family.' His eyes darted up. 'Then there's you.'

'Do you think it's wrong?' I asked. 'That the Saints are cursed, like the General said?'

A storm of emotion crossed Nico's face, like he was reliving something torturous. 'Of course not,' he whispered. 'Did you kill him, Lilly?'

The question should've been surprising, but it felt perfectly natural instead. 'No,' I said. 'I guess I wanted to. But he did it to himself in the end.'

'How?'

'Greed,' I murmured. 'He had the city key. I gave it to him. It opens a gateway to all of Castello's power. But he wouldn't let me keep even a little of my own. And then he took Liza from me. And he wanted to take Christian –'

My throat sealed over with the fear of it.

'Is that what Professor Marconi was looking for?' Nico said slowly. 'The city key? She had you searched before she let me leave the square. She said you might be wearing gold.'

I nodded, pain rising inside me: thinking of all the ways Veronica had tried to ruin my life.

'It was her idea to find it in the first place,' I said. 'Apparently, she's wanted the key since she was a kid. That's why she brought me to town – so I could deliver it to her. It would've made her undefeatable once the General was gone. The one true ruler of Castello. And I was stupid enough to go along with it.' My voice hardened. 'But she'll never get it now. It's ruined, I saw it. The General made it explode when he was trying to shoot me.'

Nico's forehead creased. 'That seems like a big mistake for him to have made.'

I shrugged, unwilling to question it – too exhausted to doubt anything right now. Shifting on the pillows and feeling a sudden ache in my side, the wound I'd gotten in the square, bandaged up but still throbbing. It brought back a flood of memories: the chaos of the crowd, the blood on the pavement. People falling and not getting up. My breath caught, eyes seeking Nico's automatically.

'It was bad, wasn't it?' I said.

'Not as bad as it's going to be.'

'You think the Paradisos will attack again?'

'Sure,' Nico said. 'Unless we attack them first. Professor Marconi is already organizing border patrols and weapons training. I think this is the start of another war.'

'But the boundary went up. The Paradisos have their side; we've got ours. There's nothing left to fight over.'

Nico laughed without any humour. 'It's Castello. There's always something to fight over. My dad used to tell stories, about what people did to each other before the General came along. The bombings and the massacres – it was a way of life. This town is like a really dangerous chess game. The clans have been playing for centuries. The General distracted them for a while, but it was never going to last. They had to keep playing eventually. Because someone has to win. Nobody ever settled for just half a city.'

'So what do we do?'

'Same thing as always,' Nico said. 'We stay alive. You'd better watch out for Christian, though. I think someone hurt him really badly. And . . . you should watch out for yourself, too. There are people who need you.'

He was leaning towards me again, eyes dark and careful on my face. I could see blood in his hair where he hadn't washed it out, the skin on the side of his neck peeling with burns. And I had the urge to reach for his hand – wanting just the simplest thing, the sturdy pressure of his fingers on mine. But that was the exact moment that Nico pulled away.

'I should go,' he said, rising abruptly to his feet. 'Everyone who can still walk is supposed to help put out the fires in the square. Professor Marconi isn't messing around running her side of town.'

I nodded, and the movement made me light-headed, wanting to sink back into the pillows and sleep again. 'Nico,' I said, when he was already in the doorway, 'are we friends now or something?'

He stopped short, turned to look at me. Something on his face: soft and aching.

'Yeah, Lilly,' he said. 'Now we're friends.'

*

When I woke again, it was dark out. All the corners of my room that had been warmed by sunlight before were in shadow. Someone had changed my sweater when they bandaged my wound, but the rest of my clothes were still filthy and smelled like fire. I slipped out of bed and made for the wardrobe, my movements agonizingly slow, balancing myself against the furniture. For some reason, the only thing I could find to wear was an old white nightgown of my mother's.

I pulled it on and chanced a look out the window, saw Castello's new panorama rising against the night sky. Two watchtowers with a jagged hole between them where Icarium's dome had been. Smoke still billowing along the horizon, telling me the fire hadn't burned out yet.

The rest of my house was silent and empty, but something strange seemed to have happened to it. The front door was hanging off its hinges, and the furniture was overturned. Drawers pulled out, chairs scattered. Papers fanned all over the floor. As if there'd been a frantic search.

'Dad?' I said, hearing my voice echo back at me in the hollow rooms. 'Are you here?'

But the house stayed silent. A sudden intuition flared in my chest, and I headed for the kitchen, wanting to check the breadbox where I'd stuffed those papers that Jack had told me to hide. The drawers had been ransacked here, too, silverware and plates smashed on the floor. And the breadbox was empty. The papers were gone. And so was my mother's diary.

For a moment, I stood still, trying to work it over in my head. Where my father might be, and what had become of the pages he'd been trying to show me. Normally, I'd have assumed he was at his office, and he'd taken them along. But given everything that had happened last night, I found that unlikely. Even Jack couldn't have worked through the church burning down. And it didn't explain the house being such a mess.

*Maybe he left*, said a voice in my head. *He told Veronica he wanted to get out of here, after all. So maybe he took what he needed and ran. And he decided he didn't need you.*

'Shut up,' I whispered. 'That's not true.'

There had to be another explanation. For the overturned house, and my father's absence. Any second, he was going to turn up and tell me what was going on. But in the meantime, I had somewhere else to be.

I descended the stairs and stepped on to Castello's streets, a web of shadows broken only by the eerie glow of fires in the distance. Moved barefoot down the icy cobblestones of Via Secondo until I reached Alex's security gate.

The latch was open, so I rolled it back carefully, pushing into the stairwell, letting my instincts lead me where I needed to go. The third-floor landing had an elegant family name plate on the door, and it occurred to me as I was knocking that I hadn't bothered to check the time. It could've been the middle of the night for all I knew. I had a feeling Alex's mother wouldn't appreciate the intrusion.

*You should've taken the roof*, I thought, just as the door swung open.

Alex stood in front of me, naked from the waist up, wearing blue flannel pyjama pants with fading superhero logos.

'Knew you'd come,' he said sleepily. 'Just wasn't sure which way.'

He looked much better than he had in Veronica's cage, something clean and innocent about him now, a lack of leather and sharp edges. Black hair tousled from bed. I felt a sudden rush of fondness, the urge to throw my arms around him. So I did.

Alex stumbled a little, stiff and stunningly warm in my embrace.

'What the hell, Deluca?' he said.

'Hug me back,' I demanded, and slowly he did.

'I'm sorry,' I whispered, once I felt Alex's arms close around me, reluctant but sturdy. 'I won't let them hurt him again. Please forgive me.'

'Okay,' Alex said. He pushed me off eventually, cheeks flushed with embarrassment. I grinned. 'Stop pretending you like me,' he muttered. 'I know you're here for Christian.'

He ushered me into the apartment, which I remembered from last time as a pristine spread of rooms with modern furniture and metal art on the walls. My shoulder clanged against one of the art pieces, and I murmured an apology, afraid of waking the rest of the house.

'Don't worry,' Alex said, over his shoulder. 'No one's

here. My mum's doing damage control with Professor Marconi. And I haven't seen my dad since the square.'

There was a faint pulse of unease in his voice, which set my own mind on edge. 'I haven't seen my dad, either.'

Alex turned back wordlessly and offered me his hand. I took it instantly, and we walked together like that, down the hall to his bedroom.

Soft light spilled from under the door, casting a soothing glow on the floor. I knew Christian was inside, could feel it from the burning sensation in my body, deeper than power, deeper than blood. Alex hesitated with his hand on the doorknob, watching me uncertainly.

'You know he's sick, right? The enforcers had him drugged out of his mind. I mean, he's alive, so I'm not complaining. But . . . just don't expect him to be okay.'

I nodded, bracing myself – letting Alex push open the door. For a moment, my pulse got so fast that I was sure my heart would burst. The room swam before me, a kaleidoscope haze, and, by the time I managed to blink my vision back to normal, Alex was gone, and Christian was before me.

He was sitting in the corner of the bed, cross-legged, head bent, curls still dirtied with soot. The sight of him was paralysing to me, because I'd never wanted someone more, and never been more afraid of what I wanted. Guilt pricked at my skin, thousands of reasons to stay away, but for once I shoved it aside. Christian raised his head, blinking in the lamplight, and said my name.

I crossed the room in a rush, knelt in front of him on the bed, letting him reach for me first: his hands greedy and urgent, like he had to reassure himself that I was actually there. Gripping the back of my neck and drawing me towards him, making our foreheads knock together.

'You're real,' Christian said. 'Aren't you?'

I nodded, scared to speak all of a sudden, the relief of his body against me so sharp I thought I'd cry.

'Because I couldn't tell before. I kept seeing you when they had me locked up. But then you would always leave.'

'You were dreaming,' I whispered. 'But not any longer.'

'You do like to leave, though,' Christian said, blinking up at me through glazed eyes. 'Don't you? Even when you promise not to. You like to run away from things before they run away from you.'

'I wasn't running away,' I said. 'I was trying to fix you. I was trying to fix the town –'

'You can't, Lilly,' Christian said. Something strangely taunting in it, his smoke-raw lips curving into a smile. 'You can't do anything about it.'

'But –'

'You can't do anything if you run.'

'I just didn't want to hurt you,' I said. 'What my mom did to your dad, I didn't want to make it all worse –'

'It's my choice, though,' Christian said. 'I get to decide what I want. No matter what it feels like. And it's you, okay? If you'll have me. It's you.'

'What about the shots?' I could see the needle marks from the enforcers all over his arms, angry and red. 'Last time, you said you only wanted me if you could have them, too.'

'I didn't mean it like that,' Christian said. 'It's just that they make everything easy –' He shook his head, eyelids lowering. 'But I want you, anyway. With or without them. Whatever it takes.'

'Okay,' I whispered. Desperate to believe him now – lacking the willpower to doubt. Wanting him to drag me down on to the bed, turn my breath shaky. Wanting to give him everything I had. 'I don't think it'll be easy, you and me. Not like the shots. But I think it'll be worth it. If we try, I think it'll be so good.'

'Then kiss me,' Christian said. 'And let's find out.'

The dream was dark and fleeting.

I was lying in Christian's arms, tangled with him under Alex's sheets, and she was standing in the doorway, watching us. Liza's chest was torn open, drenched in blood from the General's shotgun, her hair streaked with ash. Tendrils of darkness seemed to pulse from her body, her skin turned waxy below them, her veins showing pitch-black. Her green eyes, brimming with something deadly and electric. Something like power.

Teeth razor-sharp as she smiled.

'Don't forget, Lilly,' she said. 'I'm keeping you.'

# ACKNOWLEDGEMENTS

This book would not exist without the support of so many individuals. For years, it has lived with me and those close to me, and is indebted, as I am, to their care and generosity.

To my agent, Stephanie Thwaites, thank you for being such a fierce advocate for me and my writing. You've worked tirelessly to nurture and champion this book at every turn, and I'm so grateful to have you in my corner. To Isobel Gahan, thank you for guiding me through debut year with a deft hand and infinite patience, and to Jonny Geller for making it all possible.

To Jane Griffiths and India Chambers, my editors, thank you for taking up the mantle and opening your hearts to the world of Castello. It's been a privilege to work with you – you've made this story light years stronger than I imagined it could be. To Shreeta Shah for your attention to detail and graciousness with my eleventh-hour crises, and to Charlotte Winstone, Jannine Saunders, Stevie Hopwood, and the entire Penguin Random House marketing and PR teams for finding *WFITB* its readers. Beth Fennell, Sabrina Chong and everyone at PRH foreign rights, I couldn't dream up a more brilliant and dedicated group of people to fight for my book. And to Millie Lean, who fell in love with this story first, thank you for taking a chance on me.

To my parents, who have believed in me every second of every day of my life: this book owes its existence to your unequivocal love and support. Thank you for teaching me that words build worlds, and that everything is possible.

To my grandma, for being my role model and confidante, and my uncle, for keeping me grounded.

Special thanks to the early supporters of my writing who provided me a space to live and work in over the years: Sue and Trey, Pat and Tom, Hannelore and Jochen, and especially Jeanne and Gerry, who gave me a home when I needed one most. To Emily R for the mentorship; Michael S for listening to me ramble; and Gina P for helping me face demons. To Mario, Giuliana, Nico and Martina for decades of hospitality; and to Valeria for creating magic in my childhood and preserving it to this day.

To Danielle, thank you for pulling this book out of the drawer I'd locked it in and breathing it back to life with your boundless enthusiasm. And to Rowan, for picking up the phone across four time zones and three continents, holding me to my vision, editing like a pro, and never giving up on me – I'm so glad I convinced you to split that Uber to BTS. Thank you.

To my Ocean's Eight (plus one doggo): Anya, Claire, Eliza, Paloma, Sofia, Tara, Yen Ba – and Em and Gucci, who've saved my life more times than they know – thank you all for spending the last ten years being ready to bury bodies with me. Your friendship is the thing I'm most proud of.

To my Venice community, I can't imagine finishing this book without you. You opened your lives to me and have insulated me from the ups and downs with a network of unlimited kindness. Marina, thank you for literally taking me in out of the rain, making me part of the family and never letting me eat alone. To Isabella, Francesca F and the team at M, thank you for being my writing cheerleaders and partners in crime. And to Amy, Cristina, Daniele, Elena, Elga, Francesca C, Gaia, Giuliana, Maria C, Melania, Monica, Piero, Sabrina, Toma and Vanessa for having my back in every inch of this city. I can't wait to share this story with all of you.

Thanks to my fellow writers who have been on this journey with me: Megan for your optimism and invaluable feedback, and Lyndall, where to start? Your friendship and solidarity have brought so much joy to my life. Thank you for teaching me about long games, drawing Castello into reality, and steering me through many a publishing minefield. I'm so lucky to know you.

Finally, twelve-year-old Kat would never forgive me if I didn't mention Stephen King. I learned to write by imitating *The Body* and owe a profound debt to the doorways of possibility that his storytelling opened inside my head. Sometimes the smallest thing can change the course of your life. Thanks, man.